MU00714146

WAKING UP DEAD

AN END OF DAYS LOVE NOVEL

WAKING UP DEAD

AN END OF DAYS LOVE NOVEL

EMMA SHORTT

This book is a work of fiction. Names, characters, places, and incidents are the product of the author's imagination or are used fictitiously. Any resemblance to actual events, locales, or persons, living or dead, is coincidental.

Copyright © 2013 by Emma Shortt. All rights reserved, including the right to reproduce, distribute, or transmit in any form or by any means. For information regarding subsidiary rights, please contact the Publisher.

Entangled Publishing, LLC
2614 South Timberline Road
Suite 109
Fort Collins, CO 80525
Visit our website at www.entangledpublishing.com.

Edited by Erin Molta
Cover design by Kim Killion

Ebook ISBN 978-1-62266-034-6
Print ISBN 978-1-62266-035-3

Manufactured in the United States of America

First Edition September 2013

The author acknowledges the copyrighted or trademarked status and trademark owners of the following wordmarks mentioned in this work of fiction: Akido, *Alice in Wonderland*, Airwaves, Barbie, Batman, Batmobile, Bejeweled Blitz, *Buffy the Vampire Slayer*, Dr. Martens, Davidoff's Cool Water, *Dawn of the Dead*, Dumpster, Evian, *Firefly*, Frosted Fruit Flakes, GLOCK 19, *Gone with the Wind*, Gore-Tex, Gucci, Gucci Cool, Harry Potter, Hershey's Kiss, Hummers, *I Am Legend*, iPod, Johnnie Walker Black, Lynx Aftershave, Macy's, Mustang, Old Spice, Outdoor World, Prius, *Rambo*, Robin, Serenity, Spam, Superwoman, Twinkies, Wal-Mart, Weight Watchers, *Zombieland*.

To Freckles and to Bear.
More than all the numbers, in all the universes.
More than forever.

PART ONE

"ANYTHING IS POSSIBLE IF YOU'VE GOT THE NERVE...BUT
SOMETIMES A MACHETE HELPS TOO."
JACKSON HART

CHAPTER ONE

CHICAGO

Without a doubt the house with the pretty green shutters had food inside of it. Pasta, canned vegetables, tinned meats, hell, it could have a five course, good-to-go, gourmet meal in there for all Jackson Hart knew. Crouched down behind an overturned SUV she could practically hear it all screaming from inside the pantry, and she narrowed her eyes as she assessed the best way to get at it.

Not through the front door. It was probably barred tight with planks of wood, or barricaded with piled-up furniture. Maybe through the back? But the skinny, shadowed alleyway that ran between the house and its fence screamed, *horror movie showdown,* and for all Jackson knew she'd be risking it only to find a blocked-up back door too. The shutters then. How thick were they? Was the glass behind them intact? Jackson hefted Mandy-the-machete and considered the possibilities.

"You're looking thoughtful there. For the record it doesn't suit you."

Those words came from Tyrone, her friend, her only friend, if you wanted to get right down to it. He joined her behind the SUV, swinging his ax as he did so, and making absolutely no attempt to stay hidden.

"I was being stealthy," Jackson said with a sigh. "You totally just ruined it."

"Stealthy for who?" he asked. "The rats? There's only them and us. We checked the street. It's all quiet."

Jackson frowned as she looked away from the house and down said street. A backpack, probably a child's by the size of it, caught her attention, and she frowned as she noticed what looked like a rusty toy truck sticking out of the zipper. The things people had thought to take when they tried to run…it still baffled her.

"Quiet or not, they're here somewhere," she said softly. "It's been almost a day since we saw any of them."

"Let's hope for another day and then maybe another." He paused. "Better yet, let's hope for a week."

Jackson almost laughed. "Might as well wish for a working car."

"I do, sweetheart. Daily. We're surrounded by wheels and not one of them worth a damn."

"Two years and then some pretty much kills everything."

"Everything but us," Tye said.

Jackson nodded slowly at the truth of those words, tore her gaze away from the truck, and pointed her machete at the shuttered house. "Enough with the reminiscing. Take a look at that."

Tye's gaze followed the line of the blade. A frown spread across his face as he assessed the building from top to bottom. "It looks…"

"Like it probably did two years ago?"

"Yeah."

"Weird isn't it?" Jackson said. "I don't know about your end, but down there," she tilted her head to the south of the street, "the rest of these million-dollar houses are rocking the post-apocalyptic-makeover vibe. Broken glass, doors hanging off their frames, trash all over the place."

"And this one stands alone," Tye said, his frown deepening. "Could be Obama's. I heard he has a house around here."

"Had, *had* a house," Jackson said. "And I'm pretty sure the dead do not make dining distinctions based on fame, or," she added when Tye opened his mouth to speak, "government office."

"Unless he went rogue in the beginning. He could still be hanging around." Tye paused and shook his head. "That's a weird thought."

"Weird but not outside the realms of possibility," Jackson said. "Hence the stealth you just ruined. Something is off, and we can't ignore it. If there's food anywhere, it's hidden in that house. The rest have been picked clean, and this one looks like it's been protected."

Tye shot her an incredulous look. "You're seriously not suggesting there are actual people inside?"

She snorted. "Yep, I'm betting there's a whole family just waiting to open their arms to us. They'll have a meal all laid out, hot baths running—"

"Sarcasm is the lowest form of wit, Jack."

Jackson shook her head. "You goad me into it. Seriously though, I'm thinking there *were* people still living in there. Not for a while and not now," she added, holding up her free hand to halt whatever words Tye had been about to say, "but maybe they lasted out longer than the rest of the street. It'd explain why things look different. Better yet, it might mean food."

Tye's stomach gave a grumble. It was far louder than it should have been and Jackson caught his eye.

"Keep it down. That was loud enough for a pack to hear."

"Can't help it," he said. "You keep talking about food. When was the last time we ate, for fuck's sake? I still can't believe the university campus was picked clean."

"It's crazy," Jackson agreed, thinking of all those dorm rooms they'd crept through. Each had been viler than the last, full of blood and pus and a million other unidentifiable fluids. Worse, they'd stunk of teen sweat, though how that could be two and more years after those rooms had last been occupied, Jackson didn't know. "Took a brave person indeed to wander those rooms and clean them out," she added. "End of the day though, it doesn't leave us much choice but to hit up Creepyville here. We need some calories in our system as soon as possible, and I'd rather not chow down on rat again."

"There's nothing wrong with rat."

"There's so much wrong with it I can't even begin." She swung Mandy in the direction of the biggest window, forcing Tye to lean back to avoid the super-sharp blade. "I'm thinking we go through the shutters there. We'll chop through them and then the glass too if there's any left."

"That'll make a bit of noise."

"Less noise than trying to go through the front door. You know it'll probably be barricaded up, and besides, didn't you just say we were okay?"

"I said we are okay for the moment. Let's not push our luck any more than we have to."

"So we'll be quick."

He hefted his ax, giving it a swing of what Jackson assumed was agreement. "I'm always quick, sweetheart."

"I bet."

"You're not funny."

They made their way out from behind the SUV, around a Prius that seemed to have collided headfirst with a Dumpster, and across to the sidewalk. It was slippery and Jackson swerved to avoid what looked like a splatter of vomit. It was probably just decomposing vegetation but she shot it a nasty look as she passed.

"Waist-high grass and weeds," Tye said with a scowl. "Does any look trampled to you?"

She shook her head. "You're thinking zombie hide-and-seek?

They'd have been on us already."

"That they would. Bastards have no subtlety."

"Amen for that."

It took just a few moments to wade through the scraggy vegetation and approach the biggest window. Up close Jackson could see that the house did not look as pristine as it had from the street. The white of the stone was discolored in places by mold, and the wooden slats of the shutters were showing signs of wear and tear. She gave them maybe another year or so before bugs ate their way completely through.

"They're starting to rot," she muttered. "Should be easy enough to get through."

"Along the vertical?" Tye asked.

"Yeah. You take the top hinge. I'll take the bottom. One swing each should do it."

The left side shutter came off easily enough, with minimal noise, and they lowered it to the ground, propping it up against the side of the house. Once it was safely out of the way, they stepped forward and peered through the window frame into the house.

"No glass," Tye said softly. "And no pieces or shards of it either. At least none that I can see."

"It's like someone just carried them away…or cleaned up the mess." Their eyes met and Jackson frowned. "This is creepy."

"Creepier inside. There's no fucking light."

Jackson tightened her grip around Mandy as she looked into what would once have been a living room. Tye was right; although strips of light came in from the shutters, it was nowhere near enough to illuminate everything. She could make out a couch, a table, and what might be a TV stand, but nothing apart from that. "I wish I still had my flashlight," she whispered. "I'd sell you for it right now."

"Who are you selling me to?" Tye asked as he ran his hands along the ledge, probably making sure there were no slithers of

EMMA SHORTT

glass they'd missed. "If we're talking a curvy Latina I'll go happily."

"Curvy? On the post-apocalyptic diet?"

"Good point. Now stand back and I'll go in first."

"You sure?"

"It's probably my turn. Wait for the signal."

Jackson nodded as she turned to keep a watch on the street. That damn backpack was still in her line of vision and she scowled at it, unsure why it bothered her so much. It certainly wasn't the only evidence of abandoned belongings. There were other bags scattered around, most empty, but some full of moldy clothes and useless electrical items. One thing was for sure, none of them had food or bottled water inside. Stuff *that* precious was hidden away. It took creeping around, braving places no sane person ever wanted to visit, to find the good stuff.

Places like this. Jackson let out a slow exhale before turning slightly so that the empty window was in her peripheral vision. She could hear Tye moving through the eerie room and tightened her grip on her blade, waiting for the damn signal. He'd insisted when they met—almost a month or so ago, though it was hard to keep track of dates any more—that they have one, and they'd debated for hours over what it should be. Not because it was so important, but because it gave them something to talk about beyond the depressing nothing. In the end she'd agreed to Tye's suggestion of a whistle, one note for all is well and two for start fucking running. More often than not she got the two, and was surprised, was *always* surprised, when just one came.

Jackson took a deep breath, gave the street one last look, then dropped Mandy-the-machete into the room. She felt naked without her weapon and hurried to lift herself on to the ledge and pull herself up, dropping a moment or so later onto the carpeted floor.

The squelchy, stinking, carpeted floor.

What was that stench? A combination of mold and ammonia?

It was strong, almost overwhelming, and Jackson clamped her lips shut as she looked around the room. Shadows played across every surface, tiny dust motes swirled in the horizontal shafts of light, and almost immediately a feeling Jackson did not like hit, and hit hard. Over the last two years she'd learned to listen to those feelings. They'd kept her alive when so many other people—hell, practically everyone—was dead, and she picked Mandy up quickly, the feel of her smooth wooden hilt immediately comforting.

"Looks all clear," Tye said, his voice hushed. "On this floor at least."

"Something's not right here," Jackson whispered, unable to put her finger on what exactly was bothering her. "It feels…off."

"Then let's hurry."

They crept into the darkened hallway—Tye leading the way—and followed it the length of the house. It opened up into a kitchen, a large one, and the light was a little better, the gaps in the shutters wider from where the rot was making better progress. Still, the weird feeling remained, enough that Jackson tightened her grip on Mandy.

"That's gotta be the pantry, and the door is closed," Tye said. "Check it out, and I'll keep watch."

Jackson approached the door slowly, her heart beating a steady tattoo in her chest. She gripped her weapon in her right hand as she turned the doorknob, holding her breath without even meaning to. The relief that hit when nothing jumped out seemed oddly out of place, and Jackson lowered the blade only slightly, her gaze taking everything in, because whoever had lived in the house had clearly planned for a rainy day. The metal shelves were practically overflowing with food, and for a moment she just paused to look at it all, her heart racing at the sight. Beans, vegetables, even tinned potatoes. How long had it been since she'd eaten a potato? Not since that farm in Indiana and most of them had been rotten.

"Jesus Christ, take a look at this," she whispered. "There's enough food here for weeks."

Tye leaned back slightly so he could peer in. Even in the dim light Jackson saw his eyes widen, but a moment later he shook his head. "We can only take what we can carry, you know that. Unless you wanna eat here and then take more with us?"

"I want to stuff my face immediately, but," she looked around the darkened room, across the shadowed work surfaces, the sink and the oven—something like a chill slithering down her spine as she did so, "this place give me the heebies, not to mention the smell. I don't like it. It feels wrong. Let's take what we can carry and find somewhere else to eat and rest."

"Back in the direction of the campus?"

"Might as well. We need to go back that way to pick up the interstate."

"Get a move on then, sugar pie. I'll go after you."

Jackson pulled her small pack off her back and unzipped it. The sound was unnaturally loud in the quiet of the room, more so than their hushed voices. She shook her head as she caught Tye's eye. "I know. I know."

There was enough space in the pack for maybe a half-a-dozen cans. Any more than that would slow her down, and despite the spooky vibe of the house Jackson narrowed her eyes as she read the labels, wanting to make sure she picked right. After a moment or so she took two cans of beans, a tin of potatoes, and a packet of pasta. Then carefully, so as not to disturb the shelving unit, she lifted herself on her tiptoes and reached out for a tin of ham. The moment her fingertips found the first of them she paused. Tye froze too, his ax head glinting off one of the vertical shafts of light.

"Did you hear that?"

She nodded. A sound, a sort of creaking. Jackson lowered herself slowly, her feet hitting the floor with the smallest of noises, her pack held tight to her body.

Tye took a step back, so that he was closer to her, and looked upward. Jackson followed his gaze, swallowing against the sudden lump in her throat as she realized what he meant.

He gestured toward the hallway they'd snuck through, but Jackson shook her head. The stairs were there and whatever was now making its way across the roof, or maybe even inside the attic, would cut off their escape. She touched Tye's shoulder and pointed toward the French windows instead. Or rather what used to be the windows, they were just closed shutters now, but they closed from the inside, meaning they would be able to unlatch them, and slip out.

Cautiously they stepped across the floor. Like the carpet, it didn't feel right, not squelchy this time though, but sticky. Jackson shuddered inwardly as she imagined exactly what might be coating the hardwood.

"We need to be quick," Tye whispered, his mouth next to her ear. "I'll kick it through and we'll head for the alleyway on the right. It'll follow the noise and come down thinking to trap us. Don't lose that food."

Jackson nodded and slowly, carefully, put her backpack on.

Another noise from upstairs, this one sounding suspiciously like something was walking. Jackson's heart raced as she imagined one of *them* already inside the building. And where there was one there were three or four more. They traveled in packs, never alone. Food or not, it simply wasn't worth the risk to hang around.

"Now," she hissed.

Tye kicked the shutters through, and maybe it was the rot, or perhaps just the force of his muscles, but they exploded outward, shards of wood going everywhere, light filling the gloomy kitchen. A rattling groan sounded from upstairs, and where before the zombie had been stalking—trying to find a way inside, maybe not even sure there was a meal close by—now it bashed against something, the ceiling, one of the doors? Jackson and Tye did not wait to find out. They burst into the garden—as overgrown as the front lawn—and veered right, toward the alleyway that ran the length of the house.

Horror movie waiting to happen…

The words echoed in Jackson's mind as her feet pounded the ground, and she gripped Mandy so tight the bones in her hand should have ached. Should have, but didn't. Adrenaline was flooding her system, her heart was racing in her chest, and everything came into sharp focus…including the four zombies that were heading straight for them.

CHAPTER TWO

Luke Granger could hear them pounding on the ceiling of his underground bunker. The noise was constant and unrelenting, edging its way into his consciousness, pulling him from a nap that had been far too brief.

He lifted his head from his arms, glanced around the empty room, then reached for his — now cold — mug of coffee, downing the remains in one long swallow. The taste was vile, but then instant beans with powdered milk was never gonna win any medals, was it?

He scowled into the empty mug, remembering the hot lava java he used to drink, before shouting, "Give it a fucking rest."

They pounded again.

Jesus Christ. What the hell was wrong with them? You'd think that after weeks and weeks of trying to get through the thick metal they'd realize they couldn't. But no, they had to interrupt what little sleep he could get. He looked up and sent the ceiling the foulest glare he could muster. "I'm going to kill every last fucking one of you when I come out there."

They pounded some more.

"Every single one," he hissed, straightening in his chair and giving himself a shake. A sharp pain shot through his shoulder from the movement and he rotated the muscles, cursing himself as he did so for falling asleep at his desk again. The papers he'd been trying to read through before he'd nodded off were now scrunched up, and his headphones were dangling from the desk.

Luke picked them up, pushed back his chair, and stood. The ceiling was maybe three feet above him, and he walked across the room until he was directly underneath the spot they were busy bashing away at. He visualized the building above in his mind and suspected they were in the basement gym. Abruptly a meme he'd once seen filled his mind and Luke frowned. The picture had been of a house, and surrounding it were a few dozen treadmills. Zombies ran on the treadmills, arms outstretched, while a triumphant group of people looked on from inside the house. The caption had said, *zombie defense mechanism.*

If only it were that easy.

Luke sighed and stomped back over to his desk. The coffee mug was balancing precariously on the papers, and he righted it before sitting back down. The headphone cord was tangled from where it had fallen, and the jack was half out of the socket. Luke plugged it back in, then gave the cord a sharp tug. Damn thing constantly curled in on itself.

The zombies increased their pounding.

How many were up there, Luke wondered? Five. Ten. Twenty? He had no way of knowing and really, in the end, it made no difference. For all his threats, Luke had no intention of opening the trapdoor and entering the house. That many against just him? He'd probably get eaten and then he'd be…well dead, and wouldn't that be a kick in the shitter?

Ignoring that depressing thought, he closed his eyes, lifted his headphones, and put them on. The heavy padding muffled the noise of the zombie party slightly, and he sighed in satisfaction.

It would be so easy to fall back asleep…to try and go eight

hours straight without thinking about them. He could indulge in one of his little fantasies, the one that featured the battered old villa his family owned in Barra de Potosi, down in Mexico. He could almost see it in his mind. The red-tiled roof, the faded brown shutters, the scrubby brush. The sun would be beating down on it, making everything bake.

"You'd hate that wouldn't you?" he said, trying his best to ignore the pangs that remembering the old house made him feel. "The heat. Slows you fuckers down. Easy pickings."

The zombies pounded harder, hard enough for him to hear even through the headphones, almost as if they were answering him. But then it wasn't like anyone else was going to respond to his ramblings. There *wasn't* anyone else but him. Hadn't been for quite some time.

Luke sighed and leaned forward to switch the radio equipment on. A shiver of pain shot through him and, almost automatically, he reached under his shirt to rub the still-red wound by his rib cage. It itched constantly, which he guessed was a good thing. Surely it meant it was healing. And healing was essential in his lonely world. He couldn't afford to be slow, because those fuckers could run! Damn, could they run, as evidenced by the finally closed hole in his stomach where some dead bastard had dug its finger in and poked around. Not to mention the bite marks down his arms, and the particularly attractive one on his ass. His chest gave a nasty sort of ache as he remembered the kid clamping on his left butt cheek and sinking her teeth in. It ached a little more as he remembered slicing the point of his ax through her head...

The headphones crackled once the equipment was on, and Luke settled himself in the chair. He picked up a sheaf of the crumpled papers, his hand nudging his laptop as he did so. Laptop. Tablet. Phone. He wasn't even sure why he kept them—wasn't like they were much good to him now. Still...he frowned...no point thinking about that.

He turned the radio dial to find the first of the frequencies on his long, long list, his heart fluttering as a hissing sound came through over the airwaves.

He almost laughed.

How many nights had he sat in this exact same position fiddling with the radio, hoping against hope? Too many. But he had to try. What else was there?

The pounding grew dimmer as the minutes ticked by, as if they were putting less effort in, and Luke sighed with relief. Despite the fact that the zombies could not get into the basement bunker, he hated knowing they were close by. Hated the thought of them grunting and slathering on the other side of the metal.

Hated them full stop.

He flipped to the next frequency, letting his mind drift a little, imagining a lazy day on the bay, doing a little bit of fishing, drinking whiskey, eating a few olives. The last mouthful of olives he'd eaten had been out of a jar he'd found in a condo by Evergreen Park. He was sure they'd been bad. Certainly he'd suffered for a few days after eating them. Yes, a day on the beach, without a zombie in sight. He wouldn't even need to take his ax, never mind a gun. He imagined the sun shining down on him, basking in the silence...*the silence*... He bolted upright and cursed.

The pounding had stopped completely. He couldn't even hear muffled footsteps now. Sure, he wanted them to shut up, but wanting it was not enough to make it reality. They could still smell him in the sprawling mansion above, even though it had been a good month since he'd been up there, and they wouldn't stop until they gave him the steak-and-sauce treatment. No, only one thing would drag them away.

A burst of energy hit his system, jolting him awake in a way the caffeine had not. Luke stood up quickly and dropped the headphones—the wires of which immediately tangled back up, knocking the coffee mug aside in the process.

Only one thing…

Another meal close by…and that might mean…another person.

Luke's heart raced as he considered that amazing prospect. It had been so long since he'd seen or talked to someone. So fucking long…and yet… He looked upward, eyeing the ceiling again. It was possible the zombies had simply heard a dog or a fox—they didn't give much of a shit what they ate, would follow the noise regardless. He could be going out for no reason. But if it really *was* a someone, rather than a something, close by, he had to go help. Didn't matter how tired he was. How much he ached. How dangerous it might be. Even the faint possibility of someone else being out there was enough.

He righted the coffee mug, surveying his living area, or as some would call it, the heart of his bunker, as he did so. He'd been beyond lucky to find this place and he knew it, was thankful for it every single day. From what he could tell, it had been a giant panic room for the very rich guy who owned the mansion above. It was well stocked and had two exits—neither of which the waking dead had found—and walls thicker than Mary Lou's thighs. Ah, Mary Lou, his first ever girlfriend. She was dead now, of course. Lots of people were.

"Time to get moving," he said, pushing the thought of all those people to the back of his mind. "Time to go actually, finally, find another person."

Another person. The thought was almost unbelievable, and as Luke picked up his army-grade sweater from the back of his chair, anticipation curled in his gut. The hole in his stomach protested, but Luke had no time for that shit. He pulled open the desk drawer and grabbed a half-full Johnny Walker bottle, lifted his tee, and splashed some over the wound. It stung like a bitch, but the alcohol removed any possible infection, and that shit counted. Luke had no intention of getting sick, or worse, turning into one of them, though as far as he could tell it wasn't as simple as just a bite or a finger in the stomach—he was proof of that. Whiskey seemed to be the key. He'd splashed all and any wounds with the stuff and he was still breathing.

He shrugged the sweater on before bending back down to lace up his boots. A film of red goo layered the front of one and he splashed some whiskey over it. Jesus, he'd be drunk soon from the fumes, and with his current sleep level he'd probably pass out.

He snorted at the image.

Luke shucked on his leather jacket—nothing said fashion like bite marks—and locked his Glock to his waistband. A few grenades in his pocket and his ax in hand and he was ready to go. The question was—which exit to use? It'd be a lie to say he wasn't tempted to try the trapdoor that led into the basement area. Both because he was curious and because he would have liked to kill any of the zombies still hanging around—bastards deserved it, waking him up constantly. Only that'd be stupid, and Luke had not survived for so long by being stupid. He nodded to himself, mind made up, and headed across his living area to the tunnel that ran the length of the property. He picked up a bottle of Old Spice en route and splashed a liberal amount over himself. Combined with the whiskey, the Old Spice made him feel light-headed for a moment. Still it was necessary. For some reason the stench covered his tracks. Maybe they disliked the manly smell. Go figure.

Time to go save someone, anyone, he thought, and for a moment he hoped it'd be a female someone—preferably of the noncanine or nonfeline persuasion. Maybe even a luscious blonde with a dazzling smile, looking for someplace safe to stay.

He snorted again. Yeah, and why not ask for a rocket launcher, a new supply of grenades, and some way of getting down to Mexico while he was at it? The image of the villa came to him once more and he sighed. He doubted he'd ever see the place again. He'd suspected as much two years ago and nothing that had happened since had suggested otherwise.

Two years…the day nightmares came true and everything went to shit. The day the waking dead came calling.

Chapter Three

In a perfect example of timing actually working in their favor, Jackson and Tye burst out of the alleyway just as the zombies reached them. Tye was in front and he immediately lifted his ax, swinging it at the nearest one. It was a female and she was naked, dripping pus from various wounds that had yet to heal, growling in that horrible way they all did.

Tye's swing missed as the zombie swerved at exactly the right moment. He kicked out at it instead, hitting it on the hip bone, and it stumbled, falling into the entrance to the alleyway right in front of Jackson. She didn't even think about it. Jackson simply lifted her Doc Marten boot and kicked the zombie in the face—her forward momentum giving her more power than she would normally have had. Something crunched and she heard a snap. Its neck maybe? There was no way to tell and it didn't matter anyway.

Jackson skidded to a halt, lifted her booted foot again, and stamped down hard on its face. Fluids oozed rather than spurted as she made contact, and Jackson gritted her teeth as the stench of zombie filled her nostrils. Rotting garbage, urine, and a million other smells that were just as bad, all vied for prominence, making her gag. Another stomp, this one squashing the eyes and turning its nose into nothing more than a bloody pulp, then another, opening up the muscle and fatty tissues to the skull beneath.

"Balls to the walls!" Tye shouted and Jackson gave one more stomp before lifting Mandy.

A male zombie was heading straight for her. He was dressed in what looked like pajamas which were old now and had been slowly rotting. Jackson could see the mottled skin beneath them, more of those pus-filled wounds dripping. It held its arms out, those weirdly elongated limbs desperate to get to her, and Jackson swallowed down the hatred as she looked at its face.

Predatory. Feral. The bastard.

A moment later, it reached her. Jackson lifted Mandy and swung hard. The blade arced through the air with a speed that was shocking. It caught the zombie in the spot between the shoulder and the neck on the left side. About an inch of the blade went in, opening up the artery, creating a shower of blood. Jackson moved to the side to avoid the spray, pulled Mandy free, and swung again. But the zombie hit out wildly as she rotated, smacking her on the shoulder, and Jackson overbalanced, falling to her knees. She felt the impact rather than the pain, and immediately righted herself, rolling and standing in one smooth move. Her second swing worked, the blade went in to the face this time, right along the cheekbone. The force of it made her arm spasm at the shock of the contact.

The zombie shrieked. Blood was spouting from its neck, half of its face was hanging off, and still it tried to get her. Jackson kicked it in the stomach, a perfect front kick. It hit the floor and she followed it, bringing her blade down on its head, cracking the skull bone and biting into brain. Once again the contact made her arms spasm, and Jackson had to grit her teeth as she pulled the blade back out.

Her arms shook as she spun around, looking for the rest of them. One, a teenage girl, was headless, Tye's ax having cleaved right through her neck. The other, Tye was busy stamping on, and Jackson clenched her fists as she watched bits of skin and muscle splatter upward from his heavy boot.

A flash of something that looked suspiciously like an eyeball shot past her and Jackson clamped her lips shut, the disgusting thought of a bit of zombie flesh finding its way into her mouth making her mentally gag.

"Where's the other one?" she asked the moment the flesh stopped flying. "The one that was on the roof?"

Tye wiped his boot against the grass—the zombie now still—and turned to face her. "It wasn't one of these?"

She shook her head as she looked around the area. "It couldn't have got down that fast."

A *bang* sounded from the alleyway. Jackson stepped back quickly so that she and Tye were right next to each other. Another *bang*, coming from the other direction, and a nasty chill slithered down Jackson's spine. The quiet of the street just a half hour earlier reminding her that the noise could only mean one thing.

"Did you hear that?"

"Yeah."

"There's only ever five at most in a pack," she whispered.

"Four here and one on the roof."

Jackson tightened her hold on her weapon and took several, quick breaths. "No. There's more. Listen."

"Where—"

A zombie, the one that had found them, jumped from the garage, falling into a roll, before standing up so quickly that Jackson almost skittered back. Almost but didn't. That would be unacceptable. The zombie would smell her fear and would come straight for her. Like animals, Jackson had long since suspected that they could sense the weakest person, and that person would never be her. *Never.*

"Hello, Mr. Fucking Crash the Party," Tye growled.

If things had not been so tense, Jackson would have rolled her eyes. "Really?"

Tye shrugged. "Just trying to mix it up."

The zombie paused in front of them—and that in itself was odd because when did zombies ever pause with food in front of them?—before letting out a shrieking howl. The noise echoed in the space around them, unnaturally loud and menacing. It was almost like it was answering. Tye and Jackson glared.

It took one step forward, its movements jittery. Jackson could see its chest rising and falling far more rapidly than it should have done. If she stepped up close and put a hand against its chest she knew its heart rate would be frantic.

"Cross over?" she asked and next to her, she felt Tye nod.

Together they ran at it, and had it had any sense of survival it should have turned and bolted in the other direction, but of course it didn't. With painful predictability it came straight for them.

Tye swung his ax at its head and Jackson ducked below him to swing her machete at its stomach. The weapons hit at almost the same time. Her blade—her perfectly formed blade—slicing right through the zombie's skin, the fat, the muscle, and through to who knew what else. A moment later it crumpled to the ground. Jackson quickly averted her eyes, not wanting to see its internal organs decorating the sidewalk. God knew she'd seen enough intestines to last her several lifetimes.

They both paused, both slightly out of breath.

It was a zombie that broke the silence.

Jackson snapped into activity, sprinting across the lawn, the waist-high grass and scrub whipping around her thighs as she moved. Her foot wobbled slightly on an uneven patch of ground and she glanced down, surprised to see what looked like a hole in the muddy ground—a deep hole. Before she could work out exactly what it meant, Tye reached out to steady her.

She jumped over the hole, straight into a scraggly bush, before racing across the remaining lawn. Despite the fact she knew there were no zombies crouched and hiding in the vegetation—they didn't have that kind of patience—Jackson couldn't help the relief she felt as her feet touched concrete. The relief was short-lived. More zombie howls filled the air and Jackson grabbed Tye's arm, pulling him across to the overturned SUV with her.

She crouched behind it again, trying to pinpoint the source of the howls. A moment later and she realized exactly where they were coming from. Her heart sank and she had to wipe her palms on her jeans. It was only when she did that Jackson realized she was coated with sweat, and it was cold, so the sweat chilled her skin. Or maybe it was just the fact that they were completely in the shit.

"They're in both directions, cutting off our escape," she whispered, trying and failing to keep her heart from racing. "Look."

Tye followed her shaky finger and cursed softly when he spotted them. Several figures were standing on the roofs of the houses, their horrible, elongated forms outlined against the gray sky. Jackson counted five to the north, four to the south, equivalent to two other packs, and that was unheard of. Zombies never banded together in groups of more than five. Never.

"There could be more," she added, swallowing against the words. "Waiting on the ground."

"There's too many," Tye growled. "There shouldn't be this many. What the fuck are they doing?"

Jackson adjusted her position, unwilling to think about that right now. There were far more important things to consider. Like staying alive, that one being fairly high on the fucking list. "There's no way we can fight a pack each," she said. "Not right now. We'd be as good as dead."

Tye grunted at her words, most likely because he didn't want to admit the truth of them, but there was no avoiding it. Already Jackson's arms ached from the confrontation with the first pack.

Her heart was beating far too quickly, and she was beginning to shake. That was all normal, the expected aftermath of a fight-for-your-life kinda situation, but it also meant that her reaction times would be slower, her swings a little less forceful. *Fuck.*

"Ideas?" she asked.

"Not any you're gonna like."

"When do I ever?"

"We need to split the two packs," Tye said after a moment. "Lead them in opposite directions, separate them, pick them off one by one."

His meaning hit and she frowned. "Split us up, you mean."

Tye shrugged. "It's the only way. Just like when we first met, remember?"

Jackson nodded slowly, the memory of that first meeting so vivid, even now. She could recall perfectly the moment she'd realized that the man running down the street was actually alive. The first person she'd seen in what had to be well over a year. A few minutes later and they'd had no choice but to separate, Tye calling out the name of the street he was hiding on as he ran in the other direction, taking a pack of zombies with him. She'd worried all night that she'd imagined him, that he wouldn't be there when she went looking. Only he was, and a full month later they were still surviving. Two friends, maybe the last two friends, against a never-ending number of the undead.

Cheery.

"Say we do this," she said quickly. "What's our meeting place?"

"We'll meet by that chick store. The one you said looked like a Barbie brothel."

Yes, she remembered it. The sign had said Kelly's Clothing Boutique and the swooshy pink doors and windows had been oddly intact. "It's maybe a ten-minute sprint from here," she said.

"So I'll take that," Tye said, pointing to a house with its door hanging off. "I noticed a side alley behind there, leads onto a green.

I'll follow it around, baiting the bigger pack, and then come out at the end of the street. You head in the direction of the rec center and get the others to follow you. We passed it earlier remember? It's only a couple of blocks over from the Barbie brothel, wait there for a bit, then double back."

Jackson shivered as the zombies groaned. "Jesus, Tye, this feels like a bad idea in so many ways." She sighed. "I swear it's got fuck-up written all over it."

"What other options do we have?" he asked, rotating his shoulders and taking a deep breath. Readying himself Jackson thought, the plan already clear in his mind. "Don't tell me Jackson the bad-ass is scared."

She glared, as, no doubt, he'd meant her to. "Scared I'll have to come save your ass when the zombies corner you."

"You know they'll never take me alive."

"That's what worries me. You might be a dick ninety percent of the time but you're the only friend I've got to watch my back. I'm not ready to lose you yet."

He laughed, the soft, completely inappropriate sound echoing in the small space between them. "You won't lose me. I promise. And even if you did you'd do fine. You've survived two years and then some. Skinny little thing like you—makes no sense and yet here you are."

Jackson shook her head, not to deny his words, but to agree with them. *It didn't* make any kind of sense. "And if the plan goes to shit?"

"We'll find each other again. Don't we always?"

"Always doesn't mean the same thing anymore," she said eventually. "You know it doesn't."

He shrugged. "It means what it means."

"Which in today's world is precisely nothing." Their eyes met—his brown to her green and Jackson sighed, knowing when she was beaten and wishing to hell that was not the case.

If wishes were horses, then beggars would ride...and all the zombies would disappear...

"If you're not at that store in an hour, one hour, Tye," she said. "I'll find you and kill you myself."

He nodded solemnly and straightened from his crouch. "I don't doubt it. Now, come on. Let's do this."

And so they did.

Chapter Four

Luke watched from his hidden position as the pack of zombies he'd been following for the last fifteen fun-filled minutes stalked up the street. There were four in total, three males and a female. For once, thankfully, they were all dressed, though Luke could tell that it wouldn't be long before they joined the naked throngs of the dead. Modern clothing simply wasn't up to lasting two years and then some in the elements.

He took a step forward, the breeze—working in his direction he was glad to see—fluttering against his neck. A moment later and he halted. A second pack was joining the first, groaning and howling and looking pissed off. This one was slightly bigger, five members in all, and Luke sighed. Three were completely naked—it was not a pretty sight.

He edged along the wall, eyes narrowed as he tried to work out where they were heading. The street housed a number of businesses but also some apartments. Could someone be hiding out in one of those? Maybe even scavenging for supplies?

Luke had no idea. He didn't have the zombies' sense of smell.

Talking of which…the bastards must have picked something up. A scent? A noise? Whatever it was it was enough to make them run. They sped up the street, and even though it pained him, Luke couldn't help but marvel at how fast they could move. Easily as fast as a living person. Though maybe not as fast as someone superfit, like a mechanic.

He almost grinned as he followed in their wake.

A few moments later the combined pack came to a halt, stopping directly in front of one of the stores. Luke frowned, slowed, and edged a little bit forward. Who the fuck would be hanging around in—he looked at the sign—Kelly's Clothing Boutique? Groceries yeah, gas, hell yeah, but dresses and skirts? He shook his head in disbelief. Surely those items would be low on the list of any self-respecting survivor, and were in no way worth the risk they were so clearly taking.

A shiver ran down his spine as he watched the zombies pause just outside the store—no more than a few yards from Luke's hidden position behind a stinking Dumpster—their breathing rapid and almost hoarse. He watched as one, he'd once been a man in life, snarled at a female next to him. Its face was screwed up in the horrible manner all their faces were. Almost animalistic, certainly predatory. The sight of it, and the sound of its death groan raised the hair on Luke's arms and he gritted his teeth.

In the very early days, the news—what little there was of it—insisted the zombies had lost all mental abilities and were surviving only on instinct. Luke suspected the news stations had been full of shit. They ran in packs, they growled and snarled at one another, and lately the packs had taken to banding together to share food—something unheard of up till now. To Luke that kinda suggested some sort of evil mental process was going on. Like a clique of teenage girls.

The combined pack stepped forward now, their movements jittery, yet smooth. The dead did not move like the alive. Their limbs were more flexible, more fluid—though how that worked from a biological viewpoint Luke had no idea. In the end though, it didn't really matter. It was all about the effect—not the cause. And the effect was this, them fanning out around the door into a loose arc, one of their standard hunting techniques. Luke shivered slightly at the glint he could see in their eyes. Clearly they were thinking food, could smell whoever, or whatever, was inside. Yeah, they had more than instinct going on. He was certain of it. Something ticked inside them, Luke just didn't know what.

Another bunch of death groans rent the air, followed by the sound of glass breaking, and Luke knew he had to act immediately. If they actually got inside the store, the person in there would have no chance, and he'd still be alone, losing his only chance at a chess partner.

Taking a deep breath, he took two grenades from his pocket and crouched down. His ax—now strapped to his back—dug into his shoulder slightly, and Luke shifted before popping the pin from the first grenade and throwing it over the Dumpster. It landed right in the middle of the pack. They looked down at the noise, groaned, and made to disperse. But they were not quick enough. A severed arm, gushing with yellow pus landed right to the side of him and Luke grimaced. Another limb joined the arm, though it was hard to tell what type.

Luke waited a minute or so, popped the pin from the second grenade, and threw it into the melee. It took out a few more and a splash of blood hit the Dumpster. A good job he was hiding behind it or else he'd have been covered.

Ignoring the twitching limbs and pus—there was always pus—snaking its way toward him underneath the Dumpster, Luke pulled a Glock19 from each side of his waistband, positioned them at the ready, and edged out. Four zombies remained. He put a bullet in the first, dropping it in one. The second turned and bared its teeth. Luke promptly shot it and it fell on its buddy with a gurgle and a shudder.

Luke clenched his hands around his guns and eyed the

final two creatures. One had been a woman in life. Her black hair reached almost to her waist, and her breasts were obvious beneath the dirty sweatshirt she wore. He could just make out the words "Sports Mom on Patrol" printed across it and he realized immediately who she was. Not surprising, he'd had to shoot more than one person he'd known in his former life. Still…a mixture of anger and regret slithered down his spine as he looked at her, holding her almond eyes for just a moment. Recognition did not flare in those eyes and he pushed the regret away. *She isn't Lily anymore,* he told himself. *She's dead.*

The other zombie was a fairly large man, but not muscled, more like fat—and this was clearly obvious due to the fact he was naked. Luke shot him first. He did not hit the ground. *Shit.*

The zombie eyed him in a way that Luke could only describe as calculating and Luke edged back slightly. How many bullets was this going to take? He fired another one. It hit Fatombie right in the stomach but it kept on coming…almost sauntering. *Bastard.*

Another shot, missing the head by a bare inch and almost hitting the dead Lily. She growled, turned, and strode into the now-open store, dismissing him without even so much as a no-thanks. *Fuck.* He hoped the person, whoever they were, could take her down. Though the female ones were worse than the men, so that might be an issue. They were often lighter and sprightlier. He'd once seen one jump from two stories and still get her man. Intestines and all.

"Come on then, you bastard," Luke said. "Gimme your best."

The zombie launched forward, groaning as he did so, but Luke held his ground, firing both guns, riddling it with bullets. With a mere inch between them, Luke leaning back to stay out of the way of its elongated fingers, a bullet found its mark and buried itself in Fatombie's head. It hit the ground, and Luke let out the breath he'd been holding.

Thank fuck for that.

He paused for just a moment, taking in the scene around him, trying to get himself together. His palpitating heart combined with his lack of sleep was making him slightly light-headed, not a good combination. He took a deep breath and gave himself a mental shake, just as something that sounded like a roar reached him.

Luke swiveled round, and zeroed in on the wreck that was now Kelly's Clothing. His first thought was *oh shit, it really is a person.* His second, slightly more depressing thought, was that the roar belonged to a man. His blonde fantasy dissolved, his head pounded, and he ran toward the store, intent on making the Lily zombie pay. Though in all fairness it was hardly her fault. *I'll be doing her a favor,* he told himself. *She wouldn't have wanted to live like this.*

That was Luke's intention at least. Only he didn't expect to be confronted with another pack, plus Lily, eyes glinting, mouths open, emitting a series of horrific death groans.

His last thought was, fuck, where's the whiskey when you need it?

Chapter Five

Jackson wasn't sure how long she'd been waiting in the rec center, it might have been fifteen minutes, maybe even a half hour. Time seemed to stretch, or sometimes even compress, when adrenaline was calling the shots, and she had no wristwatch to tell her how many seconds had ticked by.

Part of her was antsy to head back out. The waiting was almost agonizing. But the sensible part, the bit that had kept her alive for so freaking long, held her in place, hands clenched around Mandy, legs shaking ever so slightly. But was that any wonder? Jackson had ran her skinny ass off, through gardens, side roads, over fences, managing to lose her half of the super-sized pack in the process.

Hiding out until she calmed some, and could be sure they were well and truly gone, was the sensible thing to do, and she'd taken plenty of precautions to ensure they couldn't find her. The Lynx aftershave from the last of her stash, splashed on the entrance door, would help. Jackson wasn't sure when it became common knowledge that the zombies had an issue with certain types of aromas, that they avoided places that stunk a certain way. It seemed like one of those facts that just was. Like cellulite.

The pole she'd found on the floor of the room that housed

the swimming pool gave her an extra line of defense. Jackson had pushed it through the heavy double doors, barricading herself inside. She decided to wait in the swimming pool room because of that one door. One way in, one way out, and if the pack found her, she imagined she could create a funnel effect. Picking them off just as Tye had suggested.

Tye. Her heart clenched in a nasty sort of way as she imagined him sprinting to the boutique. She hoped to God he made it. That he'd managed to kill the pack, or better yet shake them off.

Though they'd only been together for a month, he was like a brother to her. A big, annoying brother yes, but one all the same, and Jackson knew that losing him would hurt. A lot. Because despite what she'd said, she had no desire to be alone again. Two years of the solitary life had been plenty and then some.

"Be safe, Tye," she said, the words coming out as almost a croak, making her abruptly aware that she was ridiculously thirsty.

She lifted her left hand and swung her backpack off her shoulder. The food they'd risked so much for suddenly heavier than it should have been. Jackson rooted around a little until she found her flask. It was half-full of boiled and cooled rain water, and she drank almost all of it in one go. She would have liked to have poured some on her hands to remove any splatters of zombie gore that might be clinging to her skin, but there was none to spare.

She cast the swimming pool a quick look but there was no doubt that the water in there was stagnant. She'd be risking an infection having it anywhere near her. It would rain tonight. The clouds had been threatening it all day. *You'll have to wait till then,* she told herself, imagining standing out in the downpour, shivering and cursing. For one moment that image was replaced with the wondrous memory of a shower. A hot shower, with strawberry-scented shampoo and vanilla shower gel. She closed her eyes as she imagined the water beating down on her shoulders…

A muted *bang* filled the air. The sound so alien in the quiet world that Jackson froze, her hot-water fantasy wiped away in a mere moment. What the hell was that? It sounded familiar and yet she could not place it. Another *bang*, this one entirely different and far too close. Metal on metal…crunching. *Please let it be Tye. Let it be Tye.*

Something groaned.

Jackson swung her backpack on without even thinking about it, hefted Mandy and ran to the side of the door.

"Fuck, fuck, fuck." Her whispered words were for herself. A way of controlling the panic that was already flooding her body — banishing the exhaustion that never seemed to go away unless she was doing this. Fighting for her life.

A second death groan rattled through the air just as another *bang* sounded, something almost like an explosion, but Jackson had no time to consider it. The zombie was so close, on the other side of the door already. Where were its pack mates? Why the fuck hadn't she heard it get in?

Another groan and Jackson swallowed unsteadily, gripping Mandy tight. She knew what she had to do, and she had to do it fast. Because one thing was for sure, it didn't groan because it kinda felt like it. It was calling other zombies to it, and they'd come. They always did, and after today who knew how many of them would answer the call? The rules were going the same way as hers used to do after one too many sangrias.

Do it fast. Funnel it through. "I'm coming, you bastard."

The zombie hit the metal with a shriek. The sound of her voice, no, the sound of food, fueling its rage. But it was hitting from the wrong way. The door swung out, not in, so for the moment, she had the upper hand. Lifting the metal pole that ran through the handles, Jackson took short, swift breaths. Filling her lungs, flooding her body with oxygen. She was going to need it.

Another shriek and it hit the door again. Jackson pushed the pole away, where it rolled until it hit the dirty pool water. She swapped Mandy to her right hand and gripped the left handle. She had to time this right. Another *bang* and she moved into action. She pushed the door open just as the zombie pulled back to attack again. The edge of the door caught it in the face and it howled.

Not giving it time to move, Jackson kicked it right in the stomach. A nasty squelching noise smacked her ears and the stench of zombie pus filled the enclosed space. Jackson almost gagged.

She kicked it again, anger giving her power, the muscles in her legs straining from the action. The force of the impact pushed the zombie back into the other room so that it stumbled over a weight bench. It fell smack on its ass and shrieked. Jackson jumped forward, lifted Mandy, and cut straight through its leg, to the bone. A huge arc of pus and blood shot up, forcing her to move to avoid it, but she wasn't quick enough. It soaked her jeans, from ankle to thigh.

"You bastard," she screeched.

It reached out with its filthy hands, its bloodstained face screwed up in the nasty manner all their faces were. Desperate, feral, hungry.

"You want this? Fuck you!"

The machete went all the way through the leg this time, severing it. Jackson jumped over the limb, whirred behind it, and in one quick move, severed the head. A much easier job than the bigger leg. Skin, muscle, and bone were no match for Mandy's perfectly honed blade.

More blood and pus splattered but Jackson barely gave it a second glance. She had no fucking time to. Where there was one zombie there were more. Her stay at the Pool Palace was officially over.

Quickly she stepped over the headless zombie into the cardio room, skirting around a treadmill, and then another. God, she remembered when the only exercise she got was on one of those things. Instruments of doom she'd called them. She'd run for five miles a day three times a week and back then she had thought it had killed her. Not being able to run five miles at a quick trot in today's world would *actually* kill her. The irony was painful.

Pus—from the headless zombie, no doubt— was splattered over the exercise equipment. *Drip, drip, drip* it went as it hit the tiled floor. The sound amplified in the silence. She hated zombie pus. What did they do, projectile spit the stuff? She had no idea why the hell they were so full of the gacky yellow liquid.

She went through two more rooms before she reached the final door, which was open—though it should not have been. She'd carefully closed every door behind her not so long ago. Jackson paused, did a quick survey of the reception area, and then bent to eye the door handle. She was both surprised and a little panicked to see a splatter of gore on it. Had the zombie turned the handle? But why on this one and not the other? It made no sense. They didn't, *couldn't* open things. They just bashed through them. What was going on with the zombies today?

Another *bang*, and Jackson realized why it had sounded familiar. It was like an explosion, louder now, but still muted, and she felt her heart race. Could it be Tye or something completely random? She shivered as she realized she had no way to tell.

Taking a deep breath, Jackson jogged over to the curved reception desk. It was remarkably clean, the chair just pushed ever so slightly back as though someone had nipped to the bathroom or gone to get a coffee and would return any moment. A laptop sat in the center of the desk and a mug with "Number One Mom" was pushed against the extra computer monitor. They would never drink from it again.

Jackson shivered and cursed her morbid thoughts, gave the desk one last look, and headed straight for the entrance to the rec center. It was quiet, the weak sun hanging low in the cloudy sky. She crept out and down the stairs in a low sort of crouch that made her feel like a crab. Goose bumps were already dotting her skin, her wet jeans felt heavy, and her muscles were held tight to ward off the cold. If not for the adrenaline, she'd be freezing already.

She could still smell the Lynx on the entrance door as she passed. Why the hell hadn't it stopped the zombie? And where the fuck were the rest of them? Carefully, that question foremost in her mind, she sped down the steps, weaving in and out of the abandoned cars up and down the street. A mangy rat skittered past and Jackson paused, her heart hammering in her throat, dispelling the chill creeping over her. As a general rule of thumb, if you saw an animal running, you joined it. Immediately. The zombies ate animals as well as people. Heck, the bastards ate anything with a freaking pulse, as well as anything without. Jackson still kept a look out for rotting corpses even though there was no need. They had been eaten in the very early months. She felt bad feeling grateful for that, but her life was horror movie enough already. Walking past decomposing bodies on a daily basis would only make it worse.

The rat stopped its skittering to sniff at something leaking from the Dumpster onto the floor. Jackson eyed the leaking fluid and her stomach gave a nasty squeeze. She'd eaten plenty of rat meat, if you could even call it that, and it made her queasy to think about what they'd been eating before she ate them. *But it's not running* she told herself, *ignore the rest.* And her heart, as if on command, dropped back into her chest and she continued on.

She sped up into a jog, trying to steady her breathing, eyes darting everywhere, looking for the remains of the pack. They had to be somewhere, didn't they? That zombie all by itself made no sense. But then neither did the possible explosions. She scanned the horizon but could see nothing to indicate where the noises had come from. The buildings surrounding her were simply too tall.

A zombie shrieked. Jackson's heart jammed into her brain, her nerve endings tingling. She flattened herself against a building, inhaling as much oxygen as her body could manage, all the while looking everywhere for the slightest sign of movement.

She exhaled a shaky breath and gripped her machete a bit tighter, her brain demanding she *do* something. *Run, you stupid bitch*, it said, *Jesus, do you want to die?* She grimaced and tried to push the panic away—only succeeding when she realized something was tingling. Jackson found herself looking down at the source of the sensation, puzzled in an odd sort of way. When she realized what she was looking at her chest tightened and the puzzlement rapidly switched to panic.

Her jeans were soaked with zombie pus, she knew that, could feel the weight of them. But what she hadn't realized was that the denim was ripped right across the knee, and in a tumble of thoughts she recalled the zombie reaching out for her next to the shuttered house, and her knees smacking against the concrete. There had been no pain but that was only because of the adrenaline and it meant...

Fuck.

Jackson did not think. Not about the possibility of zombies close by, or the fact it was so cold. She lifted her jacket above her waist and undid her jeans, pushing them down her thighs until she could see her knee. The skin was broken.

Fuck. Fuck. Fuck.

Frantically she pushed the jeans farther, keeping her hands on the waistband away from the wet parts. They went over her boots—which were Airwaves and could take a quart of zombie blood without springing a leak—catching a little on the thick soles, so that she had to kick them off. Quickly she swung her backpack and removed her water flask, splashing the last of it on the wound. Her heart slowed ever so slightly when the water ran red—not yellow. She didn't even know if the pus was infectious. Everything she'd seen suggested it was about the bite, but Jackson could not take the risk. Her jeans were done for, and she did not have a spare pair. The only option was to grab some from the Barbie brothel and hope she didn't freeze in her panties before then.

The day was just getting better and fucking better.

Heart pounding she made to take a step forward, goose bumps already spreading across her exposed skin, but the moment her foot touched the ground she heard something… Jackson paused, tilted her head, and tried to identify what it was. A moment later she knew. She gasped, turned, and bolted in the opposite direction as fast as her bare legs would freaking carry her.

You should never have split up…you should never have gone in Creepyville…should have stayed by the university… The thoughts buzzed in her brain, admonishing her, and Jackson sped up. Because it was the sound of pounding, and it was very familiar. How many times had she heard it over the last few months? It was like the theme tune to the end of the world.

Something was running.

Chapter Six

Luke was running—lungs burning, head spinning, and...hallucinating? He took a ragged breath and tried to work out exactly what he was seeing in front of him. Not an easy job with God knew how many zombies hot on his heels, two empty guns, and not a single grenade to his fucking name.

Jesus Christ it was a woman, her ass outlined in flimsy purple panties, running almost as fast as he, straight into the local rec center. He sped up, not without some effort, just as a whiff of Lynx aftershave hit him.

Result.

Luke vaulted up the stairs, pushed through the door, pausing only to slam it shut, before following the woman. She wound in and out of the exercise equipment, through door after door, and headed straight to a set of heavy double doors. SWIMMING POOL was emblazoned across the metal in bright blue letters.

"Hold that fucking door," he shouted, pulling in some much-needed air, and the woman with the ass turned, machete clenched in one hand, shock stamped across her features. He jumped over a headless zombie next to a weight bench, almost slipped on a splatter of gore, grabbed her by her machete-bearing arm, and pulled them both through the door, slamming it shut behind him. "We need to barricade it before they get in," he gasped, looking around the room for something, anything to hold it.

"You led them here?" the woman hissed.

"Unavoidable, sweetheart," he said, sucking in more air. "And hello to you, too. We need a barricade. Now."

The woman glared. "Thanks a-fucking-lot."

He spotted a large crate full of flotation devices and grabbed a hold of it. "Help me move this."

He had to give her points. Pissed though she clearly was, she took the other end of the crate, machete still clutched tightly, and helped him drag it across the chipped tiles without so much as a murmur. Once it was in position, Luke pushed it onto its side and wedged it below the double handles. The floats, many of which were covered in mildew, fell in a sort of half pile against the door.

"That'll give us a few," he said, waving the mildew cloud away from his face. "Assuming the Lynx doesn't hold them."

"It won't. It didn't."

He took a deep breath, his lungs burning. "The zombie outside?"

"Exactly."

"Then they're gonna get in. Through the door or through those windows," Luke said, eyeing the skinny row of glass next to the ceiling. He bent down to judge their width and frowned. There were a few waking dead skinnier even than the woman who stood next to him. As well as being fast, they seemed to be able to contort themselves into all sorts of positions, not caring if they snapped their bones or removed their skin.

"The glass is very thick," she said. "Besides they're pretty high up. Too high to be a way in, I'd say."

Luke shook his head. "They'll break through them eventually when they realize they're up there. Nothing keeps them out in the end but pure, thick metal. Help me push this." He gestured to the vending machine only a couple of feet from the door. "If the Lynx isn't repelling them, we need a better barricade."

"That's our only exit, we need to funnel them, not trap ourselves. Besides, that thing weighs loads, and the crate has the door wedged shut. It's not like they can turn the handle. Well, not usually…"

Luke eyed the woman—an *actual* woman—as her voice trailed off. Where the hell had she gotten that idea from? In his experience the dead could open doors, windows—geez whatever it took to get to their food. Yeah, okay, generally they didn't, preferring the smash-away approach, but over the last few weeks he'd come up against a few zombies who were a little smarter than the rest. The one who'd stuck his finger in Luke's stomach for instance had got to him through a locked door. It had smashed the lock and then stuck its elongated fingers in to turn the mechanism. The glee in its eyes when it had accomplished that feat still gave Luke nightmares.

"Whether they can open the door or not is not the issue," he told her, not wanting to get into the subject of zombie dexterity. "They'll smash through that metal in no time, and we won't be funneling anything. We need to reinforce it until we decide what we're going to do."

"How many are you expecting?"

"Too many."

She dropped her machete on the floor and took one end of the vending machine—her version of agreement, he assumed. Luke was surprised to see a number of drinks still inside it and resolved to pop one open as soon as the machine was in place.

"One, two, three," he said and pushed. The machine wobbled a little but did not move.

"It's like a fucking elephant," the woman said.

Luke almost laughed. "How many times in your life have you pushed an elephant?"

"Never, but you got my gist."

"On four…go." Luke pushed the vending machine as hard as he could. His legs screamed against the action and the wound in his stomach radiated pain, but he gritted his teeth and heaved.

The machine screeched across the floor. "Wait," Luke said. "Move the crate. We'll need to be quick."

She nodded and pulled it out of the way—though he could see the effort it cost her by the sheen of sweat on her forehead. No wonder. She was tiny. As soon as it was free, Luke heaved the vending machine again.

"Fuck, its heavy."

The woman kicked aside the flotation devices, scattering them across the tiles, then joined him and helped push. Her face screwed up, her breath coming in short little gasps. One last heave and the vending machine settled in place in front of the double doors, rocking on its hind legs.

Luke breathed a sigh of relief and ran a hand through his damp hair. "Thought we'd never get there," he said, and then he kicked in the glass and grabbed two cans of soda.

He slumped against the wall next to the door and popped his open. The caffeine hit his system, but rather than giving him a burst of energy it made him more tired than ever. His head was pounding in a nasty way, and he knew the mistake with the zombies would never have happened if he'd been more alert. The bastards had had another pack with them; clearly that was what the breaking glass and death growls had been about. They'd probably already killed whoever was inside and were drawing the others to them. *That poor bastard.*

Luke shuddered and closed his eyes. He should have realized what was going on and the fact he hadn't meant he was lucky to be alive. Only the last two grenades had saved him, and to be fair it was only instinct that had made him fumble in his pocket and throw them at the pack before running for his fucking life.

But he was out of grenades now, out of bullets. He opened his eyes and looked around the room. They'd get in through those windows—no doubt about it. As soon as one of the smarter ones realized they were there, they'd smash their way in. *Fuck.*

"Is there another exit?" he asked the woman.

She picked up her machete, sat next to him, grabbed the other can, popped it, and took a long swallow. "Except for the windows? No."

She was shivering, and Luke looked at her properly for the first time. She was not the luscious blonde he'd hoped for. Far from it. Her hair was deep brown, almost black, and was cut short in ragged little spikes. Her skin was startlingly pale, making her huge green eyes practically dominate her face. And she was skinny. Not enough food in her system skinny. A scowl replaced the smile he'd imagined, but he could hardly blame her for that. They were in the shit.

"Total fuckup on my part," she said. "First rule: always have an exit. But this place was familiar so…"

No, she wasn't the blonde, but she was woman enough. All fire and sass, he got that from her immediately—the machete being his first clue—and beautiful to boot, in a stick-my-attitude kind of way.

"Listen," she said, turning and fixing those huge eyes on him. "This is gonna sound odd, but you didn't happen to see a guy out there? An alive one? Name of Tyrone? Tye?"

"Tye?"

"My friend. We had to split up but we were planning to meet up at that weird pink boutique a couple of blocks over. Kelly's Clothing."

Two people still alive? But…of course, one there and one here, why hadn't he realized? Luke shook his head slowly as the pieces of the puzzle fell into place. A moment later and he understood exactly what that meant. "I was just there, at Kelly's Clothing

Boutique," he said slowly.

She started. "You were there? Why?"

Luke chose his words carefully. "I was following a pack of zombies. They'd sniffed someone out, and I wanted to find whoever that was."

"Sniffed someone out? A person? You were looking for another person?"

"I'm always looking for another person," he said honestly.

"Then…it's just you? Or is there a bunch of you?"

"Survivors you mean?" he asked. "No. It's just me."

She frowned leaving Luke to wonder if she was disappointed, but then she spoke and he realized exactly what she was thinking. "And the boutique? When you were there did you see my friend?"

"No. It was just the zombies," he said, and he spoke as carefully as he could but made no attempt to sugarcoat his answer. They were, any people who were left, long since past that. "It didn't seem as if there could be anyone alive in there. I barely made it out myself."

She narrowed her eyes. "What do you mean *it didn't seem*?"

"The zombies got in before I did," he said. "And they had to have got whoever was there. There was nowhere for them to escape, and it was an entire pack." He didn't add that his last grenades had pretty much totaled the place. There was no need to mention that.

"Jesus…you mean…"

Luke reached out and patted her on the shoulder. "I'm really sorry."

She opened her mouth, closed it, and then opened it again. "We should never have split up. I knew it was a bad idea. For fuck's sake."

"Then why—"

"We had no choice," she snapped. "Zombies were everywhere."

"I *am* sorry," he said. "I didn't realize. I only expected to find one person, but it all makes sense now."

She dropped her head in her hands. "It always does. Nasty, nonstop, horrible, fucking sense."

"I'm sorry," he said again, mainly because he did not know what else to say.

Silence held for a moment, just a moment, then she lifted her head. "Forget it." She bit the words out. "Just forget it."

Her tone may have been harsh but Luke could see the pain behind it, and he knew exactly what she was feeling, had experienced the same emotions many, many times. He looked away in an attempt to give her some space. Glancing over the windows again, checking the vending machine, the swimming pool, the showers…eventually though, he came back to the woman. He couldn't help it. Couldn't quite accept that she was actually sitting next to him. It felt unreal to him and yet…clearly she was not suffering from the same intense emotions that he was. She held her drink in her hand and scowled at something he couldn't see.

Luke struggled for something, anything, to break the silence, and after a moment settled on her bare legs. "Don't take this the wrong way," he said slowly. "But why the hell are you dressed in panties and boots?"

She lifted her drink, swallowed some more soda, and scowled again. "My jeans got covered in zombie pus and I have an open wound."

"You'll freeze." He made to shuck off of his jacket and pass it across to her, but she waved his offer away.

"I'm fine," she said. "My jacket is Gore-Tex. Weighs less than a pound, all weather resistant."

"You're lucky to have that."

"It wasn't luck," she replied. "I peeled it off a dead woman."

"How…resourceful."

She shrugged. "Not resourceful enough, or I wouldn't be sitting here freezing my ass off."

Luke felt something completely inappropriate to the situation stir as he imagined that ass and maybe it was lack of sleep, or the weirdness of actually talking to a person, but he couldn't seem to stop the words that fell from his lips. "You're welcome to sit on my lap and get warm that way."

She turned and met his gaze, narrowing her eyes at his teasing words. "You're welcome to get to know my blade a bit better."

Luke laughed. He couldn't help it, and inexplicably, considering their dire situation, felt his spirits rise. Yes she was giving him a death glare, and yes she'd just lost her friend, and yes the zombies were everywhere…but she was so fucking cute. Maybe there were possibilities here, assuming they survived, of course, but then wasn't that always an assumption?

"I'm Luke by the way," he said—thinking perhaps he should introduce himself before he really tried to hit on her.

She narrowed her eyes a little more, tilted her head, and then a heart beat or two later, smiled back. A little dimple appeared in the left corner of her face and Luke swallowed, his chest suddenly feeling painfully, and oddly, tight.

"Jackson," she said.

And then the pounding began.

CHAPTER SEVEN

How many were there, Jackson wondered. Five, ten, fifteen? There was no way to know, and with the way her day was going she wouldn't be shocked to find the entire cast of *Firefly*, fully zombified, trying to bash their way in. She eyed the vending machine—which was holding firm—and ran her fingers along Mandy's hilt, comforted in a totally fucked-up way by the feel of the wood. Options played through her mind, plan after plan discarded.

"Is that your last name?"

She looked away from the seemingly unavoidable future kill zone and met Luke's eyes. Luke who was, she had to admit, a surprise in more ways than one. When she'd first heard his deep, rumbling voice, shock had filled her, and then he'd dragged her through the door, muscles bulging and testosterone seething, and the shock had amplified. Jackson wished she could say it was purely due to the fact that he hadn't tried to kill her, but that would be a lie. It had an awful lot to do with the fact that he was absolute freaking man candy, almost on a par with the *Serenity* captain himself. Maybe it was weird thinking that—what with the shitty situation and all, but she couldn't help it. He was gorgeous. There was no getting around that fact. He was also, clearly, slightly odd. What else could explain the fact that he looked completely relaxed? That he was asking her stupid questions and inviting her to sit on his lap?

"What?"

"I've never met anyone called Jackson before," he said. "It's a cute name."

She gaped. "There are zombies pounding on the door."

He took another swig of his can. "I know."

"The Lynx didn't stop them," she added. "It should have but it didn't."

"They must have skipped around it," he said slowly. "Either that or it's not strong enough. But look, there's no point whispering. They know we're in here."

Jackson frowned as she realized that was exactly what she *had* been doing. "Built-in reaction."

He shrugged. "They won't leave until they've eaten us. Makes no difference keeping the noise down."

"We're kinda fucked then."

"Jackson," he said, almost like he was testing her name on his lips, "I've been fucked so much over the last few months I might as well be a hooker."

"Not much call for hookers these days."

"The zombies certainly don't need them, that's for sure."

"Let's hope not."

For want of anything better to do, Jackson drank some more of her soda. The caffeine hit her system and her stomach gurgled. Christ, if she wasn't careful, she'd need to pee soon, and there was nowhere to *actually* do so. Nowhere that didn't include Luke.

She placed the can on the floor, next to his, and eyed him in the same way she had the vending machine. Part curious, part assessing. He stared back at her, a small smile playing around his mouth.

"Could be worse, though," he said.

Jackson raised an eyebrow. "You think?"

"It can always be worse. Imagine if they were flesh-eating zombies who could fire bolts of acidic spit out of their mouths. It'd eat right through the door."

He smiled some more, inviting her to join in with the joke and her stomach gave a funny little flip. He was just so...big! All muscles and man and her body was reacting exactly how it should to such a sight. She bit down on her lip. Stupid body was clearly not taking into account the fact that a horde of the living dead were on the other side of the door.

"I was just imagining they were the cast of *Firefly*," she said, then wondered why.

Luke shook his head. "I refuse to believe River Tam is a zombie. No way. No how."

"You're a Browncoat," Jackson said softly, surprised. "You didn't strike me as the Whedon type."

"Appearances can be deceptive."

"Always."

One of the cans in her pack was digging into her back so Jackson shifted position, trying to order her thoughts as she did so. So much had happened in such a short space of time her head was practically spinning. Creepyville. The zombie attack. Another survivor. What were the chances that she'd run into two in a month when she hadn't really seen anybody for almost a year? First Tye and now Luke.

Tye. Jackson shivered and closed her eyes, a mix of panic and worry filling her, quickly followed by a hot spurt of guilt. Here she was lusting over a random when her best friend was probably hiding out waiting for her, because there was no way he was dead. Not Tye.

She scowled as she recalled the fix they'd been in just a week ago. Camping by the shore of Lake Michigan they'd been attacked by a pack. Tye had ended up falling into the lake with a zombie grappling on to him. She'd sped over, planning to jump in after him if need be, but he'd emerged just a few seconds later, holding the zombie's head. Where its body was she didn't know, and Tye didn't say, simply asking instead if the water they'd been heating had boiled yet.

He had survived that. Of course he would survive this. Jackson had no doubt. She just needed to find him, and if he wasn't at the Barbie brothel, he'd be heading for the interstate.

We'll always find each other.

"I'm not seeing an obvious solution," Luke said, eyeing the room, and pulling her thoughts away from her lost friend.

Jackson took one last, tiny sip of the soda, wincing at the syrupy sweetness, and wiped a steady hand across her lips. "We need a plan," she said after a moment. "It would not be an understatement to say that no one else in the world has ever needed a plan more than we do now."

Luke nodded his agreement. "That we do."

"What weapons do you have?" she asked, the practicalities filling her brain. "And please tell me many grenades, a slew of guns, and a rocket launcher strapped to your thigh."

He laughed. "Just the ax, I'm afraid. You?"

"Just my machete and a small knife strapped to my ankle."

"Right…"

A particularly loud *thump* sounded, and Luke looked at the door. "They want in, the fuckers."

Despite the fact that knowing wouldn't change anything, Jackson asked the question. "How many do you think there are out there?"

Luke shrugged. "It was one pack, from what I could tell, though it looked as though there were three packs working together. Plus someone I used to know from ages ago—she was my friend Pete's wife, Lily. Who the hell knew she was still around?" He shook his head. "So four. I think I might have got one before I made a run for it but who fucking knows? You know how it goes in those situations. It's fight, run, and then try and work out what the heck went down."

"What happened to the other eight or nine?" she asked.

"I took care of them," Luke replied.

"On your own."

"Yep, with my bare hands."

She eyed his muscular form and swallowed. The man was fit, no doubt about it. She could well imagine him taking on half-a-dozen zombies, and he'd probably be smiling while he did it. "Serious?"

He laughed. "Of course not. I had the grenades. I threw the last two at the remaining pack, but I don't know if they did much beyond giving me time to make a run for it."

"Geez, at least *try* and keep the illusion of masculine strength."

He laughed again.

A plan was forming in Jackson's mind now and it seemed a do-it-or-die sort of deal. One of those crazy plans that she would, a million plans later, marvel at, and thank the crazies for it working. A particularly loud groan sounded, kind of confirming her thoughts. "I think we should just go for it."

"Huh?"

"They're gonna get past the vending machine eventually. That's a given. Why don't we pull the vending machine back slightly and drop it to the floor? We'll leave just enough of a gap for one to get through."

"Funneling them?"

She nodded. "Exactly. The longer we wait, the less chance we have. Because, and preaching to the choir here, I know, the more that are out there, the less room we have to maneuver or get away."

Luke shot her a long look and Jackson almost felt like she was going to blush—which was ridiculous. She had never been a blusher. Well no, that wasn't true. She might have been once, a few years ago. But she certainly fucking wasn't now.

"Well…that does seem like our only option," Luke said slowly. "I have a safe place not far from here that we can go to, but…" He paused and eyed her from head to toe. "You sure you're up to it?"

Jackson rolled her eyes. *Oh, so it was like that, was it?* Luke thought her a weakling girl. Well nothing else could rile her as much as a man doubting her skills. So she was skinny and short, she got that. While Luke was all tall and sculpted…damn was he sculpted… But Jackson had grown up with two brothers, had dated a cage fighter, and had won the Atomic Fallout burger challenge three years straight. She knew how to use what she had. This long in the land of the zombies? You had no choice but to harden up. It was do or die, and Jackson was a do-it kinda girl.

"Yeah, I'm up to it, and I'm thinking it's now or never."

To punctuate her point Jackson stood up, dropped her pack next to her feet, and heaved Mandy. Together they'd taken down countless numbers of the waking dead—hiding did not always work. Time to take down a few more.

• • •

Luke watched as Jackson—was that really her name?—hefted her machete and smiled. She looked like a good gust of wind would knock her over and he seriously doubted her ability to take down one zombie, never mind two. Christ, he was probably going to have to kill them all himself. Ordinarily not an insurmountable problem, but with zero weapons beyond an ax and running on hardly any sleep, he was already mentally crossing his chest and making his peace.

"If for some reason I don't make it," he said grabbing one end of the vending machine, "head north along Everdeen Park. You'll find a huge gate with a stone dragon either side—Harry Potter style. There's a gap on the left side of the hedge. Slip through there and follow the hedge around. Eventually you'll come to what looks like an overly large shed. It'll have a girder propped up against it—keeping it shut. Go through there, make sure you close the door behind you, splash some Old Spice, and look for a trapdoor. It's right in the corner, next to one of those ride-on lawn mowers. Open it, splash some more scent, and head down. Follow the path below, don't take any of the turnoffs, and you'll come across another door. Metal keypad coded."

"You serious?"

"Yeah. Code is one-two-three-four."

"Original."

"Workable, sweetheart."

"What's there?" she asked.

"Everything you need to survive. Only don't use the second door next to the bathroom. It opens a trapdoor that leads to the house above and the zombies hang around up there in their spare time."

Jackson took the other side and gave him a nod. Together they pushed the vending machine across the floor, giving them a good few of inches between it and the door. The zombies on the other side howled.

"How have you got a coded keypad working? There's no electricity."

"Generator run," he explained. "The whole bunker is completely self-sufficient."

"Impressive," Jackson said. "Ready to let it drop?"

The vending machine wobbled as they leaned back—toes out of the way. A moment later and they pushed it, making the machine topple like a drunken stripper. It hit the floor with a crash that sent the zombies into overdrive. They bashed at the double doors, and Luke could see that the doors were already beginning to crumple.

"It's good to know you have somewhere for us to go, Luke," Jackson said, stepping back toward the pool. "But I'd rather we get there together, to be honest. I'll watch your back, you watch mine."

He grinned, because whether Jackson realized it or not, those were the first words she'd said that hinted they would be leaving together. That she wouldn't be running off in the other direction the moment they were zombie-free. That thought made his heart race and Luke gripped his ax, a surge of energy coursing through him.

One of the doors buckled about halfway up, separating from the other and creating a gap about a half foot wide. "Good job we used this instead of the crate," he said "They'd have gotten in by now."

"That they would."

"They'll have their gap in a minute," he said, as the door continued to buckle inward.

"Yep."

They stood back, side by side, and Luke took a deep breath, ready to shield Jackson when the time came. He was the man, after all. But damn, what he wouldn't give right now for a grenade or two.

The double doors juddered, the metal screeched, and then the left one came away from the frame completely. Luke was impressed to note that Jackson didn't even flinch, because there, outlined against the crumpled metal, was a pack of three zombies. The dead Lily was conspicuously absent and Luke wondered if he'd finally killed her, as well as the other one. He figured he must have. Otherwise they'd be here.

As he watched them, they watched him and Luke noticed that two of the three had that same calculating look in their eyes that he'd seen more and more of as the weeks went by. Late at night, alone in his bunker, he'd found himself wondering if the zombies were becoming more intelligent. Perhaps they were, as time went on, getting back some of the human traits that had disappeared.

Half of him sort of hoped so. Maybe they'd get back a sliver of humanity, but the other part—the part that had seen so many of his friends die, and had spent so long fighting the bastards—was angered beyond belief at the thought of them becoming smarter. Surely they'd just get better at hunting their dwindling supply of food—which was him and Jackson right now.

"You ready for this?" he asked, tightening his grip on his ax.

"Always am, Luke. Always am."

The gap between the doors was just big enough for two to fit through, at a pinch. And that was what they did. Two females—it had to be, didn't it?—slithered through the hole and came at them full pelt.

They went straight for Jackson.

Luke lifted his ax and swung at the one closest but it growled and jumped out of his way, so that he severed only a hand rather than an arm. He lifted to swing again but a massive male was coming through the door now, bits of skin flaking off from the tight squeeze, and Luke had to turn and swing at him.

The ax took off most of the arm—just like he'd wanted to do with the first one. Pus and blood shot out and Luke dodged it. Another swing and the ax embedded itself in the dead thing's chest. Luke grunted in satisfaction, but the grunt turned to a growl when the blade wouldn't come back out. Fuck. It was stuck in the chest bones. He heaved and pulled but the dead guy moved swiftly and an arm wrapped around Luke's torso, squeezing him hard.

Luke lost his grip on the weapon.

The zombie lifted him then, so that his feet dangled above the floor and Luke head butted air just as he felt teeth graze his neck. Luke dropped an elbow on its shoulder but the move did nothing but anger the huge zombie and it squeezed harder. Bright spots of light appeared in front of his vision and Luke roared.

It couldn't fucking end like this! Not when he'd just found someone!

He struggled and thrashed, desperate to get free. The female zombies...Jackson...she was going to die and it would all be his fault...

The arm loosened its grip. Suddenly Luke was free, stumbling to right himself. Blood rushed to his brain and the room spun. He coughed and turned just in time to see Jackson severing the massive zombie's head. Her machete was wicked sharp and went through in one go. Like a knife sliding through butter. It didn't meet any resistance at all. Blood and pus exploded out and she jumped back before it hit her.

He could not believe what he was seeing. "Jackson?"

She smiled a grim sort of smile and pulled his ax out of the dead zombie's chest. She wiped it on the zombie's "Dave's Auto" sweater and chucked it across. He almost fumbled the pass and scowled.

"Stuck in the clavicle," Jackson stated. "Next time wrench upward, not outward. It'll slice through the lungs if your blade is sharp enough."

He gaped, his gaze following the rolling zombie head. It came to a stop next to a sausage-shaped flotation device. "Upward?"

She nodded as if this should have been obvious and dunked her own blade in the rancid pool water. "Yeah, upward. God, I fucking hate zombie pus. Where the hell does it come from? There always seems to be way too much. How does it all fit in their bodies? If I could find out the source of the pus, I'd die a happy woman. One of life's little mysteries solved."

He gaped at her again. "I—"

She shook her head. "Whatever. I suppose we have more important things to be thinking about right now."

"But... how did you do that?" Luke finally asked. "You're not even out of breath."

She pulled her blade out of the water and gave it a little shake. Their gazes met. Luke's stomach flipped.

"I am a little."

"You're not. And you killed them all."

She shrugged. "The second one almost took a chunk out of me. I got lucky. She slipped on a splatter of blood at the exact right moment. The other one tried to grab me, but she was missing a hand thanks to you."

"But—" Luke stepped back, because the pool of blood was growing, the male zombie's joined by the blood of the other two. Their decapitated corpses were leaking a whole lot of the stuff, but then that was understandable. One was missing both arms and her head, the other a head and leg.

Luke swallowed unsteadily and looked from Jackson to the undead, now dead, and then back again. She was so tiny, so delicate-looking, but clearly he'd been bang on the money. Appearances were deceptive. *Christ.* "Luck or not, that was unbelievable."

"It's done, Luke. Forget it," she said, picking her pack up and shrugging it on. "We should get out of here before any more arrive. And I need some pants. I'm fucking freezing."

"I have clothes at my place," he said. "We could go straight there."

She nodded slowly and stepped back from the rapidly growing puddle of blood and gore. "That's the worst pickup line I've ever heard, but right now it'll do."

And Luke almost fell in love there and then.

CHAPTER EIGHT

They made it to Luke's place without incident and before long he sat her down with a cup of thin noodle soup. Jackson would have liked to say she took her time and enjoyed the novelty of eating a nonrat-based meal, but that would be a lie. It took maybe a minute before she drank it all. Luke filled it back up.

It was only when that too was empty that Jackson became aware of the fact that she sat on a strange man's chair in her panties and a jacket. The panties were also a little big and may well have been gaping a bit around the gusset. She shifted, suddenly uncomfortable in a weird way, placed her cup on the table, and shot Luke a glance. He stood in the kitchen area, leaning against the counter, arms crossed.

"Have you had enough? There's more if you want it." His tone was gentle, at odds with the look in his eyes, which seemed like he was trying to figure something out. Maybe how she'd managed to take down the zombies? Jackson hadn't missed the shock stamped across his features when he'd looked around the pool room.

She fiddled with the handle of her mug and tried to remember the fight but, as always, it was just a blur. A fuzzy memory her brain was already locking away.

"Jackson?" Luke prompted, still with that same look in his eyes. She could practically hear the question his eyes were asking. "How the fuck did you take down those zombies?"

But she wasn't sure what to say. Despite two years of doing it, she couldn't explain it, couldn't really explain how she was still alive. It just happened. They attacked, she responded, and so far it had worked.

"I've had enough, thanks, Luke."

He smiled and Jackson's heart gave an odd little thud. She had a nasty feeling it was going to do that every time Luke flashed that grin of his. It was all so unexpected! Sitting with another live person who wasn't Tye, doing something as normal as eating soup, confused her. She crossed her legs and fiddled with the spoon again.

"You said something about clothes?"

He nodded and strode over to the large hamper by the fridge. He grabbed an oversize T-shirt, black, and a pair of sweats, also black. "These'll be a bit big but the sweats have a cord you can tighten, and you can roll up the legs. What color socks would you like?"

"I don't really mind."

"Here." He added a pair of bright green socks to the pile in his arms and passed them to her. "I'm sorry there aren't any girl clothes. I guess the people who set this place up weren't expecting any female company. Makes sense. I looked around the mansion up there a while back, and all the pictures were of some guy. No women in any of the shots."

The clothes smelled good, like lavender, and were soft to the touch. Jackson ran a finger across the bright green socks, marveling at the prospect of wearing clean material next to her skin.

"There are sweaters too if you want one."

"No, these are fine for the moment. It's really warm in here, and I have my jacket. Do you mind?" Jackson twirled her finger and Luke looked puzzled before he got her meaning and swiftly turned his back to her.

"Sorry."

She stood up, her muscles aching, and grimaced as a whiff of something that smelled suspiciously like old sweat hit her. Hardly a surprise. The small amount of room in her backpack was tightly rationed and deodorant was not high on her list of priorities. Still, Jackson suddenly wished that she was properly clean, especially in light of the fact that Luke didn't smell bad at all. As she'd sat next to him in the pool room her nose had tickled with the smell of what she thought was Old Spice. In fact the whole place reeked of the stuff—not in a bad way though. It was oddly comforting.

She shifted and took another surreptitious sniff. *Why do you care if Luke thinks you smell bad? Haven't you got more important things to think about?* She scowled, unable or maybe just plain unwilling, to answer those questions.

"If you want to wash up first, I have hot water. Not that you need to," Luke added hastily. "But you know…"

He trailed off and excitement shot through Jackson. She paused at the waistband of her panties. "Hot water? Are you serious?"

"Yeah, there's probably some girlie shower gel too," he added. "I collected a load from Wal-Mart a few months ago, and I grabbed whatever was left. I've been sticking to the man-gel so there should be a load of the feminine shit left."

"You realize you just became my hero?"

Luke turned back around and gave an over-exaggerated sigh. "Women tell me that all the time."

"Uh-huh, the many, many that are left."

He shrugged again and shot her a teasing grin. This time the weird little heart thud was completely expected.

"You got me there," he said. "Come on. I'll show you where the shower is."

Jackson followed him across the room, the prospect of removing the zombie gore, not to mention the stench of weeks-old sweat, dispelling some of the weird feeling. Because she *was* still a little weirded out. She could admit that. Maybe it was because of the exhaustion that was licking at the edges of her brain, the fact that she still had to find Tye, or maybe, that same sly voice whispered, *because of the look in Luke's eyes when he looks at you.* She couldn't quite put her finger on what it was but it made her edgy. Not in a bad way. Luke seemed to be on the up-and-up and a genuinely nice guy. But in a woman-meets-smoking-hot-man-eeek-eeek sort of way. Ridiculous really—they'd just fought for their lives. Hell, she was *always* fighting for her life. It had gotten to the point where she barely remembered *not* having to do so. Things like super fit men and what she'd like to do with them ranked lower on the priority list than keeping clean.

Luke led her out to the hall, oblivious to her racing thoughts. It was a long corridor with several other doors shooting off it. Jackson held the lavender clothes away from her body, reluctant to stink them up, as she looked around with interest.

"Food, weapons, extra bedroom, bathroom."

He pointed to each shut door as they passed and Jackson nodded, beyond impressed. She'd heard about such places, of course. Bunkers set up by people who had a touch of the paranoids, but she'd never been able to find one. "How did you find this place?"

"I was making a run for it about a year and a half ago," Luke replied. "Had a pack after me. Five of them, all female. Anyway, I headed for the park, thinking I could reach the condos there. I was exhausted and about one stumble away from being eaten."

"Been there."

He nodded. "Exactly, so you know how it goes."

"What's the food situation like here?" Jackson asked.

"Nothing much. Same as everywhere else, I guess. In the first few weeks the remaining survivors, including me, cleaned out the stores. I was shocked to see soda still in that vending machine—I should go back and grab the rest." He pushed open the bathroom door. "So yeah, I think the last bits and pieces disappeared completely by the six-month mark. It's not like the country you know, where food can be grown. We're in the Chicago suburbs. Not only is the zombie population huge, plenty of people lived here, but the food situation is shit. There is what there is, and it's nearly all gone."

"There's always rats," Jackson quipped.

"Sweetheart, I'd rather eat a zombie."

"Hey, don't knock 'em. Tye cooked me up rats on a regular basis. He tried to pass them off as dog or cat at first. I only realized when I saw one of the traps he'd set up. I suspect he used other things as well. Bugs and such—whatever. Protein is protein, right?"

Tye. Her chest tightened and she shivered. She'd need to head back out there soon. As soon as she was clean, and rested for just a few minutes, she would have to go looking for him. Just as he would for her if the situation was reversed.

Luke looked her up and down, nodding slowly as he did so. "Must be why you're so tiny."

Her chest tightened some more, in an entirely different way, because Luke's words in no way suggested her skinny bod was a bad thing. "Yep. I've lost a fair bit of weight since the zombies arrived," she said. "Silly to think it was something I used to worry about."

"What did you do," Luke asked. "Before all this started?"

Jackson frowned. She didn't really like to talk about that sort of thing, but Luke might think it odd if she didn't answer him, and there was no need for him to know how just strange she was—not yet at least. "I waited tables in a New York bar, my hometown, and studied at Macy's for a month or so before it hit."

"What the hell did you study at a department store?"

"Cooking courses. They offered special courses there, so I

thought, why the hell not? I was never any great shakes at school and couldn't afford college, anyway. I had planned to get a job in a restaurant or something instead of waiting tables." An image of roast lamb with all the trimmings filled her mind and Jackson sighed. Roast lamb had been pre-waking dead. It was roast rat now, at best. "Such things aren't important now and I interrupted," she continued, "you were making a run for it and…"

Luke grinned and leaned against the door. "I spotted this place. The gates were locked tight but I noticed the gap in the hedge. You can only see it from a certain angle, so I headed straight in. I'm not sure what made me follow it around instead of heading for the house." He shrugged. "The shed was right there, and I thought I could hide inside for a little bit. It was less obvious than the house. Then I noticed the trapdoor and it didn't take me long to find the keys. You saw the locks when we came in?"

Jackson nodded.

"I opened it up and went down. It was a risk. It might have just been a cellar and then I'd have been well and truly trapped, but I didn't have much choice."

"Sometimes we have to do that," Jackson said, remembering all the crazy risks she had taken over the past two years.

He nodded. "That we do, and it worked. Whoever built this place was paranoid in the extreme. I don't know if you noticed but it's not a direct path from the trapdoor to the bunker. Some of the forks go nowhere, and one doubles back in a loop. It baffles me how they managed to build it without anyone noticing."

Jackson thought about the long, steeply inclined pathway and tried to visualize above ground. "Maybe it was part of the original structure and they just improved it? It's a house up there right? A big one?"

"Practically a mansion. God knows how much it would have cost back in the day. This much land in this spot?" He pointed to the final door in the corridor. "That one goes straight into a small tunnel. There's another trapdoor at the top of the ladder. It leads to part of the basement area in the house. The zombies don't know about either exits, but they know I'm down here. They must have smelled me in the building—I went to check it out about a month ago. Stupid curiosity. So once they get tired of chasing other people, or whatever else it is they do, they come here and pound on the ceiling in the main room. It's directly underneath the gym."

Jackson shivered at the idea of the waking dead knowing exactly where they were. "The ceiling and walls are metal?"

"They are," Luke confirmed. "Place is like a giant underground panic room. The generator has enough fuel to keep it going for many more months and the water is funneled straight down from a water butt, which I assume is on the roof of the house. Pure rainwater as well. All I had to do was read the instruction pack someone had thoughtfully provided and turn it all on."

"It's perfect."

"It saved my life. Literally. I was reaching the end of my food stores and having trouble finding safe places to sleep. I don't know where I'd be without this place. Which is why I'm still here." He pointed out the shower and a timer on the counter. "It'll run for one minute before it goes freezing cold. I strongly suggest you make the most of that minute. You'll find gels and shit in the cabinet. I'll make some more food for when you get done."

Jackson reached out and grabbed Luke's hand. She wasn't quite sure why she did but it felt like the right thing to do. His palm was calloused. The skin was rough beneath her fingertips and it made her spirits rise. The hand of a man who knew the meaning of real work.

Just like her.

"Thanks for this, Luke," she said, her fingertips tingling. "I really appreciate it."

He smiled that smoking-hot smile of his and opened the cabinet. "Strawberry shower gel good for you?"

CHAPTER NINE

There was a woman in his bathroom. A kick-ass, naked woman, with the most perfect green eyes he'd ever seen. Luke grinned and picked up the Old Spice. He was running low, would need to grab some more before the week was out. Not from the pharmacy though, last time he'd been there they'd almost trapped him. It'd have to be one of the convenience stores—though which he wasn't sure. He'd cleaned so many out.

His grin became a frown as he looked at the bottle, wondering as he did so if the scent still worked to deter them, because clearly the stuff Jackson had sprayed on the rec-center door hadn't. Maybe it was too old, the chemicals in it degraded. Luke's frown deepened as he picked up a washcloth and thought it through.

He rubbed the cloth over the back of his neck, the whiskey on it stinging a little. He was pretty sure the zombie's teeth hadn't grazed the skin—the sting was probably because of his open pores—but still, better safe than sorry. A quick swipe over his shoulder too and it was all good.

Jackson had wiggled her little nose when they'd come into the main room and he suspected she was reacting to the mingled smells of Old Spice, whiskey, and man. Yeah, the place could use a woman's touch. He wondered if she'd be willing to hang around, machete in hand.

Damn, but she could fight. He shook his head and stashed the whiskey and washcloth in the cupboard. He still couldn't get over her total bad-assness where the dead were concerned. It was no wonder she'd managed to survive for so long. He wondered if the guy, Tye, had taught her or if she was naturally tough. He preferred the second idea, more because the idea of this Tye, whoever he was, had him gritting his teeth. Which was ridiculous, the man was probably dead. Luke had heard him roar as the zombies approached and there was no question they'd have eaten him before he turned—even assuming he would. With their food sources so low the zombies didn't hesitate like they had in the old days.

Luke made his way into the kitchen area, and grabbed one of his many, many packs of noodles. Everyone liked noodles. Hell, everyone liked anything they could get their hands on these days, including rat, by the sound of it. He smiled slightly and thanked the unnamed bunker builder again. He wondered for just a moment where he'd be if he hadn't had this hideaway. He was convinced the waking dead worked by following scent. They seemed to know where a human was hiding and what else could explain that but enhanced smell? Maybe in some way it was activated when the higher brain functions decreased. Like going back to the predatory days of old. Then too was their weird aversion to aftershaves. He suspected there was a common chemical in all of them that they disliked. That'd make sense with the whole enhanced smell thing. He'd have to ask Jackson what she'd learned.

At the thought of the kick-ass pixie Luke heaved a completely ridiculous sigh of satisfaction. He couldn't help it. Finally he'd have someone to talk to. Some company to see him through the long, painful nights. Though he'd admit it to no one, Luke had been lonely. By the time he'd found his bunker he hadn't seen another person for more than two months. He knew there were people still out there. After all, he was still alive, and more than once he'd thought about abandoning his safe house and striking out in search of those other survivors. Only the knowledge that he had it pretty good already had stopped him.

He wondered how Jackson had found her way from New York—she'd said that was her home town hadn't she?—and how the hell she'd managed to survive so long. Considered objectively, it was certainly possible. Not everyone who was infected and died came back, and many who *had,* died all over again in the early days, killed by other zombies, other people, and the army had bombed many areas, too. These days you'd find a couple of thousand— mostly native residents—in the suburbs, split into their little packs, each with their own stomping ground. It *was* possible to avoid them if you knew what you were doing. Possible to stay hidden. Though of course Luke had no idea what it was like in the cities, he could only draw on his own experience, there could be millions still there for all he knew. But viewed realistically survival became harder. Finding food was the number one priority, followed by staying warm and healthy. Having to do that while keeping clear of the packs was a nightmare. Luke had a hard enough time of it in his area, and he had a bunker at his disposal. Jackson sure was something for getting so far...

Well, she's here with you now. A ridiculous grin spread across his face. It was safe here. She was bound to want to stay. He'd fed her, offered up toiletries and clothes, and could watch out for her. That had to count for something, right?

A few minutes later Jackson returned to the living area, trailing her backpack in one hand, warmly wrapped up in his clothes. The T-shirt came all the way down to her knees and she'd rolled the sweats up several times. His gaze lingered on the sweats a little longer than it should have but he couldn't help remembering her bare legs. Sure they were covered in bruises and scrapes, and she clearly hadn't seen a razor in some time, but they were a woman's legs. All hidden dips and tempting curves.

"That was absolutely amazing, Luke," she said, giving her head a shake.

Her hair was still damp—there was no hair dryer in the bunker—but if the smile on her face was any indication, she didn't seem to mind. He smiled right back before spooning some noodles onto her plate and decorating them with a sprig of parsley. Dried stuff but it was the thought that counted.

"Here, eat this."

She took the plate from him with her free hand and sat down at the small table. "There's loads here," she said. "And you already gave me soup."

Luke grabbed his own plate and joined her. "Thin soup, so your stomach adjusts. Eat a little but go slow."

Silence reigned as they both chomped their way through the noodles. Luke practically gulping his down, Jackson forking up little bits. After a moment or so, she pushed her half-full plate aside.

"I never thought I'd say this again, Luke, but I couldn't eat another thing."

"It's because your stomach's shrunk."

"Yeah."

She placed her hands on the table and Luke was struck by how small and dainty they were. That image contradicted the one of her severing heads and he shook himself inwardly. The woman and the bad-ass, how to reconcile them?

"I want to thank you for all this," she said softly. "Sharing your resources and helping me take down the pack."

Luke grinned and nudged a bottle of water toward her. "Not a problem."

She took a hefty swig of the water and looked up. Their eyes met and Luke had to take a deep breath. She was so fucking pretty, and he knew it wasn't just because she was one of the few women left on Earth. Luke was fairly certain he'd have felt the same way if he'd seen her before the world went to shit.

"But it's time for me to get going."

He started, completely surprised by her words, and had to take a moment to process them. *What the fuck?* "Going?" he said quickly. "Going where?"

"To find Tye."

Tye. Luke felt an undeniable anger build at the sound of the other man's name. No, not anger, he realized, as his stomach clenched. Jealousy. It was obvious. Maybe it should have clicked immediately? Jackson and Tye were together. She wanted to go looking for her boyfriend. While he applauded her loyalty, a large part of him rallied against it. If she did, by some miracle, find him she'd probably leave, and he'd be alone again. *And what else was fucking new.*

"Sooo…" She paused and Luke leaned forward, trying to bank down the anger.

"What?"

"I'd appreciate any information you can give me on the shop. Entrances, exits. I don't think he'll be there now. It's been what over two hours maybe since we split up, but I need to be sure."

"But if he's not there," Luke said slowly, "how will you find him? I'm assuming you don't have a walkie in your pack."

"I wish."

"Then how?" he said, aware that his voice sounded a little demanding but unable to stop it.

"We'll find each other on the interstate," she said. "We're planning to follow it—well as roughly as we can—down to where it finishes in Texas."

"You're driving to Texas?"

She laughed. "You know the cars don't work anymore."

Luke shook his head as her meaning hit. "You're planning to

walk to Texas?"

"Um yeah, of course that might be harder than I thought now." She paused and Luke opened his mouth to speak, to ask what the fuck could possibly be in Texas that would make her crazy plan of walking there make any kind of sense, but she spoke before he did, and when she did his heart gave a nasty little thud. "Something's going on with the zombies. Something weird."

"Everything about them is weird."

"Apart from the obvious I mean." She paused for just a moment. "I don't know if you picked up on it, but they're banding together, almost like they're working together. Oh, I know the packs do," she said, waving a hand. "We've all seen that, four or five of them buddying up. They're like animals, right, so why wouldn't they do that? But today when Tye and I had to split up there were way more than five."

Luke nodded slowly, putting the Texas issue aside for the moment, because this was not news to him, and for a brief second there he'd been expecting something else, something unknown. But then…how could Jackson not have seen this before? The packs had been joining up for months.

"How many were there, altogether?" he asked.

She shrugged. "Fifteen maybe? There could have been more that I didn't see. They tried to cut off our escape, waiting on the roofs. And that makes absolutely no sense. They're not supposed to be able to think."

"They're not supposed to exist at all."

"Neither is tofu."

"Huh?"

She rolled her eyes. "Something my…just something someone used to say. Point is something's changing with them. I saw it today with my own eyes and I don't know what it means."

"Something meaning what?"

She shrugged and wiped away a few of the water spots on

the table. "They seemed almost like they were...plotting and planning...I know that sounds ridiculous but..."

Luke frowned because again this was not news to him. He'd seen more than one zombie acting that way, and he'd thought about it a fair bit. It horrified him—the cunning behavior, the gleam of a burgeoning intelligence—but in a weird way it made a nasty kind of sense.

Zombies should not exist.

Only they did.

Zombies should be dumb and stupid.

But they weren't.

Jackson was oddly out of the zombie news loop. It was time to bring her in.

Chapter Ten

"It's a whole lot worse than you think," Luke said, lifting his sweater. "Take a look at this."

Jackson's stomach gave a funny little flip. Damn, even sitting down, Luke had some ab muscles going on, like really going on, and she was weirdly tempted to run a hand over the hard planes. She clenched her fist to shake the feeling off but relaxed them the moment she spotted the wound. It was located just below his rib cage and was about the width of a chunky human finger. Clearly he'd sewn himself up—not very well. The edges were still shiny pink and he wasn't completely healed. On the plus side, she couldn't see any sign of infection.

"Whiskey," he said, as if reading her thoughts. "Johnny Walker Black."

"Huh?"

"I pour it over me anytime one of them bites me. It seems to do the trick."

Surprise hit and Jackson tilted her head, considering. "How many times have you been bitten?"

"Five or six in all. You?"

"Never."

"Are you serious?"

"Yep. I came close one time." Jackson closed her eyes as she remembered the incident. "It was at the very beginning, right before everything went completely to shit," she said slowly. "She, well, it, I guess, grabbed my ankle and sent me flying. She was crawling along the floor, I think maybe there was something wrong with her legs, and went straight for my thigh."

"What did you do?"

"I almost died of shock! It was just instinct that I kneed her in the face. Hard. She went down and I ran for it. I ran for so long…" She shook herself. "Like I said, those were the early days. I didn't even think to behead her or chop her up. How could I? I had no idea what was happening." The image of the dead zombie's snarling face and bloodcurdling howl, were so vivid Jackson swallowed unsteadily. Some memories just stayed with you more than others. "So why the alcohol?" she asked. "You think it counters the zombie infection in some way?"

"I'm not sure," Luke replied. "It's just alcohol. But then it's not like in the movies is it? When one bite equals death followed by waking? I've seen people bitten over and over and they've died a few weeks later of blood loss or normal infection or something, and don't come back. But others are bitten, die, then get up zombiefied."

"What about the pus?" Jackson asked, intrigued to have another viewpoint on the situation. Sure, theories and speculation had flown thick and fast in the first few weeks of the end, and Tye had been full of information, some more vital than others, but Luke had clearly seen other things. After all he didn't seem in the least bit surprised by the idea of smart zombies. Plus he'd been in one place for a long time, while she, and Tye, had been traveling for the past two years. It was bound to give him an entirely different perspective.

"I've been covered in the stuff and I'm fine," he said. "Even with open wounds. I really think it's all about the bite. The pus seems to be an internal response or something. Like snot when you get a cold."

"You might be immune to it," she suggested. "The virus I mean, not the snot-pus."

He frowned. "I doubt it. Besides I know of other people who've been sprayed too and they're fine, or at least they were, but that was in the beginning. They're probably dead now. Properly, I mean. Anyway, my point is that it just seems totally random to me. No one knows how it started. No one knows how the infection gets passed around. In the beginning, pretty much everyone I saw who turned did so because they got bit. The zombies were so fast and people were so shocked. No one ever expected this, did they?"

Jackson wiped up another droplet of water and frowned. "No, it was completely unexpected." She paused for a moment, her brow scrunched. "Except for maybe a bunch of survivalist types. Preppers and rednecks."

He snorted. "Yeah they're probably fine. Hiding out in the mountains and shooting anything that comes up their path."

"Most likely...so are you saying you think that the infection was spread purely from the zombies biting people?" Jackson asked. "Not from a virus transmitted through the water or the air or something?"

"If it was a virus, then why didn't everyone get it?"

"I don't know. But someone had to get it in the start, right? The first zombie?" She shuddered slightly saying those words. The first zombie had become almost a bogeyman in her mind, and yes, she got that that was weird. There were enough horrors already, no need to add more. But when she dreamed, which was not often, sometimes it was the first zombie that woke her up shaking.

"It's never made sense to me," Jackson added. "How many people were there in the US before the zombies?"

"More than three hundred million or so, I think," Luke said.

"And most of them just disappeared in the first few months didn't they? Dead? Zombiefied? I don't know. All I know is that one day the world was full of people and then they were gone or they were zombies. It never really stacked up," she said softly. "How it could have happened so quickly if it was all about being bitten."

"I never really thought about it like that. People were dying so quickly, zombies roaming the fucking streets." He shook his head. "I always just thought that the odds were not in favor of survival and just worked off that."

"But we survived."

"Yeah. But out of a country of millions, I bet there's only a few tens of thousands of people who are still human."

"And that's exactly my point. There are fewer every day."

"Fewer every day," he repeated.

Silence reigned for a moment and Jackson wondered if Luke was thinking about her suspicions that all was not as simple in the zombie world as it seemed, or maybe he was just thinking about all the people he'd lost. Indistinct faces started to form in her mind, and she spoke quickly in an effort to push them back where they belonged.

"So tell me where did this come from? It doesn't look like a bite mark."

"It's not. I guess I need to tell you the whole story. Come on." He motioned for them to sit down on the couch. Jackson hesitated. She needed to get moving, to go find Tye, but on the other hand if Luke had information that was important…well it would benefit them all for her to hear it.

She eyed the couch with a frown. It looked devastatingly comfortable and she knew it wouldn't take much to sink into it and close her eyes. The shower had banished some of the exhaustion, mainly because she'd gone over the one-minute mark and had been hit with a bolt of freezing cold water, but still she was feeling it. Yes, it would be so easy to just lie back, but there was Tye, and Luke who had knowledge for her. So she straightened her shoulders, gave herself a mental shake, and joined him on the couch.

"Let's hear it then."

"I've been fairly lucky so far," Luke began. "Well, lucky so far as other survivors go, I guess. It's all about the perspective. I didn't die or get eaten or turn into a zombie."

"Amen to that."

"But you're right, Jackson, something has changed. You remember when the first of the zombies started coming?"

Jackson nodded, even though the question was so obviously rhetorical. "I remember my first dead face-off like it was yesterday," she said, despite the fact it was held back by one of her refuse-to-think-about-it barriers. Though the barrier was a little shaky now, and she clenched her fists as her brain tried to replay it, speaking before she could keep it silent. "It was the woman I told you about. The one whose legs didn't work."

"You got away from her though," Luke said.

"Just about. I didn't stop running for hours."

And that woman had been a mere taster, Jackson thought, though she did not say as much. There was no need. No doubt Luke had seen his fair share of zombies running through the streets. They had come out of nowhere, were everywhere, and because no one had been expecting them, and the zombies had been able to fucking sprint, everything had been chaos.

"What did you do in those early days?" Luke asked and Jackson shook her head automatically. She so did not want to talk about the days she'd holed up in her apartment, waiting for her brothers. Or the fact that only one of her brothers had turned up... Jackson clenched her fists tighter, swallowed unsteadily, and dragged the mental barrier back into place. Stamping your first zombie brain, your brother's no less, was something best not replayed...

Silence held between them for a moment and then Luke started to speak, clearly, and thankfully, getting the hint. "They were stupid in those early days," he said and Jackson made an effort to unclench her fists.

"Yeah, they were." Though it was an undisputable fact that her brother had found his way to her apartment—something that still broke her heart if she let herself think about it—so even back then, in truth, they hadn't been that dumb.

"Fast yeah, but stupid," Luke continued, then paused. "No, not stupid, that's the wrong word. But it was like all they wanted to do was bite and eat and that consumed them. I think they were acting on their predatory drive more than anything else."

The drive to find a sibling, a family member...Jackson shivered, and before she could stop herself she started to think about how many people had been eaten by their loved ones. It was an old thought, one that refused to go away, despite all her barriers.

Luke settled back on the couch and scowled. "They smelled food, they attacked. Like a shark or something, they didn't seem to think about anything else. I remember once, I watched one almost lose an entire hand bashing through brick to get to the people on the other side, but the door was right there and he could easily have got through the wood—it didn't make any sense."

"I saw plenty of that too."

"Only things *are* different now." He pointed to the wound on his stomach. "I had one motherfucker chasing me and God, he was fast. Like really fast. I had zero weapons left, a pounding headache, and I was beyond tired, so the only thing I could think to do was find somewhere to hide. Somewhere with a locked door. It was stupid of me really. I should have just turned and fought."

Luke paused and Jackson could tell the memory still haunted

him. She didn't blame him. She had more than the one mental barrier keeping things shut away in her head. Geez, in her old life she'd go bankrupt from the hours of therapy she'd need to get anywhere close to normal again. But then normal was relative now wasn't it?

"But anyway," Luke continued. "I found a building and locked myself in. I figured I'd have five, maybe ten minutes at most before he broke the door down and my plan was to get out the other side. Before I even had a chance though, it broke the lock and turned the mechanism! I couldn't fucking believe it."

"It turned a lock?" Jackson was shocked and it took her a moment to get her head around Luke's words. She'd never heard of a zombie displaying such intelligence. "Maybe it was an accident?" she suggested. "It didn't know what it was doing and the mechanism just happened to turn?"

Luke shook his head. "No. It had this gleam in its eye, like it knew exactly what it had done. It was calculated. And it was so fast! It had pinned me down before I could even move."

"Christ…"

"Stuck one of its rancid fingers in my stomach. Honestly, Jackson, it was like it was playing with me."

"How did you get away?"

"A paperweight, would you believe? The desk in there had some sort of quartz thing and I used it, literally with the last of my strength, to smash its head in."

Jackson scowled at the picture Luke's words created and tried to get her head around the idea. "So, they really are becoming smarter? And more of them are—not just random ones."

"I'd put money on it, if that still existed."

"What does that mean for us?"

"I'm not sure yet. I'm really not."

She looked upward, toward the mansion Luke said was above, and felt her stomach sink. "If the zombies can turn locks, then surely they'll find a way into the bunker?"

"They don't know where the trapdoors are, and there's no way they can get in through the walls."

"But…" Jackson tried to get her thoughts in order. She'd always known the dead awoke changed. Biologically and mentally. But hadn't part of her always questioned things others, in the beginning, had seemed to ignore? Like why did they come back to the last place they'd been? Why did family members hunt down others? And why did they sometimes eat in a way that seemed to prolong the pain and terror? This idea of intelligence bothered her, but it wasn't as hard to accept as she might have thought.

"From what I saw with my own eyes earlier and from what you've just told me, they seem to have discovered some basic skills. What's to stop them watching us and following us through that door." She gestured to the entrance they'd used.

Luke frowned. "They don't have the patience to follow someone."

"They didn't use to plan shit out either, but now they do."

She shuddered and ran a hand through her short, damp hair. God, she missed her long black hair, but long hair in this world was the equivalent of shouting, "grab it, pull my scalp off." Another shudder and she rested her hand back on her lap, her mind a whirr of thoughts.

"Those doors are metal too," Luke said. "And the zombies don't know where they are."

"Not yet, but you know, as well as I do, that doors are always the weak point. If enough of them pound on it for long enough… How long since you checked the other one, the one that leads to the basement?"

"Not for a while," Luke admitted.

"Then maybe—"

He frowned and then nodded slowly. "If it makes you feel better, I'll go check the other door."

• • •

Jackson's green-eyed gaze followed Luke as he made his way back through the living space to the basement door. He made an effort to look cheery and awake as he left the room, despite the fact his chest throbbed, his head pounded, and he wanted nothing more than to collapse on his bed.

Trouble was he didn't want Jackson thinking he wasn't up to the job of making sure they were both safe. Especially considering the fact that she'd practically saved him in the pool room. He knew, of course, why it was important for her to see him as a rescuer. Had known the moment his gaze had fixed on her purple panties, and if not then, certainly when he'd met her very green eyes.

He ran his fingers along the entrance. It was still perfectly intact, the thick metal as sturdy as ever—just as he'd known it would be. He considered unlocking it and checking the ladder up to the trapdoor but was fairly certain that he'd find nothing amiss. The zombies had yet to find it, despite the fact that they'd haunted the rooms above for the last month. His own stupidity, of course. He deeply regretted giving in to the urge to see what was in the building above.

Idiot.

When he returned to the living space, Jackson was bent down lacing up her boots. He paused for just a moment to feast his eyes on her, and despite his extreme tiredness felt his groin stir. Part of him was extremely pleased to note his libido was working as well as ever. The other part remembered Tye and rallied against it. Why the hell couldn't he have ended up with a single woman? One who'd be glad to cuddle up on the cold nights? Life was so fucking unfair.

She stood and smiled and Luke's heart stuttered. "I'm gonna go check out that store."

"Right now?"

"Yeah. I can't leave it any longer."

Luke sighed inwardly and opened the drawer of his cabinet. "We may have killed off a few packs, but there are others, Jackson. There's at least a few hundred of them, maybe even a couple of thousand, around here. They'll come looking for us soon enough."

Jackson nodded. "Yeah, I know."

"We could end up running into them." He paused for a moment. "And we're both pretty beat."

"I hear what you're saying, Luke," she said. "I don't expect you to come with me."

He snorted. "You're probably worse off than me. When did you last sleep?"

She shrugged. "I dunno. A while ago, but I never needed much sleep even when the world was normal. Five or six hours at most. I'm not on my chinstrap yet."

Luke started, because Jackson's military slang made him think immediately of Pete, one of his friends from the old world. He'd been an army man, though Luke never knew exactly what he'd done, and swore that four hours of shut-eye a night was enough for any man to get by on. Pete wasn't around very often. His job kept him away, but Luke had met Pete's wife—now the zombie Lily—on several occasions. They'd holed up together along with several other survivors in the local police station a few weeks after everything had started going wrong. But, of course, the zombies had found them.

Pete had been awake for more than thirty hours and had insisted he was fine to head outside with Luke and two others to take down the pack before they could find their way inside. But despite his words, *it's not chinstrap time yet*, the tiredness had taken its toll and Pete had gotten sloppy. The dead had gotten in through the door Pete had been guarding, and Luke had watched through the front bolted door, unable to do a goddamn thing, as one had taken a sizeable chunk out of Lily's neck. She'd died immediately, only to awake minutes later—faster than any zombie he'd ever seen.

Luke's stomach clenched as he remembered the calculating gleam in her eyes when he'd seen her earlier. He didn't realize she'd been around all this time, busy eating his fellow survivors. Which was stupid. He should have. The zombies tended to stay where they had lived, probably because it didn't occur to them to go anywhere else. He wondered again where Pete was now, the last he'd seen of him he had been holding Lily down as she had tried to rip a piece of his face off…

"You don't have to come," Jackson repeated, and Luke shook off thoughts of Pete's whereabouts and that he'd probably killed the Lily zombie with his last grenade.

"Of course I do. You'll never make it back here alive."

"You think?"

He remembered her bad-assness and laughed, then realized she hadn't said she wouldn't be coming back… "Okay, you might, but I have no intention of leaving you to face them alone. You say you're good, but that fight in the pool room must have taken a lot out of you."

She shook her head. "It didn't take everything, and I have to be sure Tye's not waiting for me."

He could understand that. Jealousy aside, of course he could, and though Luke wanted nothing more than to sleep for thirty hours straight, there was no question whether he'd go with her. He'd only just found her, hadn't he? And if Tye *was* alive, well hell, he'd invite them both to stay. Their Texas plan was ridiculous and he had more than enough for everyone for a good while yet. The guy was probably decent. He'd hung with Jackson after all, and she seemed as straight as an arrow. And if he's dead? Luke was unwilling to even think about that yet.

"At least if I look, I'll be sure," she added. "Then it'll just be a question of heading back to the interstate. He'll wait there for me."

Luke took three grenades—his last three grenades—and a Glock out of the drawer, before passing them across to Jackson. He'd deal with the whole interstate thing later. "You know how to use these?"

"The Glock 19? Yeah. I learned years ago, long before the zombie invasion. I had my own until about three months ago. Lost it somewhere in Ohio. Gotta love the lack of a safety." She shifted and eyed the grenades. "You keep those."

"Check your gun."

She did, her movement swift and efficient, before giving him a nod.

"Luke, I'm sorry to drag you out again, especially as you went to save him the first time. I just want you to know I appreciate it."

He pocketed the grenades himself and reloaded his own guns. Unlike Jackson, he hadn't known how to check a gun over until the waking dead had arrived. He'd never even held one before then. Pete had actually shown him when they had holed up in the police station.

"I get it," he reassured her. "Of course I do. He's your boyfriend—of course you need to be sure."

Jackson paused in her gun prep and gaped. "What?"

"Tye. Your boyfriend, yeah?"

She smiled then and let out a long, slow laugh. "Ermm, no, he's not. Tye's a buddy, almost like a brother, nothing more."

"What?"

"We're friends," she said. "There's nothing like that between us. There never has been. We just didn't click that way."

Suddenly Luke didn't feel quite so tired anymore.

Chapter Eleven

The Barbie brothel was not only a ruin, it was deserted. Not a person in sight, dead or alive. Well there were parts, quite a few in fact. Severed arms, a leg, and what looked suspiciously like a shrunken penis. Jackson tiptoed around them and the charred remains of a bunch of clothes, Glock in her hand, Mandy wrapped in a tee and strapped to her waist with one of Luke's belts.

She looked all over, past the serving counter and the rooms that had once been changing areas and were now smoldering heaps of wood. When she saw nothing she started to look through the body parts. They were mostly burned, the bits that weren't mottled and vile, weeping pus and gore. None of them were strong and healthy or the amazing café-au-lait color of Tye.

He was not here and she sighed unsteadily, because part of her was starting to question if Tye really had made it out of this one. The only way to be sure was to head to the interstate, the very clear route they both had to get down south, and if he wasn't there…

Jackson scowled to dispel the tight feeling in her chest as she gathered some unburned jeans and a sweater, the possibility of getting to the interstate and not finding Tye weighing heavily on her shoulders. And though she had enough depressing thoughts, her mind abruptly filled with the image of Jayne, another companion from the early months. They'd met while hunting for food in a deserted Wal-Mart and had hit it off immediately. Why wouldn't they? Neither had seen another person for weeks at that point. But the waking dead had found them late at night while Jayne was on watch. The poor girl's bloodcurdling scream had been the only thing that had awoken Jackson from a too-brief sleep and had allowed her to not only shoot her dying friend, but to make a run for it. The image of Jayne's missing arms, zombies lapping up the gushing blood, not to mention the back of her brain exploding outward, was placed immediately behind its own never-to-be-removed barrier. She'd given a mental good-bye then. She did not want to have to give one to Tye too.

"You okay?" Luke whispered.

Jackson picked up a pair of uncharred pink fluffy socks, appliquéd with skulls and crossbones—how apt—and nodded. "Yeah."

"She's not here," Luke said, and Jackson grabbed a woolen hat to add to her pile. She stuffed all the clothes in her pack, bar the hat, which she put on, and swung it back on. It was getting heavy now and that was a problem. Weighing oneself down with goods was a stupid idea. You couldn't fight properly if you had extra pounds on your back, and yet she needed her precious food resources, not to mention the other things.

"Huh?"

"No sign of her."

For one moment she thought Luke was referring to Jayne and she looked at him, puzzled. "Who isn't?"

"The zombie Lily."

"Oh. Well, no, there aren't any of them here. I picked up on that with us being alive and all."

"I meant the pieces." Luke gestured to the limbs lining the

floor. "I can't see her head or anything."

"Maybe she got fried, or she got away?"

"But then why wasn't she with the others when they attacked?"

Jackson shrugged. "I dunno, but now's not the time to be wondering about zombie whereabouts." She pulled Mandy free of the tee, hooking it on her waistband opposite the Glock, so that a weapon would be ready for each hand. "Tye's not here either so there's no point in us hanging around."

She turned toward the entrance but halted the moment a flash of red caught her eye. It was a patch of leather, and it was very familiar to her. Jackson gasped as she hurried over to it, bending down amidst the rubble to pull it free. The patch was attached to a pack, a black one. It had been poorly applied because the person who owned the pack hadn't had much to work with at the time, but even later, when other bags were available, he'd stuck with this one.

His lucky pack.

Her heart thudded as she laid the Glock on the floor, unzipped it, and checked the contents. A lighter. A flask. A pack of purification tablets. "No…"

"What is it?"

Jackson swallowed past the lump in her throat, barely able to get the words out. "This is Tye's pack."

Luke walked over and bent next to her. "Maybe he dropped it?"

She shook her head. "He would never have left this behind. No way. These things are our life. Our survival totally depends on them."

"Jackson…"

"No matter what he would have come back for this. He's completely vulnerable without it."

"Then…"

She swallowed again, the grit in the air making her throat hurt.

If Tye hadn't come back for his pack, it could only mean one thing, and her chest ached as she imagined it. "He can't be dead," she whispered. "Not Tye."

"We can try the interstate," Luke said. "Come up with a plan."

Jackson nodded, mainly because she did not know what else to do, because she did not want to believe what was rapidly becoming reality. She lifted Tye's pack and hooked it around her arm. But Luke stepped forward and took it from her, shrugging it on without so much of a word.

The streets were as deserted as the shop, apart from the massive amounts of rubbish and abandoned cars, and, of course, the ever-present blood splatters. Jackson looked down at her feet and was unsurprised to see bits of gore all over her boots, flecks of ash stuck to them.

Luke was right next to her as they made their way down the sidewalk, his eyes watchful, his stance protective. She could see he was tired, and then some, but he'd put himself out yet again just to accompany her. And it occurred to her then—because it hadn't really, not before—how lucky she was to have met him, and she resolved to concentrate on that rather than worry over Tye's disappearance.

She often did that—concentrated on the good rather than remembering the bad. As a strategy it worked. As a way to stay even nominally sane, not so much. The bad stuff just licked at the edges…but still…she eyed Luke again. Not only did he have food, clean water, and shower gel, but he seemed like a genuinely nice guy. In the real world, aka pre-dead people rising, she'd have accepted a date from him in a New York minute, assuming they'd ever met, or he'd even looked in her direction. Jackson was not oblivious to the difference in terms of their attractiveness. Luke was one of those guys she'd always sighed over but never actually got to date. Of course, the pool was significantly smaller now and besides *she* was different too. Not the same girl at all. Who knew how different her dating prospects would have been if she'd been this Jackson in the sans-zombie world?

A quick fantasy flash shot through her mind. She imagined them finding Tye, the three of them striking out together, and the idea almost made her smile. It wasn't a lot to ask for was it? To have the man that was like a brother, and the other that was already something else entirely, with her in this ruined world.

"Careful," Luke whispered, pointing to a crack in the road. "You'll disappear down there if you're not careful."

"I got it," she said, the fantasy disappearing as quickly as it had come.

He smiled at her as they walked past an old street stall, and abruptly she remembered the light she'd seen in his eyes when she'd confessed her single state. Luke was interested, smaller pool or not, and the possibilities that created gave Jackson a weird feeling she hadn't experienced in a while, and had not expected to feel again.

Anticipation. How odd.

"I wish it wasn't getting dark," he whispered, pointing his gun around the corner.

"Does it really make a difference?"

He shrugged. "It's probably a survival thing. I always like to be back in the bunker before all the light goes. It makes no difference to them I know, but I feel safer facing off against them in the daytime."

"Because you can see them?"

"Yeah."

They passed a McDonald's and Jackson's mouth watered despite all the food she'd eaten already. Like whispering when the zombies were close by it was an ingrained reaction, because God knew she'd chomped down enough Happy Meals in her time.

"We'll be safe in the bunker," Luke added, interrupting her fast food thoughts. "And then we can start figuring out what to do from there."

"What to do?"

"How we'll get to the interstate."

His words startled her, namely the "we," and she almost stumbled into a pothole. "You're going to come with me?"

"Sure I will. If Tye's not there, you won't be able to find the way back to the bunker…"

"You don't think he will be, do you?" Jackson asked, picking up the tone of his voice and remembering his words from the pool room.

"You want honesty?"

"Always."

"Then no. I don't. When I arrived there," he shrugged a shoulder behind them, "a pack of zombies were in and busy doing something. It doesn't take a genius to figure out what. I'll come with you to make sure, but it might be that you have to accept they got him, and then we'll have to start making other plans."

"Other plans?"

"Yeah," he agreed. "You said something about Texas. Does that still hold without Tye?"

They rounded a corner and Jackson looked left and right before speaking—Luke's thoughts, his question, prodding her. *Without Tye.* It was an odd prospect. After being alone for so very long, she'd gotten used to having him around. Maybe that was stupid. Maybe she should have expected this. After all, everyone died, and in this new world, it happened a whole lot faster.

"I started this journey a while ago," she said slowly. "Two years or so ago. Mainly, in truth, because I didn't know what else to do. I had no clear plan on where to go. I just started walking, but meeting Tye changed that completely."

"Changed it how?" Luke asked.

"He'd been traveling as well, almost as long as me, but he had a clear goal in mind, and the moment I heard it, it became my goal too. How could it not?"

"What was—"

Jackson held up a hand to halt Luke's words, her heart suddenly hammering in her chest. She gestured to the side of the road and together they jogged over to the entrance of a large building. It looked like it used to be a bank, the first clue being piles of money on the floor inside. Now it was just paper.

Luke leaned in close to whisper in her ear. "What did you hear?"

Jackson shivered, not from whatever was moving, but from the feel of Luke's warm breath feathering across her skin. He could easily become a major distraction. *Priorities*, she told herself. *Remember what's important.* "I'm not sure. Wait."

They stood perfectly still, stance ready for whatever Jackson had heard and then watched as a ratty dog skittered past them. The poor beast looked like it was on the verge of collapse and Jackson's heart went out to it. Animals seemed to be immune to the virus, but were in trouble regardless. They got eaten.

"Little guy won't last much longer," Luke whispered.

"Literally." She heard the zombie before she saw it and the momentary relief that had sparked at the sight of the dog died a swift death. Jackson flattened herself against the doorway, pushing Luke back as she did so. He made to protest but she held up Mandy and hissed a warning.

The zombie was faster than the dog by a fair margin and it was less than a heartbeat before it pounced. The dog's bark was followed by a whine that screamed pain as the zombie ripped its front leg off, stuffing the limb in its mouth. Bright red blood pooled on the floor as the dog tried to crawl away. It had no chance.

Though she knew it was the height of stupidity, because the damn canine was pretty much a goner, Jackson moved forward, the image of one of those bastards doing the same thing to Tye flashing through her mind. Luke pulled on her arm but she shrugged free and stepped onto the road. The zombie paused, howled, and turned.

Despite herself Jackson's stomach lurched. It was a woman and tufts of gray fur were stuck to its chin. Its mouth was working overtime trying to chew the dog limb up and as it straightened it spat out what looked like bones.

Bile welled in the back of Jackson's throat, swiftly followed by anger. She'd always liked dogs, and the little guy had survived for so long. She shot it a quick glance and her heart squeezed. It was trying to crawl away, fangs not even bared.

"Take care of the dog," she said.

"How about let's get the fuck out of here?" Luke replied. "They travel in packs, remember?"

The zombie pounced. Jackson did not move. It was all about the timing. One, two, three...she stepped back. It landed right in front of her and met Mandy's blade. Straight through the neck.

She moved to the left, avoided the spray of blood and pus, and pushed Luke in the same direction.

"How sharp is that blade?" he breathed. "I mean, Christ."

"Not always sharp enough." The zombies head was still attached, by maybe a half inch of sinew and skin. "Take care of it, Luke. I need to help the dog out."

Jackson jogged forward, ignoring the *thud* behind her. Her heart was pounding and she had to swallow several times to push down what felt like a little ball of vomit. *Stupid, stupid, stupid*, she thought. Because there were probably others close by, and could arrive at any moment. She'd put them in danger, for what? The dog looked up at her and whined. For a quick death, her mind answered. For saving someone, something, the excruciating pain of being eaten.

Jackson thought of Tye as she brought Mandy down on the dog's neck and her heart squeezed for them both. Dog and man.

For the headless zombie she felt nothing.

CHAPTER TWELVE

"This goal of Tye's," Luke whispered a few minutes later, more to break the tension than anything else, because Jackson had been completely silent from the moment she'd killed the dog. "What is it?"

She didn't answer at first, and Luke wondered if she was going to, but after a moment she spoke, and there was an odd note to her voice. Because of Tye or because of the dog? He had no way to know.

"I didn't believe it at first," she said, her eyes everywhere. Checking and checking, but it seemed the zombie had been a straggler—which was weird but not unheard of. Luke had come across a few in his time. They didn't stay alone for long. "When he told me, I mean," she added. "I didn't believe him. I thought maybe he'd been alone for too long and had gone a bit…off…plus he was so reckless. It was like a game to him, the zombies. He was fearless."

Luke wondered if Jackson realized she was using the past tense. Probably not.

"I asked him where he was heading," she continued, "and he told me he was going south."

"To Texas?"

"Exactly. It's like forever away. It'll take months, maybe even years to walk it, and I asked him what the hell could be so important." She shook her head. "What could possibly make that walk worthwhile? I thought that maybe it had something to do with the heat. You remember in the early months people said that it affected them, that it made them slow? And it seemed to me that they *are* slower when it's summertime."

"Only summer doesn't last long enough," Luke pointed out.

"That's true."

Silence fell as they passed through a car filled street. Luke noticed that Jackson's knuckles were white against the hilt of her blade. That, even though she was so small, she slid over the hoods of cars without waiting for him to help her. A strange feeling began to gnaw in Luke's gut, more important than the information about Tye's goal, and once free of the car jam he took a deep breath before asking, "You're wondering why I didn't save the dog?"

Jackson turned to him with a start. "No."

"Because I'm kind of feeling a little like Robin here."

"Robin?"

"Yeah with you being Batman and all."

She laughed, though it was tinged with something he couldn't quite identify, and shook her head. "I've never been called Batman before."

"Superwoman, maybe?"

"How about just Jackson?"

"Look I didn't save the damn dog because what happened would have happened anyway," he said.

"The zombie eating it?"

He shook his head. "No, it dying. They always die, Jackson. Always. Zombies always get 'em in the end, and it's not like we could have taken it to the bunker even if they didn't."

"I know. Believe me, I know."

"So I was thinking more about us than it, you know. Thinking to get us safe." Why did he feel like he had to explain himself to her? Luke frowned as they jogged across the street. He didn't know, only that he wanted her to realize that he wasn't a fucking wimp. That he could take care of both of them, given the chance. *Yeah, you're off to a great start there*, his mind said. He ignored it.

"I know you were," Jackson whispered. "I get that."

He frowned some more. "But you just jumped in without thinking. Like in the pool room."

"I always jump in without thinking. Impulsive you know? Gets me every time."

They paused at an intersection and Luke's eyes swept the area. He pulled in close to Jackson as they crossed the open expanse of road and was pleased to see that she did not move away.

"And going down south?" he asked when they were on the other side of the road. "Following Tye's plan? Is that also impulsiveness?"

"No," she said. "It's all that's left. A world without zombies, that's my plan. Call me squeamish but I'd rather not see one covered in dog fur again if I can help it."

"There is no such thing as a world without zombies."

"That's where you're wrong, Luke," she whispered. "So wrong."

Luke almost stopped in the middle of the street, shock punching him straight in the gut. "What the hell are you saying?"

"That there *is* a camp down there, a group of survivors," Jackson said. "It's not many, a few hundred maybe, but it's some."

"A camp of people?" he breathed. "You're not serious?"

"I am."

"But..." Luke paused and shifted. "Those rumors were just wishful thinking in the earlier days. There aren't any big groups left. Not even the ones the army tried to set up. We'd have heard about them otherwise. *I'd* have heard about them. I have a radio in my bunker," he added. "I check it every single night. I've heard nothing on it for months."

Jackson sped up, probably in an effort to encourage him to do so. "That's what I thought," she said. "That nothing was left. But Tye came across another group in Indiana—they'd fortified a huge hospital. They weren't as big, but they knew about this other group, gave him directions."

"But why didn't Tye just stay with them?" Luke asked, trying to wrap his mind around the idea. "If he was looking for a group, why not stay with the one he found?"

She shrugged and stepped over a broken laptop. "Tye used to be a cop. He said that he didn't approve of the way that group was…ordering themselves. That they were…off. He didn't want to stay there."

"And they told him about this group instead. How did they know about one another?" Luke shot the questions out quickly, aware that he sounded skeptical but was that any wonder? The prospect of a group, groups, of people still living their lives with some kind of normality was staggering.

"They were in contact. Don't ask me how," she added. "Because I don't know, and neither did Tye. But they *are* there, we just need to go west on the highway and pick up I-35 and go south all the way to Laredo, Texas. Apparently it ends there, just by the border crossing."

"This supposed camp is next to the border?"

"I don't know about that. Even Tye didn't know where it was exactly. The other group said there are signs directing any survivors."

"And you really believe this?" Luke asked. "You're going to travel thousands of miles based on information from a group you've never met?"

"Based on information from Tye," she said. "My friend. If he believed it, that's good enough for me."

"But—"

"Otherwise what's the point?" she demanded. "What do we do? Keep on surviving and hiding? What about in ten years or twenty or, hell, forty, assuming we live that long? When we're too old to go looking for food or too old to run away? When it's our limb being shoved down a zombie's mouth as we try to crawl away? That's no life. I'm happy to risk mine on the assumption that there's something else out there. The faint possibility of getting something back. And think about it, maybe this group will know things we don't. Why the zombies are changing, maybe even a way to deal with it all. Hell, they might even have found a way to kill them a lot quicker than we can."

"That really is wishful thinking, Jackson," he said. "Dangerous thinking."

"More dangerous than the way we're living our life now?"

"No…but what if you travel all that way—assuming you even make it—and there's no camp there. What then?"

She shrugged one tiny shoulder. "Then I'll know, won't I? And I'll be down south. If the thing about the heat is true then maybe there'll be fewer dead people to fight, at least."

Luke shot her a look, trying to read her, to see if she really believed in the impossibility of what she was saying. It seemed to be her driving force and Luke knew a thing or two about that. In a world where nothing made sense anymore and all hope was sucked away, a person had to find something to hold onto. Something, no matter how little, to provide a reason for waking every day. His own motivation was the desire to kill as many fuckers as he could. He relished taking out packs and had even hoped that one day he could clear the area, *I Am Legend* style. It was probably a futile hope. After all, every time he killed a pack, another moved in, but it gave him some comfort, and more importantly stopped him from going crazy. Because what else was there for him? Unlike Tye, he'd never heard of the possibility of another group, and he had radio equipment in the bunker! If there were any left, surely they'd have broadcast something on one of the frequencies he constantly checked? But they hadn't and striking out on a vague hope would be beyond stupid. Maybe when his resources ran out...he'd thought maybe then, but for now he was safe, warm, comfortable. Why risk all that?

"You could come with us, you know," she said softly. "I'd really welcome the company."

His heart thumped. "Serious?"

"Yeah. Though you might want to really think about it. I've had two companions and they're both missing...or dead, so I'm not exactly a lucky charm."

"Everyone I knew is dead," he reassured. "So I'm thinking it's not just you."

"Perhaps."

Go south with Jackson? Go looking for a camp that probably doesn't exist? The idea whirred around his brain and he was stunned to find he didn't reject it immediately. It was odd. He'd known her for a few hours, but that didn't seem to count for shit right now. She was another person, a human! And those were few and far between. More than that though, Jackson seemed like a genuine kinda girl, the sort he'd have made an effort to get to know even before the end of the world.

They skirted around the park. Luke loved this spot. He could see all around him at this time of year, and there was no chance of anything sneaking up on him here. It was why he'd run down it in the first place when being chased, and what had led him to his bunker.

Ah, the bunker. Could he really give it up? It had kept him safe for months, offered him every single thing he needed to survive. It was his haven and he knew without a doubt he'd have been dead long ago without it. On the surface, the idea of leaving that behind to trek a treacherous road south, with only the faint possibility of finding a zombie-free land full of healthy survivors, seemed like nonsense. But there was Jackson and already he hated the thought of her riding out of his life.

What about in ten years or twenty or, hell, forty, assuming we live that long?

She had a fucking point. He couldn't deny that and he'd often wondered himself what'd happen, assuming he even lived.

"Will you think about it, Luke," she asked as they approached the mansion.

He already was but as her small hand, Glock gripped tightly, brushed his arm and he looked down into her perfect green eyes he sort of forgot that. A weird sensation shifted through his chest and he swallowed drily.

"Yeah. I will."

One last look around, Jackson's words of earlier ringing in his ears, and they squeezed through the hedge. It only took a minute or two to jog the inclined perimeter and make their way to the shed.

"I'm looking forward to just sitting still for a couple of minutes." Jackson sighed. "It feels like it's been days."

"Yeah, for me too." He put his gun in his left hand as he removed the girder that kept the shed door propped tightly shut. "Can you manage some more food?"

"Do dead people wake back up?"

He laughed and opened the door, happiness, totally ridiculous happiness, spiking through him.

"We can—Fuck!" Luke pushed the door shut as fast as he possibly could, his heart hammering in his chest, adrenaline zipping through him at light speed. The happiness of only a second ago gone, replaced with pure, crystal-clear panic.

"What—"

"Run," he roared, and of course Jackson did without so much as a word.

The pounding started mere seconds later, and then the awful sound of wood breaking. Luke raced across the lawn, sweat dripping down his spine.

"The hedge!" he shouted. "Get back to the fucking hedge."

She raced with him, both of them pumping their arms to get traction. *Please God, let us make it*, he prayed. Because a myriad of death groans were filling the air now, he heard them like a deafening roar, and if they didn't get to that gap, they were trapped, as good as dead.

"Move," she shouted and Luke saw the gap in the brush before they barreled through the space that mere moments ago had felt like a safe haven. His muscles clenched and though he didn't want to turn, Luke knew he had to. The last thing he saw as they sprinted across the street was the sight of an enraged face with far too much intelligence sparking in its eyes.

The dead Lily.

CHAPTER THIRTEEN

"This is fine," Luke said, slumping down, eyes closed, against the wall.

"It's more than fine, we're well hidden, well protected," Jackson told him, easing her grip on Mandy's abused hilt. "You did well bringing us here. We're safe for tonight, Luke. Just, let's just worry later, okay?"

They were in the office of one of his friend's garages. A dead, or possibly zombified friend obviously. The room was big enough to allow them space to fight, but small enough that it was cut off from the main building. It also had two exits, both of which were now blocked with filing cabinets. For a quick, run, flee, find shelter excursion, Jackson was feeling pretty pleased.

Luke so obviously wasn't.

Slowly she bent down, joining him on the floor, and reached out to run a hand across his head only to pull back at the last minute. He looked exhausted and...haunted. She didn't even know how to start comforting him.

He shook his head and said the words they were both thinking. "I can't believe she found the trapdoor."

"I know."

"If we hadn't gone to look for Tye, she might have found a way into the bunker. They all might have. We'd have been trapped."

"I know."

"Jesus Christ, Jack. It's completely compromised…" He shook his head and trailed off.

"Do you need to talk about this, Luke?" Jackson asked. "To talk it through? It might make you feel better. I know in the beginning there were a fair few times I wanted to talk to someone when something awful had happened. When I was so scared and so worried and every noise, every slight movement made me jump out of my skin."

"But not now?"

"Not now, what?"

"You said in the beginning."

"Oh, well yeah, but there was never anyone there *to* talk to so I got out of the habit." She paused. "Well, no that's not true. I had Tye, and Jayne at times, but for the main I've been on my own. It gets a bit pointless talking when there's no one there to answer, you know?"

"I guess," Luke said. "But we have each other to talk to now."

Jackson nodded, sort of touched by that comment, even as her head was mentally shaking. Fact was, habits usually got replaced with another habit. Like a smoker who switched to sunflower seeds or an alcoholic who started to run marathons. Her habit of talking her feelings through had long since been replaced with the habit of bottling all the bad stuff into one horrid little place in her mind. It was just her way of dealing. It happened, she locked it away, and tried not to think of it again. Of course, Jackson wasn't stupid. She knew that eventually it'd all come tumbling out. That she'd have to think about things, talk about them. She planned to put it off until she had no choice, but clearly Luke's try-and-keep-sane strategy was different. It would be good for him to talk about things.

The irony wasn't lost on her. Good for him but not for her. Her brain jabbed and admonished but she ignored it. *Whatever.*

"Now they know where the entrance is, they'll get through the trapdoor eventually," Luke said after a moment. "Even if we sneak through the house and get back into the bunker through the basement, it's not safe anymore."

"This is my fault," Jackson said, guilt prodding her. "If you hadn't come out to help us, you'd be fine."

He laughed but there was no humor in it and he didn't open his eyes. "She'd have smelled me there regardless, whether it was today, tomorrow, or next week. It has to be the Old Spice, like with the Lynx. The scent doesn't cover our tracks anymore. This is far from your fault."

"You're sure?"

"Of course I am. None of this is anyone's fault. Just bad fucking luck."

"The zombies are getting smarter," Jackson said after as moment. "Maybe smart enough to realize the smell that puts them off is where the food is hiding?"

"Maybe."

"Perhaps the virus is mutating?" she suggested, remembering a movie she'd watched long ago. "A different strain or something."

"Or maybe the brain is fighting it?"

She shrugged. "We have no way to know."

"We never do," Luke said, his eyes still closed. "You know, I thought the bunker'd be safe forever. Hell, I slept in there when they were pounding on the ceiling. Smug I guess, in the knowledge that they couldn't get in. How wrong was I?"

Jackson wrapped her arms around her knees. "We can't go back there again."

"No, we can't. All those weapons, the food, the supplies…all useless now."

"We'll find other stuff," she reassured him.

"It's like the beginning all over again. I remember when—"

"There's no point thinking about what we've lost," she interrupted quickly, thinking that maybe it wasn't such a good idea for him to be talking about it after all. Not if they were going down the early-days road again. Jackson hated remembering or discussing those times—with Tye she'd steered well clear of it. "Serious, Luke," she said. "You'll only make yourself depressed. It's gone, all gone. We have to move forward."

"I've been there for so long is all. It was the last fucking thing I had left."

Guilt squirmed in her gut and Jackson shifted. Maybe she was being selfish; maybe spending so much time alone had left her that way? It was easier for her after all. She knew it was. The bunker had felt safe for maybe a half hour, if that. As soon as Luke had told her about the lock-turning, finger-poking dead guy that fleeting feeling of safety had gone. But Luke had lived there for well over a year by the sound of it. It was home to him. Giving that up was not going to be easy. Hadn't they already lost so much?

"I know. I'm sorry, Luke," she said softly.

"We have nothing, Jackson," he said. "No supplies beyond those in the packs, and the few I have stashed."

"We have the clothes on our backs don't we? Full bellies for the moment, not to mention we're both clean. We're safe. We'll do the only thing we can do, scavenge as we go."

"I'd forgotten what it was like, before I found the bunker, I mean," he sighed, dropping his head into his hands. "Living on whatever I could find, looking for somewhere to bed down every night. I remember when I stumbled on the gun shop. Jesus Christ, I nearly wept. That's all gone now."

"I know, Luke. I know."

There was nothing she could say to make it better. Literally nothing. Luke was grieving and she knew a thing or two about that. She knew too, in that moment, that Luke had not yet managed to get to the place she had. Maybe because the bunker had shielded him from the necessity. But it was the place that you *had* to get to in order to stop jumping out of your skin at every creak or whisper. When you were in that place, when you lived it, you shook off such things as soon as they happened. The body was simply not capable of working properly under a continual feeling of despair or of supplying a constant stream of adrenaline. The only way to exist in the world of the dead was to accept something when it happened.

Accept and deal.

"I'm gonna change, Luke," she said. "These sweats keep rolling down my hips. I thought they were gonna fall completely when we ran. Could you imagine? Me running as fast as possible with my pants around my ankles?

He laughed, just as she'd wanted him to. "It might even have made the zombies pause."

She pulled off her backpack and took out the clothes inside. "In shock, perhaps? Do you want this extra sweater?"

"No. You use it as a blanket."

"You'll freeze."

"I just need to sleep. I'm so fucking tired I don't care if a horde of them comes through the door."

Not even bothering to ask him to close his eyes, what with them already being shut, Jackson stripped out of the baggy clothes and slithered into the new ones, pink socks and all. Like in the pool room, dizziness assailed her when she bent down. She needed sleep too.

Once she was dressed, with the bright green socks folded in her pack, she sat back down next to Luke and draped the heavy sweater across their torsos, followed by the sweatpants across their legs. "Warmth is warmth," she said.

"Yeah."

He sounded so depressed, and it was so freaking cold. Jackson sighed and wiggled her toes, encouraging the blood flow. She'd been colder of course. She'd *always* been more something, and that thought tended to put things into perspective.

"You know once I was trapped in this little town, somewhere on the outskirts of Pennsylvania," she said slowly, toes still wiggling. "Though it might have been Ohio—did I mention geography is not my strong point?"

"You did."

"Well the zombies were holed up at the only clear way out of the place. I'm guessing the residents had tried to run and it was just a mess. I lost days trying to scout another route out, but there wasn't one."

He lifted his head, distracted, just as she'd wanted him to be, even though he kept his eyes firmly shut. "What did you do?"

"There was at least one pack of them, and the space was so tight I knew if they got me, I'd be a goner. There was only one option, and I still can't believe it worked. Basically I walked the river bed, weighed down by stones, a plastic tube for my air."

"Fucking hell…"

"I was so lucky it was a thin river, not too deep either. When I got to the other side I rolled myself in mud and had to creep up the bank so they didn't spot me. I'm sure I looked like I'd stepped out of a horror movie."

"That is pretty damn amazing, Jackson."

"It was pretty cool," she said shooting him a smile. And it was, though she hadn't thought much about it at the time, beyond being ridiculously grateful she'd made it out and pumping herself full of antibiotics to combat the ear infections, but several days later she'd just sat in shock. Almost unable to believe she'd done it. It was one of so many weird plans that really shouldn't have worked but somehow did. So many that she'd never have believed herself capable of just a couple of years ago.

"It takes on a new view now, though," she said, almost to herself.

"In what way?"

She shrugged. "I can't help but wonder if they were waiting purposefully. To catch anyone trying to leave town. If they knew somehow that that was the only way out."

"I wouldn't be surprised," Luke said shifting his position a little. "They just found an impenetrable bunker, so if you tell me you spotted some on the moon I'd believe you."

The shift gave her a little room to sink into him. The spot right where their bodies touched was wonderfully warm and Jackson leaned in a little farther.

"You okay?" he asked.

"I'm cold."

"You and me both."

"Not to be a pervert…" She paused for a moment before she said the next words, knowing in some way that they were going to set a sort of precedent between her and Luke but knowing too, that right now he needed it as much as she did, the warmth between them already was proof of that. "We'd be warmer if we cuddled up."

Finally, Luke snapped his eyes open and looked at her. He was so tired; she could see the heaviness in his eyes and the strain around his mouth. Her own eyes pulled, almost in sympathy. She'd be getting out the toothpicks soon.

"Serious?" he asked.

"Yeah. Put your arm around me and I'll drape my legs over you. Our body heat will help keep us warm."

"That won't work," he said and Jackson felt her heart drop. Embarrassment clawed its way down her spine and she wanted to squirm. Did he think she was coming on to him? Crossing some sort of line? She wanted to say something smart-assed to cover her blunder, but before she could mull over what the hell to say Luke slid an arm under her thighs and lifted her onto his lap—in one smooth move. "This is much better."

Jackson almost smiled, relief settling across her, and laid Mandy across her thighs. Warmth spread along the parts that were touching and she sighed. "Yep, much. Now sleep. I'll wake you in a few hours."

"You need sleep too."

"And I'm going to, but like I said I only sleep for a few hours at a time. We'll be fine here," she added. "Those filing cabinets'll make a hell of a noise if they try and get in. We'll have more than enough time to wake up and deal with the situation." *Batman and Robin to the rescue.*

Luke nodded, closed his eyes, and pulled her a little closer. She'd known he was big. That he was tall and wonderfully muscular. But being swept up all *Gone with the Wind* style and deposited on his lap brought it home in a way she hadn't considered before. She stroked a finger along Mandy's hilt, wondering at how quickly things could change in such a short space of time. Only yesterday she'd been sitting with Tye in an abandoned warehouse eating old sardines and huddling under a blanket that had smelled like mold.

And now? She looked up at Luke, the last of the day's light shadowing him. A smattering of stubble was already decorating his jaw and his hair was wonderfully tousled. The hotness could not be denied. More than that though, his actions and his words cheered her in an odd sort of way. That he already trusted her enough to put his life in her hands and that the precedent they'd set felt okay for them both.

Another stroke along Mandy and she dragged her gaze from Luke and swept the room instead. All was well and that left her thoughts free to dwell on other matters. She missed Tye. That one was a given, and her heart clenched as she thought of him. Assuming the best-case scenario, he'd be making his way to the interstate about now, or maybe resting up in a house somewhere. He was probably worried about her, wondering where she was... and for the first time it occurred to Jackson that Tye had not come looking for *her*.

She must have spent well over an hour in the pool room, both before and after meeting Luke. And she had gone looking for him, hadn't she, so why hadn't he come looking for her? The answer sprung into her mind and Jackson gritted her teeth to deny it. She wasn't ready to accept it yet.

She wished instead that she were warmer, but being cold was part of life for her now, there was nothing to be done about that but shift and settle in against Luke. Which she did and felt her stomach clench as he tightened his hold. Fact of the matter was, worries and problems aside, the feel of Luke's huge arms around her waist was very distracting, extremely comforting, and disturbingly exciting.

Priorities, she told herself, but all of a sudden they seemed to shift. Possibilities filled her, sparking anticipation that helped her bruised heart heal just a little, and she knew without a doubt that she had to convince him to come south with her.

There was nothing else for it now.

• • •

When Luke awoke he woke to the smell of strawberries. For a moment he was reminded of another time. Back in the days when the dead stayed dead. Back when the world still functioned and the only worries he'd had were balancing the garage's books or making himself presentable for a date. His mom had grown strawberries on the little porch outside her house. The baskets would overflow in the summer, the smell intense in the muggy air and he'd pick one or two before walking through the door to see his folks—dead now of course, properly dead. He hadn't been able to get to them before they had been eaten.

The scent filled his nostrils now, not exact of course, the faint chemical ring to it jarring, but despite that, and having two sleepy legs and a numbly cold ass, he inhaled a satisfied breath.

"How long have I been asleep?"

"A while," Jackson whispered. "About nine hours according to the clock."

He let out a groan, opened his eyes to complete darkness, and shifted position. He was massively uncomfortable and the fact he'd slept for so long shocked him slightly—because clearly it was night. "You should have woken me."

"It's fine."

He shifted again as soon as he became aware of his hard-on. *Fuck.* "You need to sleep too," he said, more to fill the silence than anything else. She had to be aware of it, didn't she? It was clearly obvious, no doubt prodding her through his pants. It couldn't be helped though, even as embarrassment flooded him. The end of the world did not mean the end of a man's natural urges—or a woman's for that matter. How long had it been since he'd awoken with a firm ass on his lap? Not to mention two luscious legs draped over his side and a distinctly female scent surrounding him? It could only be more perfect if they had been sitting in his bunker, sans zombies. Well, no, being in the pre-dead world, in his old house would be the epitome of perfection, but that was like asking for a return trip to the Moon.

"I did, and you're gonna need to keep your voice down."

Both his erection and his musings subsided in an instant. "What's happened?"

Jackson leaned in closer to him so that her mouth was right next to his ear. "I heard noises out there about a half hour ago. Faint, but there all the same. I'm guessing zombies are close by, but they haven't found us yet."

"We need to move then."

"No, we're fine for the moment. Wake up properly first and let your eyes adjust to the dark."

"They'll smell us, Jackson, and I'm good. I can make out your shape now."

She waved a hand in front of his face, as if checking to see if he was telling the truth. When he reached out to grab it she nodded and pushed off his lap. Though Luke was sure the lack of weight should have felt like a relief, it didn't. She was so slight that her extra pounds had barely made a dent. He could just about see her reaching out a hand to steady herself and guilt swamped him. How many hours sleep had she managed?

"You should have woken me sooner," he whispered.

She stretched against the wall, miniature squat thrusts, limbering herself up for movement. "Why? We were safe enough and out here you have to take advantage of those moments. Besides if I get tired you can give me a piggyback."

The image of her legs wrapped around his waist filled his head and Luke had to take a deep breath. Now was not the time for such thoughts. Hell, there was hardly ever a time anymore. The zombies were everywhere. Intimate moments were going to be few and far between—if ever—he suspected.

"It's four in the morning," Jackson said. "If we leave now, we'll have a couple of hours of darkness to cover our tracks."

"Zombies and darkness." Luke sighed. "The perfect combination."

Jackson bent down and picked up the sweater and sweats before folding them and placing them in her small backpack. "I know, but it makes sense to take advantage of the cover. If we leave when it's day, they could be out there waiting for us, and they'll see us immediately. The dark gives us a chance to sneak away. Besides it's never completely dark. The human eye adjusts pretty well to the smallest light source."

"I know. So what are you thinking, about a million years to make it down the interstate on foot?"

"Down the interstate?" She paused while swinging her backpack on and gave him a look he probably couldn't have deciphered even with lots of light. "You're coming with me? To Texas?"

Luke took a deep breath and nodded. His mind had been

made up really the moment he'd seen the Lily zombie waiting to get into his bunker and realized it wasn't a safe haven anymore. No, that wasn't right. More like when he'd spotted Jackson's purple panty-clad ass sprinting down the road. It just took Lily in his home to make him see it. The loss of his safe house to clarify his mind. The thought of leaving Jackson to make her way to Texas alone seemed wrong somehow. Sure there was no doubt that the girl could take care of herself, damn, could she. But the border must be a couple of thousand of miles or so, and that meant a whole lot of dead things—all wanting to eat her—all of them starving. It just made sense for the two of them to stick together. The fact he was attracted to her was an added bonus. He wanted to explore the possibility of something happening between them, and he wanted to see if her dream had any chance of being made a reality.

"Yeah. I am," he said. "We'll do this together, Jackson. We'll try to find your friend and then we'll carry on. See what, if anything, is left."

"I can't tell you how happy that makes me," she whispered. "I really can't."

A peculiar judder occurred in Luke's chest and he smiled at the feeling. "So then on foot? We'll make it when we're about a hundred?"

She shrugged. "We'll be eighty at most."

"Well then it's a good job we won't be on foot, huh?"

She stepped closer so that they were mere inches from one another. "You mean…"

Despite himself, Luke savored the look he could now see on her shadowed face, finally feeling as though he was doing his part. Jackson had probably protected him while he slept but now it was his turn to protect her. He'd get them to Laredo, Texas if it was the last fucking thing he did. He'd apply the same single-mindedness to this as he had to killing the dead, and he'd be damned if anything stopped him.

"Luke?" she prompted.

"Why do you think I brought us here?" he asked, pointing to the back of the building. "It's where the Batmobile's stashed."

Chapter Fourteen

They pulled into the deserted garage midafternoon. Luke had driven past several but every time Jackson pointed one out as a possible extra supply source he'd shook his head and driven on. Eventually she'd closed her eyes and gotten some much-needed sleep.

She could see why now. McGraw's "stick and spit," was on a deserted road, plenty of open space for them to look around and be sure they were dead-free. It was a good choice for their first stop.

"Can you see anything?" Luke asked as he slowed the car to a crawl.

Jackson wound down her window, shivering a little from the chill on her exposed face, and craned her head out. The garage was an old-style structure. Painted in fading red, it was surrounded by a few bare tree trunks on the side of the road, with a couple of abandoned cars completing the picture. The weak sun shone dully on the surrounding asphalt and for once Jackson couldn't see even a single blood splatter. "We're good. Nothing but clear space. Unless they're hiding inside."

"I wouldn't put it past them right now," Luke muttered. "So

listen, I'll pull up in front of that pump and check for gas. I don't reckon they'll be any in there, though. We're probably going to have to siphon it out of those cars. I have some tubing but we should probably look for supplies while we're here. Unlikely they'll be any, but you never know."

Jackson waited until Luke pulled to a stop in front of the first pump before jumping out of the car and stretching her legs. "I'll go inside. You get started on the gas." It crossed her mind that she might get lucky and find a stash of chocolate or candy. Jackson missed chocolate—badly. She'd give just about anything for a Hershey's Kiss. "See if I can find anything useful."

Luke undid his seat belt and followed her out of the car, his brow scrunched up. "You're going in there by yourself?"

Jackson snorted. "What because I'm so fragile?"

"No, just…well, it's sensible for us to go in together."

"Don't be stupid, Luke. What's sensible is you cracking on getting our fuel while I try and find whatever in there," she hiked a thumb in the direction of the garage, "might be of use to us. We don't want to be hanging out in the open for too long. First rule when on the road: do whatever you have to do quickly and move on as soon as possible."

"I thought the first rule was to ensure your exits? That's what you said at the swimming pool."

Jackson sighed and hefted Mandy. "I'm talking about open-road rules here, not hiding rules. There's a distinct difference. Open road it's all about keeping moving. Interiors, all about making sure you have a way to be *able* to move."

"Rules aside, we'll go in together," he insisted, his brow doing the scrunchy thing again.

A nasty suspicion arose in Jackson's mind then and she rubbed her fingers along Mandy's hilt. "Are you going all me-man-I-will-protect-woman on me? Please tell me you're not, because the whole Batman and Robin thing is not going to work. I don't want to be Batman, or Robin, for that matter."

Luke frowned. "No, and the comic-book analogy was stupid. I don't know why I said it."

She shrugged. "Guy thing. But, Luke, serious, you know I can take care of myself, right?"

He frowned some more. "I know you're tough but we need to stick together. It's just stupid us splitting up and putting ourselves at risk. In fact it's the whole reason we're going to have to haunt the interstate for a few days."

"Low blow," she said.

"I didn't mean it to be," Luke sighed. "But we should stick together."

"It's a few yards away."

"Yes..."

She ran her thumb up and down Mandy's hilt again. The familiar motion made her feel grounded and right. "We're working together here."

"Yeah"

"Which means being efficient and getting things done as quickly as possible. So you do your thing, I'll do mine, and then we can hit the road again."

"Jack..."

He didn't sound convinced but she shot him a smile and left him frowning at the Batmobile before he could voice any more objections. The door to the small building was, of course, unlocked and the room itself, because it was just one room with some sort of add-on, musty in an I-haven't-been-opened-in-ages kind of way. But someone had opened it at some point because the walls and now-silent fridges were picked completely clean. Jackson held Mandy tightly as she checked the aisles, and around the counter, but as well as a lack of anything edible, there were no zombies. She doubted they'd ever been in here. The lack of droppings and pus was a clear indication. She checked through cupboards and drawers, just in case.

Mild exasperation ran through Jackson's mind as she thought about Luke's reaction to her idea of splitting the work. She got that he was naturally protective. If the world hadn't ended he'd probably have a wife, a passel of kids, and be doing the total man-of-the-house thing. He was clearly the type to want to look after the women in his life and the idea made Jackson smile, chasing the slight irritation aside. Pre-zombie she probably *would* have let him look after her. Her brothers had bossed her around constantly and it had been easier to go along with their plans than put up a fight. Two years was a long time though. Two years changed a person. Two years in the land of the waking dead could change them almost beyond recognition, and she knew she had. Jackson was not the same easygoing girl she had been. She'd never be that girl again. She'd learned to take care of herself. To train her mouth not to scream when something horrific happened, or her mind not to freeze when a dead person tried to eat her. It hadn't been easy, not at all. She'd had to become someone completely different than the person she once was, not just physically but mentally too.

She frowned and stood on her tiptoes to look out of the dusty window to see Luke bent over an abandoned car. That right there was enough to show her the difference. Two years ago she'd have looked out of this same window and given a little sigh, mooning over Luke's hotness, and wondering how she could get him to notice her slightly overlarge ass. Now? Well, now she was more concerned about how exposed he was looking and the fact that his ax was a shade too far away from his hand. And her ass? He'd have trouble finding it these days. She shook her head, fell back to the balls of her feet, and pulled open another cupboard. Nothing. Not a goddamn thing. She kicked it shut with a growl and circled the store.

Jackson heard him long before he popped his head around the door, and resolved to have a long conversation with him that was *so* going to feature the word stealth. God, he reminded her of Tye.

"Everything okay?" he asked.

She straightened from where she'd been checking under the counter. "Why wouldn't it be?"

"Because the world is overrun with zombies."

"Since when?"

Luke grinned and gestured to the back of the store. "Are you all done?"

"Give me two more minutes. I want to check that add-on back there."

He nodded and backed out of the doorway, though Jackson could see it was an effort for him. It was sweet in a goofy kind of way, even endearing, but as she watched him make his way back over to a beat up truck and pop the fuel cap, she knew it simply wasn't going to fly.

He *was* hot.

He *was* sweet.

"But you can't let it make a difference," she said, tearing her gaze away from the window and edging around the shelving units to the back of the store. "Got to keep yourself tough. Stay strong. Stay independent."

The mantra played through her mind and it was no surprise that she thought of Tye. He'd never tried to look after her, not really, but then he'd been more interested in someone he could kill the zombies with than anything else, and he simply did as he pleased, ignoring her thoughts completely. She'd often ignored his thoughts too. In that, at least, they had complemented each other. And though they'd shared their journey for more than a month Jackson hadn't once relaxed her usual guard.

Why did she think it was going to be more difficult with Luke? Even if they managed to find her erstwhile friend.

A few minutes later, after using the skanky toilet inside the add-on, she joined Luke outside. The morning light illuminated his masculine features and she swallowed unsteadily. There *was* no getting around the hotness. Maybe that had something to do with her worries over what she suspected was going to be a tendency on his part to try and be the Giles to her Buffy.

"No chocolate to be found. Nothing to be found, actually, place is bare. There is a toilet though, but it doesn't flush."

He looked up and shot her a smile, the relief in it was obvious — relief no doubt that she was still in one piece. "There's gas in these cars," he said, pointing to a tube sticking out of the nozzle of one. "So that's something, and I found this tube. Just need to suck it out."

"What are you waiting for?"

He shrugged and smiled again. "Pathetic, I know, but I hate the taste. You'd think as a mechanic I'd be used to it. The smell is fine, but the taste always makes me gag."

"I don't mind it," she said, slightly endeared by his honesty, and the smiles too. "I can do it if you don't want to."

He pulled on the tube and shook his head. "No. I'm good."

Jackson watched as he took a deep breath and popped the tube in his mouth. She rubbed Mandy again and looked around, scanning the buildings, the trees, everywhere. No sign of zombies anywhere. They were okay for the moment. She could let her mind wander for a moment couldn't she? It wandered to Luke's lap.

She grinned. It had most certainly not escaped her notice that when he'd awoken he'd had a raging hard-on. She'd felt it through his jeans a good few minutes before he'd actually opened his eyes. Their positioning meant that it had prodded her ass and she'd sort of squirmed a little on his lap as she had tried to work out what to do.

He'd woken before she could make a decision and Jackson had thought the best thing to do was just ignore it. Luke was no doubt embarrassed and she hadn't wanted to draw attention to something that was a purely physical reaction. Men always got hard-ons in the morning. And while she suspected he was attracted to her, now was so not the time to be thinking of anything along those lines. Anticipation aside, Jackson wasn't sure there would *ever* be such a time. How could there be when zombies shadowed their every move?

"Urgh…" Luke's exclamation pulled her back on track and her grin widened as he removed the tube and spat gas on the ground, before pushing the tube into the canister in front of him. "What did I say? Tastes like shit. What I wouldn't give for some gum."

"Dream on, sweetheart."

He looked up, pushed a few strands of hair out of his eyes and smiled. Jackson felt little butterflies fluttering in her stomach — though it may have been due to hunger.

"How much do you think is in there?" she asked, and even she could hear the slight catch in her voice, so maybe not hunger after all.

"A few gallons, I hope."

The canister he'd found filled up long before the tube stopped giving them their gas, and Jackson pushed another one across to take the remaining liquid. She placed the top on the first canister, then got ready to do the same with the next.

"We should get another to see us through for a few days," Luke continued. "I want to get as much here, where I know we'll find it, before we're somewhere I'm unfamiliar with."

Jackson nodded and secured the second canister. She pushed it across to Luke and stood up to do another security sweep. Still nothing. They were okay for a little longer.

"We've got a fair bit already."

They'd lucked out with these cars. Sure there was plenty of gas around but it was a question of it being contaminated in the fuel lines or some such shit, or worse getting to it. It seemed Luke knew the whereabouts of pretty much every garage in the state —

he'd visited most of them in his old job—and she suspected he could tell if it was good to use, so maybe it wasn't so much luck but the company.

Jackson *was* very pleased, protective tendencies aside, that he'd agreed to come with her. In truth she was almost thankful to the zombie for infiltrating his bunker, even though she felt guilty just thinking it. It had been Luke's home, after all. But she knew they stood a much better chance of making it to the border together. Plus there was the whole car situation.

Luke stood then and stretched. His sweater and the tees underneath rode up showing her his washboard abs again and Jackson sighed before remembering the wound below his rib cage.

"How's the hole? No infection?"

He lifted his sweater and smiled. "Nah. It's all good. A few more days and it should be healed up nicely. Good job too. I'm out of Johnny Walker."

"Couple of weeks, I reckon, whiskey or not. Hopefully it'll be healed long before we hit the south. We don't want it festering in the heat."

He laughed. "I never fester."

"There's no showers out here, Luke. Believe me, in a week or two, you will indeed be festering."

He laughed and made a show of sniffing his armpit. "All good, so far."

Maybe it would have been easier if she'd hooked up with someone a little less attractive? But then she'd done that with Tye, hadn't she, and though she hadn't had to deal with the sit-on-his-lap-and-get-flustered situation, because she'd never seen him in that way, it still hurt to lose him, just as it would hurt if she lost Luke.

Lost chances and all that.

"There's another garage a mile down there," Luke said. "Might be some food there. One can hope at least."

"We've got loads of stuff." Jackson gestured as Luke grabbed the two gas cans and placed them in the back of the car with the rest of their gear. "Way more than I've had since the world ended."

Luke shook his head. "We don't have enough food. Maybe a few days, at most."

A few days worth? She almost laughed. She and Tye had lived day to day, hour to hour sometimes. "Yeah but we've got a car! Look on the bright side, I say. I can't believe we can actually drive. Do you realize that'll take months, years, off the journey? If I'd had someone to drive with me, and a working car, I'd have been there last year."

"It'll make things easier for sure as long as we can keep it fueled." He paused his packing and gave her the eye. It was that same look he'd given her in the bunker. Like he was trying to work something out and Jackson wondered what it meant.

"It'll be good for you too, Jackson," he said. "You've had to walk for too long. I'll be happy to drive you around."

Despite the eye contact and the loveliness of his words, Jackson bristled slightly. There it was again. "Are you assuming you're driving because you're the guy?"

He nodded slowly and grinned widely. "Of course I am. You know how it goes. The man always drives."

Jackson stroked down Mandy's hilt and narrowed her eyes. "If I thought you meant that, you'd be getting better acquainted with Mandy here."

"Anytime, sweetheart."

"And, I won't actually mention that I can't drive."

He walked around the car and opened the passenger door for her. His gesture was chivalrous and playful and it took a moment for Jackson to take it in. How strange that in the world of the dead there was still a man who remembered such things, who could make her feel…a little bit weird over it.

"You can't drive?"

Jackson shrugged. "Nope, never had the money to learn or to own a car. It didn't matter before, especially in New York City. But after, well, I tried in the early days when cars were still running. A couple of crashes later I decided it might be better to walk. I didn't trust myself not to fuck up and get hurt, and then the zombies would find me and eat me, so, yup, feel free to take the wheel."

"I'm gonna have to teach you then," Luke said. "What if something happens to me? You need to be able to get yourself south."

"Maybe," she said, touched by his offer, feeling guilty even that she'd bristled at his words in the first place. "But I'd prefer we keep you in one piece instead."

Luke waited until she settled into her seat. "Okay. One piece it is. Time to get moving?"

Seat belt on she nodded. "Hell, yeah."

CHAPTER FIFTEEN

Three days later Jackson and Luke sat in an abandoned house, slightly musty blankets from the linen closet around their shoulders for warmth, the bedroom door—sluiced in Tye's bottle of Davidoff's Cool Water—barred against any waking dead that might come sniffing. It was likely the scent wouldn't work, not after what they'd seen, but they'd done it anyway, just in case. Their escape route was secure and they were taking a moment to regroup.

The last of the day's weak sunlight was filtering in through the windows, leaving Luke to scowl at what that light illuminated: a tin of Spam. The scowl was not just for the Spam, though he hated the stuff, it was for the conversation he knew they had to have.

One that was going to be painful.

He shifted under his blanket as he considered the best way to approach it. Only maybe there was no best way? Perhaps he was just going to have to be blunt. He shifted a little more as he played the last few days back in his mind. They'd driven the whole area—using a fair bit of gas in the process—and waited around the point of the interstate for three long days. Checking and checking. Only Tye was nowhere to be seen. There was nothing at all to suggest he had come this way, and they could wait no longer.

It was becoming too dangerous.

"Jackson," he began.

She looked up and shot him a smile. "You're not eating your Spam."

"I'm not a fan," he said.

She shrugged. "It's edible. That's all that counts. Unless you want to risk the big malls, we've got no choice but to eat stuff that's a bit gross. Personally, I have no problem with it. I think we ate it when I was young. Did you know that it dates back to the Second World War? It was used as a meat substitute as part of rationing in England."

His stomach rumbled. "I'd risk the malls about fucking now."

"I wouldn't let you."

Luke frowned as he looked into the small can of smushed meat Jackson had opened. The canned mushroom soup they'd eaten yesterday had been bad enough, but this was the tipping point. He too had eaten it when he was younger and had hated whenever his mom had placed it on his plate.

He shook his head as Jackson attacked her can, scooping the meat up and munching it down. Once again, as he had over the last couple of days, he was reminded of how easy he'd had it in comparison to her. Over the last year and a half he'd been safe in his bunker with access to clean water and decent food, while Jackson had eaten whatever the hell she could get. And even before then he'd been lucky, hell if he thought about it, luck had been on his side since the beginning. He'd always found food before the hunger got too much. Never had an issue finding drinking water or a place to bed down. Maybe it was because he'd stayed in an area he was familiar with?

It was the little things that brought it home to him. The way she started looking for somewhere safe to park the car as soon as the sun got low in the sky. The way she didn't even think to complain when it had rained, just shrugged and suggested they slow down. To her things were pretty good right now. He got that. They had transportation, with enough gas for quite a few days, and somewhere safe to sleep in the car. She probably still thought they were going to find her friend.

He sighed. She was tough and resilient and it almost shamed him at times that he wasn't more so, in comparison to her. Oh, he'd done his part so far, he knew that. Just yesterday, prior to the mushroom soup hitting his stomach with a ninja kick, he'd taken down three waking dead, leaving just one for Jackson. The admiration he'd seen in her eyes had warmed him as he kept watch, though his grumbling stomach had kind of negated the happy feelings a little.

He'd found them enough gas for the journey south, too, and up till now he'd provided decent food—mushroom soup aside. Yep, he was looking after her…although if he was totally honest with himself, he got the feeling she didn't need him to. Hell, she could look after herself without so much as a blink and he knew that. Didn't stop him from wanting to, though.

"Zombies like the enclosed spaces in there," she said after a moment around a mouthful of Spam. "I didn't know that in the early days. Got trapped in one, *Dawn of the Dead* style, and I vowed—never again. Now particularly is not the time to risk it. Not now they're so smart."

He could see the sense in that and nodded to her. "I get that, Jack, but we are going to need more food. We have what? Five or six cans left and a few granola bars?"

"All the more reason for you to eat your Spam."

He growled but scooped a forkful in, swallowing it quickly before the taste could register.

"If it gets to the point where we can't find any cans or whatnot, we have one other option."

He swallowed some more, shuddering slightly. "And that is?"

"Rat."

Luke winced, the Spam suddenly becoming far more appealing. But then he remembered that Tye had caught rats for her, hadn't he? He vaguely recalled Jackson saying so. Would they taste worse than Spam? Could anything taste worse than Spam? And was *now* really the right time to bring up the Tye issue?

"You want to eat rat?" he asked.

She rolled her eyes and pulled a face at him. "No. I freaking hate them. They're all stringy and it gives me the heebs to think about the things they've been eating before we eat them, but," she paused and shrugged, "it comes down to putting calories in our system so we're strong enough for whatever we need to do."

"You're right," he said slowly. "We can't fight zombies on an empty stomach. It's surprising isn't it, how much beheading one takes out of you."

"Less than it used to," she said.

"Because we're fitter. Our muscles more developed."

"Yup. Still need those calories though."

He nodded. If rat was all there was, then so be it, he'd suck it up. Because, and though it pained him to admit it, he did not want Jackson thinking he was less able to do what was needed than she was, or than Tye had been.

Tye. Why did he feel slightly threatened by the other man? It was ridiculous, really. The guy was obviously dead, and besides Jackson had told him there was nothing between them but friendship and he'd seen the truth of that in her eyes. He was sure he had. He was also pretty sure he'd seen something else too. A whisper of the same thing he didn't doubt she saw reflected in his eyes.

Attraction.

The interest he felt for her was not one-sided. Insane maybe, in today's world but still. They'd snuggled up the last couple of nights—for warmth she said—but Luke had caught a look, a stray touch here and there, and was sure there was more to it than that. What he was going to do about it he didn't know. They were in built-up areas. Nowhere seemed safe enough for them to do the sort of things he found himself fantasizing about. It'd be just his luck to have his pants around his ankles when the zombies found them. It'd be laughable if it wasn't so fucked-up.

Luke was also aware that they'd known each other for only a handful of days and he didn't want to come across as some sort of jerk taking advantage of the nearest woman—not that Jackson was a take-advantage-of kinda girl, but still.

Food was the priority right now, not getting laid, and he wanted to make sure Jackson ate enough. Where these caveman urges to look after her came from, he couldn't say, especially in light of her bad-assness, but he felt an overwhelming need to feed her and keep her safe. Ridiculous considering she was the toughest woman he'd ever met. It was also odd for him, because there were two competing drives going on. He'd worked that out as he waited by the pumps at the stick and spit for her to return. His was to make her comfortable and safe and hers was to keep being the tough little cookie he knew her to be. Her drive didn't lessen his, only increased it, and he found himself wondering exactly how that was likely to play out.

"I'd love some steak," Jackson said wistfully.

"No chance of steak but I can't believe we're driving a route other survivors have picked clean" he said, frustrated by the lack of available supplies. "Jesus Christ, there aren't that many of them. You'd have thought there'd be canned vegetables left or something. No one likes them. They're always mushed up."

"There's nothing anywhere these days," Jackson said. "So the steak really is just a wild fantasy. I read once, ages ago, in a news article, I think, that there was only enough food in the country to last a month. We've had more than two years, so all things considered, it's not too bad. And at least there are still rats and wild things growing. We'd be in the shit otherwise. Plus, I imagine the farther south we get, the more things we'll find to pick. I lucked out once on an entire greenhouse full of squash and zucchini. They gave me a churning belly but I eventually ate them all. And there was the time I found the orchard…"

Luke nodded for her to continue and ate the last of his can while she listed all the freebie food she'd found. The aftertaste of the Spam was hideous and he took a long swig of his water to wash it down. Yesterday it had rained for three hours straight so liquid was not a problem, though he'd damn well kill for a cup of coffee.

"So things aren't yet as bad as they seem," Jackson finished.

"Okay. Well if worst comes to worst, rat it is."

She smiled and gripped Mandy to her—yeah she'd named her machete, he'd laughed when she told him, but realized mere moments later why. With realization had come a nasty feeling in his gut. She'd named her weapon because it was the only real thing she had—the only thing she'd relied on for so long.

"How are you gonna catch one?" she asked, playing along. "I can in a pinch, though it always takes me ages."

"I'll use the Spam."

She nudged his empty can and smiled. "They probably hate it too. It's not my favorite food but I'll eat anything these days."

"I *am* going to find you food," Luke said, eyeing her skinny frame. She was so petite and he knew she was constantly hungry. Her food disappeared the moment it made it into her hands. The protective urge rose up again and he gritted his teeth. The urge to look after her, to keep her safe, to fill her with food. "We haven't checked out the shops around here yet and there's no better time than now. Give me one hour. Wait here, okay."

He imagined finding a stash of good stuff, Jackson's eyes lighting up with pleasure, reaching out to hug him…Jesus Christ he was pathetic! His friends, were they still alive, would say he had it bad, and they would not be wrong.

"You're not going alone."

He started from his fantasy and righted the Spam tin. "What? Damn right I am. It's gonna be dark soon. You'll be safer here."

"Not going to happen."

"Jackson—"

She shook her head. "Didn't we discuss this at the garage?"

"We did, and you said back then, correct me if I am wrong, that it made sense to split up when necessary."

"That was different. That was a few yards. I'm not losing you, Luke," she said and he halted his next words when he saw the look in her eye.

There it was again, the glimmer of interest, the same thing he felt, surely? What the hell was he going to do about it? In this world, this totally fucked-up world, what could he do?

"You're not here to look after me, Luke," she said after a moment. "You need to get over that right here, right now. I'm not some weak female that you have to coddle and protect. Nothing pisses me off more than you taking that attitude. I can look after myself. We're each other's backup and we go together. That's the way it is now. We look out for one another and we stick together when we need to and do things separately when we don't, but there's no leaving the other behind because of some macho bullshit."

Together. The word spread through him and his heart gave a strange little thump that felt almost like heartburn. He had a nasty suspicion he knew exactly what it meant.

"Jack—"

"As equals," she added. "Equal risks, equal responsibility. That's the way we roll, or we don't roll at all. And it is time to roll it, isn't it?" She paused. "I know you've been thinking it and you haven't wanted to say, but it's time we moved on."

"And Tye?" he asked, relief hitting that he hadn't been the one to bring the issue up.

"He's probably taken a different route is all," she said. "It'll take him longer to get to Laredo, but he will eventually. Maybe we'll even find him on the way?"

"Maybe," he agreed, because if that was what Jackson wanted to believe, who was he to say otherwise?

"So we'll go," she added. "And you'll leave the macho bullshit here."

Macho bullshit...was it really even that? He paused and wondered for a moment how he'd be reacting if Jackson was Jack — another man rather than a woman. It jolted him slightly when he realized that he would be treating her, him, very differently. And not just the weird heart stuttering and hard-ons. Luke swallowed some more water and took a deep breath. He *would* have to suppress the urge to take charge and protect. He got that. To stop treating her as he would have the women in his life before the zombies came. Fuck, it was going to be difficult. Jackson was a woman, a beautiful, sassy woman, but one all the same, and bad-ass aside it was his natural male instinct to protect her. His mom had brought him up to look after the women in his life and end of the world or not, suppressing those urges would be hard. Yet, he would try. What else could he do?

"Together," he said on the exhale. "We'll go together."

She shot him a dazzling smile then — and it was every bit as spectacular as he'd imagined it would be. It flickered across her face, making the green in her eyes glimmer and her soft skin beg to be stroked. Understanding dawned with that smile and Luke gritted his teeth to stop from giving a little cheer, or worse, leaning across and planting a kiss right on those curved lips.

He wanted Jackson and he was fairly fucking certain that she wanted him. Sooner or later something would happen between them because it would have to. Equals, neither one jumping first, but together. At some point, certainly not today, probably not even tomorrow, but maybe in a few days or even a few weeks, they would both jump, and fucked-up world or not, what would happen, would happen.

And so he reached out his hand, and she took it, and that was the way they went.

Chapter Sixteen

In places the interstate was impassable, so they had no choice but to try other roads. Those roads were either ridiculously deserted or very messed up. It all depended really on which they took and also how many had taken those same routes before. Not just now, as in the last of the survivors, but before, when there were still thousands—millions—of people all trying to get away.

After two years it was almost impossible for Jackson to imagine that. Both because of the barriers she'd erected and also because the thought of that many people now seemed almost fantastical. Like something out of a dream, or a forgotten story she'd once read a long time ago. To envisage a great surge of people, all of them desperately trying to find a way out of the madness was akin to envisaging a world without the dead—and that was just ridiculous. She knew that there would have been moms and dads and little children. Old people and babies. All of them with jobs and friends and hobbies. Every one of them would have had a story, little tidbits and anecdotes and interesting facts. All of that consumed by the desperate desire to get away.

Jackson understood the mindset, of course she did. When the zombies came, running through the streets at top speed and breaking through the windows, the main impulse of most people was to run, as quickly as possible. They gathered what they had and hit the road. Trouble was, thousands of others did the same, and in those days where there were people there were zombies...it had soon turned into an absolute bloodbath. Thousands of people dying only to awake moments or minutes later and eat anyone else still trying to escape. Like a fucking daisy chain.

Jackson would like to say she'd been smart back then, but in truth she'd just gone with the flow. Her brothers had decided early on that the only way to stay safe was to remain inside and barricade the windows and doors. So she had. It was only when her brothers were gone, the food had run out, and the water had started to turn brown that she'd struck out on her own. By that point all those thousands of fleeing people had pretty much been eaten or infected. All that remained were their smashed-up cars and their scattered belongings. All those stories and experiences held within each person lost forever. Consumed by the waking dead just like their flesh was.

In some ways, as they drove past wreck after wreck on the seventh day, Jackson almost felt like she was following paths set out by those people—and though she tried not to think of them, part of her couldn't help it. The barriers swayed and undulated in her mind, wanting to be let down for just a little while. She looked around at the devastation surrounding them and the feeling was almost like she was late for the party—that she'd missed it, and was only now saying, *Okay wait for me.*

Maybe it was because they were driving rather than walking? It seemed to give everything a new perspective, removing some of the danger and allowing her to view it all from a distance.

"Look," she said softly. "How quickly it changes."

Luke followed her gaze to the row of tract houses on the left of them. They were wide open, doors ajar, windows smashed. Already nature was intruding on those homes. Jackson knew if she stepped inside, mildew would be growing anywhere that was moist. Plants creeping along the pathways and paving stones. Vines and branches twisting around the exterior structures. In a few years' time, sooner perhaps, those plants would get inside the houses and start growing on people's couches and inside their TVs. Jackson couldn't help but wonder how long it would take until nature took back everything man had taken from it. Until the huge structures in the cities succumbed to rain and the beating of the sun.

"How quickly it'll keep changing," he said grimly, and she frowned.

"Not everything. Think about all those mansions that are closed up. They might last for decades in good condition."

"That they might," he agreed. "We should find some and break into them. I bet they're full of stuff."

"But then they'll be open and ruined like everything else," she said.

"We'd just be speeding the process up."

Jackson sighed and looked back out the window, the truth of Luke's words nudging her. It was odd how sometimes their positions shifted. She thought of herself as the bad-ass, the realist, but sometimes it was Luke who was the pragmatic one at heart.

"I'll keep an eye out for rich-looking zombies," she said after a moment. "They'll lead us to the mansions."

"And a rich zombie would look like...?"

She shrugged, the frown turning into a smile. "Rich."

Only there were no zombies dressed in designer clothes and dripping in gold. Instead cars sat in long lines, snaking out across the lanes. Glass glinting on the floor, sometimes frosted, marked their route. The ever-present blood and pus splatters decorated the cars and buildings, splashed in arcs, puddles, even in crisscross patterns. The blood was the only sign of the humans that once were. The bones, as always, were gone.

As they passed a billboard splattered with what looked like

several pints of old dried blood, Jackson turned to Luke. Luke who had indeed found them food inside an abandoned apartment on the fourth day. A veritable feast of canned goods and dried pasta. Luke who insisted she sleep first, rest for longer, eat more, be careful, take her time… Luke who, day by day, macho bullshit aside, was becoming more important to her, healing the hole in her heart where the loss of Tye still ached…

His hand was resting on the side of his seat, just inches from hers, and it seemed perfectly natural for her to reach out and stroke the skin on the back of it. He turned and smiled the moment she did.

"You okay?"

She nodded, her heart thudding a little as his smile widened.

"I was just thinking."

"About rich zombies?"

She shook her head and trailed her fingers away. "No I was wondering, what do you think they do with the bones?"

Luke pulled a face and maneuvered around a parked truck. "You ask some weird questions, Jack. The bones? Lemme think. Well, I guess they suck the marrow out and then discard them somewhere."

"Okay, ew with the marrow."

He grinned. "Makes sense."

"But discard them where? I've never seen any bones anywhere. Do you think they eat the bones too?" It was a question she'd long considered and had been unable to find an answer to.

"It would be hard to see how," Luke replied. "Bones are tough, and it's not like they have much in them that would be worth the hassle of chomping them down that couldn't be sucked out instead."

Jackson pointed them through a passage that was fairly free of carts and cars, considering the possibilities as she did so. The zombie's teeth were about the same as a normal person. They didn't grow or anything once they turned—they were just dead people come back to life, after all. And although there were differences— their limbs were more elongated, more flexible, their skin thinner, and their bodies a little mushier—there were no other biological changes that Jackson had noticed. They still had all their limbs, their eyes, ears, and hair. Only the force they seemed to exude allowed them to rip through muscle and flesh. Luke was right. She couldn't imagine those teeth, in essence the same as hers, eating through bone.

"Maybe they collect them as trophies or something?"

Luke gunned the accelerator as they hit a clean road, one that many of the other cars and vans hadn't made it to. She tried not to think about why that was the case, pushing the barriers back up and thinking instead of what it would be like to have a bag of fries on her lap.

"No. They don't think like that, Jack," he said slowly. "Don't give them qualities they don't possess."

Buildings flashed by and Jackson shifted slightly in her seat to watch the procession of smashed up windows and broken doors. It was weird but she could actually feel the emptiness of those buildings without even needing to check if anyone was inside— not that anyone was, of course. Her gaze moved from the doors all the way up to the roofs. Nothing looked out of the ordinary to her, well ordinary in this world.

"Qualities?" she asked. "What do you mean?"

"Like deep thinking," Luke said. "Trophy collection means they know on some level what's happening around them, to them. They'd collect them for a reason and it suggests a humanness to them. Serial killers used to collect trophies, didn't they? They knew what they were doing and they knew why they shouldn't be doing it. The zombies don't even have that excuse. They *don't* know what's happening, not really, because they're not human anymore, Jack. They're dead and somehow brought back to fucking life.

They're not us anymore."

"I know that," Jackson said. "I know they're not us."

"They don't think the way we do," Luke added as if she hadn't spoken. "They can't, else they wouldn't be able to eat us would they?"

"Bits of them have to think *something*," she said. "To open doors and smell us. So yeah, okay, they might not think exactly like us but they are thinking still. Something goes on in their brains."

"But that something is not like us."

"Maybe not," Jackson agreed. "But you don't know how they think, not exactly. No one does and that's why we're in this mess."

• • •

But Luke did know how they thought. He was sure of it. All that time alone in his bunker? He'd spent a significant part of it trying to work out the zombies. How they hunted, how they tracked people. If he hadn't gotten some sort of understanding he'd be dead now. He knew he would.

"They think like animals," he said. "Maybe that's why they hunt in packs. Even so, this new intelligence of theirs changes nothing beyond our own goals. They've lost their compassion, their empathy, their very humanity."

"Luke—"

"Serious, Jack," he said. "You need to understand this."

"I do," she replied. "Two years and then some has been enough for me to get the whole I'm-gonna-eat-you thing. But what goes on in their minds is a mystery. I've spent plenty of time thinking about it, because what else *is* there to really think about, and I can't even begin to imagine."

"I can. Let me tell you about Mr. Jenkins."

"And he was?"

"Hold on…" Luke slowed the Batmobile and pointed to the top of a four-story building. "Did you see something up there?"

"No, and if I did, I wouldn't slow down, I'd speed up. Gas it and tell me about this Mr. Jenkins."

Luke complied and took a left turn.

"He was my neighbor. I don't know exactly how old he was, but sixties at least. He was a war veteran, though he never spoke about it. His favorite hobby was tending the garden, front and back. He grew these amazing flowers. I don't remember what they were called, but in the summer they'd grow everywhere and they smelled great. I was going out on a date once and he gave me a bunch to take—she loved them."

Luke swung a right and then regretted it. The buildings surrounding them were a good few stories high on both sides. He accelerated and took a quick left before returning to Mr. Jenkins.

"He'd chide me constantly that I left my garden in such a state." Luke shook his head at the memory. "He mowed my lawn when I was at work and I'd tune his car when he was at his club—I knew his war pension would barely cover the cost of regular repairs. Neither of us mentioned it. He was too proud and it was just something we did."

"He sounds like a nice guy," Jackson said. "But, Luke, I should tell you here and now that while I'm happy to hear about Mr. Jenkins, I don't like talking about the people *I* knew from before. Maybe you haven't picked up on that yet, but it's something I tend to avoid."

"The people from before?" he said, baffled by her words. "Everyone we knew was from before."

"Exactly."

Luke shook his head and shot Jackson a quick look. She was stiff on her seat, eyes darting to the view outside. Her fingers were rubbing up and down her machete's hilt in an almost compulsive fashion. He'd seen her do that many times and wondered if she was even aware of it.

"But if we don't talk about them how will we remember

them?" he asked.

"We won't. That's kind of the point," she replied. "What's the use in remembering them? They're all gone."

"The use is because they make us feel things and often they illuminate things, which is what Mr. Jenkins here does." The image of his gray-haired neighbor entered his mind and Luke smiled as he paused to negotiate the car through a thin gap where two large sedans had smashed into one another, wondering as he did so, why he hadn't picked up on the fact that Jackson actually had *never* mentioned a single person from before. Sure, she talked about the books she missed, the drinks she'd tried, but the people, no, never the people...

"So tell me, Jack," he said now that they were through the wrecked cars, "apart from gardening and going to his club to play checkers or whatever he did there, do you know what the thing Mr. Jenkins most loved was?"

"No," Jackson said, drawing the word out. "I have a suspicion this is not leading me to a nice place, though."

"Well I'm going to tell you because it is important. So for once let me do that, please."

"For once..."

"He loved his grandchildren," Luke said, ignoring her words. "He had two. Two little girls. Bethann and Louise. They were six and eight. I know because every time they came to visit he would show them off like his most-prized possessions. Damn, he loved those children."

"Luke..."

Ignoring the plea in Jackson's voice, Luke continued. "The girls were visiting when the first zombies found their way to our neighborhood. Chicago was one of the epicenters of the outbreak, so it was bad luck all around, though I didn't know this until later. I'm guessing we were one of the first bunches to even see a waking dead. What a wonderful thing to brag about, eh? Anyway, they broke through Mr. Jenkins's windows first, three of them—they hadn't started forming their packs yet. I grabbed a mallet. It was all I had, and ran around, thinking they were burglars or something. It was one of those awful moments where you can't actually believe what you're seeing is real…"

Luke trailed off as he remembered the faces of those first snarling dead. It had been like something out of a horror movie, and even as he'd brought the mallet down to smash in one's head he hadn't really believed it was real. *You're going to get arrested…* that was the thought that had ran through his mind.

"Together we killed them all, again, though we didn't know that at the time. Me, Mr. Jenkins, and his son, well, me more than them, if I'm honest. I just sort of bashed away at them until they stopped moving," he said giving himself an inward shake. "We barricaded ourselves upstairs in my house, put the news on, and kept guard against any others. The news told us nothing of course, wild rumors, talk of terrorists—absolute nonsense. So we thought we'd wait till daybreak and make a run for it until we could figure things out. I wanted to leave immediately, get to my parents. But Mr. Jenkins was in his sixties and his son was a complete wimp. I couldn't just leave them."

"Luke…"

"We discussed all sorts of scenarios," he continued. "Could it be druggies? Could it be some sort of weird joke? But in the back of our minds I think we all had a suspicion." He sighed and gripped the steering wheel, memories overwhelming him. "And I checked, kind of sneakily, to make sure no one had been bitten. I'd watched enough movies after all, and though I felt like a total dick doing it, I looked all the same. I didn't see anything though, and as the hours passed and no more zombies came, Mr. Jenkins son took a turn to keep watch. I should never have let him…"

"I so don't want to hear this."

"So Mr. Jenkins son was taking a watch when I heard a

scream," he continued, ignoring Jackson's mumblings. "I hadn't been asleep, not really, just sort of dozing. When I opened my eyes it was to see Mr. Jenkins holding one of the girls in his arms, his son looking on just sort of horrified, almost in a stupor. I don't know if it was Bethann or Louise. I'd never been able to tell who was who. But she had these lovely blond curls and when he looked up at me, noticing I was awake, he pulled away a chunk of her brain with his teeth. I could see the hairs sticking to his chin, his cheeks, everywhere. I think she was still alive when he broke her skull and started eating her. His little granddaughter. The one he'd been so proud of."

"Luke, no…"

"He didn't even stop eating her, just looked at me and kept chewing."

If there was any memory stored in his brain that Luke would like to lose, it was this one. Of all the zombies and dead people and plain old carnage he had battled, the memory of little Bethann or Louise always pulled at something inside of him. It was the start of the nightmare that had begun his new life, and forever her blond hair would signify that.

"That's horrific," Jackson whispered. "And I believe we are being followed. Thank God. I think I've had more than enough reminiscing."

Luke almost laughed. "A pack? You'd prefer to battle a *pack* than talk about my neighbors?"

"Damn right, and it's a megapack, on the rooftops."

"Gun it or kill them?"

"I suspect we're not gonna get a choice. They're trying to round us up."

"They won't catch us."

"Uh-huh."

"Do you want to know what happened to Mr. Jenkins?" Luke asked, eyeing the rooftops.

"Not really. I wish you hadn't mentioned him. Though now that you have, if I die before I find out, I'll be mad. But then if you tell me, I'll be mad because I so don't need my head filled with any more of that kind of shit."

Luke slowed the car and unclipped his guns. "The movies again. I used to watch plenty before they came. I loved *Zombieland* and I remembered exactly what they did to them. So I beheaded him and then I left to find my parents. The son spent the entire time sobbing with one little girl dead in front of him, and the other little girl in his arms. My point in telling you this story though, Jackson, is for you to realize something. I haven't told you it for no reason. There *is* a point."

"And that would be?"

"That there's nothing left in them anymore. Nothing to even remember the love they'd once held so dear. They're animals. Worse than that, even. Family members ate family members without compunction. Hell, they probably still do."

Jackson wound down her window, took aim, and shot a waking dead straight through the head. It fell from the roof with a splat.

"I know," she said without so much as blinking. "Just as an FYI, I stomped my brother's head in before he could eat me."

Luke started in surprise. "You serious?"

"No, just thought I'd lighten the mood."

"Your brother..." he said, ignoring her sarcastic tone. "That must have been horrific."

"Don't want to talk about it," she said in a singsong voice before aiming and firing. The bullet missed, lodging in a nearby window.

"But—"

"Don't make me shoot you, Luke."

"With that aim? I don't think I have to worry."

"Try me."

He sighed. "Okay subject closed…but you get what I'm saying—"

She shot a second zombie just as Luke took aim, effectively halting his words. "Yes, I get what you're saying, but that doesn't mean we know how they think," she said. "Part of them could be looking on, horrified, watching it all happen, unable to do anything."

"I don't believe that."

She shrugged. "In the end it doesn't matter, I guess. We kill them all the same."

"Yeah."

"And if they are looking on, trapped, they're probably grateful for it."

"I suppose…" He sighed and watched as the zombie he was aiming for jumped from building to building. They were so flexible and so strong. How he hated them.

"In the end, I guess nothing really matters anymore," Jackson said slowly. "Nothing but finding that camp and seeing what's left. If there's anything we can do to change things."

"To change things?"

She nodded slowly. "I'm fantasizing that it's an army camp. Full of scientists and doctors all busy working away on a cure."

"You're not serious?"

"I said fantasizing."

She sounded so glum that Luke wanted to reach out and grasp her hand, partly because he felt guilty for telling her a story she clearly didn't want to hear, for making her remember her brother, and partly because he just wanted to. But he was all tied up with the gun and the steering wheel. Instead he shot the jumping zombie, for her, and smiled as it fell to the ground. A quick look in her direction and his heart sort of juddered. She wore her hat covering her pixie hair, her coat zipped right up to her neck, and a scowl split her face. She was probably pissed with him and with them, hell, he got the impression she was pissed with the whole fucking world.

But she was so damn pretty.

"No," he said after a moment. "You're wrong. Some things still do matter."

CHAPTER SEVENTEEN

That evening they had no choice but to stop and hide. Another super-size pack was out, and they were waiting on the only clear road out of the area. Jackson had spotted them as they scouted the route through and suggested they hole up for a while until the zombies either dispersed, or until they were both rested enough to go for a full-on showdown.

They found a restaurant with metal shutters on the windows, parked the Batmobile out front, and went in through the back door, closing it and securing it with a large table, before splashing it with Gucci Cool. They made sure the front door gave them a clear escape route to their wheels, grabbed the blankets they'd taken from the abandoned house, and settled down on the mezzanine level right next to the window.

Jackson was cold but far from tired. Like she had told Luke, her sleep requirements were minimal. Maybe it was due to constantly being on high alert. She guessed it didn't really matter. Like everything else, the cause was irrelevant. Only the effect counted anymore.

"Tell me something I don't know about you, Jackson," Luke whispered, the moment they were settled, rubbing his hands together for warmth.

"Like what?"

"Anything."

"Well when the zombies—"

"No," he interrupted. "Something before them. Something from the real world."

Jackson paused and searched her mind for something lighthearted, and non-people themed, to share with him, but nothing immediately presented itself. Even discounting the people memories, looking past the last two years was almost like looking through a veil. It was gauzy and difficult to really see. Maybe it was her mind's way of protecting her psyche. Not wanting to recall things or else it would become too depressing.

"My life before this feels like a dream now," she said honestly. "I already told you about the things I miss, didn't I?"

"Yes, but you tell me about things like food and places you liked to visit. You haven't told me anything about you, not really. I know you don't want to talk about the people. I get that. But there must be some things you can share with me. Things about you."

"Well I already told you about everyday stuff."

"Tell me about your job," he asked. "You worked in a bar, right? How did you get that job?"

Jackson's heart stuttered and a clamminess washed over her. Her eldest brother had found her that job and the memory of it was suddenly vivid... him walking her to work on her first day, them laughing... She pushed the memory back where it belonged and shook her head.

"I don't want to talk about that."

"Because it's too hard?"

"Because it's pointless."

"Jack—"

She scowled and tucked her blanket under her feet. Why didn't Luke realize that if he pushed her down the rabbit hole, then a whole lot of nasty stuff would come spewing out and maybe it wouldn't go back in? It was far easier to just live in the moment, think about the rest of the day, surviving for a little bit longer. It was what she'd done for the past two years. Taking each day at a time…

"No, Luke, serious," she said, because it was important to her that he understood this and clearly right now he wasn't. She was never going to be Alice tumbling down that rabbit hole.

Never.

"Thinking about the world as it used to be, the real world you called it, is stupid. I can imagine the food and the places I liked and the books I read, the movies I watched, because that stuff isn't really important, not anymore. But the other stuff, the actual reality of that world—the people and the activities, and the everyday tick tock of it, does not fly. It's gone and nothing we will ever do in our entire lives will ever change that. It is what it is now. Everything we knew, everything we loved, is gone. You have to let it go, too, let them go, and the only way to do that is to not think or talk about it."

"Psych one oh one would say to let things go you *have* to think about them, talk about them, let them rest," he argued.

"Well, I was just a waitress and I never took a psych class or any other classes, for that matter. But I know what works in my head and you have to respect that. You have to give it up."

"But you haven't given it up, Jack, not really," he insisted. "You're still looking for a bit of normality. It's why we're heading south. Hell, you're hoping for a fucking cure."

Jackson shifted. "Because I have to," she said. "And you know, maybe it's time to tell you why."

"Okay…"

"One time, long before I met Tye or made it to Chicago, I was walking down some street. I can't even remember where it was, but it must have been a city, because there were skyscrapers."

He nodded for her to continue, probably imagining she was going to tell him something quirky or amusing. Jackson almost stopped right then.

"A city?" he prompted and she took a deep breath and nodded.

"I'd been alone by then for months, I was ridiculously lost and lonely, and I was…" She paused and shifted. "Having a moral dilemma."

"What sort of moral dilemma?" Luke asked.

"It makes no sense now," Jackson said softly. "Not considering the person I am today, but I was having trouble dealing with the whole murdering people issue."

Luke inhaled sharply. "They're not people."

She shrugged. "But they were and I'd killed so many. It just came, comes, naturally to me, I don't even know how it works, but I kill them so easily. What do you think that says about me, Luke?"

"That you're a survivor."

"Or something else." She sighed, not wanting to think those thoughts again, because she hadn't resolved them all those months ago and she probably wouldn't be able to now. "Point is," she continued, "I was not in a good place mentally or emotionally."

"We've all struggled to accept the way things are," Luke said.

"I know. Anyway, so there I was walking down this street. I don't even remember what I was thinking, but as I walked past I looked inside the bottom floor of the skyscraper, there was a big reception desk, and I just stopped. Right there in the middle of the street I just stopped. I don't know why or for how long, but before I knew what I was doing I went inside. The front glass was shattered so it was completely open. It was so quiet, just so quiet. The only sound was my boots on the glass." She pulled her blanket a little closer as that memory undulated through her brain, aware that Luke was perfectly still as she spoke. "I don't know what was wrong with me for taking such a risk, but before I knew what I was doing I was walking up the stairs. There were so many, flights and flights of them. I think it took me over an hour to get to the top and if there had been any zombies, they would have got me. There was no way I could have fought them off in such a tight space. But for some reason I wasn't thinking about the danger, not at all. It was like something was pulling me upward."

"What?" he whispered and Jackson frowned.

"When I got to the top I found an observation deck. The type with little telescopes for people to look out across the city. It started snowing a few seconds after I stepped outside and it was so beautiful, so magical. The flakes were falling and swirling and I was enchanted. I stood there on the deck, and Mandy was in my hand, and I looked around and I realized why I'd come up. It seemed perfectly obvious to me then and I laughed. I laughed so hard my side ached. The snow got in my hair and whipped around my face and I stood there, all those floors up, and I just laughed."

"I don't understand—"

"I was going to jump off," she stated.

Luke's eyes widened and he reached out, maybe to take her hand, but he stopped just shy of where it was bundled under the blanket and shook his head. "You wouldn't have."

"You have no idea how close I was," she whispered. "I went right to the railings and I looked down and every single part of me wanted to jump. It would all be over then. All the fear and the worry and the panic. I'd die but it'd be on my terms. It would be an end at last."

"Then why didn't you? What stopped you?"

She smiled a little as that memory blossomed. "I saw smoke."

"Smoke?"

"From a fire I think. It was faint, in the distance, and I could only just make it out, but it was there."

"Other people?"

Jackson shrugged. "Maybe. I don't know. Maybe it was just an exploding transformer. Regardless, something in my mind clicked and I realized that I had another option."

She moved her hand through the gap in her blanket and took Luke's. It was resting right there as if waiting for her, and as always, it warmed her the moment their skin met. She shivered slightly even as their fingers interlocked, and she looked into his eyes as she said the next words, entreating him to understand. "I could keep walking and keep looking, that was my option. I could try and see if there was anything left, and if I died before I got there, it didn't matter. Do you get that, Luke? It did not matter. Part of me died a little on that deck and I let it."

"I understand," he said, brushing a thumb along her wrist. "It makes sense now, why you're so fearless."

She laughed softly. "I'm not fearless. I'm always scared."

"But not of dying," he said.

"No," she agreed. "I accepted that a long time ago. A few months later I met Tye, and when he told me about the Laredo camp I knew that I had been right not to jump. That there *was* something left. I just needed to find it."

"And the moral dilemma?"

"I learned to ignore it."

Silence settled between them and Jackson released the breath she hadn't realized she'd been holding. Their fingers stroked back and forth, the heat continuing to sizzle between them.

"Jack?" Luke sighed, laying his other hand on her arm. "Thank you for telling me that.

Jackson gave him a weak smile. "So now you know just how freakful I can be."

"Barely any freak at all."

Another smile and she squeezed his hand. There would be no more confessions tonight, but he'd taken her revelation so well, that Jackson felt like she had to give him something else. Share just a little of normal, not quite so fucked-up Jack, even if it hurt.

"Would you like the story of my backpack?" she asked.

A pause and she knew if she looked up he'd be smiling. "Is it good?"

"Enthralling."

"Then shoot."

"Being all coddled in your bunker and all you didn't have to worry about supplies," she began, and Luke ruffled her hair.

"Coddled?"

"Uh-huh."

"You'll pay for that comment, sweetheart."

"Bring it," she said. "So when I left my apartment I had one bag, and it pains me to admit that it was not the survival type of carryall."

"What was it?"

"A knock off Gucci. I know. I know," she said, holding up a hand. "But I did live in New York. It was tiny, and the type you have to carry. I stuffed it with way too many clothes and not enough of other things."

"What happened to it?" he asked, pointing to the backpack at her feet. "I'm assuming it's not simply stuffed in there."

"I ended up using it to throttle a zombie."

He sighed. "Why am I not surprised?"

"It was an accident more than anything. I held it up in the air and the damn thing ran straight through the straps, headfirst. And so then I had to find another bag, and I was starting to learn by that point. Guess what the shop was called where I found this baby?"

"I hate guessing games."

"It was called Jackson's."

"You serious?"

She smiled. "Yep. I got the backpack and a bunch of proper supplies from there. You asked me once where my name came from?"

Luke nodded slowly. "I did."

"I was named after the guy who owned that shop." *Deep breath.* "He was my dad's best friend."

Without a single word Luke shifted, wrapped an arm around her waist, and pulled her against him. Jackson took a deep, slow breath, her chest aching, her body flustered already to feel his warmth against her again.

"Don't you want to sleep first?" Luke asked, and she sighed.

"No. I slept first last time."

"You sure."

"Yep. It's your turn."

He settled against her, his body warming hers. A whole week of man-arm action and she was still finding it...difficult. They'd settled into an easy relationship up till now, but it was odd parts of teasing, affection, and holding back. Jackson understood it all perfectly but couldn't help but wonder what it meant for them. Despite his insistence on getting her to open up—clearly his worst character trait—and his urge to protect her in his slightly goofy way, she liked Luke.

A lot.

But they lived in the land of the dead. A place where jumping off a building seemed like a perfectly acceptable action. Where a man and a woman could never just *be*.

Jackson risked a glance out of the window. It would be dark soon but for the moment there was enough light left to see. The street was quiet, still. The breeze blew against the rubbish in the street, and into the buildings where the windows and doors were cracked or open. The emptiness hit her forcefully and she frowned, shocked to feel it. How weird was it to be in Luke's position and imagine things how they might have been two years ago—because she was sure he often did. The scrunch on his brow, the frown that chased across his face...all indications that he was rewinding the months. If he was in her position, he'd be looking at the building directly opposite and thinking that it had once been a bakery.

Jackson squinted to make out the sign, MAGNIFICENT MUFFINS perhaps? God, she'd kill for a croissant.

Despite herself she couldn't help her gaze going to the next building. It looked like it might have been a bookstore. Though there were no books in there now. They'd probably been burned for fires in the very early days. And the other one, maybe a deli? Her mouth watered and her stomach rumbled. She imagined salami and ham and cheese…oh God cheese…and crackers, and a pickle…

Who had owned those stores? Who had lived in the apartments above? When had they been eaten? Or were they even now running around dead? The questions ran through her mind and she squeezed her eyes shut. *Don't think about it,* she told herself. *Pointless, remember? Get those barriers back up.*

Luke grumbled against her and she opened her eyes, tore her gaze from the deserted buildings, and turned to look at his profile. With his eyes closed, and his long lashes fanned against his cheeks, he looked peaceful. Peaceful in a way she knew she never was. She wondered if Luke was right. If she'd spent too long on her own. If she'd become too independent, too prickly, too quick to think that the worst was going to happen. But then that was hardly surprising, was it? The world was a nasty place and nasty things happened all the time. Every single fucking day.

Maybe as the days wore on, as they made their way farther south, that would change? Jackson hoped so. Luke was the perfect companion for her. She'd been so lucky to find him, so lucky he'd agreed to come with her. Surely eventually, if she really wanted to, she'd become…a little bit *normal* again? If anyone was going to help her to do so, it was the man now holding her in his arms.

Chapter Eighteen

Luke watched the rain falling as he held Jackson in his arms on the mezzanine level of the restaurant. She slept now, at last. But not peacefully, never peacefully. She twitched and she fidgeted and sort of groaned in a silent kind of way.

He wondered what thoughts were chasing through her subconscious mind and then decided he didn't want to know. His own nightmares were enough to make him shudder. He suspected that Jackson's were a bit worse.

I stomped my own brother's head in…

He frowned as he realized he hadn't asked her before now about her family. He hadn't wanted to, but then she'd never asked about his. Maybe family discussions were something most people who were still alive held onto for as long as possible? The last little bit of them. But then again maybe not. After all, he was ready to tell Jackson about his parents, so what that said about their relationship he did not know.

"I never got to my parents in time," he whispered. "They were just…gone. The door was wide open, the windows smashed, and there was just nothing…"

She mumbled something and he held her a little closer, closing his eyes against the images of his parent's home. Those images were replaced immediately by the haunting vision of Jackson standing at the top of that skyscraper, or her stomping her boot down on her brother's neck.

"You're so fucking brave," he whispered. "I have no idea how you made it here."

Her grip on his arm tightened and his chest with it. The minutes ticked by and he thought about everything, playing it all over in his mind. Him. Her. Their journey. He even found himself thinking about Tye and wondered if Jackson had been as elusive and independent with him, whether she had even told him her skyscraper story. Luke suspected not. It was the person she was... no, he amended, the person she had become.

In his mind's eye he could easily imagine Jackson as she must have once been. Her long dark hair running down her back. Her body all curvy, a smile on her face as she served drinks and wrote down her orders. She'd told him how much she missed her iPod and he could see her striding along the street, the headphones in, oblivious to the world around her. It pained him to think she would never be oblivious to anything ever again. Neither of them would be.

She mumbled again in her sleep and he looked down to see a frown chase across her brow. Even in the darkness her skin was very pale, her lashes fanning across the dark smudges underneath her eyes, and her lips were settled into their customary frown. Yet, still, she was so pretty to him. Too pretty, maybe? It surprised Luke how much he felt for her already. They were so unlike each other, both of them having responded to this new world in such different ways. He knew that essentially he was the same person he had been two years ago. Sure he was tougher, maybe a little meaner, maybe even a little harder—but when it came right down to the nitty-gritty he was still Luke. Still the mechanic who missed his family and wished every single day that things were different.

If Jackson's idea of a world without zombies was real, he knew it wouldn't take much for him to slip back into the person he'd once been. It would be like putting on an old coat, familiar and comfortable. No trouble at all.

But the more he considered it, the more he didn't think it would be that way for Jackson. She was good at this life—odd though that might sound. Her skill at beheading the dead was a thing to behold. Nothing interfered with her actions, no emotions, no hesitation. She took the dead down one after the other and didn't even pause. Of course, now he understood why.

The skyscraper. The acceptance.

The lack of food, the lack of warmth, none of it fazed her, not in the way it did him. This existence suited her and he wondered how much she'd had to change to make it that way, or whether the person he knew had been in the person that was her all along.

"Who are you, really, Jackson?" he whispered. "And why is it so important to me that I find out?"

She mumbled some more, shifted against him, and he would have held her a little closer, comforted her in her sleep, but a noise outside caught his attention and he paused. Slowly he swiveled his head and watched as four zombies, illuminated by the moon's light, walked up the deserted street. Though maybe walked was the wrong way to describe it. It was more that they sort of stalked.

He checked his weapons slowly, carefully, and was relieved to find them exactly where they should be. Energy was coursing through him and he had to force himself to sit perfectly still.

They groaned as they moved, snapped at one another and bared their teeth. The rain didn't seem to bother them at all, even though two of them were naked. Luke wondered if they even felt the cold, or whether that sensation was long since gone. It was an abstract wonder, though. In truth, he didn't really care.

"They're outside aren't they?"

Her whispered words against him were soft on his skin and

Luke sighed, craning his neck slightly as the zombies started to move out of view.

"How did you know?"

"I just did."

"You haven't slept for long."

"I know, but now is the time to get moving. How many are there?"

"Four."

"That's four less on the road. Let's move while we can."

Luke frowned and eyed the disappearing zombies. Wondering what they were stalking, if anything. Who knew what the hell they were up to anymore? The bastards. What he did know was that Jackson had barely rested, that she was as tense as anything and he did not like it. He wanted her to rest some more. He wanted her to just take a whole day or a night or fucking something to escape from it. She wouldn't though.

"Jack—"

"Andrew and Peter," she whispered.

"Huh?

"I just dreamed about them," she said with a sigh. "It all comes out in my dreams. The first zombie. My brothers. Those were their names. Andrew and Peter, and really in the end, I guess you could say, I killed them both."

He shook his head instantly, and pulled her closer. "Jack, you didn't."

"I did," she whispered, and he felt her tremble ever so slightly in his arms. "You wanted to know, so here it is. They went out to find supplies and only one came back. He was already infected. I had no choice but to kill him. I almost didn't…I almost let him eat me…"

"He'd have killed you."

"I know," she sighed. "So I killed him instead, moral dilemma number one, and who knows what happened to Peter? I never found him."

"It wasn't your fault," he said, even as he imagined how awful that moment must have been for her. He supposed, in a way, he should almost be grateful that his parents hadn't been waiting for him, waiting to *eat* him. "He wasn't your brother anymore."

"I know that," she whispered. "But all the hundreds I've killed? They were all someone's brother, someone's sister, someone's kid. One after the other and after the other. I don't even know how I do it, Luke. I was never tough before, but the moment Mandy is in my hand I just kill them. Nothing stops me."

"We do what we have to."

"And does that make it—"

The screeching noise that filled the air had only one obvious source and Jackson stopped speaking immediately. They were both instantly still and he relaxed his arms so that Jackson could lift Mandy, poised and ready without so much as a noise.

"The front door," she whispered and he nodded.

"Quickly."

Another screech and Jackson lifted herself off him carefully, her shadowed face settling into the familiar lines. He stood too, and swiveled around as quietly as possible, before leading the way forward and down the spiral staircase to their escape route. Another screech followed by the sounds of glass breaking and they both ran. The zombies were pushing the table out of the way, but now that the window was broken they would likely just climb through the gap, not caring if they broke their skin or bones while they were at it. He scowled, even as his heart pumped double time.

How had they found them? Had they circled back around while Jackson was confessing her secrets? The questions clicked through his mind in a mere second and he tightened his grip on his ax.

"Quick, Luke," Jackson hissed and he felt her bump against him.

A howl sounded, followed by another, and Luke gave up all pretensions of stealth. He kicked through the front door and ran straight out into the rain...and one of them. Clawed hands grabbed at his arm, teeth snapped, and Luke used his ax to simply bash rather than cut, catching the zombie hard on the face.

A screech, a howl, and the zombie reared back, allowing Luke to swing the ax properly. It embedded itself in the zombie's chest, and remembering Jackson's advice from the pool room, all those days ago, Luke pulled upward. His ax tore through the zombie's chest and came out at the neck. From there it was easy to pull it free and swipe once more, removing the head. It rolled across the floor, the body hitting the wet street with a nasty squelching noise.

Luke turned quickly and spotted Jackson by a large Dumpster, two zombies were closing in on her and he ran forward, desperate to ensure she was okay.

"Get the car," she shouted and he gaped. She thought he'd just leave her?

"No fucking way!"

"Then stay the hell back," she shrieked. "Wait for the other one."

Luke looked into the restaurant, because yes, of course, one had gone around the back to flush them out. It would arrive at any moment. He went to grab his gun, but then thought better of it. The moon's light was dim and he could well end up hurting either Jackson or himself. There was no choice but to wait, but he wouldn't do so while she fought off two, no matter what she said!

He moved forward, determined to help her, but the moment he did the zombies closed in on her and Luke watched in horror as she fell to her knees. He roared as he moved, and for a second he couldn't understand what he was seeing, but the moment the now-damaged zombies hit the ground he realized. She'd sliced through them at the kneecaps, removing a leg a piece in one single, graceful arc.

She beheaded one before even looking in his direction, then took care of the other, and though really he should have been looking out for the other zombie, Luke couldn't help but admire her moves. She was so efficient, so matter of fact, and so damn cute.

"Can you believe that," she growled, pointing Mandy at one of the zombies.

They were both naked and Luke sort of shuddered as he noticed where she was pointing, a male, and he was dripping yellow pus from his dick.

Disgusting.

Another shriek behind them and Luke turned to see the final zombie, a female, charge out of the restaurant. She didn't have the calculated look the others had. She was wild and crazed—a zombie model one, as in minus the smarts. She also went straight for Jackson.

"Think it through already," he heard her say and Luke wasn't sure if she was talking to him or the zombie, but he lifted his ax anyway and cleaved it straight through the back of the zombie's head.

The skull cracked, brain oozed out, accompanied by a significant amount of pus, and the shriek turned into a dull scream. Luke flipped the ax in his hands so that the thick part was now directly above the cracked skull and bashed it once, then again, until the whole thing split like a melon.

Jackson shot him the biggest grin the moment the zombie gave its final twitch. Moral dilemmas or not when it came down to the fight, she was ruthless. They both were.

"Come on, Luke! Time to get the hell out of Dodge."

She was grinning and running toward the car and Luke followed her, exhilaration at another battle survived making him almost high. The moment they were inside, both breathing heavy, Luke took a deep, steadying breath, and turned to Jackson.

"You're something to behold, Jack. You might not know how you manage it, but damn you do."

"You're not too bad yourself." She grinned, and before he could think better of it, Luke leaned forward and deposited a kiss on her open lips.

Maybe it was the adrenaline? Maybe it was the thrill of the win, or maybe it was just her, but the moment their lips touched his chest expanded and a strange tingle ran down his spine. He lingered for just a second before pulling back and tucking a stray strand of spiky hair behind her ear.

"What was that for?" she whispered, but she was still grinning and his heart thumped some more.

"Because we're bad-ass."

Slowly she nodded, her smile widening, her beautiful eyes filled with something that made his entire body harden. "You damn right we are. Come on. Let's go kill some more zombies."

And so they did.

Chapter Nineteen

Several days later Jackson watched as, binoculars in hand, Luke looked down to the middle of the fire escape where she perched.

"How many?" she whispered.

"Do you really want me to answer that?" he mouthed back.

"Roundabout?"

Luke scowled and even from a distance Jackson could see the worry lines around his eyes crinkling.

"Put it this way, Jack," he said. "We're in the shit."

Jackson watched as he poked his head over the wall again and let out a long, slow exhale. She knew from his position that he could see pretty much the whole area, and by the sound of things, aka the shrieks and groans, it was not a pretty sight.

She took a deep breath, flooding her body with oxygen. A moment later she felt her stomach rumble, almost like it was demanding calories for the fight it knew was coming.

"Yep, totally in the shit."

"Scale of one to ten?" she whispered.

He turned and scowled. "Ten."

Jackson sighed. Why the hell wasn't she surprised? After traveling for days without any trouble beyond a couple of dead things, it was too good to last.

Of course a lack of action meant a lack of other kinds of action. No adrenaline meant no adrenaline-induced kisses. She shivered ever so slightly as she replayed their kiss. Part of her had been so tempted to initiate another. After all, he'd started the first and turnabout was fair play, right? But she knew it had to be organic, natural, and it was all about timing, and now was *so* not the time. Not for another kiss or even to be even thinking about it! Something had Luke worried, something bad, and Jackson was not surprised. *Yep, too good to last.*

"What's the deal then?"

"I'm gonna come down and you take a look yourself. Be prepared."

With some rather dexterous movements they swapped positions and Jackson, ignoring the feel of Luke's body brushing against her, climbed up until she too could look through the binoculars—a handy scavenge from an Outdoor World shop— and see out across the area. The sight that greeted her was enough for any thoughts of further kisses to subside and panic to judder through every single cell of her body. Nervous energy joined it, creating a nasty combination that made her sway slightly on the ladder. *Shit.* She bit down on her lip and steadied herself before letting the shock of what she could see settle across her. *Accept it and deal with it,* she told herself. Only way.

A minute or so later, once the adrenaline peaked and held, and the fear—because despite what Luke thought, there was always fear—settled into its usual spot on her shoulders, heavy and painful, Jackson began to think. How many were there? Then she realized that it was hard to say. The press of flesh was immense. Mottled, elongated limbs pressed up against one another, teeth snapping, pus dripping, and howls sounding. She guessed more than a hundred but either way it didn't really matter. It was a hundred too many.

They were spread out across the entire area as far as Jackson could see. In the doorways of the abandoned buildings, hanging from the lampposts, shrieking from atop cars. One in particular caught her eye, though she didn't know why. It was a female zombie, probably a retiree when she had died. The image of her snarling face against the soft flowers of her smock jarred somehow and Jackson felt vomit rise.

Swallow it, she told herself and her body complied.

Her gaze went to another waking dead. A teenager. She still had pink hair and bits of metal in her face. Piercings, of course, and Jackson's heart went out to the girl she'd been. Another face, a young boy, then another, an elderly man… Mr. Jenkins flashed through her mind.

The sheer sight of so many boggled her mind. She'd seen nothing like it since the very early days. To see a pack, a fucking immense *super*-sized pack now, scared the shit—and then some— out of her. What the hell did it mean? Why were they banding together like that? What were they living on? It didn't seem like they were eating each other.

She crawled back down the fire escape, her mind in a million different directions. A cloud of dust erupted under her and Luke's feet and they both paused for a few moments. The groans continued to sound—though distant now—and the air had that same tangible feel to it. *Danger.* It was what had made Luke stop the car with a frown a few blocks back, before suggesting they scout the area out a little.

"You were bang on the money," she whispered. "It's almost like we can feel them."

He stepped a little closer to her, so that there were bare inches between them. As always, Jackson found her gaze on eye level with his despairingly muscular chest, and swallowed carefully before raising her eyes to his.

"Houston, we have a problem," he whispered and despite the

fact that a horde of flesh eating beasts was just a few blocks away, Jackson smiled.

"We so do."

He lifted a hand to indicate the direction he wanted them to go in and Jackson crept behind him until they made it back to the car. The panic subsided ever so slightly when they were inside. *The illusion of safety*, she thought. But then there almost *was* an element of it with Luke behind the wheel. She trusted him to drive right, not to take chances, and she could actually sleep as he traversed the country.

How odd.

Jackson swallowed carefully and eyed the man who sat next to her. She'd never really thought about it. How, when she was in the car with him, she did relax a little. She'd thought it was only when they were holed up somewhere, snuggled up together, but clearly that was not the case. What that said she didn't know, but when he reached out to take her hand in his and give it a squeeze, she kind of thought that might have something to do with it.

Priorities.

"You know what this means, don't you?" Luke whispered.

For a moment she thought he was talking about her internal dialogue and gaped a little. "Huh?"

"Where they are in relation to the roads," he said waving in the direction of the fire escape, and Jackson realized he was talking about the zombies. The many, many zombies that should have been at the forefront of her mind too!

"I did mention geography is not my strong point, right?" she asked.

"That you did. So here's the deal. We have to go through them," Luke said and Jackson felt her jaw drop.

Go through them? "Have you lost your fucking mind?"

He frowned. "We have to. It's that or turn back completely and go through Kansas."

Her heart gave a nasty thump and Jackson let out an exhale, needing it to steady herself. "Kansas sounds good."

"Unless we find the same thing there," he said. "We have to assume we will. We have to assume this is normal now. Fucking hell. Giant packs."

"Let's not just assume."

"We have to," Luke insisted. "Assume the worst, hope for the best."

"But going *through* them?" The very idea made her skin crawl. "Do we really want to risk that?"

"It's the only way across the river that I know of. If we do it right, gun the car, we should sail right through them. I scoped it out when I was up there. It's one clear road once we get past them. The only danger will be in the beginning."

"You realize this plan is crazy?"

"I know. It's almost as bad as some of yours."

She punched him lightly on the arm with her free hand and he smiled. That smile…her heart thumped again, she couldn't lose it. She wouldn't!

"We have to be fast. You have to put your foot down and do not let it back up. I'll be on point."

"They won't get in the Batmobile," he insisted. "I'll be fast."

"I don't doubt it, but we're just-in-casing here." She paused for a moment, their hands still clasped together. "This is def our best option, right?" she asked, though she was fairly sure she knew the answer. Luke was at his best when confronting a problem head-on.

"Yeah."

Jackson shivered and plotted it out in her mind. It *could* work, assuming they drove fast enough, but the thought of being in the midst of that many waking dead made her feel slightly sick. It wouldn't, once she was actually in there. She knew she'd be fine when they got going. The anticipation was always the killer and right now it was scaring the fuck out of her.

"Let it go," she whispered. Because this *was* one of those moments where doing that was the only thing that made any sort of sense. Letting go was all about putting yourself in a place where you could think, *yeah I might die, let's hope I don't, but I'll roll with it either way.* It was like recapturing the exact moment when she'd been poised to jump off the skyscraper. That exact, slightly insane moment.

"Jack?"

And she trusted Luke, didn't she? If he thought they could make it, then surely that was good enough for her?

"Okay..." she said slowly. "Let's do this."

Luke nodded, squeezed her hand once more before releasing it, then readied himself to restart the car. But at the last moment he paused and shot her a look. "Spit it out, already."

"Spit what out?"

"Whatever's going through you mind. I know something is. Your brow's all scrunchy."

Jackson shrugged, but Luke must've seen it anyway. After a few weeks together now she and Luke were pretty much in sync. He picked up on what she was thinking before she even thought about telling him. It was vice versa, as well. When she looked into his warm eyes she got what was there. It was slightly scary but exciting too. Just one more thing in the constant catalog of things she liked about him. One more thing that made the nights more and more difficult...well, that and the kiss.

"Going through is what it is," she said slowly. "I'm ready. But I'm just wondering...why are they here in the first place?"

Luke gripped the steering wheel and shook his head. "Who gives a shit? The important thing is that we're not. They'd tear us apart, Jack. Into pieces. We'd be like a doughnut at a Weight Watchers convention."

She gave him a smack on the arm. "I went to Weight Watchers a time or two. Don't be snarky."

"Just making the point. And we should go. Now. Get this done."

Jackson spread her hands wide. Trying in some way to explain the feeling that had hit her. "Something feels weird," she finally said. "Why are they all there? Think about it. When have you ever seen that many together apart from in the early days?"

"Well… I haven't," Luke replied. "They formed their packs. Fighting among one another and eating anything with a pulse that crossed their paths."

"Exactly. So what the hell is going on? That many in one place? What the fuck are they up to?"

"I have no idea. I don't much care, to be honest. We need to leave. *Now*."

"Yes we need to leave, but just think about it for a moment, Luke," she said, because it felt important to her that he understand. "They all looked pretty healthy, not skinny or feeble. I only got that off a quick look, but the ones I could see you know, they looked fine. They weren't snapping at each other, eating each other. But then more than that, they looked as if they were waiting."

Luke frowned. "For what?"

Jackson thought of the zombie crowd. Visualizing them in her mind. Yes. She was sure of it now. They *had* looked as though they were waiting.

"I don't know. That's my point. And I can't help but wonder…"

"You wonder too damn much," Luke said. "They are what they are. This is what it is."

Jackson sighed, took a sip of water from her Evian bottle and frowned. Luke was getting impatient. A state he rarely seemed to be in. Wasn't he always the understanding one? The most easygoing? So really, that right there should have told her how dire the situation was. But still, she couldn't help thinking…

"Jackson?" Luke prompted.

Let it go. Just let it the fuck go and get your mind in the game.

"Yeah. Okay. Let's do this."

Luke turned the ignition and backed the car up. The noise split the silence and Jackson almost winced. Sure, the zombies were a fair distance away, but they could still hear the faint howls, which mean the dead could probably hear them too. The element of surprise was going to be their best bet now. They needed to plow through before the zombies even realized they were there.

"You ready for this?" Luke asked.

"Always am," she said.

They shot out a side street, heading straight for the horde. It would take maybe a couple of minutes at the speed Luke was going before they hit the very center of them and already Jackson could feel the panic settling into a steady resolve. *Time for some Superwoman-style balls.*

"Come on then," Luke said making the final turn before they hit the clear road to zombie central. "You might as well tell me what you're wondering about exactly. If we die before I know, I'll be super pissed-off."

"We're not gonna die," she said as the first zombie, one straggling on the edge of the crowd and still some distance away, spotted them. "Not before I get another kiss."

It shrieked and before she knew it, the entire horde was turning, their snarling faces all zeroing in on the one little car.

"Then we're definitely surviving," Luke growled.

"That we are."

"Quickly," he said. "Zombie mash coming right up."

"If they're massing here, it's for one reason only," she replied, the suspicion seeming even more obvious now that so many of them were in front of them. "And it isn't us."

"Shit," Luke said and the zombies began to run. "You mean…"

"Yeah. Doughnuts."

Chapter Twenty

A hundred zombies running at full speed was something to fucking behold and Luke's grip on the steering wheel became painful. He put his foot down on the accelerator, getting up to top speed, and gritted his teeth.

"You ready for this?" he asked.

"Too late now," Jackson said and laughed. "We're so past the point of no return."

He glanced at her. She was poised on the edge of her seat, Glock in one hand, Mandy in the other. She looked almost serene and he shook his head as the car moved faster, unbelieving that she could be so calm.

Part of me died a little on the deck.

The part that any normal person needed, he thought, and shook himself. He wished he could be so calm but if suicidal thoughts were what it took, he'd deal with the nerves instead.

"Look," she whispered. "That one looks just like my fifth-grade math teacher. God, I hated him. Run that one over first."

He did as she asked, more by accident than design. Math zombie hit the car with a *thud*, its body thrown into the air, landing direct in the horde. The other zombies didn't give it so much as a look. They simply kept running, straight at them.

They were so fucking fast!

"We need to go faster," Jackson urged, and Luke pressed his foot down as far as it could go, because he could see her point. The press of flesh was extreme and he did not want to risk them stopping the car.

A *thud* sounded on the roof and they both looked up. "Shit."

The zombie started banging on the top immediately, and the other zombies on the edges of the horde began to climb up lampposts, fire escapes, hell, the buildings themselves.

"They're copying," Jackson breathed. "The bastards. They'll overwhelm us."

"We'll be through in a minute," he said. "They won't have time to. Just hang the hell on." But sweat was slithering down his back, almost declaring him a liar, and Luke was starting to wonder how good an idea this had actually been.

Another *thump* on the roof and he jumped. They were banging hard now, the metal beginning to show slight dents.

"Here we go," Jackson whispered, and a moment later they hit the shrieking horde.

The zombies, as had always been the case, showed absolutely no sense of self-preservation. None of them tried to jump out of the way, and those directly in the path of the Batmobile were hit—hard. They smacked into the surrounding zombies, wet flesh squelching against wet flesh. Some were just clipped and they hit the ground. Luke ran over them without a second thought and held his breath as the bumps made the car shudder and shake, praying the zombie bodies were not damaging the car. The idea of coming to a stop in the middle of this...

He looked out of the side window, a huge mistake. Snarling face after snarling face pressed against it, and even speeding he could see the hungry, calculating gleam in their eyes. It made him feel sick and he tore his gaze away, back to the front where a clear road was now visible.

"Almost there," Jackson whispered. "You're doing good, Luke. Oh shit!"

A zombie attached itself to the passenger side, hanging off the wing mirror, and before Luke could do a goddamn thing it lifted an arm and began to pound at Jackson's window.

She moved quickly, pressing the electric button to wind it down, taking aim, and firing. The bullet when straight through the head and the zombie fell away. Luke took a deep breath and pressed harder on the accelerator. They were through the worst of the horde now, though he could see in the rearview mirror that the zombies were running after the car, desperate for their food to not escape.

"Quick, quick, quick," Jackson chanted and he swallowed drily.

"Almost there, Jack. Get that window up." A few seconds more and they were free. Only a couple of stragglers were still in front of them and Luke ran them over too. They fell onto the road with howls and groans and Luke felt a deep sense of relief and satisfaction thrum through him.

Jackson was pressing on the button, practically bouncing on her seat as she waited for the window to close, but it, or she, was not fast enough and Luke cursed as a hand entered the car.

"Shit!" Jackson spat.

"Jesus…"

He couldn't work out what was going on but a moment later realized. The zombies on the roof. And just as he thought that another hand started on his side of the car, pounding the window.

"This isn't going to work," she hissed.

"Just shut the fucking window," he said. "I'll deal with them."

The window moved up but the zombie's hand did not retreat. It grabbed at her, looking for any flesh it could find. On Luke's side, the other zombie continued to pound the window, only its position was stopping it from having enough force to actually break through. In the distance he could hear shrieks and howls, but they were falling away, becoming less pronounced. Another few minutes and they'd have left the zombies in the dust.

"It won't move its hand!" Jackson shouted. "Fucking bastard, let's see him go for this." She leaned back in her seat, angled her body, lifted her knee up to almost her face, and kicked out.

A shriek sounded and the hand that was clawing at the window went limp.

"Just a couple of minutes," he shouted back. "Keep it from getting inside."

She kicked again, and then again, pus began to splatter the window. Then with something that sounded like a curse, she lifted Mandy and chopped the hand off. It fell between her legs, blood coated the window, and she gagged. "That is fucking disgusting."

Luke leaned forward, foot down hard, grabbed the hand, and threw it out of the gap in her window. Just a wrist was poking through now and it couldn't grasp anything. Jackson pressed the button once more and the window closed tight.

"The smell…" she said, and Luke nodded.

"We'll get it cleaned up."

They barreled down the highway, the tires eating the cracked asphalt underneath them, the pounding from their unwanted companions continuing. It didn't matter. Luke was drenched with sweat, his entire body clammy. All he wanted to do was get far enough away that he could bleach his mind of the press of zombie faces so fucking close!

"They're going to get in," Jackson said.

"No they're not. Brace yourself."

He slammed down on the brakes. Hard. The zombies were not expecting it, or maybe they weren't yet smart enough *to* expect it. They flew off the top of the roof and hit the road in front. Luke did not pause. He slammed his foot back down on the accelerator and did not let up.

Neither of them said a word as they sped along the road. The interior of the car was heavy with emotion. Relief and a sense of disbelief. Worse it competed with the stench of the zombie pus that was dripping down Jackson's window.

After a few more miles Luke brought the car to a stop, the tires screeching from the pressure on the brakes. They both looked up, scanning the surrounding area, but a handful of zombies right now seemed like something they could take care of in their sleep. Nothing could ever seem as bad as what they'd just made their way through.

"Jesus fucking Christ," Jackson breathed, echoing his thoughts. "I can't fucking believe we survived that."

"I know."

"When that zombie's hand came out of nowhere..." She shook her head some more and placed Mandy across her thighs.

"We did it though," he said. "We fucking did it!"

"You did it, Luke. You totally had that."

She was still pushed against the back of her seat, her eyes wide, and her words made exhilaration run through him. He reached forward, placed a finger under her chin, and turned her gaze to his. "Someone said something about kisses?"

She laughed, the last of the adrenaline leaving them, making them both feel shaken and stirred. "Never mind a zombie horde. All you're interested in is the kisses, huh?"

"Can't be helped," he replied. "You're far too pretty for your own good, Jackson."

"And you're far too hot."

Their gazes held, and Luke could see the excitement so clear in hers, reflected no doubt in his. He took his hand from her chin, wrapped it around the back of her neck, and pulled her forward. The kiss was not brief this time, and it was not gentle. He put all of his relief and elation into it and Jackson responded in kind. By the time they pulled apart they were both panting.

"You sure know how to kiss, Luke," she said and he smiled.

"Snap, but that'll have to hold me for now. We're not free and home yet. I want to get a few good hours driving between us and them."

She looked behind her, the smile fading ever so slightly. "I gotta get this pus cleaned off first. Apart from the stench I don't want it on me. I know we're not sure if it infects but let's not take the risk, huh?"

"Grab a towel from the trunk."

"Got it."

She opened the door and jumped out and Luke sighed as her very firm ass filled his vision. His lips were still tingling and apart from the lingering horror of it all, he felt better than he had in weeks. It had to be the adrenaline. He was still pumped up on it. Part of him barely able to believe they'd just survived a fucking zombie horde.

It was scary as hell and they'd done it!

And then there was Jackson. The kisses. He remembered in the pool room, when he'd hoped for possibilities. Those same thoughts filled him all over again but he knew it wouldn't be as simple as that now. This was Jackson and he…he paused…his feelings were so far from what they had been. But he wanted her, how he wanted her.

"Luke do you—"

Her voice cut off and he frowned, twisting around in his seat, wondering what was wrong. A second later and he heard her scream.

Luke was out of the car before he even thought about it, pulling his gun free in a mere instant. He ran around to the back and felt his heart leap into his chest as he saw what was happening. Jackson lay on the ground, a huge zombie on top of her, only Mandy against its neck holding it back.

"Luke," she screamed.

He lifted his ax to cleave its head but paused. The blood and pus would soak her if he did that, and she was right, they didn't know where the infection lived. Instead he moved to the side and kicked the zombie hard. It fell back onto the road and Jackson scrambled to her feet. It reared up too, its teeth bared, its eyes gleaming with something that looked suspiciously like hatred.

Luke shot it, taking out half of its brain. It fell back to the floor, a puddle of blood and pus soaking the road around them. He shot it again, close up, removing the rest. It twitched once or twice before going completely still.

"It was under the car," Jackson said, and there was a catch in her voice, something that he'd never thought to hear. "I didn't even think to check. I was too…" She shook her head and ran her hands up and down Mandy's hilt.

"Me neither," he said, pulling her into his arms. She pushed back a little but Luke refused to let her go. "It held on? Even after all these miles?"

She nodded against his chest and pointed to the zombie. The skin across its legs was all but gone, just nasty oozing grazes visible.

"Shit…" He bent down quickly, checking there were no more, but they were clear. "We should get out of here," he said. "Just to be on the safe side.

"Agreed. Put your foot down and get some distance."

"I'll clean the pus first."

"No I—"

"I'll do it," he said. "I got this."

She nodded slowly and held Mandy close. Luke frowned. He'd never seen her look so shaken, but shaken she clearly was. Her face was paler than usual and her hair was sticking up in clumped little spikes. He raced around, grabbed a towel, cleaned the pus as best he could, and washed his hands in bottled water—a waste but a necessary one.

Then he carefully walked her to the passenger side and shut the door behind her. One last look around and Luke started the car again. Jackson was quiet, her face blank, and he felt his chest tighten.

Had he distracted her with the kiss? Had they both been too quick to forget the danger they were constantly under? To think themselves safe when they so obviously were not? Those questions raced through his mind as he drove and they stayed with him for the rest of the goddamn day.

CHAPTER TWENTY-ONE

That night, wrapped up tightly in blankets, in the passenger seat of the car next to Luke, Jackson felt herself shivering. It had been some time since she'd had such a reaction and she couldn't quite work out why it was happening now. Maybe it was due to the shock of that zombie wrapping its hand around her ankle and pulling her to the floor, or maybe the fact it had pinned her down before she could even get Mandy into position, or hell, it could be a million things and then some. *Or maybe it's because you saw like a freaking hundred zombies!* Either way she couldn't sleep, even though she knew she should because it was Luke's watch.

Wrapping her arms tighter around herself Jackson tried to instill some warmth. She was reminded ridiculously of a time when she'd spent almost a month walking in constant rain. It had been winter then and toward the end of it Jackson felt like she would never be warm again. Only she had. The feeling had passed.

They always passed.

This one would too. Just not yet it seemed.

She'd thought about the zombie horde nonstop as they drove, hours and hours to think, and nothing good had come out of those thoughts. Getting to the survivor's camp seemed more important than ever now. Hell, it was crucial, because how long could she and Luke survive alone?

She looked down at her hands, surprised to see them shaking a little, and was thankful all over again that she and Luke were together.

Right to the end. Whenever that might be.

"Jack?" Luke whispered, obviously alerted by her fidgeting. "You okay?"

Jackson swallowed. She didn't want to admit to Luke what was making her feel odd, but at the same time every part of her ached to talk. Turnaround much?

"I'm fine."

"Talk to me, Jack," he said softly. "You know you can talk to me about anything, right? Anything."

"There's no point."

"There's always a point. It'll make you feel better, for a start."

The minutes ticked by and Jackson kept silent. It was only when Luke reached out and took her hand that she spoke.

"I feel fine," she said and he sighed.

"No you don't."

He squeezed her hand gently. Jackson closed her eyes and concentrated on the feel of his skin against hers. Soft and warm and oddly comforting. She squeezed back and took a deep breath. It wasn't talking about *them*, her family and friends, so maybe just this once it was okay to open up to Luke. Maybe it would make her feel better?

"I keep thinking about the people."

He frowned, she knew he did even though she couldn't see it, and rubbed a thumb up and down the side of her palm. "What people?"

"The survivors in the town."

"There were no survivors."

"I think there were," she whispered. "I've thought about it

for hours and I think that's why the zombies were massed there. Probably there were a group or two, and they hadn't been able to get to them, so they called in reinforcements. They call each other with their groans or something. I'm almost positive it's how they communicate."

"You're speculating."

She shrugged, her shoulder aching from where the zombie had slammed her against the floor. "It makes sense."

"Well, we killed a bunch of them, hurt a bunch more, so we helped."

"I know we did, but if there are survivors, they're not safe."

"No one's ever safe," Luke said.

"And you expect me to sleep with those words ringing in my ears?"

"I didn't mean—"

"I know."

"We're safe here, for the moment, I promise," he reassured her. "Let me be the one to worry for once, Jack, just me. I'll keep watch and you can sleep for as long as you like."

She could see nothing through the dark of the night except for a shaft of moonlight illuminating the windshield, but she knew he was right. They'd found an old, roofless barn in the middle of nowhere. After checking it out, they hadn't found a single dropping or pus stain. If zombies had been in the barn, it hadn't been for many, many months. Still, safety was relative. They were okay for a handful of hours. Five being the limit they'd set between them. After that it was a question of moving onto the next safe spot they could find. Moving was good, Jackson thought. Staying in one place for too long was too much temptation. It became too easy to lure oneself into a false sense of security. Like Luke with the bunker, like her stepping out of the car like she was on a fucking country jaunt!

She was aghast as she remembered how happy she'd been,

how it hadn't even fucking occurred to her to do a security sweep! How stupid. How ridiculous. It was like walking up the steps of the skyscraper all over again. Only this time she'd been thrumming with desire, exhilarated and happy and *stupid*. So stupid.

"I don't know what's wrong with me," she whispered. "I'm used to this stuff."

"Not this you're not."

"I am," she insisted. "I've squatted in rotting Dumpsters for hours on end to hide from them, surrounded by smells the likes of which I've never known. I've stood on a tiny ledge, eight stories up, in the pouring rain for more than fifteen hours because the zombies were all over the building. One time I had the flu, though how you can still get it when there's no other people around, I don't fucking know, and I spent a week shivering in an abandoned mine. It was the only shelter for miles and it looked as though the roof was going to cave in at any moment. I was so ill I didn't care. Truthfully, part of me wanted it to. At least then it would all be done with."

"Jack…"

"I'm not telling you this as some sort of pity party," she said. "I'm just trying to explain that this is my world. I live it. I shouldn't be feeling like this."

"Maybe for once you should just feel it?" he suggested. "You're far too contained, Jack. Talk to me, lean on me. I'm here for whatever you need."

"I need…" She paused and tried to untangle her thoughts, because in that moment as Luke continued to stroke her palm, his words soft in her mind, she knew exactly what she *did* need. It seemed obvious now. Like the thought had been teasing her for days and was now clarified. But how the hell would Luke react?

"Whatever you need, you know it's yours," he said and her heart thumped wildly.

She needed Luke. She needed his arms around her and his

lips on hers. It was as simple as that. The last couple of weeks, every touch, every smile, had shown her that he was just right for her in every way, and though marriage and babies and happily ever afters were things that no longer existed—because who the hell would take the risk—there was nothing stopping them from finding some enjoyment in each other, was there? To seize the moment and hold it? And she needed it. Damn, did she need it. After Tye, the bunker, the dead horde, and the out-of-nowhere zombie, she wanted to lose herself in the pleasure she instinctively knew Luke could give her. To forget for just a few hours that the whole damn world had fallen apart. That they could be minutes from their deaths, mere moments from the end of everything.

"I want you Luke," she said softly.

His head snapped around so fast Jackson worried he'd given himself whiplash.

"You serious?" he asked.

"Aren't I always?"

A moment passed and the intense light in Luke's eyes was enough to tell her he would not deny her.

"I've wanted you since the first moment we met," he admitted. "When you were in your purple panties."

Warmth filled her then, banishing the chills and the odd feelings she did not want to name, and she held her breath as Luke reached forward and cupped her face. Maybe it was the last of the rush or maybe it was just him, but Jackson didn't hesitate before wrapping her arms around Luke's neck and tilting her head. He responded instantly, and once again his lips were on hers.

They were firm, yet so soft, and when his flesh pressed against hers she felt a shiver flow from her mouth, down her neck, before it wrapped itself around the base of her spine. They moved against one another, softly, exploring the taste and the feel, the sensation of unexpected contact. In that moment zombies no longer existed, nothing did but the two of them, the experience of him and her, and something…something she thought was lost but she had now found again.

She moaned softly beneath him, encouraging more and Luke complied. Taking her whole mouth, covering her lips with his in a gesture that was unassumingly male. His tongue tickled against hers, his fingers tracing a path down from the hollow of her throat to the base of her neck, before pulling back to look in her eyes.

"You're so beautiful," he whispered. "The last bit of beauty in this world."

And though Jackson knew full well that she was far from beautiful, that in the pre-waking-dead world Luke would have been so out of her league, in that moment his words made her feel like she was—like he meant every damn word.

Probably he did.

"Kiss me again, Luke," she said. "Make me forget it all, just for a little while."

And he did.

. . .

The feel of Jackson's lips was like going back in time. To a place where the world made sense again. Luke relished her softness, the little mews of satisfaction she made, and the heat he could feel rising between them.

He wished for one moment that they were in a bed. Somewhere he could spread her loveliness beneath him and savor every moment, but beds, like everything else, were a thing of the past, and right now Luke was grateful for whatever he could get.

He traced her lips with his tongue, her soft skin with his fingers. The curve of her jaw, the sharp length of her cheekbone, even the arch of her eyebrow. He exulted in the feel of her skin beneath his fingertips. She responded by running her fingers along his back, before moving to the front and skirting over his stomach. Her touch was soft and delicate. A stark contrast to the way he knew those hands could be in other situations. But there was no anger tonight, only this, the two of them, finding some sort of peace in each other.

"Let me see you, Jack," he said and she nodded.

It took only a handful of moments to remove her sweater and toss it in the back, a handful more to remove her vest as well. She was bare to him then and her beauty in the dappled moonlight took Luke's breath away. She was pale, so pale and so delicate. Not in reality, he knew that, but here in the darkness she looked fragile, and the urge to protect her rose again within him.

To keep her safe.

Something he'd almost failed to do today. Something that he'd never let happen again.

He shuddered as he ran his fingers along her skin, pushing away the memory of the zombie trying to eat her, and concentrating instead on how fucking pretty she was. He peppered kisses along her neck, over the arch of her shoulder, and up to her ear. There he nibbled on the lobe, smiling when she shivered in his arms. Her skin was hot, though he knew not just from him. They were in hotter climes now, the feeling of freezing through the night almost over.

"Luke…" she whispered and he heard the plea in her voice. Heard it and felt like shouting in satisfaction. How long had he waited and hoped? Praying that eventually this would happen?

At last.

In one quick move he pulled her onto his lap so that she straddled him, her thighs either side of his, her back bathed in the moon's glow. Her weight was negligible, yet it comforted him, made sense somehow, there on top of him. He placed one hand on the small of her back and the other on her shoulder before leaning in and taking one pert nipple between his lips.

It budded immediately. Its hardness ripe against his tongue. He laved it once, then again. Enjoying the feel, the sensations, the amazing experience of her against him, like this. Jackson arched her back, encouraging more and muffled a moan with her hand.

He pulled away. "Scream if you want to."

"But the zombies—"

Luke reached up and laid his hand against her face. It covered the entire side and he let it rest there. She leaned into it and sighed softly.

"They aren't here," he said. "Not tonight. It's just you and me."

He ran his other hand up and down her side, along her arm, over her back, relishing the feel of her skin. She lifted his sweater and tugged until he allowed her to remove it, and it joined the pile of her clothes.

Luke had experienced many erotic moments in his life, but this, the two of them, naked from the waist up, stiffened him to the point of pain. He wanted to be inside her. To fill her and stretch her. To make her cry out...

"I want to have you, Jack," he whispered against her lips, "but we have no protection."

"We don't need it."

"But—"

She placed a finger against his lips and sprinkled kisses along his jaw line. Sensations fled to his groin and Luke groaned. He had to be inside her. God he had to!

"I'm too thin, Luke," she whispered. "Or maybe too athletic. Whatever. I don't even have periods anymore, so I can't get pregnant."

"You sure?"

"Yeah."

He lifted her up so she braced against him and shimmied out of her jeans. All that remained now were the purple panties and Luke smiled when he saw them.

"I'm going to keep these on," she whispered. "Just in case."

So she wasn't forgetting like he'd asked. But could he really blame her for that? The dead hovered on the edges of his mind too, and he knew their sex would be fast and frantic—a hard edge of need driving them, spurring them on.

He unzipped his jeans and freed himself. He was unbelievably hard, desperate to feel Jackson's warmth, and Luke hoped he wouldn't disgrace himself.

"I—"

He meant to ask if he could proceed. To treat Jackson with the courtesy so long ingrained in him, but she didn't give him a chance. She held either side of the headrest and, panties to the side, slipped onto him. Her body sheathing him in one rapid movement.

"Ahhhh…" The sound left him before he even knew he made it, and he gripped her hips. His large hands spread across her belly and back. She felt fantastic. All hot and wet and warm. It felt like coming home.

"I want to ride you, Luke," she said.

"Do it."

She moved on him then. Lifting herself up so that she worked him, over and over. Luke gritted his teeth, the sensations so amazing they bordered on unbearable.

He ran his fingers down her spine, along her hips, every bit of her making his body ache.

"Luke." She sighed his name, kissing her way along his ear, and he removed one hand from her back, knowing instinctively what she wanted. He placed it between them both, resting it against her clit, giving her the extra cushion she needed as she came down.

"Yes, Luke. Do that," she whispered.

He followed her as she moved. His fingers pressing down on her warmth, rubbing along and around. She gasped against his lips, whispered his name, told him how much she liked it…

It was indescribable. Luke began to move. One hand on her hip pushing her down as she rode him. His hips bucking into her, driving as deep as he could possibly go.

"Jackson, God…"

"Luke, I—"

They moved and they moved and rational thought fled to be replaced by pure, exquisite sensation. He tingled all over, blood pooling low in his gut, his thigh muscles tightening every time Jackson pushed down on him.

He opened his mouth, to tell her perhaps that he might not be able to last much longer, but then she came and satisfaction made him groan.

He felt her orgasm. Felt her muscles clench all around him, begging him to drive deeper. With one last thrust he did, coming, too. The amazing orgasm blocked everything but the feel of his body finally shooting into her, all the anger and stress pumping out, singeing his brain with endorphins.

For one perfect moment nothing existed in Luke's mind but the pleasure Jackson gave him, and the pleasure he gave her. They held on to one another, their breathing ragged, their hearts beating a steady tattoo in perfect unison.

And then it was over…and they looked into each other's eyes, and they laughed.

Chapter Twenty-two

"So planning to have your way with me every night, are you?" Luke asked.

From her position on the passenger seat, with her legs draped over him, the morning sun lighting up the barn, Jackson smiled. "Probably."

"You'll wear me out."

"Of course I will."

He smiled too. They both did. Their smiles egged each other on, and it was ridiculous but Jackson felt happy. Happy! An emotion she'd long since relegated to the scrap heap. Maybe it was due to the orgasm? It had been pretty incredible, and with it, Jackson had felt months of tension drain from her shoulders—not completely of course, but the amount of drainage was good. All due to the endorphins. Something she'd been sadly lacking for so long.

"I'm on top next time," he said. "I am the man after all. I should get some control over things."

The smile creased his face, and his very blue eyes twinkled. Jackson thought for the millionth time how she'd have totally dated him pre-dead people. If she'd served him a drink, or saw him in Macy's she'd have done something. A hello, a smile, maybe he'd have offered her his number or taken hers. And they'd have dated, and then who knew what?

It pained her for a moment to think that Luke would never meet the woman she once was. Would never get to see what had been some of her best qualities. He'd gotten Jackson the independent bad-ass, not Jackson the smiling, carefree girl. The world did indeed suck at times.

"You let me have so little control over everything else."

"You think?" she asked.

"I think…" He paused, his smile dying, to be replaced with something else. Something intense and Jackson found herself holding her breath. "I think I'm very lucky to have met you, Jack. That the way you make me feel is something pretty damn special. More so than before the zombies, because it is so unexpected now."

Jackson sucked in a shocked breath. She hadn't expected that. She'd expected them to tease and laugh with each other, not to talk about their feelings, but then hadn't Luke been unexpected from the very beginning?

She shifted a little, not sure how she felt about the whole "bare all-athon." It was way outside of her comfort zone and she didn't quite know what to say.

"I—"

"You don't have to say anything," he said quickly, as if, as always, he'd read her mind. "I'm not asking for a declaration here, babe. But time is so often…not short…but unknown, I guess. And if something were to happen to me, I want you to know that this past month has really been something."

"Nothing will happen to you." The very thought was enough for Jackson's heart to clench in on itself and panic to wind its way up her spine. She couldn't imagine the journey without Luke. Not now. Not when they were so close. It had been a mere blink in time, yet she felt like they'd spent months together. That they'd been watching each other's backs forever. More than that though, she knew that the chances of getting to safety without him were slim, and even more than that, she didn't want to. Going it alone now was not even an option. The reality of it scared her but it was there all the same.

Can't give away any independence… But even as the thought formed Jackson knew it was too late. She had given a little just yesterday when the zombie pulled her to the ground, but she'd gotten a lot back, hadn't she?

"Nothing is allowed to happen to you," she said slowly, forcing her mind around the thought of losing Luke like she had Tye, and though it made her feel awful for thinking it, she knew losing Luke would hurt much more. Tye had been her friend. He'd often annoyed the hell out of her but she had cared for him and had grieved for his loss. Wondered still where he might be. The way she felt about Luke was something else entirely. Jackson knew she wouldn't be able to put him in the same compartment as the other companions she'd lost.

"We're both going to get to Laredo. Safe and well."

"We will," he agreed.

"Well then. Don't say things like that," she chided.

"Jack —"

"It has been special to me too," she said quickly. The words leaving her before she could even think to hold them back. Because Luke was right. Who really knew how much time they had? They could both be eaten today, or both be dead, properly dead, before tomorrow. Now, more than ever, was not a time to play games or to act coy. Now was the time to be honest. To put aside all the previous conditioning, simply accept the feelings, and then share them.

"I've felt more normal with you than I have with anyone," she continued, blurting the words out. "Even though we're not safe at all and the world's a complete fuckup. But it's not about proximity of the dead, or likelihood of being eaten. It's just you. You make

me feel like I'm the old me, at times, even though I'm not at all...
Am I even making any sense?"

Luke nodded. "No. But yes. A contradiction, Jack. Which is
what you are. One huge contradiction. The woman and the bad-
ass. If I had weeks and weeks more, I don't think I'd ever quite
figure you out."

"I like you a lot, Luke," she said. "That's all you need to figure."

And he laughed before answering her in a solemn sort of
voice. "I like you a lot, too, Jack."

The happiness expanded then, until Jackson was sure it
inhabited very pore of her being. She shook and shivered, shocked
by it. The desire to be at the camp now, to have attained their goal
assailed her, and she reached out to run a finger along Luke's jaw
line.

"My mom used to teach ballet classes," she said softly. "She
tried to teach me but I failed so bad. I could never get my head
around the moves. She'd take me with her every single week, and
even though I was so awful, she kept me there. In the end my dad
had to have a quiet word with her and suggest that perhaps ballet
was not my thing."

"Jack," Luke breathed. "You don't have to—"

"I found out later," she continued, taking a deep breath, "that
she didn't care I was so awful. She took me because she wanted
there to be something we could share. My brothers went to
kickboxing with my dad, they were awesome, and so she wanted
this to be our thing."

"And was it?" Luke asked.

Jackson smiled. "No. But that did not stop my mom. She was
determined! She took me to God knows how many other classes,
one after the other. We finally found one we both liked, and really,
when you think about it, I have her to thank that I'm still alive."

"What was it? The class?"

"Akido. I may have only spent a year or so doing it, I may

have been a kid, but I think perhaps those moves came back to me when I most needed them. Almost like my mom was there protecting me. She died long before all of this, both my parents did."

"She sounds like a remarkable woman," Luke said.

"She'd still be alive," Jackson whispered. "There's no doubt in my mind about that. And she would have done whatever was necessary to find safety. She would not have stopped until she found a way to make everything right again."

He reached out and took her hand, planting a little kiss on the palm. "You're like her then."

"I was always more like my dad…like my brothers…you have no idea how much I miss them all." Her voice cracked on the last word and Jackson clamped her lips shut.

"I know how hard it was for you to tell me that," Luke said. "But as time goes on it will be easier. I promise, Jack, much easier."

"It never gets easier."

"That was because you weren't with me before."

"Is that right?"

He kissed her palm again and Jackson shivered. "We fit. We work. We would have even if the world didn't end."

"I want to get to safety," she whispered. "I want us to be able to lie on a bed somewhere and sleep at the same time and know that we don't have to keep watch. I want us to walk out and about, holding hands, not guns. I mean, obviously I will keep watch because that would just be stupid, and I'd have Mandy still, but…"

He nodded slowly, interrupting her babbling.

"I get what you mean. Though you've never struck me as a hand-holding kinda girl."

"A time or two."

"Then that's the first thing we'll do when we get there."

"And if we don't?" she asked, all seriousness now. "If the south is as overrun as up north? If there's no camp in Laredo? There's no safety but in our minds? What then, Luke? What will we do?"

It was the first time she'd asked him that question, the first time she's suggested that it might not all be as she wanted. But Luke did not mention that. He simply nodded slowly, ruffled her hair, and smiled.

"Then we'll have each other," he said moving forward for another kiss, maybe more, "and Jack, there's no doubt you'd look fucking fantastic with a tan."

CHAPTER TWENTY-THREE

The little girl sat on the edge of the sidewalk, the place where the lawn of the house behind her was starting to overtake. She was dressed in a dirty white dress, with dirty white bows at the end of her braids, and held a patchwork doll under her arm.

Her head was lowered, her face shadowed, and she was perfectly still.

Luke slowed the car to a halt but kept it running. The sound of the motor ticking over the only noise beyond their rapid breathing. Finally, it was Jackson who broke the silence, her words soft and halting.

"Why is she so still?"

"I'm not sure," Luke said, trying and failing to understand the sight in front of him. He swept the area carefully, taking in everything he could see. But the quiet, residential streets, baking in the afternoon sun, gave nothing away. A chill crawled down his spine all the same. It would be impossible to say how much was wrong with this situation beyond a lot.

Jackson shifted in her seat. "I thought for a moment there…"

"What?"

The little girl sat, unmoving, a mere fifty feet in front of them.

Only the very slight breeze ruffled the lace of her dress.

She shifted again. "She almost looks normal."

"You know she can't be human," he said softly. "Not after this long."

An arm moved, the one holding the doll. The barest of a twitch but they saw it all the same. Luke waited, expecting more, but the arm remained in place.

"I've never seen a zombie so still," Jackson whispered. "Especially not a child one. She can hear us, smell us. Her instinct alone should have her attacking."

"Then what?"

"I don't know, but…"

"What?" Luke prompted.

"That dress looks weird," Jackson said.

"Weird how?"

She shook her head. "I don't know. But after near on two years it should be much dirtier, ragged, but it's not. I mean, how many naked zombies have we seen? And those braids, they look like they've just been done."

"The dress has mud all over it."

"But the patches without mud look clean. Like it's fresh on but she got it messy. And she's holding a doll, Luke. How many zombies have you ever seen holding dolls?"

"Meaning?"

"Either she's only recently turned, or she's still human."

Luke sucked in a shocked breath. His mind instantly rejected what Jackson hinted at. "What you're suggesting is impossible! Completely fucked-up."

"A horde was impossible two weeks ago."

He scanned the street again, his gaze going from building to building. He felt antsy and oddly panicked. He hadn't wanted to come down this way in the first place, but it was, once again, the quickest route. They were just a few hours or so from Laredo, a few more miles. Surely nothing could stop them now?

Famous last words he thought and clenched the wheel tighter.

"Jackson," he began, "there is no way in hell that girl is still human, and if she was, whoever is looking after her sure as hell wouldn't let her play outside like a free meal."

"It's hotter here. The zombies might not come out."

And it was hot. Luke agreed with that. The further south they traveled, the higher the temperature, especially this close to the border. They'd dispensed with their sweaters a while back and the sight of Jackson in only a vest was enough to put a smile on his face as they drove the long road south. It was enough to make him smile at night as well. As he held her. As they pleasured one another. Finding time, even in the horror, to love. But the waking dead, well, they were hungry and the heat would not be enough of a deterrent.

"They'd come," he argued. "They'll take the heat if it means food. Sure they'll be slower and easier to kill, but still, slower hardly matters when there's twenty odd of them."

Jackson turned in her seat, squinting out at the small, still child. "So she must be one of them, then." She didn't sound convinced. "There's no other explanation."

"So we should go."

"No. First we should check. If only to understand how she looks so pristine. Why those braids haven't unraveled."

Luke sighed at the resolve in her voice but said, "She'll just try to kill us."

"I know."

"And then we'll have to sever her head."

Jackson sucked in a shocked breath, loud enough for him to hear, and jerked to look at him. "You're seriously not suggesting we behead her? She's just a child."

"We have no choice, not if she tries to take a chunk out of us. You know that."

"Yes…but…it's just a kid."

"I…" Luke paused, unsure how to continue. He'd had to take down more than one small zombie in his time, and though it had torn him up after, he'd had no choice. Logically he knew they were zombies, that they thought only of eating him, but he could also see where Jackson's protest came from. The girl in front of them still *looked* like a child. The first instinct was to protect. Only she wasn't really a child at all, and it would be stupid to forget that.

"She's a zombie," he said finally. "She's no longer a child."

"I know that," Jackson said. "I don't want to behead her though—call me a wimp if you will—but it feels wrong. I'll sink Mandy through as many zombies as I can, but not children."

Luke shook his head at the differences he once again saw in Jackson's personality. Like her hands, soft and supple, yet deadly, she was now showing him something else. She had killed hundreds of the waking dead without so much as a murmur. He had watched mesmerized as she swung Mandy through limb after limb, but now, because this one still wore the skin of a child, she hesitated. He wanted to rally at her for being weak, but he knew deep down that it was not weakness. It was compassion, something she had buckets of underneath her hard exterior. "You realize that makes no sense."

"Promise me, Luke."

Luke gritted his teeth and tried to ignore the soft inflection of her voice. He was often helpless against it and she knew it, damn it!

"Fine, we won't kill her. But we need to leave."

"After we check," she insisted. "Something feels off and it'll bug me until I find out what. The dress, the hair, the doll…" She paused. "It doesn't make sense."

"You planning on asking her those questions yourself? As she tries to eat you?"

"I just want to look. Something isn't right, Luke. Please. Don't make me beg or threaten."

He growled. "Holy hell, Jack, we're a few hours at most from the end goal. We don't need this now. If something is wrong here, I don't want us to get in the middle of it. Looking isn't going to give you any answers."

"Please, Luke," she asked again, laying a gentle hand on his, and with that he was helpless to say no. She was so in sync with him! Their physical relationship only added to the mental one that was already well established. He had a nasty suspicion that she'd have been able to wrap him firmly around her finger in the prezombie world. Hell, he was barely hanging on now.

"Okay," he said, "we'll drive past slowly. As soon as we confirm she's a zombie, we'll gun it and go. Just in case."

"We won't behead her?"

"No."

"Okay then."

Slowly he pressed down on the gas, edging forward carefully. He intended to give the girl a wide berth, use the other lane. That way when she turned, snarled and came after them, he could get them away without breaking his promise to Jackson.

"Luke, wait…"

He eased off the gas and opened his mouth to say something but didn't need to. It was obvious what was happening. As slowly as he'd pressed on the accelerator the girl rose. Her movements were smooth, not jerky, and as she stood, her dress fluttered around her knees.

"Oh my God," Jackson breathed.

The child's legs were tanned, ending in frilly white socks and black patent-leather shoes. Bits of mud clung to the lace, to her dress, her hair, but Jackson had been right. Underneath all that dirt there were no weeping wounds, no blood splatters—she looked like a normal little girl. She *was* a normal little girl.

For a moment Luke had no idea what to do. A human girl,

alone, on a deserted street… How could it be?

"It's a trap," he whispered, knowing somehow that the words were true the moment he said them. "It can't be anything else."

The girl lifted her head then and her eyes found them. Bright blue eyes, in a muddy little face. No. Terrified blue eyes, in a human face. Tears tracked down her eyes, she shook her head, and then the little girl ran.

• • •

Jackson didn't even think before she opened the door. Her hand grabbed the handle, pulled and pushed, and then her feet were hitting the road, Mandy in hand.

"Jack, what the fuck?"

She heard Luke's hissing voice, of course she did, but the only thing she could think about was the small child running in front of her. Four yards, five — she needed to move, and quickly.

The road was almost melting in the heat, making the air undulate oddly and Jackson's heart went out to the child who had no doubt baked half to death on it. No parent would leave a child out alone in this weather. The girl was there for an entirely different reason. One that screamed danger.

But she *was* just a girl, and Jackson could not leave her.

She pulled her gun from her waistband as she sped up, so that both of her hands were weaponed up. Part of her wondered if that would scare the child, a ridiculous thought considering. God knew what the child had seen.

The child in question swerved as she headed not for the front door like Jackson had expected, but toward the garage. Even as she ran, Jackson's heart gave a horrible lurch. Spaces that had not been prechecked were bad news in so many ways, especially in this heat. But she couldn't leave the girl, damn it. She was human, and a child. Just a little girl. It was ridiculously impossible that she was even alive!

"Wait," Jackson shouted, then regretted it immediately when her voice rang out in the silence—only her own rapid heartbeat a counter point to it.

The little girl turned slightly and shook her head, making her braids fly about, and then she crouched down and slipped under the half-open garage door.

"Fuck."

She heard Luke's footsteps behind her, about the moment she skidded to a halt.

"Jack…" Luke hissed, grasping her arm. "What the hell are you doing?"

"We need to get her out."

"It's a trap!"

Jackson bit down on her lip and took a deep breath. Her heart was racing and sweat was already gathering along her back. She needed water. No doubt the child did too. The child had been waiting in the street, the heat baking her poor little body. How long had she sat out there waiting to lure someone in?

She sighed and gripped Mandy tighter. "I know, Luke."

He growled, his eyes darting everywhere. "Then what are you doing? You can't go in there."

Despite the fact she knew it was an ambush, Jackson knew too that without a doubt she could not leave the child. Something was screaming hard at her and she had no choice but to listen to it. "I will not leave the girl here."

"I know it's totally fucked-up," Luke said, "but Jack, you go in there, you get eaten. You know it, I know it."

"Get eaten?" She shook her head at the words and then gasped. "You think…the zombies…"

Luke started. "Who else?"

"I thought people."

"No, Jack," he said quickly. "It's them. I can feel it."

His words made vomit rise and Jackson almost gagged. The

idea of a houseful of feral survivors was bad enough, but the idea of one of the dead braiding the little girl's hair, pus dripping, skin flicking off, was infinitely worse.

"But the girl—"

He growled again. "I'll do it. I'd have told you that if you'd have waited. Stay here. Now," he said, and then before Jackson could even stop him, Luke ran around her, sprinted across the sidewalk, bent down, and shimmied under the garage.

Her heart gave a horrible lurch and for one moment dizziness hit. Jackson gripped harder on both weapons to gain her equilibrium, before she ran after them. Her foot slipped as she hit the space where the parched lawn met the concrete, and Jackson looked down. What she saw there made her breath catch in the back of her throat.

A hole. A deep hole. *Just like the one at Creepyville.*

Head spinning she jumped over it, ran up the path, and toward the garage. The smell hit the moment she got close. Mold and ammonia, and oh God...she turned to look at the house... the windows did not have any fucking glass in. The same feeling slithered down her spine as it had all those weeks ago, and Jackson's chest heaved as she bent down and entered the garage.

Her adrenaline peaked to the point of implosion when she spotted Luke and the girl. They were in the corner of the room, Luke pulling the girl into his arms. Jackson swallowed down the lump in her throat and looked around. She'd expected to be confronted with something, other people, a pack, but there was nothing, not even the usual odds and ends such a garage would hold.

"We have to get out of here," she stammered. "Right fucking now."

"I told you to wait. Jesus Christ, Jack."

"Right now, Luke."

She ran over to them and grabbed the girl from Luke, right

into her arms. Up close she could see that she wasn't eight or nine like she'd first thought. The distance changed her perspective and Jackson knew now that she was six at most. Her small, mud-covered body quivered in Jackson's embrace. Her eyes wide and terrified.

"It's okay," Jackson reassured, running back to the door. "We're leaving."

The child let out a small moan and wrapped her free arm around Jackson's neck. The weight of her little body was negligible but it sent a deeply maternal thrum through Jackson. She'd always loved children, always imagined having a big family. Of course that would never happen now. *So don't think about it.*

"You're safe," she said, swallowing the lump in her throat. "We're gonna get you out of here."

The little girl shifted so that her lips were now level with Jackson's ear and her breath was oddly cold, shivering along her skin.

"They're coming," she whispered. "The monsters."

And in that moment Jackson knew with a horrible certainty that Luke had been right. That the trap was not one designed by humans at all but by zombies.

CHAPTER TWENTY-FOUR

As soon as he heard the kid's whispered words, Luke crouched down and looked under the door. What he saw was enough to make him feel sick. A quick count and he was about ready to check right on out. He lifted and turned to Jackson, their eyes met, and that was enough.

"How many?" she whispered.

Déjà vu hit and Luke's head pounded. It was always "how many," or "how close," or "where are they?" Would they ever get any peace? Couldn't the damn things leave them alone for more than a week?

"Luke?" Jackson prompted, and he made a concerted effort to get himself under control.

"At least fifteen."

He checked the garage door and was unsurprised to see that it had been jammed in place, jammed just enough for a person to fit through—like a fucking burrow. No way at all to loosen it, no way to shut it.

"Too many."

Sweat was snaking its way down his back now and the grip on his weapon was moist.

"Three packs?"

"Yeah. At least."

The girl buried her face in Jackson's chest. Small sobs erupted from her. With Mandy in her hand, holding the girl, Luke was struck forcibly by the image. Despite the weaponry, and the impossibility of the situation, it had an almost Madonna feel to it. Jackson did not know the child, yet she was willing to risk it all to save her.

But I can't save her. I can't save either of them.

Panic shot through him and impotent dread held him in its clutch.

"Let's be glad it's not a horde," Jackson whispered.

But in the end it made no difference. A horde, fifteen? Any more than one pack was too much in this situation, and Jackson knew it just as well as he did. And there was another difference now, one that couldn't be ignored. Before it had only ever been about him, grabbing what he needed, killing the dead, and making his way back to the bunker. Now it was all about Jackson. Keeping her safe, and now, by default, the child, too. From here on in she would be their responsibility—for who else could possibly step up to the plate?

But how? Luke bent down again and eyed the dead through the gap in the door. They were fanned out in a loose arc—their usual hunting technique—their mottled gray legs lined up in all directions. As usual, some were naked, some clothed in months-old material. He could see wounds on the limbs of some. Those strange wounds, created perhaps because their skin was so thin and so easily broken. How many times had he had to flick the stuff off his own clothes? The wounds were, as always, dripping pus. It stuck to their bodies and the stench was disgusting even from where he stood. The smell of death and mold. Like heated garbage.

How he hated it. How he hated them.

"Ideas?" Jackson whispered.

Luke shook his head slowly and signaled them to move farther back into the garage. He needed a moment to think.

He heard Jackson shush the girl, her words soft and comforting, and his mind swiveled in about a million different directions. *What to do?* His heart pounded so heavily that combined with the heat, he felt light-headed. He was reminded irresistibly of the moment in the bunker when he'd set out to help whoever was attracting the zombies. The start of all this really. The start of him and Jackson.

He shot a look at the two females huddled against the wall, Jackson's stance protective, her eyes darting from him to the child. Her pixie hair was fanning around her head in little spikes. He'd promised her a haircut soon. She did not like it getting long, fearing the dead would use it to grab a hold of her. Sweat was beading along her brow and down her chest and he swallowed down the lump that threatened. They'd eat her quickly, that was something to be thankful for. She was so thin it wouldn't take long at all. And the child? She too would be eaten in no time. They wouldn't suffer.

The child. It really was the perfect trap, he thought. Maybe that was why it had clicked so quickly with him. A child as bait, who the hell wouldn't stop to save her? And the zombies knew it. They'd really become that clever. How the hell had they gotten a hold of her? And how long had they had her? How had they communicated with her? He couldn't wrap his mind around it all and the horrific image of one of the dead holding the little girl's hand filled him, making him swallow down the bitter bile.

He had to find a way to save them all. Fucking hell he had to. He couldn't just give it up. *Think*, he told himself. *Think it through.* Their access to the car was completely blocked, though that was his fault more than anything on the part of the dead. But it was too far away to make a run for and there was no way they could run from that many waking dead on foot. No way out of the garage except through the locked door.

The door.

Luke nodded slowly and walked backward to Jackson, his gun trained on the gap in front. "What type of lock is it?" he whispered.

Jackson knew what he meant immediately. "Nothing fancy. We can easily break it."

"In and through then? Out the back door and we can go back around to the car?"

"We can try."

He ignored the note in her voice. The one that said she didn't hold out much hope but would give it a go. "Don't you worry, Jack. I got this."

She laughed softly. "You've always got it, baby."

Because so often he didn't, her words meant so much.

"Put her down. You can't fight and carry her."

"No. It's safer with her in my arms, and if it comes to a fight against that many, we're pretty much fucked anyhow. I won't risk them getting her."

He nodded. "Okay then. I'm gonna break the lock and there's no doubt they're gonna hear. So we need to be quick. I'll break and cover. You go through. Head for the back door, then circle around. I'll be right behind you."

"You make sure you are," she said, reaching out to him. "I mean it, Luke. Don't be a hero."

He nodded and wrapped an arm around her, and the kid. Gave them one swift hug. It wasn't enough. Not at all. He wanted to enclose her in his arms properly and squeeze her until they both ached. To lose her already…to lose everything when they were so close to the goal. Luke could barely comprehend it. But things were not looking good. He knew they weren't. If they survived this, it would be a miracle and already in his head he was plotting the best way to ensure Jackson's survival. If he had to sacrifice himself, he knew he was ready to do it. It was like he'd almost promised himself the moment they'd first kissed. He just hadn't known it then, and besides, when it came right down to it, he knew that he'd had a damn good run. The fact that they had gotten this far? Two years and then some after the end of the world? Yeah, he'd done good. What more could a man ask for than that?

"Ready?"

Jackson hefted the girl, hooked Mandy into her waistband, and lifted her Glock. "Yeah I'm ready."

Luke lifted his own gun ready to smash the lock, his eyes finding Jackson's—a message arcing between the two of them, promising something neither knew if they'd ever be able to give again. One quick swing and—

An explosion rocked the room, enormous in its size, the sound of it filling everything. The entire structure shook, bits of plaster and stone raining down. Without even thinking, Luke crouched down, protecting Jackson and the little girl with his body. *Thuds* sounded against the garage door. A ringing filled his ears and he staggered onto his knees. "What the fuck?"

A dead limb rolled under the open garage door, followed by another and then…rain?

"Jack—"

She shook her head, eyes wide, and they both turned to see liquid dripping onto the floor from the door. Even through the dust and plaster they knew what it was. Pus and blood. The *thuds* on the door were zombie bodies.

Jackson heaved the girl, stood and ran forward. "Come on!"

Luke followed immediately, looking for a space where they wouldn't be showered with zombie fluid, and together they slipped under the space, choking on the dust and grime around them.

"Jesus…"

The sight that greeted them as the dust cleared was enough for Luke's jaw to drop. He wasn't even sure what he'd expected, even if he'd had time to think it through. He just looked and he reeled and eventually a feeling of deep, and completely unfamiliar, relief filled him.

Because the bodies now standing in front of him did not belong to the dead. They were people.

PART TWO

"WHEN THE IMPOSSIBLE BECOMES THE POSSIBLE IT TAKES TIME TO
BELIEVE IT, FOR SOME MORE THAN OTHERS."
LUKE GRANGER

CHAPTER TWENTY-FIVE

TEXAS

There had to be at least thirty people, men and women, and shock held Jackson still as she looked from one to the other. Were they army? Their outfits suggested as much. They were all cammoed up, dripping in weapons and such, and they were hench. She saw that immediately by the fact they were busy beheading the zombies. Not in an angry fashion but systematic. One after the other, after the other. Until nothing remained.

Jackson's heart slowed its frantic beat with each swing of a weapon. Yes, she was still amped up, still feeling the despair that had settled across her in the garage, but now it was joined by something else. Shock, disbelief, relief? She didn't know, couldn't even pause long enough to work it out.

Her eyes zeroed in on one of the soldier-type people and watched as he shot a smile at the woman next to him and then high-fived her. Their spirits were up, the camaraderie obvious, and it shocked Jackson to see it. It'd had been so long since she'd witnessed people just being silly. The zombies had put a stop to anything like that, or at least she'd thought they had.

"Did we get all of them?" someone asked.

"Yep, all dead."

"Reckon they might stay dead this time, the bastards?"

Laughter echoed around the space and unsure what to do, not to mention slightly off-balance by the riot of emotions running through her and the amount of people right in front of her, Jackson edged closer to Luke. Her grip on the girl tightened, and she was pleased to feel Luke's arm enclose them both.

"What should we…?" Her voice trailed off as a large man shot through the crowd. He had to be well over six and a half feet and he was built like a linebacker. He too was dressed in full camo gear and had the biggest gun Jackson had ever seen. In an odd way he reminded her of Tye. He was out of breath, had clearly been running, and sweat beaded across his forehead. He certainly wasn't the only one sweating. Jackson could feel her vest damp against her back.

His gun arm dropped the moment he set eyes on them and to Jackson's surprise he choked off a cry. "Sammy?"

The girl's head whipped around and she let out a squeal before wiggling her way out of Jackson's grip. "Daddy!"

The girl ran to him and was enveloped in his arms. Everything made sense to Jackson then. The trap the zombies had set up, the fact she and Luke were still alive. It was all so clear, and ever so slightly horrifying.

"Survivors," she whispered. "The zombies were trying to trap these survivors. We just got in the way."

"I knew it," Luke replied, his breath tickling her neck. "I could feel it."

Everyone turned to look at them then, their whispered voices drawing the attention. Thirty-odd gazes went from Sammy and her dad and then back to Jackson and Luke again.

"Feeling the nerves here," Jackson whispered.

Luke laughed softly in her ear. "Nothing to be nervous about, babe."

Sammy's dad stepped forward, the girl clutched in his arms, a grin creasing his face, relief so obvious in his eyes. "Can't even begin to thank you people enough. Can't even believe she's here. Thank you, thank you so much."

Jackson shrugged, slightly embarrassed to be the center of attention though the embarrassment went some way to overriding the other, nastier emotions.

"No thanks necessary."

"I thought…" The man squeezed his daughter to him and shook his head. "Well you can imagine what I thought when I saw the pus in her bedroom."

"It's what we all thought." The second voice came from a lithe Latina woman. She grinned at Sammy then at Jackson, and held out her non-gun-bearing arm. "That one—it couldn't have been more than one—had snuck into the camp and took her. But we never imagined she'd still be alive. It makes no sense. Nancy, by the way. This is Mack."

"A zombie snuck into your camp?" Luke asked as Jackson took Nancy's hand. "An army camp?"

Nancy shook her head. "We're not army. Not in the conventional sense of the word at least. Though our camp is as well defended as any army base used to be." She scowled. "A zombie's never managed to get in till now. Never. Well, they've got close but never past the inner perimeter. We're locked up nice and tight."

"If you're not army then," Jackson said. "Are you the Laredo camp?"

Nancy's scowl turned into a grin. "Is that what they're calling us?"

"They?"

"People up north." She shrugged. "I'm assuming that's where you've come from. You're not tanned enough to be from these parts."

"Yeah we've come from Chicago," Luke said. "We're looking for the camp that's at the end of the I-35."

"And where did you hear about this camp?" Nancy asked.

"Another group, in Illinois," Jackson said.

"Not the university?"

Jackson frowned. "What university?"

Nancy paused for a moment and eyed the rest of her group. "Don't you people have zombies to kill? Might as well clean house while we're here."

They grumbled and muttered but the majority of them went quickly enough, heading for the houses lining the street. Jackson noticed each smaller group that branched off from the main had four people in it. One for each pack member maybe? She was unsurprised to note that Mack did not join the groups. He took his daughter over to one of the trucks she could now see parked up and sat her inside.

"There's someone there," Nancy said, dragging Jackson's attention back from the man and his daughter. "At the university campus in Chicago. Polly her name is. She's sent a couple of survivors our way, to our camp, and yeah, you can call us Laredo if you like."

Jackson gasped, her heart thudded wildly, and her legs felt ever so slightly weak. *At last. After all this time. Just like Tye had promised.*

"There aren't any survivors around that way," Luke said, interrupting her frantic thoughts. "I lived by the campus and I never saw anyone."

"Polly tends to keep to herself," Nancy replied, gesturing for them to follow her over to their parked trucks. "I'm not surprised you didn't see her. But the other group, the Illinois crew, they're a weird bunch. Be glad you didn't stay there."

"How do you know all this?" Jackson asked, her head spinning. "Are you in contact?"

"We are." Those words came from a skinny Asian guy, who was chewing what Jackson assumed was gum, in a maniacal fashion.

Jackson's heart thumped some more. How she'd hoped...it was unbelievable!

"But we can tell you about all this later," Nancy said. "First, Sammy. What happened here? Like I said, she's been missing since they took her night before last." She lowered her voice. "We never expected to find her alive. Thought this would be a revenge mission rather than a retrieval."

"Well..." Jackson exchanged a look with Luke and he nodded.

The remaining people—seven in all—clustered around them then, a loose circle of more people than Jackson had seen in many months. She swallowed unsteadily, a little surprised by how disconcerting it was. She'd been so used to it being just her and one other.

"She was bait," Luke said, straight to the point as always, beating Jackson to the punch.

Gasps filled the air, followed by low murmurs.

"What?" The question came from the gum-chewing guy. "What did ya say?"

"What Luke means," Jackson replied, nudging him. "Is that as far as we could see they left Sammy on the open road as, well, yeah, bait."

"What do you mean?" Nancy asked.

"We saw her as we were driving past and she was just there," Jackson replied. "We thought she was a zombie at first, but we realized pretty quickly that she was still alive. We followed her in there." She hooked a thumb at the garage. "But it's been no more than a half hour since we found her. We were totally in the shit before you guys arrived. They had us trapped."

"You think they left her in the road to trap us?" Nancy asked, and the tension in her face was obvious. "That's impossible."

Jackson shrugged. "But it's what happened."

"Jesus Christ."

They turned, all of them, to look at Mack and his daughter. He met their eyes—shock stamped across his features—before lowering his gaze back to her. "Where have you been, baby?"

Sammy gasped a sob and clutched her dolly to her. She sat on the driver's seat, her little legs not even reaching the floor.

"Baby?" Mack prompted.

"With them." The girl's words were just a whisper, and everyone leaned forward a little closer to hear it.

"With the bad guys?" Mack asked.

Sammy nodded. "They made me sit in the road and I was thirsty and then they made me run."

The crowd exchanged looks and Nancy shifted uneasily, her gaze scanning the street. "Made you how?" she asked.

"They told me."

"They spoke to you?

Sammy shook her head. "No."

"Then how?"

"They just did," she cried and her little lip wobbled. "They were waiting."

"For who?"

Sammy stroked down her dolly's dress and looked from one shocked face to another. Her braids bobbed slightly as her little shoulders shook, and tears tracked down her face, creating a path free of mud. "For everyone."

Chapter Twenty-six

The drive to the survivor's camp did not take as long as Luke thought it would, just over forty minutes in total. He looked around as he drove and realized pretty quickly why that was the case. The camp was not in Laredo, but rather in a small town called Realitos, a little farther from the border.

"Used to have a population of about two hundred," Nancy said as they passed the town sign. She'd jumped in their car, that uneasy look still on her face, and had peppered them with questions. Only when she was done did she start answering theirs. "About six months before it all went to shit some big-shot developer bought a lot of the land around it. He started building a gated community. Not sure who the fuck he thought he'd be able to sell the houses to." She shook her head. "But it worked in our favor. He had some issues with theft, and so the guy walled off the construction area—made it into a fucking fortress. By the time everything started to fall apart most of the houses were built—not finished internally, but built."

"Then it's a safe zone?" Jackson asked.

"Sure is," Nancy agreed. "And most of the original residents of the town came straight here. One of the construction guys had the keys. I knew about it because I lived a couple of towns over and we don't get much news. This development was a huge deal."

Jackson nodded slowly. "So the army didn't set it up in the beginning?"

Nancy snorted. "Like I said there's no army here. Not anymore."

"And the zombie population?" Luke asked.

"There's a fair few," Nancy said. "Mostly hanging around in Benevides and San Diego. We try and clean them out as often as possible, but they tend to keep coming."

"Why did the zombies take Sammy so far from the camp?" he asked, the question swirling in his mind. "And more to the point, how?"

Nancy shrugged. "I have no idea. None of this makes sense. They're getting smarter, we know that, but to set up such a trap? It goes against everything we thought we knew about them."

"It'd take them hours to sprint this distance. Hours."

"Yeah. Like I said, it doesn't make sense, just like the fact that one snuck in the camp, and I don't need to tell you how much it's worrying me. You'll see what I mean when we get there," she added. "We're like a virgin's panties—or at least we used to be. I'll need to get everyone doing a thorough sweep, see if we can find where that fucker got in."

When Nancy showed him where to turn off the road and onto scrubland, Luke saw immediately what she meant. He whistled a low breath, turned the steering wheel, and cast Jackson a quick look. She nodded, seemingly as impressed as he.

The survivors had inherited a fortress. Literally. The ground all around was cleared bare, leaving not a single place for a waking dead to hide. In the distance, a wall at least eight feet high extended for a good distance before curving in on itself, no doubt completing a circle. The wall boasted sentry towers every couple of hundred yards and they were clearly manned.

"You added the towers?" Jackson asked.

"We had the materials," Nancy replied. "They were just there and so we got to work. Like I said, the original residents saw what was happening across the rest of the world and knew we had to do something. We were luckier than you guys, though. The heat makes them slow. It has to do with their increased metabolisms and ability to sweat or something. Sebastian understands it better. He's our resident zombie expert. Basically the same thing that makes them hungry makes them struggle in the higher temperatures." She shrugged. "Those that turned headed straight for the shade. Bunkered down under houses and stuff, waiting till nighttime when the temperature dropped before attacking. Except we turned the tables and flushed them out."

"There were so many though," Jackson said. "So many."

Luke reached out and took her hand, giving it a squeeze, ignoring the fact that his own was far from steady. He felt oddly shaky. He'd thought the end was nigh, so no fucking wonder. The fact that they were alive was nothing short of a miracle and he had to take a deep breath to get a hold of himself.

"Like fucking rats," Jackson continued, her voice hardening. "The bastards."

He gave one last squeeze. No one, least of all Jackson, liked to remember those early days. Thousands of zombies chasing anything still alive. It was the stuff of nightmares and everyone in their convoy had lived those nightmares. Many times over.

"That there were," Nancy agreed. "Thousands and thousands. They ate plenty, believe me, despite the heat. We were lucky we had this place. Lucky so many thought to come here."

Luke leaned forward, slowing the car slightly to get a better view of the approaching building. "How many does it hold?"

"A good few hundred, though we're hitting capacity. We have to save a fair bit of land for growing food and for the chickens."

"You're growing food?"

"Yep. We're doing okay, though rations are tight. We have other farmland but it's risky going out to cultivate it. The zombies have those places pinged now they're getting smarter and they wait around hoping to get their hands on us, despite the heat. It's better to stay inside the walls when possible."

Luke eased off the gas as the cars in front slowed, waiting for the huge gate to open. It cranked apart bit by bit and as it did Luke saw groups of people milling around in the front courtyard.

"We're expected," he said.

Nancy leaned forward and showed them a walkie-talkie. "Mack would have called ahead."

"Walkies huh? You have other technology working?"

"Yep. We got all sorts. We scavenged a whole load of solar panels a while back, and Miguel, one of the teens, is a whiz at hooking things up to them."

"Radio?" Luke asked but Nancy shook her head.

"We've not been able to find one of those."

They drove through the gate and Luke noticed Jackson shifting as all eyes hit them.

"This is unbelievable," she whispered.

Luke almost laughed at the expression on her face, emotions churning inside him—the main one being absolute satisfaction that they'd made it. That they'd done as they planned, and now Jackson at last, was safe. The Madonna moment image of her holding Sammy again came to him and his almost laugh died. How close it had been.

"You thought this would be here," he said softly. "It's what you've been looking for. Hell, you had me believing it."

She turned in her seat and their eyes met. The same feeling that had arced between them in the garage erupted again and Luke swallowed drily.

"No, not like this…"

"Well I'm glad you're impressed," Nancy said with a laugh,

lightening the moment, and Luke turned from Jackson's muffled words to look back at Nancy.

"Beyond impressed," he said. "I never expected this. When Jack spoke about finding other survivors down south I thought a ragtag bunch at best. That we'd hook up with you and scratch out a living of some sort. But this? Nah, I never even dared imagine it."

"We're doing okay," she said, the pride in her voice obvious. "The dead aren't gonna take us down. Not if Sebastian has anything to do with."

"Who is this Seb...?" Luke trailed off as he braked to a standstill behind the other cars. They were all lining up against the wall, each ready to move at a moment's notice, and when he could move again he had to squeeze the Batmobile into a small space by the gate. The spot gave them a view of the entire courtyard and camp area.

The others started jumping out of vehicles, grabbing gear and stuff, but Luke simply remained in his seat wide-eyed. He looked from house to house, all laid out like some sort of little village, and then finally to the group of people hanging around the large carport. He couldn't really believe what he was seeing, and it was only when he looked closely at the group did he realize exactly what he was having trouble trying to process. He felt Jackson give him a nudge and shook his head.

"I don't believe it."

She laid a hand on his arm. "What's up?"

"How many did you say were here?" he asked Nancy, giving Jackson's arm a rub back.

"A few hundred," she replied. "Three hundred and seventeen if you want an exact head count. Nineteen now, I guess."

Maybe his eyes were playing tricks on him? Maybe he was imagining things, but he didn't think so. "And how many came from up north like us?"

"I dunno, fifty maybe? We've had some come in bunches, some

in pairs like you guys, and the odd lone survivor. Why?"

"That guy there," Luke pointed to one of the cammoed guys helping to unload one of the cars. "I know him."

"In a world of millions—now thousands," Nancy said, "it's unlikely that you'd know someone."

"I'm positive."

"I don't know…"

"Come on." He jumped out of their car, ignoring Nancy's words, waited for Jackson to join him, and strode forward. The floor was packed mud and dry as a bone, the heat here was palpable, and the noise… The noise was what startled Luke the most. So many people laughing and joking. It almost felt normal. Like a bit of the old world was left. Which he guessed it was. Here in the heat of the south, in this conclave, part of humanity remained. Well, normal apart from the gun digging into his back.

"What's going on?" Jackson asked.

"You remember the Lily zombie?"

She shivered. "That I do."

"That guy there." He pointed. "That's her husband."

Jackson gaped. "Are you serious?"

"Yep."

"Oh my God. The odds…"

"Yeah what are the odds, huh?" They rounded one of the cars and when the guy came into view Luke knew he hadn't been mistaken. "Pete?"

Pete turned and straightened, a wrench in his hand, shock stamped across his features.

"Fucking hell…"

"I knew it!" Satisfaction spread through Luke and he raced forward, grabbing the other man around the back and hugging him for all he was worth. "I thought it was you. Jesus Christ, man."

Pete, Luke's friend from so long ago, the guy that had brought his Mustang in for a service year after year, grinned and clapped him back. "Well, well, well. Never thought I'd see you again."

Luke shrugged. "Me and you both."

"I haven't seen you since that fuckup at the police station," Pete said, shaking his head and grinning widely. "But you made it here? Fucking hell, buddy. You're gonna need to tell me how. In detail. I thought that they'd got you. I never imagined you'd survived."

"No. I made it out okay in the end," Luke said. "But you? The last I saw of you, well…" Luke shifted uncomfortably; Pete would not want to be reminded of that incident.

"Yeah." He waved away the words. "Last you saw me was when my wife was trying to eat me. Suffice to say she didn't succeed."

"I'm sorry, man."

"No. It's fine," Pete said, but Luke could see the pain in his eyes, the difference in the man he'd once known. "We've all lost everyone right?" he added. "Lily's dead now, just like everyone fucking else. But you guys are here, and other survivors, that's a blessing. A total blessing. We have to be thankful for that."

Luke turned and met Jackson's eyes. An unspoken message ran between them and he shook his head ever so slightly. The image of the snarling Lily filled his mind. Her self-satisfied look as she had stood in the only safe place he'd had left in the whole world. Her howl of rage as they'd escaped across the park.

She'd smartened up, would have eaten them both in a heartbeat. There was no doubt about that. But underneath it all, somewhere inside whatever remained of her brain, she was still Pete's wife. Maybe she'd forgotten it all? The laughter and the teasing, all the times they'd spent together, the three of them. Or maybe she did remember but no longer had the ability to care or even process the information. Whatever. It made no difference in the end. So far as the world stood now she would never be Lily again. She was one of them. The zombies. Their enemies and he fucking hated them all.

"Yeah, buddy," Luke said as Jackson took his hand and squeezed. Telling Pete of Lily's continued existence would help no one. Least of all the broken man he could see in front of him. "She's at peace now."

Chapter Twenty-seven

Jackson awoke the next morning and automatically reached for Mandy. It was only as her hand moved across the soft comfort of the mattress that she realized and remembered. She was in a bed. An honest to God bed!

Luke shifted next to her and let out what sounded like a satisfied sigh. His face was relaxed in sleep, his weapons laid down carefully on the side table next to him. Jackson shook her head and curved her fingers around Mandy's worn hilt. She'd placed her under the pillow, ready to grab at a moment's notice. Luke had raised an eyebrow at her action but said nothing. She knew that he assumed they were safe now. She suspected they might be, but *suspecting* and *might* were not definite and Jackson couldn't even imagine sleeping without the familiar feel of the wood within her grasp. She imagined she'd sleep with Mandy under her pillow for the rest of her life.

Jackson took several deep breaths as she ran her fingers up and down the hilt. The often-repeated action comforted her, made it seem like everything was normal. Though what the hell normal was, Jackson didn't know.

Carefully, so as not to wake Luke, she lifted herself up and looked around the room, marveling all over again at the cleanliness of it. After being introduced to Luke's friend Pete, and then a bunch of other people whose faces blurred after a while, Nancy had shown them to their room. It made sense that they'd share a room. Space was limited and Jackson didn't mind. Luke didn't seem to either.

Their room was in one of the smaller houses, off to the side of what seemed to be the main house, the place they'd eaten their dinner the previous night. A huge bed dominated one corner, the sheets crispy white and smelling of lemons. A dark blue couch and chairs grouped around a blond-wood table took up the other half, creating a kind of bedroom-living space. It was the most peaceful space Jackson had seen in a long time and she couldn't quite get her head around it. It reminded her of the time she'd hidden in a huge library. She couldn't even remember what city it had been, but it was on a university campus, and she'd ended up there more due to chance than anything else. The stacks, as high as the vaulted ceiling, had mesmerized her, and though Jackson had never done well at school, she did love to read.

She'd wanted to stay in that library and devour all the volumes, probably because there was an innate peace to it. A sort of majesty that suggested it would endure long after the zombies, long after her. The atmosphere in her little room now was kind of like that. Sort of paused. Maybe it was because she could barely believe that they'd actually made it. Against all odds, they'd traversed the country and found the south, and survivors. An actual survivor's camp. Just like Tye had promised.

Jackson lifted a sheet and inhaled the scent. Basking in the freshness of it. Everything felt surreal and she knew it was going to take a little while for that feeling to fade. Her life had entered a new phase, a different phase, and once again, she was going to have to adjust.

Luke shifted again, mumbling something, and Jackson smiled

slightly before running a finger along the curve of his lower lip. He was damn hot and her body clenched as she remembered just what those lips had been doing last night. Another smile and she moved carefully, slipping out of the bed and padding over to the couches. She settled on one, tucked her feet underneath her, and placed Mandy on the armrest.

"Here at last," she whispered. "You made it, girl."

And damn, hadn't it been tight? She'd thought there in the garage that it was the end of her road, and she'd gathered her strength to face it. She'd need her strength for something else entirely now. Not least, the prospect of sleeping without always keeping a part of her brain on the alert. She hadn't lied when she'd told Luke that she had, at most, slept for four or five hours a night before the zombies had arrived, but at least that had been four or five hours uninterrupted. In the last couple of years, Jackson doubted she'd slept for more than a handful of hours straight through. Her body had wanted to but her brain hadn't allowed it. Maybe it had been the constant flood of adrenaline, or the unrelenting terror. Regardless, she'd have to adjust all over again now. She suspected it was not going to be that easy.

"Jackson?" Luke's mumbled words caught her attention and she met his sleepy gaze.

"Right here."

"What time is it?"

Jackson shrugged, struck by the silliness of his question. Time meant nothing anymore beyond the length of a day and the reach of a night. "Time? I don't know. Does it matter?"

He sat up and rubbed at his eyes. "Yeah, it does. I promised Pete I'd check out the garage this morning."

Jackson pulled the curtain aside, running the fabric over her fingers, and looked out onto the courtyard. A couple of people were walking past, obviously on their way to do something, but all in all it looked pretty quiet. "It's early, I think. The sun looks weak, probably five or six or so."

"I should get up then," Luke said, stretching. "Don't want to keep him waiting."

"When did Pete ask you this?"

"Last night during dinner. You know when I went to get us some water? He collared me there by the taps and asked if I could help out. If I'd be happy to be the designated mechanic. Apparently there are a couple of people who know the odd thing or two but no one who can fix the in-depth stuff. They have a whole bunch of vehicles but some of them no longer run. It makes sense to keep the fleet here in good shape rather than replace them. Batteries go flat, rust kicks in etc. Looks like I've got a whole bunch of work on my hands—if I want to do it, that is."

"So you'll be useful here then?"

"Looks like it. It's what I used to do. It makes sense for me to help with it here if I can."

Luke the camp mechanic. It suited him. "That's good to hear, Luke."

"What are you planning to do this morning?" Luke asked. "Maybe you could go back to bed for a bit? God knows you deserve the rest. Or you could come with me to the garage?"

Jackson paused, suddenly startled. She hadn't even thought about what she'd do. The previous evening at dinner she'd simply marveled at the food, the people, the laughter. Taking it all in, Jackson had simply let it wash over her. It had felt weird to do that. No need to plan the next step or worry about the next move. And then she and Luke had taken the obligatory tour—seeing pretty much the entire camp. After that they had each showered before falling into bed and practically ripping one another's clothes off.

Zombie-free sex. *That* was something she could get used to very easily.

Afterward she'd drifted off for an hour or two, waking at intervals to do a security sweep and be reassured by Mandy's presence. Everything was good, or rather everything would be once she got herself settled in and used to the oddness of it all. And the first step would be finding something to do, because clearly she'd have to do *something*. In a camp this size everyone was expected to have a role. To contribute. And it certainly wasn't the place to laze around, even if she had been that sort of person, which she wasn't.

"No that's fine," she said slowly, considering. Last thing she wanted was to get in Luke's way.

"Fuck. I didn't even think," he said, jumping out of bed, his face scrunched with worry. Jackson took just a moment to enjoy his muscles moving as he walked. He was a fine specimen of a man, that was for sure, and already she was wondering if she could drag him back into bed. Maybe being in the camp would turn her into a sex maniac? She'd exert all her energies between the sheets. The thought made her smile and she held her hand out to him.

"Are you okay with me doing this, Jack?" he asked, taking her hand. "I don't want you to feel like I'm abandoning you or anything. Pete asked and I just said yes. I didn't think. If you'd like, I could go to the garage this afternoon or even tomorrow. We can spend the day just here, just the two of us."

"Don't be silly. There's no reason to put work off if it needs doing."

"You sure?"

He looked unhappy, clearly thinking he'd fucked up and Jackson was quick to reassure him.

"Totally." She didn't want him changing his plans to babysit her. The very thought horrified her. Their time in this camp would be decided by their actions over the next few days. She couldn't allow the people here to see her as Luke's woman and nothing else. Like she needed looking after. She was bad-ass and it was important that the other survivors got that from the get-go. Quickly she came up with a list of possible activities. Anything to keep Luke from insisting on keeping her company. "I'll be fine. There's a whole bunch of stuff I want to do. I need to explore properly for a starters. Scope out the lay of the land. See if there are any weaknesses in the security."

"They have guards, babe, and it all looked pretty good when we looked around last night."

"I know this, on the surface, yeah, but a zombie got in and took Sammy," she reminded him.

"Well yeah…"

"Exactly. I won't be able to relax here properly unless I know that everything is okay. Speaking of which, I'd like to go find Sammy, too. Make sure she's okay. And then maybe I can speak to whoever's in charge around here, find out as much information about this place as I can, then maybe see what I can contribute."

"There's plenty you can contribute."

"Serving dinner?" The moment the words left her lips Jackson wanted to take them back.

"What?"

She shrugged and ran a hand across Mandy's hilt, annoyed with herself for betraying her insecurities. "That's what I used to do isn't it? Serve food and drinks. I'm not qualified to do anything else, not like you are."

"Don't be silly, Jack. There's loads you can do. You're bad-ass."

"Everyone here is bad-ass, Luke."

"What makes you think that?"

"They wouldn't be alive if they weren't."

Luke squeezed her hand. "You don't need to do anything at all right now, Jack," he insisted. "Why not just enjoy being safe for a few days. Relax and rest. God knows you need to! You've been running on nonstop energy for years."

Jackson's fingers ran up and down the hilt—familiar, comforting strokes. "You're going off and contributing."

"Yeah, because I was asked. To be honest, I'd have preferred a day or two to get used to everything. Only I can hardly say no, can I? And besides, it's only this morning and I had all that time in the bunker when I was okay. Not having to look over my shoulder constantly. It was different for you."

"I suppose…"

"But seriously, if you want me to stay with you, I will."

"No." What was wrong with her? Jackson paused and let Mandy be, trying to figure out exactly what was making her nervous. Because something *was*, she realized. Despite the loveliness of the room, the food, the obvious lack of snarling zombies, and the feeling of safety battling with her usual feeling of doom, something felt…off. She'd made it to Camp Laredo, actually done what she'd spent so long trying to do—so why did it seem like now, when she'd reached her destination, that something was unfinished?

"No. I'm fine," she insisted, pushing away the questions nagging her. "Just because we're together, Luke, does not mean we have to live in each other's pockets."

"Are we then?" he asked.

"Are we what?"

"Together?"

Jackson tilted her head and looked into Luke's eyes. "Well, we just spent the night wrapped in each other's arms, and neither of us said anything when we were given one room so I kinda assumed so…"

"Not the entire night. It was a few hours. I heard you get up on and off."

"Sorry, I just…"

"I don't mind," he said quickly. "It's you, I get that, and I wanted us to have the same room. I loved sleeping with you, Jack—even just for a handful of hours. You know that, don't you?" At her nod, he continued, "I just wanted to be sure being here doesn't change that. Because you know I'm not the only choice now."

She laughed. She couldn't help herself. "Luke, don't be silly.

You're still the only choice. What I said stands. I like you, I like you plenty."

He smiled and leaned forward, capturing her mouth in his. His lips were supersoft, and she sighed as her own lips moved with them. Kissing Luke was addictive. The feelings it aroused in her had no name as far as she could tell, not yet at least, but feelings they most certainly were. Delicious ones.

He pulled away after a moment and peppered the side of her face with kisses. Each a little peck and goddamn it, she nearly giggled. *Giggled*! Jackson was fairly certain she'd never giggled, not even before the zombies.

"I like you, Jack," he whispered. "A whole load of lots."

Heat pooled throughout her body, like everywhere. "I guess really the only difference between us now is that we get to explore whatever this is between us without being on the alert for dead people trying to chomp down on us. At least I hope so."

"I already know what this is," he said, gesturing between them, settling next to her and taking her hand.

Her heart gave an odd little thump. "What do you mean?"

He laughed and squeezed her hand, the whole thumb-rubbing thing happening again. "Nope. Not saying a word. Not until you know, too."

Panic bubbled and her eyes widened…could Luke be saying what she thought he might be saying?

"I—"

He leaned forward and planted another kiss, effectively silencing her. Minutes later when they came up for air, he whispered against her lips. "We can go out holding hands."

The panic subsided a little and Jackson took a deep breath. "You are so sappy," she said, deliberately lightening the moment. "But I guess I did promise. Believe me, though, Mandy stays strapped to my waist and the Glock in my jeans. I'll never go anywhere unarmed no matter what."

"It's different here, babe. You don't need to be on a constant guard. Just keep the gun on you and let's hope they have some more ammo."

She sighed, her worries rushing back all over again. "Everything *is* different now, Luke, only not in the way you mean. It's going to take some time to get used to it all. For me maybe more than you. I've wanted this for so long, hoped for it. I fantasized and imagined, and now…" She shrugged. "I'll need to find a place here. You've found yours."

"You'll settle in. You'll be settled in before you know it. And I'll only be gone a few hours. We'll meet back up here at midday, okay?"

He took her in his arms and ran fingers up and down her back. Jackson closed her eyes and allowed the sensations to settle over her. Both comforting and exciting her all at once. But underneath that, prodding her from deep inside, the feeling of safety battled with the nagging unfinished thoughts.

And even as Luke's hands made their way down her body and tugged at the waistband of her pants, Jackson couldn't help but wonder what the hell she was going to do next.

CHAPTER TWENTY-EIGHT

The survivors had an excellent fleet of vehicles, and Luke whistled as he walked up and down between the rows. "Where the hell did you get the Hummers from?"

Pete laughed. "There was a guy in a town over. He fixed them up for some big security firm. His son ended up here and told us about them."

"And the guy?"

"Dead probably," Pete said. "Like all the others. His kid's doing well though. He helps out in here."

"So does everyone have a role here, then?" Luke asked, thinking of Jackson. He knew he'd fucked up royally this morning by not considering what she was going to do with herself. He'd just been so excited at the prospect of fiddling with cars again—something so normal, and she was so fiercely independent he didn't consider her in those terms. Jackson did what the hell she wanted when she wanted. She'd find her place, he didn't doubt it, but the more information he gathered from Pete, the more options he'd have to suggest to her. "People are given stuff to do?"

Pete handed him a tool bag and together they bent down to start separating everything out.

"Yeah," he said. "Nancy pretty much runs the place. She started all this in the first place. Building the towers, looting supplies. I think she used to be a cop and she led most everyone here. Anyway, she comes up with the strategic plans, which are then put to a sort of rough vote. Hands-in-the-air style. Mack kind of backs her up. We have people who do the cooking, some clean, some look after the kiddies, others make stuff. We've got techie people who spend their time trying to get shit running again. Sebastian is our doctor, total geek, and then there's Layla, she's the midwife — though, as you can imagine, there's none of that happening. Who the hell wants to bring kids into this world?"

"And you?"

Pete shrugged. "There's a bunch of us who are, well, for all intents and purposes, the army I guess — ironic huh? Considering my former profession? We man the boundaries of the camp, go out foraging, killing off any zombies who come too close. It's the tough bastards in our group. The ones who've nothing left to lose and can't quite accept this place."

"What do you mean?" Luke asked. "Isn't everyone happy to be here? Somewhere safe?" He was a fair way to accepting it already, overjoyed to finally find himself in the mix with so many people again. He was almost annoyed with himself for leaving it so long to strike out. If Jackson hadn't been there to push him...

As he'd made his way to the garage, he'd spun all sorts of fantasies. They'd grow, gather more people, maybe even have a fortified city someday. More than that though, he was delighted that Jackson was safe. After that moment in the garage, when he'd thought the end had come for both of them, something had clicked inside of Luke. His protective tendencies had been pushed to the back by her natural take-no-shit attitude. Now they came roaring to the fore again. It had felt so amazing last night to settle into bed with her. To brush her spiky hair and plant a kiss on her cheek without having to worry that a zombie was going to come barreling in at any moment. Now, he knew there was no need for her to constantly look over her shoulder, to spend all her time so stressed out. Waking up to see her this morning relaxing on the couch had filled him with a happiness he hadn't felt in a long time. Obviously, things weren't completely normal. The zombies were still out there, and she was still twitchy. But here in this camp, he and Jackson could have a little bit of ordinary, and the thought filled him with pleasure.

Pete passed him a crescent wrench. "Some people, and I'm one of them, by the time they get here they're not—ah shit I don't even know how to explain it."

"Pretend we're back in my garage and you're trying to explain the ticking noise in your Mustang."

"I miss that car."

"I miss my garage."

"Well, look, I lost Lily, you saw that," Pete began. The shadow that crossed his face spoke plenty on his thoughts about that. Pete and Lily had been inseparable. The love between them had been obvious for all to see. The lack of that now in Pete's life was apparent. Despite his cheery facade, he was a broken man. It pained Luke to see it. "I made my way down here purely on instinct and because I had nothing else to do," Pete continued. "I was planning to cross over the border and head into Mexico when I saw the signs."

"The signs?"

"Nancy had a team go out a year or so ago and paint some of the walls around the crossings. Basically instructions on how to get to a drop-off point, not to the camp you understand, we have to be careful, but somewhere we can check for survivors."

"Smart move," Luke said.

Pete shrugged. "Only one of the guys came back so it wasn't that smart, but we've only added about fifty extra people because of them…so yeah…maybe it was."

"And you found these signs?" Luke prompted.

"Well yeah," Pete said. "I thought if I could find others, I could start putting myself back together again. I was on the edge, seriously considering shit you do not want to know about."

Luke thought about Jackson on the observation deck. "I can understand that."

"Trouble is…" He paused and stood. "It doesn't work that way."

"We've all lost everything."

"It's easier for people like you," Pete said, though there was no resentment in his voice, just a sort of deadness. "People who come here with a skill. Look at you. Already you're here and you'll be lucky if you ever leave this garage again. We need you. You wouldn't believe how pleased Nancy and Mack were when they found out you were a mechanic. I've fiddled with the cars and Jace has helped, but pretty soon we'll need someone with more knowledge—hell, we already do. It's like that for Sebastian and Layla and some of the others. They have a purpose. So they can forget at times about the zombies and concentrate on doing something for the community. That sort of shit keeps you going, you know?"

Luke popped open the hood of one of the Hummers, nudging Pete aside. "I guess. I mean, I can understand where you're coming from. But surely in a community this size everyone is needed?"

"Yes," Pete agreed. "But mostly they're needed for defense. So everyone who isn't needed for other things does that. We're the goddamn army. Which means we never get to forget, even for a minute, about the zombies. We're fighting them daily. They're hungry now. More willing to risk the heat, and we can't let them build up and mount an attack. So that's what we do and here's the thing…" He paused again and Luke waited, knowing that Pete would get there when he was ready.

The sounds of activity washed over them both. People going

to and fro about their business. Kiddies on their way to lessons, maybe, little Sammy probably one of them. Meals being prepared, gadgets fixed. It was like an echo of lost times and Luke reveled in it.

"We like it," Pete finally said.

"Killing zombies?"

He nodded. "It's what we are now. More than that, it's *who* we are. Being here in normality again, or as normal as things can be today, doesn't work for us. Little things get to me. The kids playing, the sound of laughter. I get itchy, antsy, and the only way to fix that is to go out and kill some zombies. There are loads of us like that here. We'll do it until we can't do it anymore, or until the zombies take us all out. I think it's kind of like those vets, you know from the old wars, who never really got used to civilian life again."

Luke struggled to think of a response and buried himself in the car, playing for time. He understood what Pete meant. Hadn't he himself taken down as many as he could? Trying to clear his area? But always underneath that had been the desire for a sliver of normality again. The wish for the world to return to how it had been, how it was supposed to be. Here in this little camp he got that. He could forget for a time that the zombies wanted to eat him. That they prowled in those houses he and Jackson had been trapped in just an hour away. What Pete was suggesting seemed absurd, that some people were now too far gone to want to forget them, to crave normality again? That being reminded was too much?

The image came to him then of Jackson on the couch in their room, running her hands up and down Mandy's hilt. Over and over again like some ritual. The vision of her placing Mandy under her pillow, of waking up throughout the night to do her "security sweep."

A nasty feeling slithered down his spine and he tried to push it away. Because Jackson had wanted this hadn't she? Had been searching for it for so fucking long. Her entire life had been about finding some sort of safety…and yet…

"How do you know who those people are?" he asked slowly.

Pete passed him a screwdriver and laughed humorlessly. "Give them a day or so after arriving and they're ready to head right back out."

• • •

With Luke busy in the garage, Jackson slipped into her jeans and vest — smelling a bit ripe, she had to admit — and left the room. They were on the top floor, at Jackson's request, and she padded down the staircase carefully. It was habit now to take each step one at a time and to pause to minimize any possible creakage. Her feet fell into that familiar rhythm without her even thinking about it. She looked back and forth after each step, wincing slightly as her boots left little brown marks on the clean stair boards. Mandy's wooden hilt felt warm in her hand and she let out a soft sigh, clenching and unclenching around it. Though she knew nothing would be waiting for her at the bottom of the stairs, or likely to come from the top, she didn't actually *know* it. A zombie *had* gotten into the camp, after all, and like she'd told Luke, now was not the time to let her guard down completely.

At the foot of the stairs Jackson looked left and right, letting out a deep breath when nothing lurked, howled, or ran. Her hand was sweaty and she took a moment to wipe it on her jeans.

She made her way out of the thick wooden front doors, pausing for just a moment to gauge both the thickness, and the quality of the locks before stepping outside. The air was warm, muggy even. She imagined the dead trying to fight their way through it, each step getting slower and slower. Nancy had said something about them not being able to sweat properly and Jackson spent a minute thinking about that as she looked around the outside area.

The building she and Luke had been housed in stood at a right angle next to another building, which was then at an angle to the next, creating a C-shape. They were clustered off from the other sets of buildings, a couple of minutes' walk. Directly opposite, Jackson could see the same arrangement of buildings, and that was repeated again next to them. She did a quick mental calculation, working out the number of possible rooms, and could see that there was easily enough room for a few hundred people—just like Nancy had said.

Smells invaded her senses as she walked forward down the building's path. It seemed that the garden areas, either sides of the flagstones, were taken up with various plants, and Jackson recognized a few, including wild garlic and tomatoes. She wondered what other foodstuffs—maybe things she hadn't eaten in what seemed like forever—were dotted about and resolved to find out at some point. She did have a whole morning to fill.

Her mind flickered across to Luke and she sighed, wondering what he was up to. *Fixing cars*, she answered herself. *Busy finding his place here.* She sighed and swung Mandy back and forth. She wasn't angry with Luke, not at all. It was good that he'd found something to do, that he was contributing, but she did feel a little lost. Would there be something for her to do here, as well? She knew she didn't have any real qualifications. She wasn't a doctor or a dentist or even a qualified cook. The only thing she had any skill at now was slaying the dead.

Jackson walked across the courtyard, tense and a little nervous. She looked back and forth, taking everything in, trying to assimilate all the information in one go. The main courtyard was a damn good size, made of compacted mud. It would allow every survivor to stand with a good few feet around them. She noticed people laughing in the towers around the perimeter fence. Other people hung around outside the houses, chatting. One in particular seemed to be a focal point for activity. It was a little larger than the others, and had a wide, wraparound porch. Jackson swallowed and took a deep breath. She'd have to go and talk to someone at some point. She knew this, and yet she was strangely reluctant. *It's because you haven't been around people for so long*, her mind said, *and also maybe because you've got a touch of the paranoids.*

A tall, thin guy walked up then, from the direction of the houses opposite hers, a burlap sack in his sinewy arms. He smiled and jogged over. "Coming up to the main house for some breakfast?"

Jackson nodded slowly. "I think so. I wasn't sure what to—"

"You can follow with me if you'd like," he said. "I'm Sebastian, by the way. Oh, and its Frosted Fruit Flakes. Breakfast is always Frosted Fruit Flakes. We found a factory not far from here and took about a year's supply. So every morning is the same thing. Dry Frosted Fruit Flakes."

She couldn't help but smile at his accent, which was British and like cut glass. She half expected him to give a "tally ho" or "cheerio." How long had it been since she'd heard those sorts of tones? Years, at least.

"Pleased to meet you, Sebastian," she said, casting a glance up and down him. He was about thirty or so, she guessed, but his hair was completely gray, and it stood in loose spikes around his head, as if he'd been pulling at it over and over. But he had the most amazing blue eyes Jackson had ever seen, and she'd definitely put him in the yum-yum category. She fell into step behind him, Mandy still held loosely. "Oh, I'm Jackson. Sorry, my manners deserted me a while ago. I guess I'm gonna have to relearn them."

"You don't really need that here," he said, nodding at her machete. "Or the manners even, and I already knew your name. Is it your actual name?"

"Force of habit, and yeah, of course, why wouldn't it be?"

Sebastian shrugged. "People change their names when things like this go down. We had a 'Shadow' once. He was a rather shady character though, and left after a couple of weeks. So where's your chap?"

Jackson smiled slightly. Already it seemed she and Luke had been lumped firmly together. That pleased her in an odd way. She didn't want anyone thinking of her as Luke's wimpy woman, but she was happy for everyone to see them as a couple. "Luke, you mean?"

Sebastian nodded. "Saw you both last night. I only nipped in to get some food and it was straight back to work for me. It was fantastic though to realize we had two new survivors, especially young people like yourselves."

"You're not exactly a senior citizen," Jackson said.

He laughed. "Apart from the hair. Premature graying, what can I say? I have a stressful job. So, where is Luke?"

"He's with the cars," Jackson answered. "He's a mechanic." She felt a weird kind of pride saying those words, something totally new to her.

"Thank God!" Sebastian sighed. "We needed a mechanic, badly. Last time I made the trip up to the shack we broke down. We had to wait to be picked up and ride back cramped on each other's laps in the second car. Not the most pleasant experience, especially as I was seated on Jay. He growled at me the entire journey home."

"He's happy to help out," Jackson assured him. "We both are."

"So what are you, then?" Sebastian asked. "Or rather what were you before the end of the world?"

Jackson shrugged, the uncomfortable feeling returning. "Nothing special. What about you?"

"Oh, I'm the doctor."

Something clicked in Jackson's mind then and she halted. "Yes, of course. Nancy mentioned you. You know all about the zombies. About why the heat affects them."

Sebastian heaved at the sack and rolled his shoulders. "Well…"

"Is that too heavy for you?"

"No, of course not!"

Jackson raised an eyebrow, transferred Mandy to her left hand, and took the sack. Sebastian spluttered slightly but she ignored him and carried on to the house with all the activity, her mind whirring in a million different directions. Was it finally time to get some of her questions answered? "I need the exercise. Don't want to go soft. Now, Sebastian, tell me, how much do you know about them, the waking dead I mean?"

He frowned and gestured to the sack. "I can carry my own stuff, you know. It's just awkward. I might not be a soldier-type like you and the others but I'm not a complete wimp."

"Like I said, I don't want to get soft."

"No one goes soft here." He snapped his fingers. "Of course. I know who you are now. Polly was talking but I wasn't really listening. I was busy. But I am almost certain she said Jackson, and yes that's good. Perfect, in fact."

"Huh? Who is Polly? You lost me."

"She's a friend of mine, a scientist," he said, as if that should have been perfectly obvious.

Jackson hefted the sack a little. "Did I meet her last night?"

"No," he said. "She doesn't live here."

"Where does she live?"

Sebastian waved a hand in a vague kind of direction. "In another place entirely."

Another place? Jackson frowned, wondering if Sebastian had all his cents to the dollar, because Nancy had said nothing about another camp close by. She frowned and racked her brain, a moment later and she remembered. "Polly is the woman in Chicago? At the university there?"

He smiled. "She is."

"And she mentioned me?" Jackson said, wondering if her and Luke's arrival was already a topic of conversation at the camps that seemed to be dotted around the country, camps the Laredo people were in contact with.

Sebastian gestured to the group by the door, one hand tugging at his gray locks. "I'm not entirely sure. Like I said I wasn't really listening. But look, there's so much to do, Jackson! And never enough hours in the day to do it. The others help me out. They don't like it much, though, and Colin quit a few days ago. Said he couldn't stand the smell anymore."

Jackson gaped, completely lost by the good doctor's rambling. "The smell?"

Sebastian nodded forcefully and tugged at his locks again. "I can't say I blame him. It is quite awful and I've had a couple of years to get used to it. Still, it's very annoying losing them one after the other. I'm getting down to the last few. What will happen then, I ask you? Nancy will have to force them into it and they won't be happy."

Jackson frowned, glanced at the group by the door, who gave her what looked like a knowing look, and then back to Sebastian again. "You know you're not making any sense, right?"

He smiled, and that smile of his was quite brilliant, crinkling his eyes and making him, Jackson had to admit, look a teensy bit maniacal.

"You're good with that blade I assume?" he asked.

Jackson nodded. "Of course I am."

"Good enough to take down a pack on your own if you have to?"

"I have done," she said slowly. "But it isn't easy when it's five on one."

"It's never easy. Why would it be?" he agreed as if this should have been perfectly obvious. "But unfortunately it's necessary. Now tell me, how soon can you be ready to leave?"

CHAPTER TWENTY-NINE

It was almost ten o'clock by the time Luke put down his tools. He was sweating profusely and ridiculously grateful for the fact that Pete had thought to bring a supply of water with him. The water came from some sort of well on the property, sunk when building of the new housing development began. Just another thing, Luke was beginning to learn, in a long line of positives about the place.

"Time to take a break?" Pete asked.

Luke nodded. "I'd kill for a coffee."

"Then you are in luck, my man," Pete said, clasping him on the shoulder. "We have tins and tins of the instant stuff. Found it in the same warehouse we got the Frosted Fruit Flakes." He shook his head. "They're grim. I never thought anything could taste worse than some of the shit we ate on patrol, but morning after morning of that stuff?"

"Might be a bit more palatable with milk," Luke said. "I had loads of the dried stuff in my bunker."

"Can't believe you found that place," Pete said. "You lucked out."

Luke wiped his hands on one of the rags, oddly cheered to see the grease there. The smell of the garage, the feel of it. Once or twice over the course of the morning he'd almost found himself humming. He'd forget, for just a few seconds, the reality of the world. Whether that was a good thing or not, he did not know.

"I mean who the fuck was so paranoid in the Chicago suburbs they built a fucking bunker?" Pete added.

"Someone I am eternally thankful to. I only wish—" He paused and shook his head. "Doesn't matter."

"That you'd found it sooner?" Pete asked. "That we'd all managed to hole up there?"

Luke dropped the rag and turned his back on his friend. A nasty feeling slithering through him. How the fuck could he say that Lily *was* busy holing up there? That she'd found the bunker. Was probably even now trying to find a way in on the off chance that someone might be in there? No it was impossible. Would hurt his friend immeasurably to mention it, and yet…Lily was still around, and Luke had no idea how.

"What happened?" he asked slowly. "With Lily I mean, after. You don't have to talk about it if it's too much," he added. "But…"

Pete sighed and kicked the tire of the Hummer. "Knew you were going to ask me this."

"Tell me to mind my own fucking business if you want."

"She was your friend too," Pete said. "You remember all those nights we went out to dinner? She wanted to set you up with her cousin, Martha. You dodged a bullet there, bro."

"I vaguely recall her mentioning that name."

"I put her off. Told her you could find a wife of your own well enough, but that was Lily. She wanted everyone to be happy and settled."

Luke nodded, even as the image of her snarling face filled his mind. Lily was the only zombie he'd seen that he'd ever known personally. There had been some he recalled from around the area. A customer here, a shopkeeper there, but Lily was the only one he'd really known, and he couldn't quite fit the two together.

The woman she had been versus the thing she'd become.

"I couldn't do it," Pete said after a moment.

"Do what?"

"Kill her. When she turned, and she was there trying to eat me, even then I couldn't."

It was as Luke suspected and he reached out to place a hand on the other man's shoulders. "I understand."

"It was still her," Pete continued. "But she wouldn't have wanted this. She was so fucking scared, so worried. I should have done it. Should have killed her and then turned the gun on myself, but I couldn't."

"Pete…"

"And then I was fucking trapped," he added, as if he hadn't even heard Luke's whispered word. "I couldn't off myself then, knowing she was still around somewhere. I didn't know what else to do but head south. Charlie Foxtrot all around." He kicked the tire again. "Assuming another zombie hasn't taken her down, my wife is still out there somewhere, and she'd try and kill me the moment she saw me."

"Look—"

A beep sounded and Luke halted his words. Pete held up a hand, turned around, and strode over to the workbench. His walkie was on there, it crackled some, and Pete gave it a shake before heading to the garage doors, mouthing the word signal as he did so.

In a way Luke was grateful the conversation had been halted. Should he have told Pete he'd seen the Lily zombie? He wasn't sure. Which would hurt the man more? Knowing or not knowing? Luke frowned. How would he feel if Jackson were ever to…he shuddered…that was not an option. Even the thought of it made something inside of him twist.

"We have an issue," Pete said, striding back into the garage.

Luke looked up and immediately noticed the change in his

friend. Whatever feelings he'd been battling for Lily were now buried. "What kind?" Luke asked.

"Couple of packs of zombies over in Concepcion, small town not far from here. We tend to keep it cleaned out as it's our drop-off point."

"So…"

"So I need to take a couple of teams and clear it out. You okay here?"

Luke nodded. "Of course. Go."

Pete was out the door a second later, talking into his walkie as he did so. Luke grabbed his tool bag and placed it on the workbench, before taking a swig of water from the large bottle there.

It was long before their meet time but he decided to go see Jackson. At the least she'd want to know about the zombies Pete was planning to go kill. Hell, she'd probably want to go help. He almost laughed at that thought as he hurried from the garage and across the courtyard. Jackson had spent forever trying to find this camp. No way would she want to head back out again so soon. She was full of questions. Was probably finding someone to answer them for her—maybe even Nancy. He imagined the two women together and smiled. They'd be friends in no time.

He nodded to himself and sprinted to the house that was now part theirs. If he was very lucky she might even still be at home. Maybe curled up in bed, sleeping. Christ knew she needed to. He'd die a happy man if she would sleep ten hours straight.

His heart thumped as he imagined her in just her vest and panties. Or better yet naked as she had been in his arms this morning—the purple panties no more. She was so fucking beautiful. Would he ever get enough of her?

Doubtful.

I know what this is…because he did. Luke knew exactly what it was between them, had known it from the moment he'd given her that too-brief hug in the garage. It was the two of them now. Even surrounded by three hundred-odd others, it was still just the two of them.

He grinned as he pushed open the door to the room slowly, so that she'd have ample time to realize it was him. She didn't like surprises.

"Hey," he said.

But no one answered, because Jackson wasn't there.

• • •

Sebastian had indicated that the drive to the shack would take fifteen minutes at most. More than twenty minutes later—courtesy of the watch he had strapped to his wrist—and Jackson was having serious doubts about the doctor's time-keeping skills.

"Is it much farther?" she asked.

He frowned and pulled on the stick shift. "I don't know. I've never driven here myself before. Someone else usually drives and I get on with some work. So maybe it might be a little bit longer. I don't know."

She shook her head and cast him an exasperated look. Nancy was right. Sebastian was a bit kooky, but he was also honest to the point of blunt and she respected that about him.

"I'm starting to wonder about the wisdom of this, Sebastian," she said. "I'm also starting to wonder why I let you talk me into it, and I should have told Luke what we were up to."

"You have to check in with him?"

"No, of course I don't, but he'll be worried if he gets back to the room at midday and I'm not there. We said we would meet up."

"Everyone meets up at midday, so I wouldn't worry. He'll have plenty of people to talk to."

"That's not quite what I meant."

She thought of Luke busy in the garage, fixing things up, and suddenly regretted not checking in with him. She didn't want him worrying, but in truth, she just hadn't thought things through at all. She was lost and feeling a bit like a third wheel and Sebastian's need for her help had seemed like a godsend. Despite the fact she couldn't drive, he'd insisted they needed to make one quick trip— and he'd been so goofily persuasive. He'd do the driving if she was willing to be guard. Before Jackson had a chance to ask what the hell he was talking about, or anything else for that matter, he'd dragged her off to find Nancy and pass it by her.

Nancy had sighed when Sebastian told her his plan, but had nodded before taking Jackson aside.

"He's a bit odd, but the work he does is of the utmost importance, Jackson. It's fairly safe from here to the shack, so you'll be fine, and I don't doubt you can take care of yourself. You might come up against a stray zombie or two, no packs around here, though I doubt you'll even see that. I've got several teams out doing sweeps as there's an issue over by Concepcion, but that's not in your direction. That does mean, of course, that I can't really spare anyone else to go out with Sebastian, not with the internal checks we're doing, and it'd be just like him to go on his own and get himself in trouble."

"The shack?"

Nancy sighed again. "Best to see it. You'll understand what it's all about then." She shook her head and gave Jackson a long look. "I'd really appreciate it if you'd do this for us. We need you."

How could she refuse that? A role, a way to contribute. She couldn't—it was exactly what she needed at just the right time. But then there was Luke. She needed to be back by midday. She'd have to be quite stern with Sebastian about that. It would be hugely unfair to leave him worrying. *I should have checked in, damn it.*

"We're back by midday, okay? I don't want Luke to worry."

Sebastian frowned and pressed down on the accelerator. "I get the impression you can take care of yourself, Jackson. Which is why, as you put it, I asked you to do this. But don't worry, we'll be back well before then. We've got hours and hours."

"I'm having serious doubts about your math skills. It's already after ten. We'll have to turn around as soon as we get there."

"I only need to make a quick check," he insisted. "Besides you'll be glad I talked you into this, believe me. I've never understood why everyone at camp stops work in the middle of the day. For my work, at least it is the perfect time. It's hot, which means the wakers are at their most sluggish."

"The wakers? Do you mean the zombies?"

He nodded. "I do."

"So why not call them that?"

"Because of my work."

Jackson frowned. Once again he wasn't really making sense, and yet she sensed there was something important going on. Answers to her questions maybe. "You still haven't told me what your work is."

"And I won't. Like I said, you need to see it to appreciate it. All you need to know right now is that I need your help. Really need your help."

"Well at least Nancy knows what we're doing. I don't want everyone thinking I've upped and left already!"

He grinned and pressed the accelerator too hard. They jerked forward. "Ah here we are."

In the distance, on the edge of a long field, Jackson could see a large building. It might have been a warehouse once, or some sort of depot. Her first thought was that it was the perfect place for hiding zombies.

"Do you do a security sweep when you arrive?" she asked.

Sebastian shot her a look and shrugged. "Whoever comes with me handles that, I guess. I haven't ever. That's your job."

"I think one is most definitely in order. That place is huge and they could be hiding."

"No they don't hide. Their intelligence may be increasing at an alarming rate, but I don't think they've quite got the patience for that yet. Besides it's all locked up."

"Luke and I have seen some things. Including them disabling locks."

Sebastian actually smiled, as if the idea pleased him. "Really? Well that is interesting. Almost as interesting as how the wakers got Sammy to do what they want—which I've yet to find out. Mack won't let me speak with her." He shook his head, clearly annoyed. "But actually, Jack, can I call you Jack? You haven't seen anything yet."

He pulled the car up in front of the building and made to get out, not even pausing to park properly. Jackson laid a hand on his arm to halt his progress. "How about you wait here while I check stuff out."

"You don't want me to come with?"

She nodded to the rifle in the foot well. "Can you actually use that?"

Sebastian shifted in his seat and scowled. "Sort of. I mean, I can if I need to. Just point and aim, right?"

That was hardly what she wanted to hear, and Jackson was seriously doubting the wisdom of her actions. Where the hell was Luke when she needed him? Luke… They'd only been apart for a few hours and already she missed him… She grimaced and gripped Mandy nice and tight before checking the Glock's position—now fully loaded courtesy of Nancy—on her waistband. Now was not the time to go all Juliet.

"Wait here," she told Sebastian. "Keep the gun aimed and ready. I'll give you a shout when all is clear. Then you can open up for me and I'll do a sweep inside. If I'm not back out in five minutes, leave."

Sebastian paused for a moment before shaking his head. His hair sort of bounced as he did so. "No. I'm going to come with you. You might be startled by what you see and you'll need me to explain so you don't…upset things."

"What's in there for me to be startled about?" she asked, the curiosity burning.

"Best you see rather than me tell you."

"Geez, come on then."

Jackson led the way as they did a check around the outside perimeter of the area. Sebastian strode along and muttered to himself. She couldn't help but compare him to Luke—who would be alert, treading with sure footsteps, probably planning how to get her out of harm's way.

Once she was assured of the building's zombie-freeness they went in through the small locked door by the parked car, Sebastian fumbling with the key and fumbling again as he relocked it behind him. The smell of lemons hit immediately and Jackson frowned. It wasn't fresh, clean, zingy lemons, but ever so slightly rancid. She held a hand to her mouth as they moved inside and she wasn't even sure what she expected to see, but wasn't massively surprised to see the whole inner space had been opened up into one huge laboratory—all apart from one small room at the end. Sebastian was a doctor, so a lab was a given. Only thing she didn't understand was why it was so far from camp.

"What gives with this place?" she asked. "Why isn't it in camp? Surely that would be easier?

Sebastian smiled and gestured her forward. Skylights gave them plenty of light as they strode through the lab, though the metal bars spaced a half inch apart sort of sent it in shafts, giving the room a checkered look. "Easier in some ways," he said. "But not in others. Come on."

The smell got stronger as they made their way through the room, and Jackson exhaled on a whistle. "Why can I smell lemons? Old lemons?"

"Waker defense," Sebastian replied. "Citrate interferes with their sense of smell. Or it used to. Doesn't seem to work on the smarter ones anymore."

"Yeah, we noticed something like that too," Jackson said, her heart leaping at the first of what were sure to be many answers. "Do aftershaves have citrate in them?"

"Indeed they do."

So that explained it all. Jackson wondered how people had known in the beginning, how Tye had known, and felt a pang. He would so have loved this setup. She could easily see him striding alongside next to Sebastian breathing it all in with a smirk and a swing of his ax.

"It's in here that I need you for, Jack," Sebastian said, picking a key from the bunch and pulling her thoughts from her lost friend. "Mostly you just stand guard and keep an eye on the situation. Plus, if any wakers should come here you'll need to take care of them, though that's never happened before, so I wouldn't worry about that."

Something in his tone alerted Jackson and she hefted Mandy into position, ready and waiting. A shaft of light glinted off the machete and Jackson frowned. The blade needed sharpening— soon.

"I don't like surprises, Sebastian," she said. "Like, really don't."

He laughed and tugged at his hair. "Jackson, that is a damn lie. I barely know you, but I know that much already. You thrive on surprises. You need the adrenaline. It's part of who you are now. Admit it. You're a bit excited to be here. I am too. It's how we work."

"No," she began to say but paused when he gave her another laugh and pushed the door open.

Jackson didn't know what was going to be inside but she knew it was going to be something she was not going to like. Damn it, Sebastian was right. It felt weird, it *was* weird, and she *was* almost… excited? Her heart was pumping hard and her hand was twitching on her blade.

They'd spent just a night in the camp. Only yesterday she'd escaped the zombie trap, and yet here she was, out and about, and it felt almost normal to her. An image of her nice, clean room came to her. She could be sleeping on that wonderful bed, sitting on the comfy couch, even showering, but none of that appealed as much as this. Doing something, contributing in a small way... being back in the thick of things, finding answers. It was what she'd come all this way for and yet...she couldn't help wondering what the hell was wrong with her.

"You ready for this?" Sebastian asked and moved inside. Jackson followed, opening her mouth to ask what she was supposed to be ready for. But she never got the chance. The smell hit her instantly, making the rancid lemons seem almost sweet, and then the sounds. Both were horribly familiar and as Jackson moved forward, she gasped, because right there, strapped on the table in the very middle of the room, was something Jackson had hoped to see, but never expected in a million years, or two if she wanted to be accurate.

"Is that...?"

Sebastian smiled with obvious enthusiasm, rolled his sleeves up his arms, and grabbed a lab coat. "It is indeed. Jackson meet patient two hundred and three. Or as I like to call him, Two-h-ee."

She stepped forward, halted, and then took a step more. Her heart was racing, and every cell in her body was tingling. It was unbelievable. Exciting. Amazing. *Christ.*

"You're not fucking serious?" she gasped.

Sebastian glared at her tone, perhaps taking her words of surprise in completely the wrong way, but then Two-h-ee glared too, and he had no way to understand nuances. *Two-he-ee*...or as Jackson would call it, the fucking zombie.

CHAPTER THIRTY

The camp was not that fucking big! Where the hell was she? Luke growled as he made his way across the courtyard for probably the hundredth time, wondering where the hell he could possibly check next. It was half past twelve, well past their agreed time to meet, and yet no one seemed to know where Jackson was, except for the fact that she was with Dr. Sebastian—the resident medical man and zombie expert. A few people thought Nancy might have more information. But Nancy was nowhere to be seen either.

Luke passed by one of the housing clusters—waved back absently to an elderly woman who was in one of the upstairs windows—and took a deep, trying-to-be-calming breath. If Jackson was late because she was busy working on something with the doctor, fine. It was inconsiderate of her, but he could suck it up if she was doing something that made her happy. What concerned him was *where* she was doing it.

Pete's words rung in his ears—*we head straight back out*—competing with the things Jackson had told him. How badly she had wanted to find safety. The fact she had walked for years on the slim chance that there might be something more. And yet as the minutes ticked by, as he thought about Pete's words and Jackson's behavior the whole time he'd known her, his certainty that she was somewhere in camp began to wane.

Images filled his head as he walked past another trio of houses. Images he'd never really even considered before. The rubbing of the blade's wooden hilt over and over again—probably she didn't even know she was doing it most the time. It was obsessive. Like the actions of someone with OCD in the old world. The emotionless look in her eyes as she cut through zombie flesh. Luke had never seen her scared or even angry when she had beheaded them. Sure, beforehand, maybe even afterward, but during? No. She locked it all away and just did what she had to do. And the lack of sleep— four hours a day, at most. Surely no one could live on such little rest forever, not without some sort of effect?

She's good at this life. Why hadn't he realized that before?

"Sorry, didn't see you there…oh…"

Luke turned the corner to see a tall, skinny, gray-haired dude dodge out of his way, a pile of papers in his hands, a pen hanging out of his mouth.

Dr. Sebastian in the flesh.

"Not a problem," he told the doctor, his jaw practically grinding. *Keep calm.* "I'm Luke, by the way."

"Ah," Sebastian said, pushing the pen into the front pocket of his shirt. It was such a geek gesture that Luke wanted to roll his eyes. The guy was like a fucking walking cliché. The gray hair, the abstract air to him. Really he only needed a pair of glasses to be the epitome of a man of science. "Yes, Luke. Of course. It's good to meet you."

He held out a hand, which Luke took. The other man had a firm grip and Luke raised an eyebrow in surprise. He hadn't expected that.

"I'm glad I've bumped into you, actually," Luke said and Sebastian dropped his hand.

"If it's a medical issue, you're better going to Layla," Sebastian

said, taking a step back. "She's a fully qualified nurse, and I only
deal with our major injuries."

Luke shook his head. He was fit and even the hole on his
stomach was beginning to turn a dull pink now, the skin stretched
taut across where the wound used to be. Jackson had taken the
stitches out for him two weeks ago. She'd done a poor, poor job of
it, but Luke had not complained. He never did when she had her
hands on him.

"Not a medical issue," he said. "I'm just wondering. Someone
mentioned you were with Jackson earlier and I wanted to know
where she is."

Sebastian shifted and moved the papers he was holding from
hand to hand. "Last I saw she was heading for the main house."

"I checked there."

"Oh, well I headed back to my room after," Sebastian said,
finally settling on which hand to hold them in. "So I don't know.
She's probably here somewhere, though. It's not like there's
anywhere else for her to go is there?" He ended on a laugh and
Luke's eyes widened as he took in the doctor's feeble attempt for
a joke.

"Right…"

"Maybe check your room again?" Sebastian suggested. "She's
probably waiting for you there."

"Will do."

The doctor nodded, muttered something unintelligible, and
strode off in the opposite direction to the way he'd been going.
Luke shook his head and let the other man go, before turning and
heading back to their room. Hoping to God Jackson had actually
returned.

As angry and worried as he was, when Luke approached their
room he opened the door slowly so Jackson wouldn't be startled.
Relief—pure, unadulterated relief—filled him as Jackson turned
from where she'd been unlacing her boots and shot him a smile.

It seemed both happy and relieved—and maybe a little bit guilty. He couldn't help but notice she'd reached out for her machete too.

"Hey," she said, "you all done?"

A million thoughts hit Luke then—each wavering for prominence. Pete's words of warning. Her flushed face and sparkling eyes. He closed the door and leaned against the closet, taking a deep breath as he did so. She was back, that was the main thing, safe and well. The rest could wait for just a fucking moment.

"Where have you been?" he asked, trying to keep his voice calm, but realized almost immediately that actually the words sounded the demand all by themselves. They hardly needed a tone to make them worse.

She frowned and tilted her head. "Finding something to do, of course. It took *way* longer than I thought. I'm so sorry I'm late. I didn't want you to worry."

"I did worry though," he said. "I thought we were going to meet at midday? I came to find you, but you were nowhere to be found." He knew he sounded ridiculous. Like some sort of possessive idiot, but he couldn't seem to stop himself.

"Oh, well. I got kinda busy," she said, kicking one unlaced boot off before making a start on the other. "It took longer than I thought it would. I'm sorry, Luke."

"I've been looking everywhere. I was worried about you."

She frowned and shifted. "Again, I'm sorry. I didn't mean to worry you. You know I'd never do that on purpose."

"You did though, Jack," he said. "I've been fucking panicking." *Deep breath. Don't get worked up.*

"About what?" she asked. "What did you think would happen?"

He growled, his anger increasing with her words. Had it really not occurred to her that he'd be concerned? That after their weeks together he'd want to make sure she was okay? *Ah but you left her this morning,* his mind whispered, *you went first.* He told it to shut the fuck up.

"Luke?" she prompted. "Do you think there's something off about the camp? Are they planning to feed us to the zombies?"

He started and shook his head. "No. Of course not. It's fine. Everyone's good. But Christ, Jack, I checked everywhere. We live in the world of the dead. Many things could've happened. I surely don't need to list them for you because it all kind of starts and ends in one. Zombie."

"You keep telling me we're safe here," she said slowly. "And you encouraged me to go out and about and find something to do."

"Yes…" *Fuck.* She was totally twisting his words and Luke scowled, his mind a whirr of confusion, before latching onto the only thing he really had to complain about. "I thought we were going to meet at midday?"

"Yeah," she said. "Like I said, I am sorry. I tried to get back here in time but it was just madness. But I'm here now."

She stepped forward, her movements accentuating the sway of her hips and Luke groaned inwardly. Now was not the time for this. He wanted to know what the hell she'd been up to!

"Jack—"

"I'll tell you about it later, okay? For now, how about you put your arms around me?"

Luke rubbed a hand through his hair and tried to hold onto the anger. Jackson had to realize that she had to consider him, just as he'd resolved to consider her. "We need to talk first," he insisted. "About what happened today. About what you were up to."

She shook her head. "No, we don't. Not yet."

"But what have you been doing? Why were you so late? What did you find to do?"

She closed the distance between them, tilting her head to look into his eyes.

"Later. I need this right now, Luke. Take me in your arms,

please."

How could he possibly refuse that? With a sigh, Luke reached forward and pulled her the last foot or so to him. She was so slight that his arms completely enveloped her.

"I need to know."

"After," she said.

"You'll tell me," he insisted and she nodded.

That was all he was going to get right now. It would *have* to do. Luke pushed all the other thoughts from his mind, concentrating instead on the feel of Jackson's lips as soon as his touched hers.

Soft. Always so soft. He moved against them, holding them within his own. Jackson moaned slightly and his tongue lightly brushed against hers—just the way he knew she liked it. Jackson responded by tugging at the hem of his tee, and he allowed her to lift it up, pulling apart only so she could push it over his head. He did the same to hers, before dragging her vest off until they were both naked from the waist up.

"I want you, Luke," she whispered and his whole body thrummed in anticipation even as he called himself all sorts of a fool for falling for her wiles. But she tied him in knots. Had done since he'd seen her purple panties running down the street.

"Immediately."

He lifted her, she wrapped her legs around him, and he carried her to the bed, where he gently deposited her. She reached for the button of her jeans, undoing them in one quick movement and he mirrored her actions. Eyes fixed on one another they each removed the last of their clothing until nothing remained between them.

"I dreamed about this," Luke said, kneeling in front of her.

"Us?" she asked.

"Yes, but this exactly. Seeing you on a bed, spread out before me. Nothing to worry about, nothing to hurry for."

She smiled and held out a hand. "It's not the first time we've christened this bed, babe."

"I know," he agreed. "But last night was fast and frantic. We were both desperate weren't we?"

"Uh-huh."

"Besides it seems like days ago," he added. "The hours pass far too quickly when nothing is jumping out from the shadows."

"The shadows are still here."

"Not right now."

"No, maybe not."

"And it's the first time without Mandy under the pillow," he whispered, wondering even to himself why that seemed important.

Her eyes flicked to the weapon and she frowned ever so slightly. "Just this once, Luke, because I worried you, I promise to leave it there and not to even think about it."

"Just you and me, Jack," he said. "Let it just be about us. Not about the dead or the world. Just let me love you."

She shivered beneath him. He could actually see her pale skin move and Luke's heart thumped harder than it ever had before. Both before the end of the world and after. *I know what this is…*

"Come here then," she whispered. "Just us. I promise. Just me and my Luke."

Yes, he knew what it was. It was clear and obvious to him now. Why the hell else had he been so frantic for her? So worried about Pete's words. So worried full fucking stop. He loved Jackson. The kind of love that a man waits for. The kind of love that nothing can ever really put a stop to. Not even a horde of zombies or the end of the goddamn world.

But even as he leaned forward and kissed the smile from her perfect lips, turning it instead into a sigh of pleasure, he knew something else. Though *he* knew it through and through, from the tips of his toes to the ends of his hair, Jackson did not.

• • •

After two years of what had to be the closest to hell a person could ever get, the only peace Jackson had ever found was in Luke's arms, and she needed it now more than ever. Because today she'd found out that the struggle and the pain and all the other stuff was not at an end, not even close.

It was just beginning.

She sighed as Luke's lips left hers and pressed against her neck—one of her most sensitive areas. Closing her eyes tightly, Jackson pushed away the thought of Two-h-ee, concentrating instead on the way Luke's touch made her feel. Because what else could make her forget, even if only for a little bit? Nothing but Luke, of course, only he had the ability to make the worries recede.

Guilt battled with the pleasure. The guilt of leaving him to worry and wonder. Jackson resolved never to do so again. Luke would always know where she was from here on in. Not because she was obligated to, or because Luke demanded it, but because it was the right thing to do. Because he deserved that from her, that and so much more.

"I love the taste of you," Luke whispered. "Even when we were running for our lives and showering was—how shall I put it?—infrequent, you tasted so good."

"What do I taste like?" she wondered.

"Like Jackson."

His lips fired her nerve endings. One slight touch against her neck and the most delicious shivers made their languid way along her collarbone and down through her belly. And then he moved, kissing another spot and this time the shivers zipped around her neck down her spine, centering right at the bottom and radiating out. How could she describe them? Like the kisses were actually inside, under her skin, but superfast, running and racing and sizzling. Jackson sighed and lifted a hand to hold onto the back of

Luke's head. His hair ran through her fingers, soft and silky.

"Luke," she said. "Let me feel you against me."

His breath fanned against the cool spots he'd just kissed and he laughed softly. "I'll crush you, you're so skinny."

"I want to feel you," she insisted.

"How is it you can make me do whatever you want?" he asked.

"Can I?"

"I think so. If you tried."

"Then do this."

He lowered himself, proving his point, until his whole body covered her, holding his weight on his elbows. Jackson sighed as his skin touched hers. Chest hair brushing against her nipples, his muscled arms against her sides, holding her in place. Then too she could feel the length of him between her legs and she smiled, because soon she would feel him inside of her and it would feel like nothing else in the entire world could. It would brush away all the worries about Sebastian and his crazy, amazing, plans for just a little while—plans that she had a nasty suspicion she was inexorably linked to. Because how could she walk away? The questions that had plagued her for the past two years could be answered now. Sebastian could answer them and she was too damn curious not to let him.

She was trapped.

By him.

By herself.

Worse, by the zombies still.

"So pretty," Luke breathed. "I could spend hours just looking at you."

Jackson sighed, letting Luke's words carry away the thoughts of Seb and the dead and anything else. "You'd get bored."

"Never."

He moved his lips to her ear, pressing little feathery kisses, and she moaned, practically melting into the fucking bed. "No, no, no," she said. "Not the ear."

But he did, licking his way up and down the lobe until Jackson had to press her thighs around him, holding him in place, shifting beneath him, wanting, needing more.

He tugged on the end of her lobe and she pulled her head to the side. The sensations were too exquisite. They made her feel frantic inside, almost unbearable. A gentle hand brought her back to center and Luke took her mouth. His lips completely wrapping up her own, devouring everything she had to give. His tongue danced in and she chased it back into his own mouth, he doing the same, over and over until they were both panting. And then with one slight movement, one difference in the angle, he slipped into her. Jackson gasped and arched her hips, wrapping her arms tightly around him, reveling in the feel of him on top of her, in her, around her.

She was completely consumed in Luke and she loved it.

He drew out before moving oh so slowly back in. Jackson tightened her thighs and moved with him. Together in and out, back and forth. His length worked her, pulling along her nerves and making her entire body clench.

"Jackson," he groaned. "I…"

The inner kisses started to chase through her body all over again but this time they were far more intense. Sizzling up her spine and scorching along her thighs. Burning her entire body and she moaned, before realizing Luke was speaking.

"What is it, Luke? What?"

He shook his head, making other parts shake and moved again. "Nothing…"

She kissed the nothing away from his lips. Tiny kisses that ran across the flesh and along his jawline. She threaded her hands in his hair before moving down to his back. Slight scars raised under her fingers and Jackson trailed along them, caressing them.

He groaned again as she settled each hand over his lower

back, pushing him into her, positioning him just as she liked. Over and over, again and again they moved, and Jackson forgot what she meant or even what he meant, it was all lost in the fire, all consumed by the scorch, and throughout she didn't look at Mandy.

Not even once.

CHAPTER THIRTY-ONE

She might have been sleeping. Luke wasn't sure. On the off chance that she actually was, he crept out of bed slowly, trying to remain as quiet as possible. He paused for just a moment at the foot of the bed, he kinda couldn't help himself, and looked down at her tousled form. Her short, spiky hair framed her delicate face. It was slightly damp and he imagined how it would look falling in waves down her back. Beautiful, no doubt. But that was the old Jackson. This was the new, and this Jackson was his. The spiky hair was beautiful in its own way.

He padded across the room, the peace he felt after their lovemaking warring with his previous worries and Luke sighed. *Not now. Just leave me for a little bit, damn you.*

It was startlingly bright out and he pushed the curtain aside to look around. A few people walked back and forth but all looked fairly calm. Nothing was amiss. Whatever had allowed that zombie to get in seemed to have been dealt with. He hoped so, at least. Jackson would not begin to relax until she felt marginally safe. Though whether the camp was going to be safe enough for her, he didn't know.

Where was she? What was she doing? Why do I get the feeling that I don't want to know? The thoughts assailed him and Luke gritted his teeth as he opened the bathroom door. He used the toilet—one that actually flushed—washed his hands, and then ran some water over his face. It was icy cold and that was welcome. The heat at this time of day was particularly brutal and he could understand why the rest of the camp paused and why both he and Jackson had been slick with sweat by the time they had finished.

He eyed himself in the mirror, pushing the bad thoughts away, rubbed along his jaw, and frowned. A shave was so needed and soon. The stubble he'd sported for the last few days was not looking good. Jackson would probably be covered in marks for the next couple of days. He grinned slightly and rubbed the stubble again. Why did that make him feel good? That he'd marked her with his loving. Maybe because she had so many scars. Not in obvious places. But they were there all the same. On her back and her chest, one running down her thigh, another snaking its way around her left arm.

Stretching, Luke pushed open the shower door. He'd planned to save his shower for later, but he was sweaty and knew he smelled musky. The cold water would do him good. Almost ready him, in a way, for the conversation he knew was going to come. The moment Jackson told him whatever it was she'd been up to. Whatever had made her late.

And he was fairly fucking certain he knew what it was now. Her reaction had told him plenty. Jackson was going to tell him that she was helping to defend the community...and what could he say to that? He could hardly forbid her. Despite whatever thrummed between them, Jackson would not stand for being told what to do. She was far too independent for that, and though he sort of thought she'd listen to him and hear his concerns, she'd still do whatever felt right to her. But then where the hell did Sebastian fit into it all? The doctor was up to something. Luke was certain of it, but for the life of him he couldn't work out how it involved

Jackson. And a small part, just a little bit, really, wondered if he was going to have to tell Sebastian exactly what the lay of the land was. That Jackson was his and to stay the hell away.

Luke stepped into the shower stall and turned the water on, scowling as his thoughts ran and whirred and pushed inside him for prominence. A minute earlier and he would have missed it, but a minute could often make all kinds of a difference and just as the spray hit the shower floor he heard an odd sound from the bedroom. His scowl deepened because clearly Jackson was not asleep and he wanted her to be. She *needed* it. If she'd just do eight hours, he'd be a happy man. But what was that? What was she doing? It sounded like…he paused and carefully stepped back out of the stall, tilting his head back to look into the bedroom. Yes, just as he'd thought.

Jackson sat on the bed, legs crossed, feet tucked under her. Her pack was open on the bed, she wore nothing but her skin and had Mandy's wooden hilt draped across her thighs, the blade against the mattress. She held an ellipse shaped stone in her right hand. Up and down it went, *swish, swish, swish.*

She must have crept out of bed to get the machete and he wanted to rally at her for that—but how could he? How could he possibly even think to? Her face was set into a look of pure concentration, her hands finding the rhythm so easily. *Swish, swish, swish.*

She was sharpening the blade. Readying her weapon for use, and he realized then that his thoughts had probably been on the mark. Bang on.

For a few minutes he stood there, half in the bathroom and half out, watching the play of her hands and the stone moving back and forth, back and forth. Conflicting feelings, conflicting thoughts all running through him. When he could stand it no longer he spoke.

"Jack?"

She looked up but her hands did not cease her motion. *Swish,*

swish, swish. "Yeah?"

"You were going to tell me," he said slowly. "Tell me what you were doing today. Why you were late back here. What you found to do."

Jackson shifted, though the stone continued to move, and shot him a look he couldn't quite decipher. "You don't want to shower first?"

Luke's gut did a kind of flip-flop and he swallowed. "No."

"But you're wasting the water."

And water was not to be wasted. It was one of the main rules of the camp. In this heat, it was a precious commodity. "Here's the deal then," he said. "You tell me exactly what you were doing today. Then, because I'm probably not going to like it, I'll go shower and think it over and then we can talk. Deal?"

"Why do you assume it'll be something you won't like?" she asked. *Swish, swish, swish.*

"Because of that." He pointed to Mandy, and even he could hear the catch in his voice. "Because you're sharpening her for something and it no doubt involves them."

"I found a job," she said, nodding slowly. "Something useful, Luke."

"A job?"

Swish, swish, swish. "Yep," she said. "Go and have your shower and then I'll tell you. Because, it seems that fantasies really do come true, and Mandy and I are needed after all."

• • •

Jackson frowned as the pounding of the low-powered shower spray almost, though not quite, covered the sound of Luke's mutterings. He was angry with her. She thought he would be—the whole protectiveness thing rearing its head again—and because part of her understood the reason for it, she also wondered if she should have been a little bit more diplomatic. But diplomacy had never been her strong point and she sure as hell wasn't used to explaining her actions to anyone. She just seemed to blurt things out these days and before Luke there'd been no one to care. Tye certainly hadn't. *But Luke is different.*

She sighed. Yes, Luke was different, but then everything was different, and right now Sebastian's offer was the only thing making sense to her. It was exactly what she had dreamed of. What getting south was all about, and even now, after all the things Sebastian had shown her, she could barely believe it was real.

"Luke will get it," she told herself.

Luke always got her. Even though she knew she was a bit off he'd never once made her feel odd about it. She frowned and finished rubbing Mandy's tip. The man showering just a few yards away played on her mind. She felt so damn guilty about making him worry about her. It was a mean thing to do, and though it was mainly Sebastian's crappy fault, she couldn't blame him completely. She'd wanted to find out everything about Two-h-ee and all the others that had come before it, and what it all meant.

Jackson bent down until she was eye level with her blade and squinted at the tip. She could see a knick on the top and wondered whose skull bone had caused it. There was no way to tell. She'd killed so many. Hundreds and hundreds... She made to smooth the dent out but pulled back just in time. Mandy was wicked sharp now and the blade would break her skin. Still, all in all, she was standing up to the demands Jackson had put her through. There were many more years left in the old gal yet.

The sound of running water ceased and Jackson placed Mandy on the small bed table next to her, the silvery blade glinting in the light. A harbinger of death to any zombie who dared cross her path. An odd image of herself, sitting, gray-haired, shaky hands, polishing the blade, filled her mind and she half smiled. It was a ridiculous idea. She'd probably be dead by then.

"Time to spill, sweetheart."

Luke stood in the doorway, jeans hanging low on his hips. His chest was sprinkled with water and she couldn't help but give a little sigh. His hair was mussed and he hadn't shaved yet. She hoped he didn't. The rough stubble so worked.

"Of course."

He sat himself down on the edge of the bed and held his hand out to her. Jackson didn't hesitate before scooting across, placing her hand within his. His skin was cool to the touch and she paused for just a moment to allow her gaze to drift up his chest, down his arms, and then back up again. Like most people left in the world, Luke was very toned. They had to be. It was all about being able to use a weapon or run like an athlete. If you couldn't do either of those, you were as good as dead. She too was toned and looking down at herself now it occurred to Jackson that she would have had a runner's body back in the old days. All sinewy muscles and perfect abs. She'd have had to work herself to death in the gym to even come close but she suspected that the abundance of food back then would have defeated her perfect body plans. It would not be a lie to say she'd once had a lot to love.

"What have they got you doing, Jack?" Luke asked, pulling her thoughts from her old shape.

"They haven't *got* me doing anything."

"Okay," he said. "I phrased that wrong. Let's start again. What are you doing? This job you mentioned—what is it?"

He was uncomfortable. She could tell and it made *her* uncomfortable. She wanted Luke to be happy. Happy with her decisions. Happy with her. It was such a weird feeling, so hard for her to get her head around. For so long, Jackson had counted on and thought of no one but herself, but now Luke was part of those thoughts and she had to consider him when she made a decision. They were together, and that meant something.

"First off, let me just say," Jackson began, "that I did not complain when you told me you were going to work in the garage.

I was happy for you."

Luke squeezed her hand and frowned. "Now I'm worried, because you wouldn't be qualifying your answer beforehand if it was something I was going to like."

She almost laughed. Luke was so on to her. "Well, you thought that anyway. But no, I'm just trying to explain it to you. No, not explain. I don't need to explain myself. I meant try and make you understand."

"Shoot then."

"Have you met Sebastian yet?"

He scowled. "Briefly."

"You know he's the doctor?" she asked, deciding to ignore the scowl.

"I do."

"Well, after you left for work this morning I went out. I was planning to have a look around, scope out the place, like I said. Anywhos I didn't get far. I ran into Sebastian straightaway. He grabbed me some breakfast and then he asked me for some help."

The scowl remained. "What kind of help, Jack?"

"He's not a normal doctor, Luke."

"That he's not. The guy's got some weird vibe going on."

Jackson tilted her head. Had Luke already heard what Sebastian was up to? She hadn't even considered that, but he'd been out and about all day, so why the hell not. "What's that supposed to mean?"

Luke shrugged and tickled his fingers along her palm. She shivered. "Nothing. Just that he's a bit odd."

And that he was. Jackson had met some weird people in her life, more so since the end of the world—in the early months at least. But there was no doubt that Sebastian took the crown.

"Well yeah," she agreed. "He is, but then so am I. Hell we're all a bit odd these days, apart from you, of course. You're the most normal person I've met."

"Hardly. So come on then, spill."

How to start? She wished Luke had been there when she'd encountered Sebastian. That it had all been explained to them together. "He's doing things," she began. "Amazing things."

"What sort of things?"

"With the zombies."

Luke paused in his palm strokage and sucked in a deep breath. "And…"

She paused too before she spoke again. Wondering exactly what Luke was going to think. How best to frame it? Because it would be so much easier if Luke could actually see it, rather than hear it, and then maybe he'd get what Sebastian was doing and why she now had to do what she'd agreed to do.

"It's complicated and I think you're going to be shocked."

"You constantly shock me, Jack."

"Yes…" And then she frowned, because it suddenly occurred to her that there wasn't any reason Luke *shouldn't* see it. Sebastian was planning to head back out tomorrow morning, but there was absolutely nothing to stop her and Luke from going now. They weren't prisoners in the camp. They were free to come and go when they chose, and she remembered the route perfectly. "You know," she said after a moment. "It *is* better for you to see it. That'll explain everything in a way I'm not going to be able to. Come on, get dressed, and grab your weapons."

"Are you serious?"

Jackson tugged his hand, jumped from the bed, and grabbed her jeans. "Aren't I always?"

"We don't need weapons in camp, though. It's safe here, Jack. I mean, yeah, okay admittedly, I've been carrying my gun, but there's no need for the ax."

She pulled her jeans on, shivering a little from the rough denim on her sore skin. Knowing too that Luke was not going to like her next words. Not one bit.

"Yeah, but we're not gonna be in camp."

He sighed and shot her a scowl. "Please tell me you didn't."

Jackson picked up her wrinkled vest and pulled it overhead, playing for time more than anything.

"Didn't what?"

"Go back outside without me."

She bent down to find her boots. One was on its side under the blond-wood table.

"Of course, I did," she said without apology. "That's where the zombies are. Now get dressed and I'll show you exactly what Sebastian is up to. Believe me Luke, once you've seen this, nothing will be the same. Then you'll understand."

Chapter Thirty-two

Why the hell they called it a shack, Luke didn't know. It was far from that. In fact, the building was a little bit too big for his tastes and he pulled their car up slowly. On the plus side, it wasn't a built-up area, and he couldn't see any zombies, so he had to take the points where he could. He eased off the gas, applied the hand brake, and grabbed his ax. His gun was digging into his back and the sweat wasn't helping any. For a moment he imagined the cool air of the north, but then he remembered the zombies and he imagined it no more.

"Security check?" he asked and Jackson beamed at him.

"Exactly what I said when we came here. Sebastian doesn't have a fucking clue about security. But I think he was right about one thing. I don't reckon they'd be able to get in here. It's all locked up pretty tight."

"What's it for?" he asked. "You've been extremely tight-lipped."

She shook her head. "Nuh-uh, like I said, you gotta see."

He sighed. "If it's locked up tight, how are we going to get in?"

Jackson lifted her hips and pulled a small key from her jean pocket.

"Sebastian gave me this. Seems like I'll need it in the future."

Luke took a deep breath and shook his head. "Jesus, the more I think about it the more I have a feeling I don't want to know."

She smiled and planted a quick kiss on his cheek. His skin tingled all around the spot.

"Let's do a perimeter check and then we can get started."

They saw nothing out of the ordinary as they walked around the building, apart from the fact that it was all perfectly quiet — which in itself was a little unusual. No groans or grunts or howls or signs of anything not quite alive. Luke took everything in as he walked, almost enjoying the somnolent air of the area. The birds chirping in the trees, the smell of fresh grass, not to mention the company.

Despite his anger and his worry, and hell, his nerves, it was almost a relief to be back out with Jackson. Even though he couldn't quite believe that she'd proved Pete right already. How long had she lasted, a few fucking hours? His mind grabbed at the thought and batted it back and forth but he pushed it away. It might not mean anything in the long term. Pete could well be wrong. And besides, it had not escaped his notice that Jackson clearly thought that she needed to be doing this, and it pleased him in a strange sort of way to see her happy—well, as happy as Jackson seemed to get. And then there was the fact that whatever she was doing with Sebastian didn't sound like it had to do with protecting the community, so maybe he'd just have to suck it up and take the good with the bad. Yes, she'd be out of the camp getting her slay on, but at least it would be here in this quiet field…

"Feels like old times," Jackson said, dragging his thoughts back to her.

"Old times being yesterday?"

She laughed and twirled Mandy in her hand. "Seems like ages ago. Maybe my mind's making it sort of distant so I'm not traumatized."

Luke shook his head slowly at her tone. "You? Traumatized?"
"Yep."

"Jack," he began. "There's no doubt you're that, but you'll never admit it, so it doesn't even count. Yesterday we barely survived and yet here you are out again in the thick of it."

Despite his own internal reassurances he wanted to say more. He wanted to tell her what Pete had said but he didn't even know how to start. She'd be angry. Worse, she'd brush off his concerns, and when it came right down to it he didn't know which idea he hated more: that she might pull away from him or that she'd be indifferent.

She waved a hand around. "We're fine here, and I'm going to ignore that comment. You'll see why in a minute."

"Right."

She stood in the shadow of a large tree and he couldn't help but sigh inwardly. She looked so damn pretty. Her hair was spiking up wildly around her face. Her beautiful face. And she looked more rested than he'd ever seen. Yeah, okay, her hand was clamped around Mandy and she had "the look" in her eye, but she was grinning at him. Plus there was the fact that at least now he didn't have to spend his time worrying about what she was up to or what she might be plotting. Here out in the open was like their default mechanism. They'd spent so long on the road together it felt oddly normal and in that brief moment he had a little flash of what being in the camp might be like for Jackson.

Not normal at all. And she probably didn't even realize.

"Come on," she said.

They made their way back around the building and Jackson opened up the small front door, ushered him, and turned to lock it behind her. "To keep them out when we're in here," she said before pocketing the key. "Though they've never actually come here before, according to Sebastian. Maybe they know what this place is."

Luke was not shocked by what he saw. The size maybe, but not the actuality. Of course, it made sense. Hadn't he thought the doctor was some sort of kook? But as Jackson tugged him forward and began to point out various things on the shelves Luke realized exactly what was going on. Realized and felt his heart sink all the way down to his shoes. Kook didn't even begin to cover it.

"Where is it?" he asked. "Or maybe I should say they."

Jackson's jaw dropped and she gaped at him. "How did you know?"

"It's obvious."

She heaved Mandy and gestured forward. They walked to the door at the far end of the room and Luke took a deep breath, the smell of old lemons settling on him. This wasn't the first time he'd seen such a lab. In the very early days scientists all over the world had searched for a cure. They'd given up after a couple of months though, mostly because they'd been eaten. But they'd tried and he remembered seeing one on TV—before it too had died. So it didn't surprise him now to see that someone was still trying, and Sebastian was just the type to give it a go.

"Lemons," he said and Jackson nodded.

"Zombie defense, at least for the ones that haven't smarted up yet. It's the citrate, like in aftershaves. How did you know they didn't like aftershave?" she asked and he shrugged.

"I don't remember. Someone knew and it just…" He paused. "It became a sort of fact I guess, like the heat."

Nodding, Jackson unlocked the second door, with the same key, and pushed it open. Luke turned his head slightly from the stench, which was suddenly overpowering in such a small space, taking shallow breaths.

A hand settled on his and Jackson spoke. "Meet Two-h-ee," she said and though he didn't really want to, he shifted and he looked.

The zombie, a male in life, was strapped down on a long

wooden table. It actually looked like a dining room table and he frowned. Clearly Sebastian had been short on supplies. The table was secured to the floor by dint of the fact that it was surrounded by concrete a good half a foot higher than the surrounding floor. This had the advantage of both stopping the zombie from lifting itself up with the table and putting him at about the right height for whatever Sebastian was up to. Thick lengths of rope were secured around its middle, legs, and arms, which were positioned outward, like some sort of sacrificial victim. Which, Luke guessed, it kind of was.

Handcuffs added another layer of security as did the metal chain links around the thighs. Yep, it was wrapped up properly all right, but Luke knew it wasn't safe. He knew this because he and Jackson wouldn't be here if it was.

"So," he said, after a moment. "What has this got to do with you?" He suspected, of course, but he wanted to hear it from her.

"Well he needs help," Jackson said, circling Two-h-ee. "Nancy won't let him work on them in the camp. It's too much of a risk, so he brings them here instead."

"That's not how one got into camp then?"

"Nope. She's been firm on that from the very beginning."

Luke scowled and bent down to check Two-h-ee's handcuffs. He couldn't help himself. The damn thing was right there, just sort of looking at them. "That's something, at least."

"She's been assigning him guards to go with him and wait here while he works," Jackson continued, "but it is not a favored job at all. The smell for one thing. He's run through mostly everyone, and I guess he thought since I'm new and all, that I'd be willing."

And there it was. Luke tugged on the metal rope length, holding his breath while he did so. Maybe because of the smell, maybe because he knew what she was going to say to his next question. "And are you?"

She shrugged and tugged on the rope bindings. "It sounds

like important work, Luke." She paused and pointed to Two-h-ee. "He's looking for a cure."

Luke laughed. It really could not be helped. "Yep, I got that, Jack. It's kind of fucking obvious. But you know he's in dreamland right? There is no cure. The zombies are dead. How the hell is he gonna cure that?"

"Well, I don't know exactly. I didn't understand a lot of what he said. But he thinks he's on to something. He wasn't a regular doctor before this. He was a biochemist or something.

"Yeah well he doesn't exactly seem like doctor material, does he? He'd have a shit bedside manner."

"Luke."

"I'm sorry, Jack," Luke said, though he wasn't, not really. "But this is totally fucked up. You've got a weird doctor who thinks he's going to save the world and you're going along with it? People tried in the beginning. Did you forget that?"

"Of course I didn't."

"And they failed," Luke added. "Hoping for something like this now, it's…" He shook his head. "It's wrong. Some things can't be fixed, certainly not by some guy in a half-baked lab in the middle of nowhere."

Jackson glared. "You don't know him."

"And neither do you," Luke said. "You only just met the guy. For all we know he could be a complete nut job. Something this important, Jack, I'd need to know a lot more before I can even began to hope for it."

"There is more," she said, waving a hand around the room. "He has all sorts of research, from the beginning, when there wasn't time to make a proper go of it. The zombies bit too many people and then they were either turned or were eaten. There wasn't anyone left to have a go at finding a cure."

"Jack," Luke said, stepping back from Two-h-ee, who had now begun to groan and snap its teeth. "That's my entire point.

There's no one left anymore to *actually* cure. This," he pointed to the zombie, watching as a rivulet of pus dripped from a wound on its head, down its cheek and into its mouth, "is dead. They're all dead. You can't cure dead people."

Jackson looked up at him then, and of all things, grinned. "Well, that's the point, Luke," she said. "And brace yourself now. But the thing is…they're not actually zombies."

· · ·

She'd never seen Luke look so uncomfortable. Throughout it all, for weeks and weeks, he'd been watchful, protective, easygoing, just about everything but this. He started at her words and ran his gun hand through his hair, the pistol pointing to the ceiling. A groan sounded and Jackson tore her gaze away to chance a quick glance at Two-h-ee. It surprised her to see that it too was looking at the pointing gun—maybe because it knew? Sebastian had said Two-h-ee was one of the "clever" zombies. The ones who had started to think. Could it recognize a gun and understand what that gun could do?

"You lost me," Luke said slowly, pointing the gun back at Two-h-ee. It groaned and snapped its teeth. "Of course they're zombies."

Jackson thought about what Sebastian had told her and tried to work it through in her mind so she could explain it to Luke. Most of it was science stuff, and she knew fuck-all about that. Sebastian had gabbled on but it had got to the point where she had just nodded, feeling more and more stupid as the moments went by, but she kind of got the gist, enough to tell Luke anyway.

"No," she said eventually weaving around the tangled thoughts, "not in the strictest sense of the word. Zombies are dead people reanimated, right? Like they die and then something wakes them back up."

"When they were fiction, yeah, that *was* how it worked"

"And now they're fact and they're different. And we always thought, or guessed, that it was a virus. It infected them and when they bit other people it infected them and then they died. Sometimes they woke back up."

"Yeah, because we saw it," Luke interrupted. "They actually did die. No heartbeat, no nothing."

"Well Sebastian says that the zombies might be reanimated but they were never dead."

Luke shook his head. "Of course they are! Jesus, Jack. I saw people die, one after the other, and once they're dead, they're dead. Whether they're still walking around now is irrelevant."

"It's not, though," she insisted, trying to remember exactly what Sebastian had told her. "It's a virus. Definitely a virus. It does something to the immune system, sends it into overdrive."

"And kills them."

"No. The moment it infects, it slows the heart and decreases brain activity in some areas, increasing it in others. Once the heart stops completely, and it depends on lots of factors for how long that takes, people either die or they come back to life. Only changed."

"That's impossible," Luke breathed. "There's no way that," he pointed to Two-h-ee, "is still alive."

"But he is," she insisted and just like when Sebastian had told her this, a queer feeling snaked through her body. The fact that the zombie was just a very sick person. A person who was riddled with a virus that had changed him. As she looked at Two-h-ee she began to wonder what his life might have been like before he changed. And that shit just did not fly, because Jackson did *not* think about things like that, not since the moral dilemma all those months ago. It was not the way she worked! It couldn't be.

"Hold on a minute…we shoot them and they get back up," Luke said. "They lose entire limbs and don't give a fuck."

"They don't really feel pain and they have a highly increased rate of healing," Jackson replied with a shrug. "So if we shoot them in certain places they can survive it…though Seb did say it's likely those people, if they were ever to become normal again, would be damaged for life or something. But it doesn't work that way at the moment and they can still try and eat us."

"Serious?"

"Uh-huh."

Silence held for a moment as they both looked at Two-h-ee. He quivered and snapped his teeth.

"Assuming I believe this," Luke said after a moment. "Does the doctor know why they're changing? Why they're getting smarter?"

"He thinks it's because the virus depresses certain parts of the brain. Kind of stops them working. But the brain is quite a clever thing. The synapses—is that the right word?—they can start moving around, regrowing and stuff. Sebastian says that you can trick the brain into doing things in one part that it used to do in another. So the part that the virus makes work better, the part that makes them fast and flexible and hungry, that's picking up the slack."

"But it's not picking up the empathy is it?" Luke asked. "It's not making them human again."

Jackson frowned and walked across to Luke. His very blue eyes were full of confusion and maybe a little bit of anger. Her heart gave a thud and she sighed. Luke was so lovely and she was so glad he was here to share all of this with.

"No," she said, the weight of the words heavy on her shoulders. "It doesn't seem to be doing that yet. It makes them smart, but the things that made them human—the empathy and the feelings— they're not back. Sebastian thinks those parts of the brain are not working at all."

"And will they ever be?" Luke asked.

Like in the garage, when he'd just lost his bunker and he'd seemed so sad, Jackson reached out to touch him. Only this time she actually could, and she did. She pressed her hand against his chest, feeling his heart beat against her palm.

"I don't know."

He shook his head and grimaced, but did not pull away from her touch. Jackson got the feeling he never would.

"Then he's looking for a cure? A way to bring them back completely, right?"

"Yeah."

"And you, Jack. What's your part in all of this? You keep an eye on them. Protect the doctor, is that it?"

"It is." She thought of the moment earlier when Sebastian had explained her role and how easy he'd made it all sound. Well almost all of it…

"And is that all?"

She shifted, removed her hand, and turned to look back at Two-h-ee. It was spraying pus bubbles now, little breaths that shot the pus up, though of course, gravity brought it back down and it landed on its face. Little puddles around the snarl glinted in the light and Jackson had to take a shallow breath through her nose. The smell really was atrocious. No wonder people got sick of it.

"Jack?" Luke prompted.

She knew he wasn't going to like her next words and Jackson had to kind of gird herself to say them. "Well…I have to catch them too."

Silence for a couple of moments and then Luke exploded. "I hope you're fucking joking."

"You know I don't joke. But it's not as bad as it sounds. Around here, the packs are destroyed pretty quickly, so you can find an odd zombie now and then. And the heat slows them down."

He growled and stepped forward, nose scrunching. "Jesus Christ, Jack. We spent weeks trying to find our way here. To find safety. At last we have that. But the moment it lands in your lap, you throw it away again. Explain that to me please. Why would

you do that? Why search for something for so long if you were
only going to reject it when you had it?"

"I was searching for answers," Jackson said "You know that.
Seb can give me those answers."

"Yes, but you don't need to go zombie hunting to get them."

"It's not just that," she said, trying to make him understand.
"The moment Seb started talking I just knew this was where I was
supposed to be. All the questions I've had. Their weird behavior?
Seb can answer all of that. Yeah, he's a bit odd, and I didn't really
get most of what he said, but if there's any chance at all that he's
right, Luke, I have to help in whatever way I can." She paused the
rushing words as Two-h-ee gave a howl. "You understand right,
Luke? How much it means to me to be able to contribute, to have
a purpose. To try and help. After all," she added, "you're doing the
exact same thing with the cars."

"I'm fixing fucking engines, not putting on a two-man stand
against the end of the world."

"Hardly that."

"It could all come to nothing," he said. "But that is not the
issue. Why *you* is what I want to know. Why not someone else? We
just got here."

"Well, because…" She frowned, trying to think about how to
explain it to him. That she'd fantasized and hoped for so fucking
long. That this, it was almost like a dream come true.

"Because what, Jack," Luke said when she did not reply. "You
don't even know do you? You don't even get it."

"Get what?"

"The reason you're doing this."

"I just told you why."

"No," Luke roared. "Fucking hell you didn't. Don't get me
wrong. If this is real—which I have to say I have my doubts—but
if it is, I agree it's an amazing thing and we should all help where
we can. But that's not your motivation. Not really."

Jackson wasn't really sure what he meant. She shook her head, both to get a grip on her thoughts and because Two-h-ee was groaning his horrible death groan.

"Then what is?" she asked. "You tell me, Luke, because I sure as hell don't know what you're getting at."

Two-h-ee groaned again and Luke snapped at him, "Shut the fuck up." Before turning to Jackson. "You're doing this because you can't *not* do it."

"Huh?"

"This, them, the whole thing. It's who you are now. Jackson the bad-ass, Jackson the fucking zombie slayer. I don't think you're actually capable of living a normal life anymore."

She gaped. "There is no normal life anymore. Those days are gone. Gone, Luke."

"But there is, damn it," he insisted, and the anger in his voice was palpable. "It's why we came south. Why you wanted it. To find that sliver of normality. That was the whole fucking reason."

And then Jackson paused because hadn't that thought been buzzing around constantly since she returned from the shack? Hadn't she begun to question everything, her motivations, her plans. Everything? She thought of all the times on the road. The times she'd had to hide or run or curl up somewhere waiting for daylight. All along the aim pushing her on.

"Is it?" she whispered, finally, and firmly, admitting the truth to herself. "I don't know, Luke. I think in the end I came south because I didn't know what else to do. Because on that observation deck it was the only option beyond jumping, and then with Tye…it just seemed like it made sense."

"Just like Pete," he whispered back, and even though she didn't really know what he meant she knew it was not a good comparison. Knew that by the tone of his voice.

"Luke…" She reached out to do something, a hug, or a touch, whatever, but he pulled back, not giving her the chance.

"I don't want you doing this, Jack," he said, and there was a hard note in his voice she'd never heard before. "I'll spend all my time worrying and panicking, but more than that, because my feelings aren't important really, more than that, you'll be putting yourself in danger again. Daily. I want you somewhere safe. I don't want you to have to fight over and over, day after day…*I* want you to have some normality."

Jackson frowned, her mind whizzing. "I thought we got past this at the stick and spit. You and me as equals, that's how we've worked this."

"The journey, yes," he agreed. "But we're here now and I was so happy to think that you might be able to be you again."

"Me?" she said, confusion thrumming through her. "This is me. This has always been me."

Luke threw his hands in the air and growled. "You without the zombies is what I mean. Just Jackson."

Why didn't he get it? When it was so freaking obvious to her? How could he not realize. "There is no 'just Jackson' anymore," she said. "The zombies are part of everything and we can't escape that. We can't ever escape it."

"Here we can," he insisted. "For a little bit we can."

"You might be able to, Luke. But for me? There is no escape. Why don't you get that? There won't ever be an escape. It's who I am now."

Luke shook his head, slowly now, without any of the anger—almost like it had drained from him. "I don't believe that," he said.

"Well, you have to," she replied. "Because it isn't going to change. Not now, not ever. It'll be this way until the end." And Two-h-ee groaned, almost punctuating her point in a way she would never have been able to.

CHAPTER THIRTY-THREE

A knocking on the door in the early hours, two days later, awoke Luke. He sat up quickly but Jackson was out of bed in one swift move, Mandy in hand, poised and ready.

"Zombies don't knock," he said, his voice still muffled with sleep.

"People don't either in the early hours unless something is wrong," she replied. "Though for all you know, the zombies might have learned."

She moved quickly, quietly, across the small place and eyed the door. Luke sighed to see her stance. She was in fight mode. Hell, she was always in fight mode and it had not slacked off over the last few days. If anything, it had gotten worse. He suspected it was being in close proximity to the zombie that had her strung so tight, because she constantly looked like she was a hair trigger away from sending Mandy slicing through someone, and just last night she'd woken up screaming.

"Then by all means invite the courteous zombie in," he said.

She turned, scowled at him, but gripped the handle. She was still in a snit about their conversation in the lab. Not to mention the fact he'd witnessed her full-on nightmare, something he suspected bruised her bad-ass ego a little. So yeah, it was snit all around. He knew it, she knew it, and right now there was a certain sort of barrier between them. Oh, it wasn't a breaking barrier. They still spent time together, eating and talking and making love. But the barrier was there, and they were both aware of it. It colored their conversations, gave a hard edge to their time in bed, and it would have to be resolved. Only Luke didn't have any clue how.

"No need for the ax," Nancy said when Jackson opened the door.

"Force of habit, and it's a machete not an ax."

Nancy shrugged. "Same difference.

Nancy looked the same as she always did. Harassed. She was wearing an outfit very like Jackson's. Jeans, a tee, boots, and a healthy dollop of attitude. Her hair was scraped back into a braid but strands of it were falling free and as he looked at her she brushed one back impatiently. Luke got the impression the woman was personally offended by her unruly hair and he jumped out of bed with a smile.

"Something funny, Luke?" she asked and he shook his head before pulling on a tee.

"Nope. Just wondering what's up."

Nancy grimaced. "We have a situation."

"Which is?"

Nancy turned from him and fixed her gaze on Jackson. "One that needs you, apparently," she said. "Sebastian asked me to get you ASAP."

"Right."

There was no need for her to get dressed. Jackson slept in her clothes. Jeans, tee, and socks. All she had to do was slip into her boots. He, on the other hand, loved the fact that he could just wear a pair of boxers. It reminded him of the old days. He dragged his jeans on, slipped his gun in his waistband, and grabbed his ax. Nancy saw his action and frowned.

"We only need Jackson," she said.

"I'm coming."

His tone left no room for argument. The last two days had been bad enough. Jackson setting out with Sebastian and leaving him behind every goddamn morning. When she got back she told him what she'd been dong, taking great pains to let him know that everything was safe, and that it had been almost dull. She spoke of the experiments and the possibility of a cure but Luke didn't want to believe too much in it. It seemed impossible, really.

That, combined with the worry, ate away at him. He was angry and riled up and he hated the distance between them—but didn't know how to fix it. He did not want her working with the zombies and the weird doctor. She wouldn't give up something she thought was important—and hell, maybe it could be! Just because he was skeptical didn't mean anything. They were in a stalemate.

"We'll go together," Jackson said surprising him, and he smiled automatically.

"You sure?"

"Yeah, come on."

They sorted themselves out and followed Nancy out the door. Jackson somehow made her way to the front and made her way down the stairs ninja style. Despite the fact it pissed him off to see it, Luke couldn't help but admire her style. It was the dual desires all over again. The desire to see her a little bit more normal, the desire to make her happy, and then the knowledge that she was bad-ass, good at this life. But that it was dangerous, and no matter how bad-ass you were, your luck always ran out in the end...

As they stepped outside the air was noticeably cooler than it had been in their room and Luke wished he'd thought to grab a sweater. There was no time to go back though because Jackson was striding forward. Her gaze was fixed on Nancy.

"So what's up?" she asked. "Sebastian surely doesn't want to hit the shack at this time of night?"

"It's madness going there at night despite our security sweeps."

Jackson laughed softly. "Yeah, well he wouldn't see it that way if he got one of his ideas in his head."

"I know," Nancy said, "and sometimes it is necessary."

Her words sent a chill up Luke's spine and he was glad he'd insisted on coming along, sweater or no. Something was up and whatever it was he was going to be part of it. Jackson out and about in the heat of the day was one thing. The cool air of the night was something else entirely and she'd need him. Whether she wanted to admit it or not. He flexed his ax a little and was surprised at how good the wood felt in his hand. Though not as gung-ho as his girlfriend, Luke too had missed the feel of his weapon.

They made their way across the courtyard, around the opposite cluster of houses, and past a long row of greenhouses. Luke couldn't help but look around the perimeter and was pleased to see people up there on the towers, chatting softly, laughing now and then but, more importantly, keeping an eye on the outside. At this time of night they stood between everyone and the zombies, and though Luke didn't want Jackson doing it, he was grateful to those who *were* doing it, would probably take a turn himself at some point.

"Here we go," Nancy said.

She opened the door of a large bungalow-type building.

"Whose house is this?" Luke asked.

"It's the medical building," Jackson replied. "Seb lives here. Keeps his stuff here."

"It's always useful to have things on hand," Nancy said. "Things are necessary sometimes."

She gestured to the end of the hall, and they followed her into a large kitchen. Of course, it wasn't a kitchen anymore. The cooking equipment from every house—at least in those that it had been installed in—had been moved into the main house to create a large kitchen where everyone could eat their rations.

And it was clear immediately that Sebastian had turned the faux kitchen into some sort of workstation. Luke gaped a little as he looked over the equipment because it had been so long since he'd seen anything remotely like it. Several laptops were plugged into an overflowing circuit breaker, and though he had no idea what was on the screens, something was. The laptops worked! Not to mention the printer he could see plugged in and a small circular thing that looked suspiciously like a satellite dish.

We have some things working. He remembered Nancy's words and whistled slowly. This was more than he'd thought possible, put his shitty radio set to shame.

"Does he have Bejeweled Blitz?" he wondered and Jackson smacked him in the arm.

His muffled words were enough to pull Sebastian from whatever world he was in, because he started, his hair standing on end, a puzzled look chasing across his face. Luke opened his mouth to speak but Jackson beat him to it.

"What's going on?"

"Erm, we have a small problem," Sebastian replied, the puzzled look still in place. "We need your help here, Jack."

"What sort of problem?" Luke asked, stepping forward.

Sebastian shot him a grin, surprising him and beckoning him forward. "Good to see you too, Luke. We're going to need plenty of hands. Mack's sent some people to get Pete and a couple of his friends."

"For what?

Sebastian's grin slipped into a frown and he pointed across the room. "For that."

• • •

The red-haired zombie was inside some sort of cage, like one people would have used in the old days for a large dog, so Jackson guessed that was what Nancy meant by Sebastian keeping stuff here that was necessary. There were no dogs in the camp and he had several of these same cages at the shack. The zombie was also unconscious, and Jackson knew there was no way in hell the doctor had bashed it that way. No doubt he'd shot it to shit with something.

"How did it get in?" Luke asked, before Jackson could. "I thought after last time…"

Nancy scowled and walked across the room to look at the zombie. "We found something odd today when we swept the northern end of camp."

"What?" Jackson asked.

Nancy scowled some more. "We might even have missed it the first time around for fuck's sake. Who knew to look for that?"

"What?" Jackson repeated.

Nancy tucked her hands in her jean pockets. "A hole."

"A hole?" Luke asked, breaking the silence that had fallen with those words. "Where? In what? One of the gates?"

"Not the gates, no," Nancy said. "I wish."

"Then where?"

"In the ground."

Nancy turned at Jackson's hushed words, shock on her face. "How the fuck do you know that?"

Jackson frowned, her heart giving a little thump. The words had just tumbled from her lips, but the more she thought about them the more she knew she was right. Images flashed through her mind. Creepyville. Sammy's trap. "I've seen it before, more than once," she said slowly, her throat suddenly dry. "At the time it just struck me as odd, but now…"

"What?" Nancy prompted. "What?"

Jackson bent down to look at the zombie and noticed the patches of mud covering it, just like Sammy. "I wonder if maybe they're…burrowing…"

Sebastian gasped. "That's…well…that's impossible. They do

need oxygen you know, not to mention they would be deliberately trapping themselves."

"Only if they went too far down, and they could be working in tandem, one burrows, the other removes the dirt. Like tunneling or something." Jackson shrugged. "It's just a theory. But every time I've seen those burrows the place where they've been has been some sort of trap. Almost like they're creating dens or something."

"Fascinating," Sebastian said. "Adapting their behavior to hunt their food." He paused and picked up a notebook and pen. "I'll have to start smothering them, see how long they can last without oxygen."

Luke shook his head at the other man. "That is completely fucked-up."

"It's necessary—"

"Necessary or not you need to follow that hole," Jackson said. "Follow it to the end."

Nancy gaped. "You expect me to ask one of our people to go down a fucking zombie burrow—Jesus, I can't believe I'm even saying those words—and see what's there? Are you serious?"

"You'll have to," Jackson insisted. "You need to see where it comes out."

"She's right," Luke agreed. "You'll need to fill both ends."

Nancy stepped back from the cage, pulled her hands from her pockets, and ran them over her hair, smoothing the stray bits back in place. "This creates a real problem."

"If they did it twice…"

"Then they'll do it again," she snapped. "We're surrounded by mud! We grow all our food in the fucking mud! How far are they burrowing?"

"No way to know until you find the other end of that hole," Luke said. "Let's hope it's not too far."

"I would imagine it isn't," Sebastian said, as he scribbled something down. "A few meters at most. Which means they are somehow sneaking as close as possible to the perimeter and then burrowing in. That's what she probably did, and now that you mention it," excitement filled his eyes, "it would explain why she is covered in dirt."

"And why Sammy was," Nancy breathed, her eyes meeting Jackson's, realization dawning.

"Did she say anything about a burrow?" Luke asked.

Nancy bent down so she too was able to get a good look at the zombie. "No, but she's had some difficulties since the incident and Mack doesn't want her being shook up again, so I can't ask a lot. She isn't even telling us how they communicated with her. It's like her mind's blanked it out."

"I can understand why Mack wants her to have some space," Jackson said. "Especially if the zombies dragged her through a hole in the ground. She must have been terrified."

Her heart clenched at that thought. They'd seen Sammy a few times over the last few days and Luke in particular seemed to have taken a real liking to her—no surprise there, he'd have made a great dad if the world hadn't ended. Jackson enjoyed spending time with her too. She was a sweet little thing, and that moment in the garage had created a bond of sorts which both intrigued and terrified her. Luke and Tye were the only people in the past months that she'd allowed to get really close and the idea of letting little Sammy have a piece of her heart worried Jackson. The girl had nearly died once. It could easily happen again. Still, she was no trouble to spend time with, though whether the girl had been so quiet before the zombies had kidnapped her was something Jackson couldn't answer. She certainly was now. But many of the children around the camp had that air to them. Watchful, considering. Jackson couldn't even begin to imagine how it would feel being raised in the world of the waking dead.

Silence reigned in the room for a moment as everyone followed Nancy's example, craning their necks to get a good look at the zombie. Sebastian was the first to speak.

"Entry method aside, she's an impressive specimen, I must say." He turned to Jackson, pulling some of his hair as he did so. "And think about it, Jack, now that Two-h-ee is pretty much done for, we can start on her. You won't need to go and find one. We'll call her Two-h-four, or maybe Red. So really, it's a stroke of luck."

"Are you serious?" Luke asked, gaping at the other man. "We have a real situation here—zombies coming out of the fucking ground like some sort of old-school horror movie—and you're lining up your next lab rat? Giving it a nickname?"

Sebastian grinned. "Just looking for the silver lining. Besides, I can joke if I want. I woke up to find her standing over me, looking at me funny, I might add. I barely had time to grab the syringe before she took a chunk from me."

"You did good, Seb," Nancy said. "Very good."

"It was instinct more than anything," Sebastian replied. "I know, compared to the rest of you, I'm seen as a bit of a wimp. But I haven't survived this long without taking out a few myself!"

Jackson snorted. "You've killed hundreds in the lab." She'd looked through his files during the time they spent at the shack, and though she didn't really understand the science behind his work, the roll call of dead zombies was impressive. One after the other he had captured them, worked on them, and then, once they were dead, discarded them. In many ways, Sebastian was as deadly as she. Only his weapon of choice was a syringe rather than a machete.

He shrugged. "Not quite the same thing, Jack."

"Ummm."

Jackson walked over to the zombie, surprised how calm she felt, considering. Sure it was unconscious but she didn't even lift her blade, just sort of gripped it to her. She wondered if this was due to being used to Sebastian's lab, around Two-h-ee. Listening to it groan and gag from whatever Sebastian fed it. At times, though she didn't dare say so to Luke, or even really think about it after the fact, Two-h-ee seemed almost normal. Once when Sebastian had pumped it full of stuff and it had tried to curl in on itself it had seemed sort of vulnerable—ridiculous though that sounded. Jackson recalled the time the doctor had gone into the other room to get more chemicals or something. Two-h-ee had spent the previous hour screaming in what she assumed must be pain, though she'd never seen them do that before. The moment Sebastian left the room its screams had ceased and it turned its head on the table to look at her. Jackson's gaze had held his, because there was no fucking way she was backing down from one of the bastards, and she'd waited for the usual hatred to rise, but it hadn't. Her old moral dilemma had instead.

Its eyes had been filled with something that, for once, wasn't hunger, and she remembered how it had once been a person, how it wasn't even really dead. It groaned and shifted and its eyes begged for something. Part of her had wondered if that something might be death at last and she'd been tempted to simply finish it off, but before she could make a decision Sebastian had returned and Two-h-ee had resumed its screams.

Those screams had featured heavily in her nightmare last night. The one Luke had woken her from. *Nightmares!* Her brain had protected her from them for so long she couldn't quite work out was happening.

Nothing good, Jack. No shit, Sherlock.

Shaking the thoughts off, Jackson bent down to get a good look into the cage and frowned. The smell was bad, but she'd encountered worse, and though the square grids of metal distorted the view slightly, Jackson could see the zombie fine. It was sprawled out on its side, one arm resting by its face, and maybe it was because it was out for the count, but Jackson realized that its face was more… normal?…than any zombie she'd seen before "You're right, Seb," she said slowly. "There is something about her."

"It's because she's not groaning or snarling," Luke said as he made his way over. "She looks almost human."

"She?" Nancy asked from the other side of the cage.

Jackson pointed to the zombie's top, which seemed to be the remains of a red sweater — or maybe that was just dried blood. Its breasts were obvious, despite the mud, as was the curvature of the hips, not to mention the wild red hair. It reached to at least the waist and was a marvelous hue, despite the dirt, knots, and grime. "She was a woman."

Nancy stood up, brushing her knees down and glared. "She's not anymore. *It's* just a zombie now."

"It's a sick woman is all," Sebastian corrected. "Zombie or no. If I had my cure, she'd be back to normal in no time."

"But you don't, Seb," Nancy said. "Not yet."

Sebastian shrugged. "I just need the final thing."

Something passed between the leader and the doctor and Jackson eyed them with interest. She knew Sebastian was missing one element of the concoction that he called his cure, but he couldn't get his hands on whatever it was. He'd told her there was only one way but Nancy refused to let him try it. So he was experimenting, trying to find a way around it. Only it wasn't going too well, and now that their brains were changing, it was even harder.

"Let's not get into this now," Nancy said. "You know the rules, and like or no it *is* a zombie."

Jackson sighed and stretched, feeling the politics and not really enjoying them. "No. She'll be Seb's latest experiment, which means she's got what?" She looked over at Sebastian. "Two weeks before she's dead?"

"Steady on," Sebastian said, a frown chasing his face. "Two-h-ee lasted for nearly a month!"

"A few weeks then."

"The reason for calling you here," Nancy said impatiently,

fixing her gaze on Jackson, and putting a halt to their conversation. "Is that the zombie cannot stay here. I won't have them in the camp. It's too dangerous and besides it is one of our main rules. This here is supposed to be a safe place. I can't have zombies running around, or burrowing for that matter." She shook her head, and muttered. "Who the fuck am I going to get to go down that hole?"

Luke stepped next to her, his solid warmth banishing the chills Nancy's words created. Despite the distance between them it comforted her as always and Jackson reached back with her free hand to brush against his. She took a deep breath and gripped Mandy tightly. "You don't mean?"

Nancy nodded grimly. "Yep, you're gonna have to take it to the shack."

CHAPTER THIRTY-FOUR

The drive to the shack was completely different at night and Luke found himself wishing they could have waited until the morning. But even as he thought it, he knew Nancy was right. They could not leave a zombie in what was the equivalent of a human buffet. She'd proven herself smart enough to burrow into camp without anyone stopping her. Who knew what else she could do?

So drive they did. He, Jackson, Sebastian, Pete, and a huge, silent guy called Jay. He'd nodded, cocked his gun, and ignored everyone. Luke had raised an eyebrow in Pete's direction, but he'd merely shrugged. This was all Nancy could or would spare. Everyone else was on the walls or checking for burrows.

At first Luke couldn't help but wonder why she was so willing to let Sebastian—the fucking wonder doctor—leave the camp at such a dangerous time. It was cool, which meant the zombies would be bolder, and driving at night was always precarious. But he'd discovered that Sebastian did as he pleased, went where he wanted, and no one, least of all Nancy, was willing to stop him.

"It's a good job we moved Two-h-ee into one of the cages," Sebastian said as they turned down a particularly bumpy road.

The doctor was in the back sandwiched between Pete and Jay.

Jackson rode shotgun with him and if he ignored his passengers, Luke thought it could be almost like old times, as Jackson called them. Just the two of them making their journey. Less than a week ago in reality, but much longer in terms of events. It surprised Luke how much he missed it. At least then he knew where and what Jackson was doing and could try and protect her in his own way.

"We'll strap her down straightaway," Jackson replied, her eyes scanning the area. "Are you going to dose her up tonight?"

"Thought I might try something different with this one actually," Sebastian said. "The current treatment regime is not working seeing as how I can't get my hands on what I need, so I've got to start thinking outside the box as they say. Get a bit creative."

"And what is it you need, exactly?" Luke asked. He couldn't help himself. The undercurrents between Nancy and the doctor hadn't escaped him and he wondered what precisely Sebastian needed for this cure of his.

"Oh, well, I'm not supposed to say," Sebastian muttered.

Pete let out a laugh. "Everyone knows anyway, Seb. You spent weeks moaning and moping about it."

"I did not!"

"Yes you did. We all locked our doors just in case."

Locked their doors? Luke frowned, took a left, and accelerated forward. The headlights were on highbeam so they gave him a good view of the surrounding area, but still he wanted to get a move on. There and back in two hours at least, before morning proper began. "Okay, spill then," Luke said. "You've dragged my woman into this after all."

"Luke." Jackson swatted him on the thigh. "Less of the caveman, please."

"It's true," he defended himself, shooting Jackson a quick glance. "The least the good doctor can do is tell us what we're up against here. 'Cause look, I'll be honest, I'm not even sure this cure idea of yours has got any kind of legs. For all we know you could be tinkering around with no idea what the hell you're doing."

"I've been working on this from the moment it hit," Sebastian said. "It was my job before any of you even knew what was happening, so say what you will about me, but do not cast aspersions on my qualifications."

"The moment it hit?"

The doctor shifted, and out of the corner of his eye Luke noticed Pete elbow him. "I worked with all sorts of diseases," Sebastian said. "You know, before the end. That's what I did as my line of work. They call me the doctor here but truth be told, I've never practiced proper medicine. I was always much more comfortable in research." He shrugged. "Viruses were my thing."

"And you worked on *this* virus?" Luke asked, intrigued despite himself. "Where? The CDC?"

Sebastian shifted on his seat. "No, I worked for a pharmaceutical company here in Texas. I got the job offer right after I finished my PhD. It was fascinating work, adapting viruses for other purposes, specifically drug delivery. When we heard about this one…" He shifted some more. "I couldn't believe it. It was a virus unlike any I'd ever seen, and it fascinated me. There had to be a way to beat it. I knew there was, but there was so little time. Just a handful of months before nearly everyone was gone. Before they overran us all. If I'd just had more time…"

"You've had two years now," Luke said. "Granted, alone in the wilderness but how much more do you need?"

Sebastian shrugged. "It's not a time issue anymore. It's about the missing ingredient."

"Which is what?"

Jackson swiveled in her seat and nodded slowly. "Luke's got a point, Seb, and I've been dying to know myself. We won't tell Nancy you told us."

"This is so school yard," Pete growled. "For fuck's sake, I'll tell you myself. Seb needs a live one."

"A what?"

"He needs someone recently infected. Like within a few hours. Right, Doc?"

Sebastian muttered something unintelligible before shuffling forward so that his face was between the two front seats. "It's not as bad as it sounds," he said. "We discovered in the beginning, before everyone got eaten or bitten or died, that the body makes antibodies in the very early hours of infection."

"Right."

"I need to harvest those," Sebastian continued, his enthusiasm clearly overtaking his previous desire to keep quiet. "They're not enough on their own. We tried that back then. The virus depresses the immune system at first, but then sends it into overload. By the time antibodies are made, the virus has taken hold and they make no difference *because* of the immune response. It actually uses our own immune system against us." He scowled, as if personally offended that the virus could do that. "The antibodies need to be combined with other things," he added. "And I think I've isolated what—that's what I spent two years doing, playing around with immune suppressants. But it's all theoretical because I don't have any antibodies now."

"So you need a fresh zombie," Luke said slowly.

"Yes, only there aren't any of those anymore."

"Because the zombies eat you as soon as they get you. No one has a chance to be infected anymore."

"Exactly. It's a real quandary."

Luke scowled out at the landscape around them, wondering how many hungry zombies were close by and whether Sebastian would put up a fight if one tried to eat him, Jackson, Jay, or Pete. Maybe not. It would fit his plans perfectly. "So you're trying something else?"

"It probably won't work." Sebastian sighed. "Because I really need those antibodies."

A nasty thought hit him then and before he could even consider the wisdom of his actions Luke braked, hard. The truck came to a juddering halt and exclamations filled the air. Luke turned in his seat to see Sebastian half sprawled across Pete.

"What did you see, Luke?" Jackson whispered. "Zombies? Burrows?"

"No." He took just a moment to cup her face and look into her very green eyes. They showed no fear. Just resolve. "Nothing like that."

"What gives, man?" Pete pushed Sebastian off and the doctor mumbled something before squeezing back into position.

Luke ignored him and the querying glance of the silent Jay, locking eyes on Sebastian only. "You dare touch her," he said, and he knew his voice was deadly.

Sebastian gaped "What?"

"You even think of infecting her, and I will find you and slice you up bit by bit. Don't even consider allowing your thoughts to drift in that direction."

"Luke." Jackson gasped. "He wouldn't."

"We have no idea what he'd do," Luke said. "We barely know him."

Sebastian spluttered and leaned forward. "That's an outrageous thing to suggest. Jackson helps me. I need her, but not like that. I'd never knowingly infect anyone."

"You sure about that?"

"Of course!

Jackson laid a hand on his arm and tugged him around. "I *do* know him, Luke. He's a good guy and he wouldn't dare. Besides I'd slice him up myself before he even got the chance." She swirled Mandy in the air to make her point, and Luke saw the doctor swallow.

"Let's all calm down," Pete said slowly. "Luke, get moving. We've got a zombie in the trunk and who knows if there are more prowling about, or waiting underground, for that matter."

Luke scowled but did as Pete asked. They shot down the road, and he tried to grab at some calm. The thought had come out of nowhere really and *was* probably stupid. But who knew what went through the mind of these science types? The doctor was odd and Luke didn't trust him not to block out everything in his attempt to find his cure. After all, Luke knew a thing or two about single-mindedness, didn't he? He saw it every day with Jackson.

"I'd never infect anyone, Luke," Sebastian insisted after a few minutes. "There are so few of us, I'd never do anything to harm anyone. I'm trying to save people. I want to make them well again. It's been over two years and every day I wake up and it's all I think about."

His tone was earnest and Luke shifted again, feeling a slight twinge of guilt.

"There is no one else," Sebastian continued. "No one who can do this. It's just us now. We're the last hope."

"We are," Pete said.

"I need Jackson's help," he added. "And yours, and Pete's, everyone's really. But if we do this. If we find a way to pull it off…"

He trailed off and silence filled the car. Luke knew what they were all thinking. They were imagining a world without zombies. A world where Sebastian's cure could bring everyone back… And then out of nowhere Luke thought of Lily. The zombie whose husband sat just a few feet away. He thought about what it would mean for her, for the redheaded zombie in the back, for the tens of thousands everywhere. And lastly what it would mean for him and Jackson. No need to be on guard, no need to worry. Normality. A normal world. And he sighed as he said the next words, because part of him didn't want to, part of him still didn't believe it, and was unable to imagine it actually happening. But he said the damn words anyway.

"Then we'll help. We'll do whatever it takes."

Jackson found his hand with hers and squeezed. "Whatever it takes.

• • •

Strapping the zombie onto the table was going to take some effort, and Jackson tried to work it all out in her mind. They could carry her in of course, she was superlight, but it took time to arrange all the restraints and she was starting to rouse now, low snarls leaving her lips, muffled groans sounding.

"Can we drug her again?" she asked, but Sebastian shook his head.

"No. That stuff I shot her with was ketamine. It used to be used on horses. I gave her enough for five. But any more and it'll do weird things to her. I need her normal for work tomorrow."

"We need to be quick then," she said. "In and strapped up ASAP." She turned to the others, who were waiting patiently for instructions. "Jay, do a security sweep of the outer perimeter, check for holes in the ground especially. Luke, Pete you take her. I'll lead the way in and take care of any issues. Seb, you're with me."

The men raised their eyebrows but complied. The thought crossed Jackson's mind that if the zombies had done anything worthwhile, it was to finally remove the last vestiges of sexism. In the world of the dead, or rather the thought-they-were-dead-but-really-they're-alive—and especially in this camp—everyone was valued for what they could bring to the table. Gender, color, sexual preference didn't come into the equation

Jay turned to them and pointed to the back of the building. "If there's an issue, I'll holler out, okay?"

They were the first words he'd spoken and Jackson nodded. "Make sure you do."

She gestured Sebastian forward, pulling the multiuse key from her pocket as they moved. It didn't take long to open up the door, check the main room of the shack, and open up the smaller room.

Once inside, her gaze went straight to Two-h-ee. He was lying on his side in the cage they'd placed him in and from the lack of snarls, growls, or moans he'd finally passed on. She tilted her head to get a good look at him and was almost glad to see his features relaxed slightly now. He wouldn't be screaming anymore at least.

"Jackson?" Sebastian laid a hand across her arm, halting her.

She turned to look at the doctor, who had, despite what Luke said, become a friend to her over the last few days. Yeah, he was weird, and yeah, a little bit maniacal, but she got him—just as he got her.

"Yeah?"

"You know I'd never hurt you, don't you?" he asked, and his gaze was intense.

"Of course I do. I'd kick your ass."

Sebastian grinned. "I don't just mean because of the fact that you can lay me out. I mean because we're friends and I count on your help here."

"I know, Seb." She patted his hand. "We're all good, and I *do* believe in what we're doing here. I'm proud to be part of it, to have something useful to do." She paused for a minute, looking over Two-h-ee again. He was leaking pus now from its mouth and nose and she resolved to flip Sebastian the finger if he dared suggest that cleaning that shit up was part of her job. "You know it's weird. I used to hate them, still do, if truth be told. It's hard to get over the things we've done and seen in the last two years, you know?"

"I know," Sebastian replied. "Believe me, seeing my colleagues eaten was nothing I ever want to live through again. There was this one girl, we were making our way here…" He shook his head. "Doesn't matter anymore."

"Point is," Jackson said after a moment. "That knowing they're not dead, that they're still people, changes things a little. Don't get me wrong, I'll still kill any fuckers that come my way, but it makes you think a little different."

"Yeah, it changes things."

Their conversation was halted as Luke and Pete came through the door. They held the redheaded zombie by her arms and legs and Sebastian hurried forward to help them move her onto the table. Jackson joined them and together they began to strap her down.

"Quick, quick," Sebastian said, as he pulled one of the ropes. "She's starting to wake up, and we do not want those teeth anywhere near us."

Luke looked up. "It is the bite that does it, then."

The doctor nodded. "The virus lives in the saliva, not the pus or blood. I don't quite know why that is the case, because feasibly speaking, it should travel in the other fluids."

"I've been bit," Luke said slowly.

"Doesn't infect everyone either," Sebastian said. "Again, I don't know why. But then no virus does. Even Ebola, back in the day, didn't."

"I used to coat the wounds with whiskey," Luke added and Sebastian laughed.

"Wouldn't have made any difference, and sometimes one bite will do it while another won't. It just depends."

Jackson cuffed the redheaded zombie's hands in place with a *click*. She, like Two-h-ee, was now spread on the table, and Jackson frowned as she imagined what they'd be doing to the zombie this time tomorrow. Smothering her perhaps? Luke finished tightening the ropes and took a step back before casting her a smile.

"That wasn't as bad as I imagined."

It awoke then, and not slowly or muggily, but in an instant and shot forward. The various restraints held the zombie back but it howled and snapped its teeth. Pus dripped from its lips and pooled on its grimy chest. The smell was suddenly overpowering and Jackson took a step back.

"Just in time by the looks of it," Pete said. "Bitch is hungry."

And she was at that, the look in its eyes was very familiar to Jackson. Hunger combined with calculating. It wanted to eat them all, and Jackson wondered what was going through the zombie's mind. How much could it actually think? Did it even know they were people, or did nothing like that remain? More to the point, what was with the fucking smell? She turned to Two-h-ee and noticed that his pus pool was now leaking onto the surrounding flooring of the cage. She was so not cleaning that up.

"We should get moving," Luke said and he stepped around the table to run a hand up and down her back. Jackson leaned into the contact and was surprised to feel ever so slightly cheered by the thoughts of crawling back into a warm bed. "Let's not push our luck, eh?" he added.

A smile shot between them. Jackson's stomach clenched. Distance and problems aside, Luke was just so damn hot. It hit her like that at times, shocking her a little, and she was reminded of the moment they had met, when he'd pulled her into the pool room and she'd practically drooled at the fine specimen of masculinity he had presented.

"Yeah—"

The sound of footsteps filled the room and they all turned to see Jay come through the door. He was clearly out of breath, sweat beads obvious across his buzz cut. Jackson took one look at him and felt anticipation disappear, replaced with adrenaline. It zinged through her veins, clear and immediate.

"What is it?" she asked stepping forward, breaking the contact with Luke.

"There's…" Jay pulled in a ragged breath and pointed to the outer door of the shack. "We need to leave now."

"Leave?" Sebastian looked up from whatever the hell he was messing around with next to the zombie. "We haven't finished yet. Might as well get rid of Two-h-ee while we're here."

"No," Jay gasped. "Now. They're coming." And Jackson could

see fear in his eyes, and that shot something through her, because the big, silent man didn't seem like he would be the type to feel that. She'd pegged him as one of those who were past that point.

"What the fuck's going on?" Luke asked. "What did you see? How many are there? Are they coming through the ground?"

Even as he asked the questions both he and Jackson moved toward the door, Pete bringing up the rear. Everyone pulled their weapons free and Jackson's head cleared of all thoughts. There and then the redheaded zombie, Two-h-ee, the virus and its odd workings, everything faded into the distance and she put herself in battle mode.

"How many?" she asked Jay, repeating Luke's question. Visions of a superpack ran through her mind, or even zombies rising from the ground—proper old-school style.

"I—"

But there was no need for Jay to say anything else because they all heard it then. A groan followed by another, and then another and another. A veritable symphony of them and Jackson shuddered because those awful death sounds were not coming from the redheaded zombie, but her question was answered at least. A super-size pack—there was no doubt about that.

"Time to rock and roll," she whispered, and Luke stepped forward so that his body heat pressed against her and she knew it was because he alone had heard her.

"Let's do this," he said. "Quickly."

"Yeah—" The death groans continued, making Jackson pause. They were far louder than they should have been, but worse they were combined with something else. Pounding. And only one thing made that sound. Wasn't it what had alerted her to Luke's presence before she even knew him?

The others heard the exact same thing and Sebastian gasped at the same time as Pete let loose a strong of cusses. "How the fuck did they find us?"

"They've never been here," Sebastian said. "Never."

Jackson stroked Mandy's hilt and rolled her shoulders, already envisaging the battle in her mind if they didn't mosey on out right now.

"Well they're here now," she said. "So let's move."

They practically sprinted through the large space of the shack, no time to even lock the door to the small room. Sebastian muttered as they ran but even he was smart enough to know that shit was about to go down and the experiments had to come second place.

"Straight to the truck," Luke said. "We'll gun it and move out immediately. Sebastian, get the door open and then stand as far back as you can just in case any of them are out there. We'll take them out first, then get to the truck."

The groans increased in volume as Sebastian stepped forward to grasp the handle to the main door, and maybe that might not have meant anything but the way they sounded, almost like a melody, kicked something to life in Jackson, a memory, maybe her worst memory, and she skidded to a standstill. Her brain supplied the knowledge that had quivered around the edges up till now and it hit her. With that realization her heart raced and her stomach dropped to her knees. She looked to Sebastian, to Jay, then Pete, and finally to Luke.

"Oh my God…"

"What the hell is that? What is that sound?"

The question came from the doctor, his hand paused on the door, and she realized then that Sebastian had no idea what the melody of groans meant or what the volume said about how close they were. Only she and Luke knew, only the two of them understood, and before either could even say another word, they walked forward automatically and took each other's hands. The barriers they'd lived with for the last few days swayed before crumbling completely and green eyes found blue.

"Lock the door, Seb," she said softly, her eyes still held with Luke's. "They're too close."

"What?" Pete pushed the doctor aside and made to grab the door handle. "Of course they're not!"

"Listen," Luke said. "Just listen."

And they all paused, even Pete, and they listened. The death groans were reaching a fever pitch now and combined with the sounds of God-knew-how-many feet pounding on the earth floor. Jackson guessed the zombies were maybe a dozen yards away at most. There was no time to run for the truck, no time to run at all.

Luke reached out a hand and stroked down the side of her face. Jackson leaned into his touch, shivering slightly from the feel of it.

"What the hell is that?" Pete asked. "What is it?"

"It's pretty much the end," Luke said, and Jackson nodded against his hand, surprised to find how much that thought hurt.

"It is at that."

Pete growled, stepping forward, his face tight with anger. "The end? We can take down a bunch. Don't count us out yet."

And Jackson sighed, her hand clasping Luke's. "A bunch yes, but not this many."

"What many? What is it?"

Green to blue, green to blue, and nothing else but that.

"It's a horde."

Chapter Thirty-Five

The possibilities of getting out of this one were slim. Luke knew that instinctively. This wasn't like the fight outside Kelly's Clothing or the bakery or even the garage. This was a whole other shit storm.

Fuck.

"We should move back into the secure room," he said. "There are too many places out here for them to breach."

Jackson nodded her agreement and without waiting for any of the others, they sprinted back to the smaller room. The redheaded zombie snarled when she saw them and pulled against her bonds. Her groan joined that of the horde, and Luke wondered if maybe she could hear her brothers and sisters on the other side. He looked into her calculating eyes and scowled. Alive or dead, human or no, he hated them all. The nature of their virus did not change that for him. A zombie was a zombie and the only thing they were good for was beheading.

"What's the plan then, baby?" Jackson asked and he laughed, just like she'd wanted him to do.

"Isn't the planning your job? You make the plan, do the plan, live the plan."

"Yeah, ideas aren't exactly whizzing right now," she said.

"Maybe we could tunnel out? Zombie style."

"Um, we'll use Sebastian's equipment, won't take long at all. A year or two to make camp?"

She shrugged. "A couple of years is nothing, took me that long to walk from New York to you."

"Let's get right on that then."

Pete, Sebastian, and Jay barreled through the door seconds later, the doctor clearly out of breath. "I locked and barred the door," he spluttered. "But what are we going to do? A horde means a horde, right? Like a lot?"

"Yeah," Jackson said. "A lot."

"So what are we going to do?"

"Just working that out right now," Luke replied.

The outer shack door juddered and Luke swallowed the ball of frantic energy trying to leap up his throat. He worked out the layout in his mind, options for escape discarded one after the other. The shack was made of some sort of concrete, and there were no windows beyond a couple of small ones in the ceiling of the main room. They were barred though and he doubted the zombies were thin enough to get through them—his group certainly wasn't. Already they were pounding on the main door so there was no chance of getting out that way, and the only other exit door—here in the small room—had been barred up when Sebastian had taken over. Jackson had told him it worked as a possible escape, *always have an exit, baby,* by removing the bars. But that it would take a while to get them all free.

"Luke?" Jackson prompted. "What are you thinking?"

"That we need another door."

The redheaded zombie groaned.

"There's only that one." She pointed to the corner. "It's secure but we could leave through it from this side. Just need to get those bars off. It'll take about ten minutes between the two of us."

"And then what?" Pete asked. "You said loads. How many is

loads?"

Luke shrugged, trying to look composed but failing epically. "About a hundred."

"You're fucking joking."

"I wish."

They pounded again, only this time zombies were pounding on the front door, the sides, and even a couple on the ceiling. "There's the weak spot," Jackson said, pointing upward. "It's sheet metal. Will keep them out for maybe ten minutes."

"Same time it takes to get the bars off."

"Yeah," she agreed. "But like Pete said, we go out there and then what? We can't fight twenty odd each."

"So it's a choice between fighting and dying in here or doing it out there."

"This room is secure," Sebastian said. "I made sure to reinforce the roof. We can stay safe in here for maybe a half hour before they get through the second layer, or maybe go under." He shook his head and began picking up syringes. "So yeah, a half hour?"

A huge judder sounded then and they all turned to look into the outer room and watch the main door begin to buckle.

"Fuck," Luke breathed. "A choice between running and hoping to make it or trapping ourselves in here. Which are we going to do? Which gives us more of a chance?"

Another huge smash rumbled through the building, and the door frame began to bend. The metal door was being removed from the concrete itself, and Luke knew there must be dozens pounding against it to get that sort of effect. He swallowed drily and played the options over again—seeing nothing that would possibly work.

"Maybe we should—" He began, though he didn't really even know what he was going to say, not that it mattered anyway, because the moment the words left his mouth the outer door collapsed, crumpling in on itself, and behind it stood more zombies than Luke could even begin to count. It was like the drive through them all over again, their snarling faces so fucking close, only this time there was no quick escape, no getting away in a handful of seconds.

"Shut the fucking door," Pete roared. "Now."

And Jackson leaped forward before Luke even began to move, shutting it just as the horde filled the main room.

• • •

The door shut with a *thud* that perfectly matched the racing beat thrumming through Jackson's chest. She secured it and took just a moment to pause against the metal, taking a deep breath as she did so. Seeing the horde before—was it even the same one?—had been pretty skeevy, but this kicked its ass. Because they weren't driving through them at high speed now. Now the horde was right outside the fucking door.

Another *thud* followed the one she'd created as they tried to make their way in—the bastards—and she stepped away from the door, back to Luke.

"A half hour?" she asked Sebastian. "Until they get in here?"

"About," he said. "Give or take…well according to my calculations…but obviously they're theoretical…so ah, yes, I haven't actually tested them or anything."

Jackson frowned, knowing how prone Sebastian's calculations were to error. He was no mathematician. "Let's say fifteen then."

"How long before the people at the camp realize?" Luke asked, and Jackson looked to Pete, because this was his territory more than hers, even though this was her job now, and what were the fucking odds of that? Three days in and she got a horde. Just her luck.

"That we're dead? Or that we're dead?" Pete asked.

Luke shrugged. "Either or."

"Enough with the negatives already," Jackson said. Though

she knew they were right. There really was no way out of this one.

Another *thump*, a strangled groan and a series of wails accompanied her words. Jackson gripped Mandy as hard as she could to the point where the bones in her hands actually hurt.

"Maybe in a couple of hours," Pete said. "Nancy will sound the alarm then."

"It'll alert camp, at least," Luke said, "that something's wrong, so there's the silver lining."

Jackson took a deep breath as she thought about that lining and in a way it made her feel better. That the camp would survive, one of the last bastions of humanity remaining. Nancy was smart and she'd know something was definitely up when they didn't return. Likely she'd have all the guards out manning the wall. Of course, any chance of a cure would be lost after today. With Sebastian dead there would be no one to continue his work. No normality, no pulling the world back to how it was. Right about now Jackson couldn't find it in herself to think about that. Her mind was focused on one thing and one thing only: the bloodbath to come.

"Well," Pete said, breaking the silence, "I have to say I never saw this one coming. The bastards are ganging up, are they? Building hordes?"

"We saw one a week or so ago," Luke replied. "Jack thought they were massing to take down some survivors."

"It was the only thing that made sense," she said.

"And on that basis it means they're coming after the camp here," Luke added. "Though whether it's the same horde, I don't know. Probably not, considering the logistics and the fact we took quite a few of them out, so this is something they're all doing. Maybe like the burrowing. Fuck."

"Took them out how?" Pete asked and Luke shook his head.

"We ran them over."

"Ah…"

"So maybe," Sebastian interrupted, his gaze not lifting, because he was busy sorting through various liquids, "they're just passing by here on their way to the camp? They don't know what we're doing here at all, and if Jay wasn't outside, they might not even have spotted us?"

"Maybe," Luke said slowly.

"Seb, what are you doing?" Jackson asked.

"Looking for a defense," was all he replied.

She eyed his potions but couldn't imagine what he could possibly find to take down hundreds. One-on-one no doubt, he could pump the damn things full of stuff to make them scream. But this many? No, the doctor wasn't going to save them. "The door," she said. "What do we do? Out or in? We need to make a decision now."

"I'd rather fight them here," Pete said. "Restricted space and all."

"Unless they all get in," Luke said. "We'd be fucked then. They'd overwhelm us."

"So the door then?"

She sighed and pushed past them to grab the bars. Now was not the time for a fucking debate. "I'm making the decision for us. We'll go for it. Only way."

The bars were set in a complicated system of interlocking grooves—Sebastian's design of course—and Jackson got started on the first one immediately. Luke joined her after a moment and took hold of the right-hand side, followed by Pete and then Jay.

"Do we run or fight?" Luke asked as he turned a cog.

Pete twisted the bar and pulled at the same time Jackson pushed. "Fighting seems a bit kamikaze, but you know me, I never get tired of killing the bastards, and if this is my last stand, I want to make it count, not be pounced on while I'm running away."

"Same," Jay said. "I'll go down fighting."

The first bar was removed in no time and they all began on

the next. "We'll make it count," Jackson said. "What else is there to do but that?"

They twisted the second bar at the same moment a large *thud* sounded. Everyone turned—even Sebastian, who was still rifling through his stuff—and looked at the door. A large dent was obvious right in the middle and Jackson knew that such a dent meant the beginning of the end. The strength of metal was in its rigid qualities. Once that began to fail it was a whole lot easier to get through.

She wiped a hand across her sweat-soaked brow and began to pull on the second bar with Pete. It came off and they all moved down to the next. Just three more to go but the space was getting tight.

"You guys should hunt out any extra weapons," she told the two men as they pulled on the third bar. "Help Seb with whatever he needs. There isn't space here for all of us."

"Saw some hatchets over there." Pete nodded in the direction of the cage where Two-h-ee was leaking. The two men hurried over, and she and Luke began to remove the third bar.

"The things you do to get me alone," Luke said, and Jackson smiled—despite everything—she smiled.

"What can I say? I'm helpless against you, Luke."

"I wanted to tell you something," Luke began, as they pulled off the third bar.

He was right next to her. The two of them half crouched, his breath fanning against her face. She was reminded irresistibly of the time outside the bank when it had tickled her neck, and she'd thought that he was going to be a major distraction. And hadn't she been right?

"That you had the rocket launcher all along," she said. "You were holding out on me? Damn you, Luke."

He shifted and turned one of the cogs. "Not quite."

Another cog and Jackson pushed, her arms aching. "What

then?"

"Kind of hoped we'd have more privacy," Luke said slowly. "When I imagined it, I mean."

The tone of his voice told Jackson plenty and a flush traveled up her skin. Her heart race increased to the point of pain and she wondered if the zombies banging on the metal could hear it. *I know what this is…*

She paused for just a second before pushing again, her voice suddenly serious. "No, don't do this. Not now."

"Because it's the end?" he asked softly.

"Because I don't want to think you're doing it because it *is* the end."

Luke sighed. "You think way too little of me, Jack."

The flush reached her hairline and Jackson swallowed, super aware that the zombies' death groans were increasing in volume, the pounding getting louder, and the others moving frantically to find things to help them fight a war that was already lost. "I think way too much of you, and that's why I can't do this right now."

"There won't be another time," he said. "As much as I want to believe otherwise, you know there won't be. When we leave here, we're probably going to die."

Jackson pushed the bar free. They moved down to the final one. "I know. Seems almost like it's past due."

"Don't say that."

"Even if it's the truth?

He sighed. "I wish right now…"

"What?" she asked as she pushed the bar and Luke pulled.

"That we'd just kept traveling. We'd never have argued, we might even have reached the coast eventually. You could have sunbathed and I'd have rubbed lotion on you."

"And we wouldn't be about to die."

"Yeah, exactly."

One final push and pull and the bar was out. It hit the floor and they moved it aside to the pile with the others before picking their weapons back up. Jackson stood up and looked around the room—at their little team. Sebastian was filling syringe after syringe with some sort of murky blue liquid. Pete and Jay were pulling out Sebastian's cutting equipment—the thing he went through bones with. In a few seconds they would have to leave, and not a one of them didn't know they were going to die. Not one.

"Let me say it, Jack," Luke said, taking her chin and pulling her face around so that her eyes met his.

Jackson shuddered. "I can't…"

His thumb brushed against her lips and he sighed. "Well, I'm going to say it anyway, and you're going to hear it, because you need to, Jack. And then, when I'm done, we'll go out there together and face death knowing the truth."

"Hand in hand, is it?" she asked and she wanted it to be a quip, a way to lighten the mood, but it didn't come out that way at all.

"To the end, Jack," Luke said. "Always to the end, because you know that I love you, don't you?"

And Jackson's skin shivered and her heart raced and she wanted to scream to the sky, because it was all so fucking unfair. Everything! The months of traveling, of hiding, of starving—and always watching, always waiting for death. A death she expected and had readied herself for too many times. The day she'd left her apartment. The time she'd stood on that observation deck with the snow swirling around her face. Even the time when they'd driven straight through the horde. It had always been there. Always lingering on the edges. And now here, when it came to claim her at last, it gave her this. This one moment of something she'd never thought to find. Something that now she would never have.

She swallowed around a lump and in that moment it seemed like all the lumps. Tye's lump, and her brother's lumps, every single person's she'd ever known lifted themselves up and lodged there, desperate to burst free.

"Luke…"

Her voice faltered, the groans dimmed to be replaced by a roaring in her ears, and she looked into the perfect blue of his eyes, wishing she could say the words back to him. But even as she opened her mouth Jackson knew that if she spoke again the lumps would be set free, and she couldn't let them, couldn't even begin to give them the chance. Because that would be all it took, she realized. They'd leave her and as they did they would strip out everything she'd put in place to keep herself hard. Everything that allowed her to kill zombie after zombie.

"I know," Luke said and he bent forward and he placed a kiss on her forehead. "I know."

She wrapped her arms around him and for no more than a heartbeat they held each other as tightly as they possibly could. Jackson saying everything with that hug that she couldn't say with her voice. And then they were pulling apart and the others were coming over with their stuff, Sebastian handing them each a syringe, and Pete pulling on the cord to charge the cutting equipment.

"It'll buy some time," Sebastian said. "It's all I can do."

Jackson secured the Glock in her waistband, put the syringe in her left, and held Mandy in her familiar right grip before facing the door.

"Are we ready?" she asked.

Luke reached out and wrapped his hand around hers and by default, Mandy's hilt. "Ready," he said.

Death groans sounded around them, a continual pounding in time with her heartbeat permeated the room, and warmth raced up her arm from the feel of Luke's hand—held so tightly to hers. How strange to think this would be the last time she'd ever get to feel it, to feel anything. That in mere moments she'd be dead at last. Nothing more than a very sick person's meal.

"Jack?" Luke prompted and she took a deep breath, pushing

the horrific thoughts to the very back of her mind. They'd do her no good now. If anything, the thoughts would work against her. Make her slow and sloppy. She couldn't be Jackson the bad-ass if she was filled with regrets, could she?

She lifted Luke's hand to her lips and placed a quick kiss on it, her way of both saying good-bye and putting her mind in fight mode. Drawing a line. Maybe the line between life and death.

"Let's do this then," she said, and Jackson kicked the door open and together they went out to meet the end.

CHAPTER THIRTY-SIX

Why hadn't he realized it would be dark? That the only light would be from a full moon and the room they had just left. Why hadn't it fucking occurred to him?

"To the trees," he said to Jackson, noticing that the moonlight shone in a clear circle in the middle of them. "We'll get to the trees and make our stand there, okay?"

"Did you see a light—"

"The trees," he repeated, barely considering her words, and with her hand on his, started to sprint.

She ran next to him, easily keeping up pace and maybe they would have had a clear go of it but the first of the zombies spotted them and it too ran, so fast Luke could barely comprehend it. It groaned and leaped at them. Pete turned around, swung forward, and took its head off in one go, the power tool cutting through it in one smooth move. More were coming now though, alerted by the groan, and Luke sped up just as one landed on his back. He let go of Jackson's hand, shrugged it off, and lifted his ax to take the arm off. But since it was so fucking dark the farther they moved away from the room, he missed, cutting instead through its shoulder.

"It's too dark," he roared. "I can't see the bastards."

A swing sent him reeling back and he scrambled off the ground, just as one landed next to him, snapping its teeth. He grabbed Sebastian's syringe from his pocket and buried it in the fucker, depressing the top only when it was so far in it'd never come back out.

"We have to move," Jackson shouted but he couldn't see her. "It's too dark to fight here."

"Jack?" he shouted, panic evident in his voice, but she was by him then, her arm pulling him onward.

They ran, as fast as they could, making for the trees bordering the field, the circle of light that was their last hope. Luke could hear heavy breathing next to him and knew that the others, some of them at least, were still alive. But he could hear groans too, and grunts. The zombies were on their heels.

Luke wanted to keep on running, to just go and go until he heard no more, but he knew he wouldn't. They'd make their stand at the trees. It was the only option. The zombies were too hungry not to chase them and sooner or later one, then another of them, would falter, until none of them were left. That was unacceptable. So they sprinted until their feet were bathed in the moon's silver glow.

"Now," he shouted and they all halted, breathing ragged, and lifted their weapons.

The zombies were just yards away now, dozens of them, their faces screwed up into their usual snarls, their teeth snapping, pus oozing. The smell from their wounds warred with that of the fresh vegetation around them and something else…a smell that was familiar to him but he couldn't remember from where…

In that moment everything crystallized for Luke, in the way it does when it's all it can do. He didn't try to fight against the inevitable and he didn't try to sweep Jackson behind him. There, in the circle of the moon's glow, as the dozens of hungry zombies came at them, he knew exactly that this was the point his life had led him to and that at the end this was where Jackson belonged too.

Next to him.

Fighting.

Until it was all over.

Why had he tried to change that?

He lifted his ax, freed his gun, and took a deep breath. This was it...

The firebomb came from nowhere, because obviously there wasn't anywhere anymore. But come it did and fell right into the middle of the horde, spitting out and throwing its flames everywhere. Luke gasped and shook his head, trying to understand what the hell he was seeing. The zombies screamed, the fire spitting between the front line and the middle, consuming their thin skin and eating them up.

Another firebomb and then another. One after the other they rained down. Luke looked up to the trees, realizing exactly where they were coming from. And the smell... he knew what it was now... Lynx aftershave.

"To the truck," Jackson screamed and though Luke wanted to try and find the person who'd saved them, he knew he had to follow Jackson, to run with her, the five of them still. They sprinted around the fiery horde, up the field back to where they'd been. Escape—wondrous escape—seeming suddenly possible.

The light of the fire illuminated everything now, and as they darted forward Luke looked behind him to see several of the zombies breaking away from the horde, only small burns on them. They'd never make it to the truck he realized. It was parked on the opposite side of the door they'd come from.

"Back in the room," he roared. "They're still coming."

They veered in the other direction and Luke gave it everything he had, speeding up by pumping his arms. It should have been enough, but it wasn't. Three of them, enraged by the fire, caught him before he could make it into the room, and he was overwhelmed.

"Luke," Jackson screamed.

In the next instant she was pulling one off him, slicing through it with Mandy, and then Pete was there, cutting through the other, and they pulled him out from under the final one, which he shot straight through the face the moment he could reach his gun.

They scrambled back up, ran, and finally stumbled into the room, slamming the door shut behind them, but of course they didn't have time to rebar it and so they ran straight for the second door.

"How many are left?" Sebastian gasped.

"I don't know."

Jay got open the second door just as the other opened. Maybe a dozen or so zombies spilled into the room and ran straight for them.

Luke lifted his ax and swung, unable to fire his gun in such a close space for fear of hitting one of the others. It sliced through one of the large zombie's shoulders, cleaving down until the arm came off. Pus arced and splattered him, but now he knew it was harmless Luke didn't give a shit. He kicked the zombie aside before embedding the ax in its head—straight through skull bone.

Another came and again his ax buried itself in the thing's head. It hit the floor just as a groan sounded. Luke turned to see a massive female zombie coming right at him. She was huge, the biggest Luke had ever seen and he eyed her fleshy folds wondering where the hell his weapon would make a dent. "Come on then," he roared. "You—"

But the scream hit him then in tandem with another groan, the sound zinging throughout every cell in his body, and it was so unexpected and so alien that really Luke shouldn't have recognized it, but of course he did. Jackson was his now. Everything about her was inexorably tied with him.

Luke whipped around to see the woman he loved crumple

against a jagged piece of metal on one of the shelving units, the zombie's massive hands pushing her against it and saw with perfect clarity the metal slice into her face. Her perfect, pretty face.

"Jackson, no!" he roared, and he stepped forward, forgetting about the massive female zombie.

That lapse in attention, that minor slip up was enough for the zombie, and she launched herself on him, her mass sending them both to the floor. Luke actually heard his skull crack against the stone floor at exactly the wrong angle, and pain exploded outward, licking its way through every part of his brain. Nausea reared and blackness colored his vision. He tried to battle against it, but even as he gained a bit of ground and the explosion died just a little, another pain erupted and he heard himself roar.

He lifted his arms to push against it, to push it away. But it was too late and as he pushed she ripped, and the pain was so intense, the wetness flooding across his body so exact that the blackness rushed back at him, like a tidal wave, and before he could even call out Jackson's name again it swallowed him.

And Luke knew no more.

• • •

Time slowed for Jackson when Luke roared. She pushed away from the metal shelf, so that the length embedded in her cheek was pulled out, and kicked out at the male zombie. It stumbled back and in one move she whirled around, taking Mandy with her, straight through its head. Gore arced out across them and only habit, two long years of habit, had her ducking at the last moment to avoid the spray. Its body hit the floor with a wet *thud*, and Jackson shouldn't have even noticed how squishy it sounded, but her senses were on high alert—maybe because of the pain now screaming across her cheek, or maybe because of Luke. And yes, the battle raged around her, Pete fighting three or four as far as she could tell. And Sebastian holding one off by the redheaded zombie with a syringe, and Jay stuck in the carnage, but in that moment Jackson didn't care.

She jumped over the zombie's prone body, brushing at the wetness dripping down her face, and almost skidded across the slick floor to where Luke lay, crumpled on his side. As if in slow motion she saw droplets of blood and pus flick up from her feet and hit the back of the huge female zombie on top of him. They dripped downward, falling onto his denim-clad legs and Jackson lifted Mandy to her highest point.

The waking dead, once a woman, was beyond obese and maybe that should have slowed her down under any normal sort of circumstance, but it didn't. It hadn't. She'd gotten Luke and now she turned, teeth bared, blood dripping, emitting a death groan that hit Jackson's ears in a perfect melody and jumped. One swing. That was all she had. Once chance, and Jackson took it. She brought the machete down with every single bit of power her arms had left in them. Screaming as she did so. It hit the zombie woman on the sweet spot. The place where the skull bone was at its thinnest, and cleaved through.

But this was a zombie and the cleaving happened so quickly that it didn't register immediately and it kept coming. Its weight barreled into Jackson's diminutive frame, knocked the breath right out of her and she let out a muffled "oohh" as they both hit the floor. They skidded along it, gore soaked her back, Jackson turned her head just in time to avoid the spray of blood from the woman's brain. The zombie growled and Jackson let go of Mandy's hilt so that she could concentrate on lifting her knees, even though the effort it took was almost too much. But Luke was there, and vulnerable, one of the others would spot him soon—who knew how many had survived the flames? With this thought in mind, Jackson gritted her teeth and pulled her knees into her body, right under the huge roll of fat hanging from the waking dead's middle. She pulled and then she pushed. The zombie moaned and gurgled, but it was dying now, finally dying, and that was enough for Jackson to heave it from her. It collapsed backward, onto its knees, away from her and Jackson grabbed Mandy from where the machete was embedded in its head, and with the very last of her strength she sliced across the zombie's neck. Straight through the artery, which sprayed outward, a blood and pus arc, combining with that of the brain to soak the floor around it.

Jackson vaulted over it, ignoring the zombie's final gurgles and twitches, ignoring everything really, and fell beside Luke. Her knees didn't even register the puddle of blood beneath them, or the fact that the groans continued to sound around her.

He was on his side, almost curled up, and Jackson's entire body shook as she saw the bite marks across his shoulder. The zombie had gotten a good purchase. There was no doubt about that. Its teeth had sunk in a good inch both above and below. Two perfectly round crescents they should have been, only it had ripped, the way they always did, and all that was left now was a ragged hole about the size of half of a large orange. The hole was leaking blood. Luke's entire upper body was covered with the stuff. Worse than that though, she could see other fluids. Fluids that weren't his. And there was skin, rotted bits of skin and flakes of flesh.

She pulled those zombie parts away, desperately wiping at his wound—even though it was coating her own hands and the slash across her cheek was dripping on him—because she had to clean the wound. The saliva, the zombie saliva was in there and as she frantically wiped at it Sebastian's words came to her. *It's only about the bite because the bite holds the saliva, and the virus lives there. In the mouth fluids…*

And this, this bite, she shuddered. She's seen the scars on Luke's body, knew that the other bites hadn't been like this at all. They were shallower, barely even breaking through the skin.

"Luke, can you hear me?" she asked, and her voice broke on the last word. Deep breath she told herself. Stay calm. But the calm was not coming and as much as Jackson tried to get it, the more it wiggled away. "Luke?"

He moaned. Fear lanced her almost to the point of immobility. The moan sounded like one of them and only the years of barriers and holding everything back had Jackson gritting her teeth, taking him by the shoulders, and turning him so that she could look into his eyes. Only then would she know. *Please let it be him…*

They opened just as hers met his and the blue was still the blue, and the sparkle, though dim, was still there, and the fear exploded out of her so that she was speaking before she even really thought the words. Speaking past the lumps, because they paled into insignificance now against this. "Oh God, thank God. It's me Luke, it's me. Jackson. I'm here. I love you," she sobbed on the last word, her body shaking. "I do. Luke, I do."

He took a raspy breath and she could hear the effort it cost him. "Jack…

"Don't you die on me!" she shrieked. "Don't you dare fucking die on me, not now. Not now I know… I should have said earlier. Luke, I'm so sorry, stay with me, okay."

He shook his head ever so slightly to the side and tried to lift himself up, but it was too much. His head was bleeding and the bite to his shoulder and God knows what else all combined to overwhelm him. He fell back against the floor, moaning again.

"It's going to be okay," Jackson said, her voice spitting out the words. "Everything will be fine, Luke. You hear me? This is nothing. We'll get you fixed up in no time. You'll be fine. You've been bitten before. I remember you told me…" *But not like this. Not like this…*

Her hands shook as she pulled the material of his shirt away from his body. Trying again to clear the wound of everything. But it was thick material and she knew she'd have to cut it away. She grasped Mandy, lying in the pool of gore around her, and wiped it on her jeans. It removed some, if not all of the blood, and Jackson lifted her ready to cut. But the glinting metal, her savior so many times, outlined the reflection of another one of them, hunger burning in its eyes, coming straight at her and Luke.

Jackson screamed. Not in fear, not in anger, just in pure frustration. When would it ever end?

She swiveled around, her arms aching, her whole body sore and battered, knowing that she had almost nothing left. The wound to her cheek began to sting in a whole new way and she lifted a hand to it, trying to close the skin into place. The adrenaline that had filled her when they arrived was almost depleted now. Jackson knew that because she could feel so much pain, and she wanted nothing more than to sink back down next to her man and find his perfect blue eyes and hold his rough hands and let everything else just bleed away.

Just us. I promise. But it never had been, and as the male zombie emitted its death groan and stretched out its clawed fingers to grab her, she knew the truth of that. She'd never let *it* be.

Because she was changed.

The zombies may have woken back up but they weren't the only ones who'd done so through those first awful months. Jackson had awoken too, only different. Luke was, and only ever had been, her chance of getting some part of the old her back, but she'd never really let him.

Her Luke who was now dying beneath her...

Heavy with lethargy and screaming in agony, Jackson lifted Mandy, her constant companion, and blinked away the moisture coating her eyes. The first tears in more than two long years, all for Luke. But rather than swing through the neck, because she doubted her arms even had it in them, she simply stepped forward and buried her machete in its stomach. The zombie roared, the blade halting its forward momentum, and like she had with Luke Jackson's eyes matched with its eyes.

Green to brown, human to hunger.

"I'm sorry," she whispered, and then she pulled Mandy out, waited until the creature fell to its knees and kneed it as hard as she possibly could in the face.

Pain radiated from her kneecap making Jackson shriek. More tears, only these ones full of pain, filled her eyes. She blinked them away and screamed out the hurt, letting it wash over her because she wasn't done yet—she was never fucking done—it wasn't dead and she knew that her arms held no more in them—not even enough to try and cut through the head. So she hobbled over to the prone zombie, and she lifted her good leg and she slammed her steel-toe-clad boot down on its head. Once, twice, three times, over and over, until the thin, papery skin that covered it mushed under the force. And then the eyes and the muscle and the fatty tissue, on and on she went until she found the skull bone and cracked through it.

A roaring filled her ears so that all peripheral sounds were lost. Her vision closed in so that all she could see was the area around her boot and the zombie's brain revealing itself little by little under her force. "I'm sorry," she whispered again. "I'm sorry." And she didn't know who the hell she was telling, him or her or Luke or even the goddamn world.

CHAPTER THIRTY-SEVEN

Luke awoke in an instant. Awareness filled him, the sound of a repetitive *crunch* assaulting him. He sucked in a deep breath and the pain was almost enough to knock him back out again, but he gritted his teeth and pushed the blackness back. It wasn't easy and sweat broke across his head from the effort—or maybe that was just the gore.

Thoughts came then, in perfect order. *Zombies. The horde. Jackson. Where is she?* He lifted himself up, almost buckling from the pain. Dizziness buzzed in his head and it took a moment for him to take it all in. He blinked not once, but several times at the image his blurred eyes could see. The zombies were all but finished, all but the redheaded one strapped to the table, but she was quiet now, she too looking at the corpses littering the lab, lying in piles, and puddles of gore. Flames were still flickering outside and zombies screamed their dying screams.

The band of survivors were formed in a tight semicircle directly in front of him, and Luke saw that Pete and Sebastian and Jay were all okay—though looking like shit, but even as his gaze found them and rejoiced it went straight to the person in between them. She stood there and he knew then what the repetitive *crunch* was. Soaked through with blood she was like something from a horror movie herself. Her leg came up, and down, up, and down. And each time it crashed into the zombie's now-smashed skull she whispered. "I'm sorry."

Up and down, *crunch*, *crunch*. Up and down, *sorry* and *sorry*.

Luke's gaze found Sebastian's exhausted one. The doctor shifted, his eyes full of the same questions as Luke's.

"Jackson?" Luke called to her.

Up and down, *crunch*, *crunch*. Up and down, *sorry* and *sorry*.

"Jackson?" he said. Louder this time, though the effort made the nausea well up. But it was worth it, her movements ceased. She turned to him then, confusion writ across her face.

"Luke?"

"Come here, baby." His words were soft, encouraging, even around the dizziness, and she must have got that immediately because she took a step toward him. Moments later she winced and fell toward the floor. Pete rushed forward to break that fall and hooked an arm under her.

"It's okay," he said and pulled her forward until she could collapse next to him.

In all their time together Luke had never seen Jackson look anything like this, and not just because his vision was blurred. Blood covered nearly all her skin. A ragged gash bisected her cheek, dripping more blood, and her eyes were full of something… not pain, no he couldn't call it that…

"It's okay," he said again.

"Luke," she whispered. "I didn't… I lost it a bit… I'm…"

"It's okay." He wanted to lift a hand and run it across her face, maybe remove some of the blood, but his shoulder was screaming in pain and his vision was blurring in and out, a weird roaring filling his ears. *Concussion*, his mind said. *You have a concussion.*

"I'm gonna go check outside," Pete said. "Make sure there's none left. Jay?"

The two men nodded at one another and ran out to the flames, maybe to behead the burning corpses of whoever was left. Sebastian limped across the room, picked up a bag of some sort, and began pulling out vials. Luke ignored him, focusing completely on Jackson.

"We're okay," he said. "We're okay. We've survived. The horde's gone."

"I know," she whispered. "I know that, but Luke…"

"What, baby?"

"It bit you," she said.

Yes, why hadn't he remembered that? The zombie'd ripped his skin away, the worst bite he'd ever had.

"I'm all right," he reassured her, though he wasn't entirely sure that he was. "I've been bitten plenty in the past. This one's a tad worse is all."

"Yes," she agreed. "You'll be fine." Her hand took his, squeezing. Luke tried to apply some pressure back only he didn't seem to have very much strength left.

"You have to be fine," she added. "I need you, Luke. Without you I'll never be me again."

"You are you," he said.

"Me the way I was," she insisted.

"I don't want you the way you were," he whispered. "I like you just fine as you are. I should have realized. I didn't, but I do now. You're mine, Jackson. And I'm yours."

She let out a small sob and lifted a hand to her mouth, pulling away only to look at her blood-covered fingers and shake her head.

"Freak and all?"

"Freak and all."

Sebastian sat down next to them, passing Jackson a towel and a pack of antibacterial wipes as he did so. "Pressure to the wound, then clean it," he said.

She nodded and pulled some wipes free before pushing the

towel against his shoulder. Luke gritted his teeth at the pain, which was all consuming now, licking at the edges of everything. His strength was pretty much depleted. He'd told Jackson what he needed to and just wanted to sink into the blackness.

"Stay with me, Luke," Jackson said, but her voice came as if from a distance.

"Let me give him this," Sebastian said and through his blurred vision Luke could see a syringe.

"What is it?" she asked, pressing the towel a little harder. Pain exploded and he sucked in a deep breath. "Pain relief?"

"No."

"Antibiotics?"

"No."

"Then what?"

Sebastian shook his head and Luke couldn't help but notice that the gray hairs were tipped with blood. He looked exhausted, his hands shaky. "It's an immune suppressant. An accelerator if you will."

"A what?" Jackson was rubbing against the wound on his head now, cleaning blood away, maybe. Luke wanted to tell her to clean her own wound, wanted to do it for her, but he could find neither the words nor the strength to lift a hand.

"An accelerator," Sebastian repeated.

"And what will that do?"

Sebastian paused before answering, or maybe Luke just imagined that, things were not making perfect sense. "If he's infected," Sebastian said slowly, "this will speed the process up. It depresses the immune system allowing the virus to take hold."

Jackson gasped. "Speed it up? Depress his immune system? Are you fucking insane?"

"It's best we find out immediately. We can't take him back to camp like this, and we need to get moving. God knows if there are more hordes coming. We're lucky to have survived this one."

Jackson wrenched the syringe out of Sebastian's hands, her movement blurring in front of Luke's eyes. "You want to wipe out his last moments? Jesus fucking Christ, Sebastian. What the hell is wrong with you?"

"If he's going to turn, we need to know," Sebastian insisted. "We can't take him back to camp if we don't."

Jackson crunched the syringe on the floor, lifted a leg, and stamped on it. Luke saw the wince chase across her face and guessed she was injured. He wished he could help her, but he was barely hanging on. Could he be infected? He had no idea how he could tell. His head was pounding but maybe that was the concussion. He felt sick but was it any wonder? And there was so much pain. Did that mean the virus was already consuming him? Did he want to know if it was?

"We can't take him back to camp," Sebastian insisted. "Nancy won't let him in. You know she won't. But we can't stay here, either. It's too dangerous. The fire will draw even more."

"Fine. You go," Jackson hissed. "All of you go. I'm not losing the last minutes of him so you can feel better."

"It's better for him this way. He—"

"He what?" she screeched. "Will give you the antibodies you need. You're a piece of fucking work, Sebastian."

The doctor reeled back. "I wasn't thinking that! I just want to make this easier for him. Do you have any idea what it'll feel like to turn? It will hurt him if it's drawn out."

"He's going to be fine," she insisted. "I'll look after him."

"And if he turns?"

"Then I'll behead him myself. That's my job, as it would be his."

Jackson slicing Mandy through him. The image was clear in his mind. Her face would set into its battle lines and she'd grit her teeth and do it—he knew she would. But Luke knew too that it would be the end for her. The last little bits of normality she had would disappear if she had to behead the man she loved. He knew this because that was how it would be for him. Some things you never came back from, and this would be one of them.

"Get Pete," he said, and the effort of those words was almost too much.

"It's all right, Luke," Jackson whispered, turning herself so that her body covered his wound. "I'm going to look after you." She wiped the cloth against him, humming and mumbling words his ears were not able to pick up.

"Jackson…" he breathed, his voice catching on the word.

"And then we'll start our journey again," she said, her voice suddenly louder, but not because she's raised it, he got that, just because his ears weren't working properly. "We'll go all the way to the coast. Sit on a beach and rub lotion on one another. Everything will be fine because we've got each other. That's how it is supposed to be. I'll catch fish. You like fish. Remember you told me? I'll make a net or something and you'll make a fire and we'll eat them… and…" Her voice broke and Luke's pain intensified in so many ways.

"I—"

She bent forward then and placed a light kiss on his lips. "I love you, Luke. I need you."

And he loved her, so goddamn much, which was why he was going to do this.

"Pete." He beckoned the other man forward, Sebastian trailing behind. Jackson moved back so that he could pull the other man down, until his mouth was level with his friend's ear. He thought then of how it must have felt for Pete to watch his wife turn, how it was no wonder he hadn't beheaded her. Pete too must have known it was something he'd never come back from. "Take her away," he whispered. "Until it's over. And then let Seb have me okay? Let him get his antibodies."

Pete reared back, his gaze finding Luke's, and even through

the blur he saw the other man nod. "Take care, buddy."

"Luke, what—"

But Jackson's voice was cut off by an arm snaking around her waist and pulling her from Luke's prone body. She screamed and shrieked and pushed against Pete. Luke swallowed the nausea, gritted his teeth against the pain. It occurred to him then, in an abstract sort of way, that maybe Sebastian would get his cure after all, but that was secondary really. Only Jackson mattered now.

Only she had mattered for a very long time.

So he sucked in a deep breath and he screwed up his courage and he said the words he had to say. "Do it." And the last thing he felt was the prick of a syringe, and the last thing he heard was her sobs, and the last thing he saw was the tears, and everything exploded.

CHAPTER THIRTY-EIGHT

If she could have, Jackson would have screamed until her voice was hoarse. Screeched until her head throbbed, but it felt almost like her voice was lost somewhere, grabbed away by the pain.

Pete held her fast, and any other time she would have been able to get away but her knee was stiff with pain, her cheek slicing agony each time she moved, and a horrible, despairing weariness had settled over everything. It just seemed to her that, of course it would be this way. They would survive the horde, but she'd lose the one thing worth surviving for.

"I'm sorry," Sebastian said as he moved away with the needle.

"I'm going to fucking kill you," she growled, finding her voice at last. "You bastard."

"This is Luke's choice," Pete whispered. "Let him have that, Jackson. Let him. He deserves that much at least."

She sobbed, her chest heaving, the noise so ridiculously loud and unfamiliar that for one wild moment Jackson wondered where it was coming from. But then she realized it was *her* acting this way. *Her* falling apart. But this was Luke…

"I can't lose him," she whispered.

"I know," Pete said. "I remember." He turned to the doctor.

"How long until we know?"

Sebastian shrugged. The redheaded zombie groaned. "I've never used it on a person. Maybe a few minutes. No more than five."

Luke screamed then, a deep guttural roar that filled the room. Jackson winced. "Is it hurting him?" she whispered, her chest hoarse.

"Yes," Sebastian said. "But less than the alternative."

"You have to let me go," she said over Luke's second scream "Let me go to him, Pete. I won't let him turn alone, not if it comes to it."

"You'll try and kill him," Pete said softly, "if he turns, and Luke knows as well as I do what that will do to you. He's doing this for you."

Jackson shook. "I don't have the strength left. I just want to hold his hand. Let me go."

"He asked me not to."

"And I'm telling you that you have to." A memory came then of a story Luke had told her. They'd been in an old store and she'd nearly fainted when she'd found a stash of canned stewed apples. They'd taken turns eating from three cans, both enjoying the unexpected treat. Afterward he'd held her in his arms and shared stories. Luke had shared so many, she realized, while she'd shared hardly any. If only she could go back.

"You have to because of Lily," she said.

Pete stilled. "What?"

"You held her in your arms even after she turned, even when she tried to bite you, and you didn't behead her."

"How do you know that?" he demanded.

"Luke told me. You did it for her. Let me do it for him."

Pete sighed and relaxed his grip. "You promise not to behead him? Because there's more than just you two at stake here. I'm sorry if that sounds harsh but it's true. The whole fucking world could rest on what happens here."

"I know." Jackson staggered forward, pain radiating out from her knee, until she could crumple next to Luke. Feeling no guilt at all that she would break that promise if need be. A horrific image of him trapped in one of Sebastian's cages hit, and Jackson almost vomited. Spending his final days as one of Seb's experiments?

Never

This was Luke. He was hers. She'd be here for him. That was more important than any cure ever could be.

"Me and you," she whispered. *Until the end. Whenever that might be.*

She reached out a shaky hand and wiped at the blood dripping down his face. Was it his blood or hers? Did it even matter anymore?

Her free hand found his and she held fast. "I'm here, Luke. I'm here."

He screamed and writhed beneath her. His body so clearly racked with pain that she vowed here and then that Sebastian would fucking suffer for this. *But it's not his fault*, her mind whispered. *I don't fucking care*, she whispered back.

"Careful," Pete said and Jackson realized he'd followed her over, probably to wrench her away again if need be. She ignored him.

"I've got you," she said softly. "Right here, Luke. With me."

He screamed again before turning ever so slightly and vomiting all over the floor. The vomit was green, not the color of their pus, and a kernel of hope blossomed in Jackson. She lifted the wipes and ran one along his face. Her hand shaking so much that she almost missed the parts that needed cleaning.

"We'll hold hands soon," she whispered. "And go for a walk. You'll like that, baby. I promise I won't even take Mandy. I'll leave her at home."

"Jackson…"

His word was muffled around a scream and she gritted her teeth tight. "I'm here."

His body bucked, almost like an epileptic fit, up and down, shivers racing across his skin. Jackson placed a hand on his chest to try and steady him and felt the heat through his shirt. The fever burning.

"No…" she whispered. "No."

Another scream, this one long and drawn out, and his body seemed to curl in on itself. *Just like Two-h-ee…*

"Almost done," Sebastian whispered.

She felt Pete move closer behind her. No doubt ready to grab her away. Jackson knew then what she would have to do if he did.

Luke bucked again, another scream left his lips, and then, to Jackson's absolute horror, he became completely still. His body locked tight. She gasped and sucked in a shocked breath before reaching out an unsteady hand. "Is he?"

"Move back," Sebastian said, a warning note in his voice. "Move away from him."

A groan sounded then, replacing the screams. A groan that lifted the hairs on Jackson's arms and made everything crystallize. The last few years flashed through her mind at light speed, memory after memory filling her and she let the lump out.

Let them all out.

They erupted one after the other. *Mom. Dad. Andrew. Peter. Kelly. Katie. Anne. Fiona. Jayne. Tye.* Her family, her friends, everyone she had ever cared about, ever loved. She let them all out, and just like on the observation deck — as they left, a little part of her went with them.

Another little death.

Luke.

The last lump. The *only* lump. Her throat tightened as if refusing to let him go. Everything shifted into place. He would go and she would not be far behind. It was the only thing that made sense now.

"Move away," she heard Sebastian say again, but his voice was distant, meaningless almost.

"Come on." It was Pete, his gruff voice so close to her as he reached out to lift her up, his knees bent.

Jackson didn't even think. She moved swiftly, with the deadly accuracy that had kept her alive for more time than she could even fathom. The accuracy that had been there from the very beginning, it and the strength, almost like she'd been given the good parts of the zombies, but never the bad.

Almost like she'd been a little bit of them all along.

A flick and a turn and she smacked Pete in the nose, hard. He reeled back, hitting the floor straight on his ass.

Mandy was there, right there next to the obese zombie and Jackson reached across to grab her, the effort making everywhere throb, but in a distant sort of way, as though she was already past even that. Pete staggered up just as Jackson stood, her knee almost failing her.

"Don't do it," he roared. "You won't be able to come back! Don't!"

But he didn't even realize, did he? She had no *intention* of coming back. And so Jackson lifted her arms high, tears filling her eyes, blurring her vision, taking away every single little bit of herself that she had left.

"I love you," she whispered and then Jackson moved to bring the blade down.

CHAPTER THIRTY-NINE

The blade stopped a mere two inches from his head, and Luke's eyes widened on it, the metal glinting, the gore quivering off it.

A strangled cry. "Luke?" and then the blade was no more and a body crumpled against his. "Oh my God it's you."

Everywhere hurt, every single cell within him, but he was him and he knew her and that meant only one thing.

"I'm not…"

Sebastian rushed into his vision, and the doctor was there pulling and poking and prodding before a grin creased his face. "No. You're okay. Damn it to hell, Luke. You're okay!" He injected another needle before Jackson could stop him. "Pain relief," he said. "That's all."

"He's okay. He's okay." Jackson chanted the words across him, her hands running up and down, up and down, not even noticing what Sebastian was up to.

Liquid cool raced through Luke's veins. The pain started to recede. "I'm not one of them. Fucking hell…"

"You're you," she whispered. "Just you."

"You were going to behead me," he said, the image of Mandy's blade dancing through his mind.

"Yes." She planted a kiss on his cheek. "I'd never let anyone else. Just like you'd do it for me. How could I watch someone else remove your head? No, it would be wrong."

"But you didn't," he said and he couldn't even feel the burn on his shoulder anymore. "Why?"

"I saw your eyes," she said, and he couldn't help but notice that *her* eyes were ever so slightly crazed. *What else was new?*

"My eyes?"

"The blue," she said. "The you. And no zombie could ever look like that. Of course it was you. You're just really lucky that I realized in time and that I'm so weak right now. If that'd been a full-on swing, I wouldn't have been able to stop."

"Come here." Luke raised his good arm and wrapped it around her. She sort of collapsed even further against him and he swallowed unsteadily. How close it had been and how fucked-up that he totally got what she meant? That yes, in the end, perhaps their love in this world came down to things like that. To being willing to take off the head of your other half because it was the right thing to do.

"I shouldn't have made Pete pull you away," he said slowly. "It was wrong to take the choice from you. I just worried that you wouldn't be able to come back from it."

"Well I wouldn't have," she said. "But it wouldn't have mattered anyway. I was only ever going to be a step behind you."

"Jack…" he whispered. "Don't talk like that."

"It is what it is," she said. "But, Christ, I never want to have to make that choice again."

"I never want to make it at all," Luke said. "Never."

He pulled her closer, holding tight, and all at once he knew that no matter what they did from here on in, it would be together. Beheading and all.

"I love you," Luke whispered and he felt her smile against him.

"Love you too, baby."

Their lips touched briefly and maybe if he wasn't exhausted, and she wasn't still dripping blood, everything would have dissolved in a haze around them...a haze that had the distinct smell of something...but this wasn't a romance novel and with their combined wounds all they could do was slump against one another, relief filling them both.

When they finally pulled back slightly Jackson looked up into Luke's eyes, and he into hers. Those perfect green eyes which would be his forever now—zombies or not, and vice versa, and then she smiled, and he knew he'd never forget the sight of her blood-splattered face, filled with relief and love, not to mention the jagged cut.

Not now.

Not when he was an old man reminiscing about the past.

Not ever.

Not until the end.

"You look kinda crazy," he said and she laughed, shaking slightly.

"Was teetering on the edge there, baby, not gonna lie."

"I'd have pulled you back."

"You'll always pull me back."

"We need to fix your cheek," he said, moving slightly to lift himself up. Whatever Sebastian had given him was fucking fantastic. He couldn't even feel the bite now. "It could get infected."

"You both need treatment," Sebastian said. "As soon as we're back at camp I'll sort you out—though I make no claims to being a proper doctor so you'll both just have to make the best of it. It *is* bed rest for both of you for a good few weeks though. I can promise that."

"I think she broke my nose," Pete said and Jackson turned to him.

"I'm sorry, Pete."

"No you're not." He sighed, wiping away a splatter of blood. "But it's fine. I've been there, remember."

"I'll treat you, too," Sebastian said. "Perhaps some sort of compress? What about Jay?"

"I'll go look," Pete said. "He was beheading the last of them."

Jackson pushed a hand under his arms and helped Luke lift up into a sitting position. He shuddered slightly because though the pain relief felt great, he was exhausted. He wanted nothing more than to curl up with Jackson in his arms and sleep for a week.

"We should get moving when Pete gets back," he said.

Sebastian nodded and began to pack things up. "That we should. Gonna have to move to my other base as well now. This place is compromised."

"You have another?"

The doctor nodded. "Never put all your stars in one stellar nursery, Luke."

"We should…" Jackson paused and lifted her head. "Did the accelerator have citrate in it?"

Sebastian frowned. "Of course not. The formula is made up of—"

She waved his words away. "I don't need to know."

"It's just stuff to make every single part of my body scream like it was on fire," Luke said, shivering at the memory. He pulled her to him and squeezed because the feel of her exhausted body against his was enough to push it back.

Jackson frowned again and wrinkled her nose. "I could swear I smelled…" She shook her head. "It's probably nothing."

"Lynx," Luke said slowly, taking a deep breath, wondering if the concussion was messing with his mind. "You can smell Lynx. It smells exactly like the stuff you sprayed outside the rec center…"

"It's useless," Sebastian piped up. "No good to anyone apart from as a deodorant."

"Which *is* its actual purpose," Luke said.

Sebastian shrugged. "If my own specially mixed citrate spray doesn't repel them, you can bet the weak amounts of citrate in that stuff won't. Anyone still hoping it will is dead wrong. Literally. And besides," he added. "I confiscated all the aftershaves and deodorants from camp months ago."

"Then how—"

A roar sounded from outside—the noise splitting the air around them. Luke felt Jackson jump. She placed a hand on his shoulder and made to stand.

"Wait," he said, because the sound was teasing around the edges of Luke's battered brain as he tried desperately to place it.

"I can't believe it," Jackson whispered. "It can't be."

"What is it, Jack?" he asked, worried for just a moment that more zombies were approaching, maybe even burrowing. How could they possibly fight off more? But...the roar had not been a groan...it was something else entirely.

"The fire," she whispered.

Luke shifted, remembering the moment the fire had rained down. Where had it come from? What was going on? "I don't—"

"Look," she said.

She squeezed his hand and pointed toward the open door, where the flames were still flickering in the distance. Luke narrowed his eyes, trying to work out what she meant, a moment later and understanding dawned. "There's someone else out there."

"Someone else," her words were whispered, her eyes wide. "It can't be."

"Can't be what?" Sebastian asked. "What the devil's going on?"

Someone screamed, another roar sounded. Luke tried to lift up a bit farther to see, but Jackson's hand on his shoulder halted him. She turned, met his gaze, shock stamped across her features, and then, oddly, she smiled.

"Tye," she said. "It's Tye."

• • •

Jackson stood up, wincing as she did so, fucking tears threatening all over again. Her entire body shook, pain radiating out from everywhere, but it was almost as though those feelings were secondary to the alarm going off in her head...the possibility that she was right, that he'd found them at last.

Tye.

She narrowed her eyes against the smoke. Looking, searching.

When a figure emerged from the gloom—illuminated by the last of the flickering flames—it emerged in a way she had not expected at all. It was running, but slowly, because held in its arms was something Jackson had never thought to see in a million years.

Tye. But he was not alone.

She gasped as the light brought his face into focus. Those features, so dear to her, the brother that had helped to fill the hole of those she'd lost. It was almost too much to comprehend.

"Jack?" She heard Luke's words and swallowed down the lump in her throat. Her knees were shaking, the damaged one in particular feeling like it could go at any moment.

"It's him," she whispered. "It's him."

Sebastian rushed past her—his limp barely slowing him down—as he too caught sight of the figures. A moment later and they were all in the room. Sebastian. Pete. Jay...and Tye...

Jackson shuffled forward, reaching out, needing to touch him to convince herself he was actually real, but he sprinted past her, blood pouring down his face, and the heavy bundle in his arms bleeding even more.

"Tye..."

Jackson made to step forward, but her knee failed, and she would have fallen. Only Luke was suddenly there, struggling as much as she, but he caught her in his arms and held her fast. His presence was like cold water over a heated wound, and

Jackson half slumped against him. The pain, the shock, everything overwhelming her.

"Help me! Help her!" Tye's words were wrenched from him, and Jackson's heart thudded at the sound.

She looked down at the woman who Seb and Tye were laying on the floor. She was tiny, her cloud of curly brown hair spread out like a halo around her head. She was also covered in blood and pus, her eyes closed tight…and she was curled in on herself.

"Has she been bitten?" Seb demanded.

Tye nodded, his jaw locked tight as Seb peeled back the woman's T-shirt, exposing a deep bite on the side of her belly.

"I thought it was dead," Tye growled. "It was in the ground. I thought it was already dead. Oh God…"

"You need to stand back," Seb said, just as the woman gave a bloodcurdling scream.

"Help her," Tye demanded. "Fucking fix her."

The words held so much pain. Everyone in the room felt it. Each looking from one to the other, understanding passing between them. Jackson's eyes met Seb's and she immediately suspected what he was thinking. When he gave a slight, almost imperceptible shake of his head, she knew for sure.

She stepped forward, Luke helping her to do so. "Tye?"

Tye turned, confusion chasing across his haunted features. "Jack?"

She laid a hand on his shoulder. "Yes, it's me."

"I knew I'd find you here," he said. "Polly promised. The fire was her idea." He reached out and stroked his hand across the back of the woman's face. The gesture was so tender, so loving, that Jackson's heart hitched. Tye had found his Luke…and she was so happy for him, but then she realized what was about to happen and her heart sank.

"How long ago was she bit?" Sebastian asked, pulling a syringe from his bag.

Tye shook his head, pain pinching his face. "I don't know? Five minutes? Maybe more?"

Sebastian plunged the syringe in and the woman, Polly—where did Jackson know that name from?—let out a shriek. It made them all, all but Tye, jump back, because the sound was so familiar to each and every one of them.

"No, no, no!" Tye leaned across and started to gather Polly into his arms. Despite the screams and the shrieks she was completely limp, her head lolling as he tried to move her.

"Don't do that," Seb said, pulling the syringe free. "Leave her there."

"The floor's cold," Tye snapped. "She hates the cold."

"I know." Sebastian held the syringe aloft. The blood inside it seemed almost to glint in the light. "Pete? Jay?"

The two men stepped forward, ready Jackson knew, to pin Polly down the moment she tried to attack. Because she *would* attack. It was simply a question of time now.

"Get away from her," Tye shouted as Pete and Jay moved in. "Get the fuck away from her."

"It's okay," Sebastian said, but his words were drowned as the redheaded zombie groaned, as if sensing the awakening of one of her own.

"Fix her," Tye roared, placing kiss after kiss on the Polly zombie's head, rocking her stirring body in his arms. "Fucking fix her."

Sebastian stood up, the syringe still in hand, the deep red, antibody-rich blood almost pulsing. "I intend to."

Acknowledgements

Firstly, I want to say a huge thank-you to my editor, Erin, for taking a chance on this novel. I'll forever remember the day I got the call. You rock! Also thanks to the team at Entangled, including Libby, who kicked my ass on a million plot points (quite deservedly, too), my awesome publicist, Danielle, and, of course, to Liz.

Writing is a solitary business but in my little world it is made a hell of a lot easier by the support of my writing buddies and my family. A big kiss to Vix for being my cheerleader from the very beginning all those long, long years ago. We said we'd get there in the end, didn't we? An equally big kiss to Sarah for all the computer notes. I started each writing session with a smile on my face because of you. Pickle, Reuben, need I say more? Major hugs to my husband, Stel, for making all the dinners and accepting the fact that marrying me meant he'll never again have matching socks, or even a clean house for that matter. And to Andy, because it was me and you from the beginning, and no matter what you'll always be kid to me.

David Bridger, dear friend, and fellow Browncoat, thank you for reading this when it was still in its early form, even though you were superbusy and it gave you nightmares! To the BoE gals, Alexandra O'Hurley, Cat Kelly, Marie Medina and Xondra Day, your support has kept me going when my fingers have been cramping and my head pounding.

And lastly, to my readers. It still blows my mind that you guys go out and spend your hard-earned money on something that I created. How freakishly wonderful is that? Thank you all, your support means more than you'll ever know.

Additional Entangled Select releases…

Deep in Crimson

by Sarah Gilman

Kidnapped by humans and raised in a research facility, Jett was taught to believe his own race of demons insidious and violent. Jett wants to bring his captor to justice, so he join forces with the demon Guardians, and the demon child's older sister, Lexine.

Irresistible attraction grows between Jett and Lexine, but if Jett goes through the all-consuming process of becoming a Guardian, he may forfeit any chance they have of being together.

Malicious Mischief

by Marianne Harden

Career chameleon, Rylie Keyes, must keep her current job. If not, the tax assessor will evict her ailing grandfather and auction off their ancestral home. When a senior she shuttles for a Bellevue, Washington retirement home winds up dead in her minibus, her goal to keep her job hits a road bump.

Forced to dust off the PI training, Rylie must align with a circus-bike-wheeling Samoan to solve the murder, while juggling the attentions of two very hot police officers.